Pursuing Prissie
A Pomeroy Family Legacy Novel

By Christa Kinde

Yahavim

PursuingPrissie
A Pomeroy Family Legacy Novel

ISBN: 978-1-63123-028-8

"Cosmos" watercolor by Ekaterina Byakova

“Peace, friend.”

While *Pursuing Prissie* can stand alone, the author would like to remind readers that this story is a reprise. To catch all the significant references and allusions, you'll want to begin with the Threshold Series [Zonderkidz] and two of Christa's companion stories: *Rough and Tumble* (where you'll meet Ethan) and *Angel on High* (which details Koji's beginnings).

ALSO BY

CHRISTA KINDE

THRESHOLD SERIES

The Blue Door (Book 1)
The Hidden Deep (Book 2)
The Broken Window (Book 3)
The Garden Gate (Book 4)

THRESHOLD COMPANION STORIES

Angels All Around
Angels in Harmony
Angels on Guard
Angel on High
Angel Unaware
Rough and Tumble
Tried and True
Sage and Song

Angels: A 90-Day Devotional about God's Messengers

Table of Contents

CHAPTER 1

The Usual Things

When the Faithful gather, it's usually for song, but the six angels in the Pomeroys' hayloft stood silent. Boots scuffed the straw-littered floor. Fingers tapped a restless rhythm. Expressions were easy to read. Confusion marked both apprentice Guardians. Their mentors were concerned, and their respective captains were at a loss how to comfort them.

Jedrick tried first. "This is not the first time Miss Pomeroy has been at the center of mysterious ways."

Tamaes's flame-hued wings trembled with emotions his voice didn't betray. "While that is true, this is unusual in the extreme. *Prissie* is my charge."

Taweel grunted. "Show Jedrick."

Obeying his mentor, Tamaes extended a large, sun-browned hand. Letters etched their way across his palm in heaven's language, spelling out a name—*Hezekiah Pomeroy*.

"Her brother," Jedrick mused aloud, his gaze switching to a Guardian with pearlescent pink wings. "*Your* charge."

"Zeke," confirmed Ethan. Although the bristle-haired angel was clearly the youngest of their gathering, he seemed to be taking this new Sending in stride. With an apologetic air, he offered his palm. Proof of his altered status showed against fair skin—*Priscilla Pomeroy*.

"An interesting trade-off," remarked Conrad, who mentored Ethan. "Any idea why two Guardians would be asked to switch places?"

Tycho, the tall archer who captained the Flight to which Conrad and Ethan belonged, asked, "Have either of these children done anything unusual?"

Taweel snorted.

"*Lately?*" Tycho amended.

Tamaes rubbed at the letters on his hand. "Prissie's days have been quiet. She stays busy." In a gentler tone, he added, "She misses us."

Ethan shrugged. "Unless football practice and profiteroles are newly added to the perils we guard against, Zeke's days are also quiet. For him."

"Meaning they aren't," Conrad said.

Fondness warmed Ethan's tone. "Zeke is Zeke."

Jedrick folded muscular arms across his breastplate. "Since the siblings both reside here and work together, you will often remain close to the one whose name is on your heart. But with this changing of the guard, your first responsibility must be the one whose name is on your hand."

Tamaes's wry smile tugged at the scar running down the side of his face. "I look forward to the challenge."

Ethan touched Tamaes's forearm and warned, "Zeke still pulls stunts."

"Prissie still watches for miracles," Tamaes confided.

"He means well."

"She trusts too easily."

"He never stops."

"She always hopes."

Ethan tipped his head to one side, catching the more bashful Guardian's gaze. "Zeke *will* stretch your wings to their limits."

Clasping the younger warrior's hand, Tamaes said, "And your wings will delight Prissie."

Folds of translucent pink shimmered in the dim loft. Ethan bemusedly said, "Her favorite color has long been established, but she is unlikely to see them."

Tamaes shook his head. "She will. Be ready."

"Jasper Reece, are you *crazy*?" Prissie asked, eyeing the small mountain of baked goods heaped beside the register.

"Just hungry, ma'am."

"Don't you *ma'am* me." Twenty-four wasn't old enough to be ma'am-ed. Especially by one of her little brother's best friends.

"Grandmama taught me manners, and I'm not afraid to use 'em!" Jasper replied, all sass and sweet talk. "You wouldn't turn away a hungry customer, now, would you?"

Jasper's whole family was close as kin to the Pomeroys. Pearl Matthews, who worked the register every morning at Loafing Around, was Jasper's aunt. And Jasper had been friends with Prissie's brother Zeke ever since they were both wearing diapers in First Baptist Church's nursery. She supposed that made the duo lifelong friends. Although normally they were a dynamic trio. "Where's Timothy?"

"He's got lessons," Jasper replied, miming a trombone. "Which definitely works up an appetite." Leaning over to inspect the contents of the glass bakery case, he pointed. "I'll take those last two cupcakes. And all the cookies, too."

"Did Zeke put you up to this?"

"Yep. Pitched in, too. Three-way split." Jasper drew himself up to his full height, which was impressive. The soon-to-be high school senior would be the West Edinton Warriors' best linebacker this season. "It's simple, Prissie. If you sell out, you lock up. Don't you want to call it a day?"

She smiled wearily. "Yes."

Jasper knew he'd won. "Don't fuss with boxes. We'll eat straight out of the case. Won't leave a crumb. I swear."

Laughing, she rang up his order, giving him the family discount. If Zeke and his friends wanted to free up a summer afternoon, she'd thank heaven for small mercies. Today was too hot for kitchens. Flipping all the signs to *CLOSED*, she snapped the lock and said, "I'll let Zeke know you're here."

"Just gimme a fork for this pie, and I'm set." Jasper hesitated, then took it back. "Unless there's milk."

"I'll check," she said, pushing through the swinging door into the kitchen. The room was at least ten degrees hotter than out front. "Jasper cleaned us out again. Shall we thank him with a gallon of milk?"

"Sure, sure." Her dad leaned against the back counter, arms folded over a spattered apron, testimony to a morning spent processing blueberries. Jayce Pomeroy was watching Zeke, whose nose was practically pressed against an oven window. "Will young Mr. Grable be joining us as well?"

"Later," Zeke replied, jumping back with the timer *ping*ed. A wave of hot air billowed into the stuffy room as he lifted out a pan of madeleines. "Timothy knows to come to the back door."

Prissie escaped into the walk-in refrigerator, keeping one foot stuck in the door while she reached for the milk shelf. Hooking a fresh gallon, she basked in the coolness for five blissful seconds before backing out and letting the heavy door swing shut. A trip to the library was definitely in order. Days like this were made for air conditioning, *not* baking.

Zeke bounded over, bobbling a madeleine between his hands like a hot potato. "Try one, Sis!"

The shell-shaped sponge cakes smelled wonderful, but Prissie bypassed him, aiming for the shelf where tall glasses were kept. "If it's too hot to touch, it's too hot to eat."

Disappointment flickered briefly through her brother's blue eyes, but Zeke took her statement as a challenge. He bit off half the madeleine, then puffed out his cheeks, sucking in air. His words were muffled by his mouthful. "Burnt muh tongue!"

"Of course you did," she chided, splashing cold milk into a glass for him. "Be more careful!"

"Too late. Damage's done," Zeke mumbled around his food. Downing the milk, he popped the rest of the cake into his mouth. "What if I brought 'em home for later?"

"A fine idea," their father interjected. "Your mother and grandmother will want a sample."

Zeke hadn't changed much since he was a kid. His blond hair was as unruly as ever, and he still came up with insane plans. But Prissie had to admit that he was fun to work with … provided she didn't have to clean up his messes. In a way, she admired her younger brother. Zeke had always known exactly what he wanted. Not to follow in his father's footsteps, but to work side-by-side with Dad. So he did. Simple as that.

"Taking off?" asked Mr. Pomeroy when Prissie returned from her milk delivery.

Leaving her apron on one hook, she took her purse from another. "I'll be at the library, same as usual."

"And checking in on Mr. Truman?" her father pried.

With a tight little smile that warned against teasing, Prissie repeated, "As usual."

Prissie wasn't the only person who knew that West Edinton's one-room library had the best air conditioning in town. After a quiet hour spent flipping through magazines, perusing the new release shelf, and chatting with friends and neighbors, she felt refreshed. And ready for another treat.

She hurried her steps along Main Street to the door of Stained, the small business that had taken the place of Harken's used bookstore. Chimes twinkled when she stepped through the door. They were one thing that hadn't changed when her friend Marcus Truman took over the space after Mr. Mercer retired. Prissie's heart lifted at the familiar cascade of notes, but she stopped short at the state of Marcus's workshop.

Crowded tables were in typical disarray. Smudged papers with curling edges. Snips and coils of metal. Bits of colored glass arranged in neat patterns. These were future works of art—stained glass windows, sun catchers, wind chimes, lamps, and nightlights. But in the center of the room stood a stone arch.

"What are *you* doing here?" Prissie circled the unexpected prop, searching her memory for anything Marcus might be involved with. Could it be part of a theater production? Or some kind of biblical reenactment thing? Prissie touched chalky white stone, so different than the dark gray stuff they quarried locally. "It's real," she murmured. Each block must have weighed a ton.

Her fingers trailed across a surface so smooth, it felt powdery. Moss clung to the carved base, as if the mysterious structure had once stood in a forest. There were delicate carvings along the inside—twining canes of climbing roses, with three-dimensional blooms surrounded by thorns. If anything, the workmanship reminded her of Abner's doors. But her old friend was halfway around the world.

"Wishful thinking," she sighed.

A shuffle came from the corner, and Prissie turned. Wide eyes peeped at her from over the top of a formidable workbench. This was no place for a child! She glanced toward the back room, frowning. Where had Marcus gotten to? And how could a child have wandered in? Taking charge, she asked, "Does Mr. Truman know you're here?"

The boy leaned out of his hiding spot. "Are you talking to me?"

"Who else would I be talking to?" As soon as the crisp retort was out of her mouth, Prissie was hit with a sense of *déjà vu* so keen, she placed her hand over her heart.

Impossible.

Well, perhaps not entirely impossible. Ten years had passed since Prissie met a boy she shouldn't have been able to see. Koji had been the kind of friend who comes once in a lifetime … if you're lucky. But twice?

With a small shake of her head, Prissie stuck to practical matters. "Mr. Truman has lots of sharp things in his shop. Hot things, too. So it's dangerous for children. Did you come in here by mistake?"

"No."

Holding out her hand, she urged, "Come along … hmm … what's your name?"

"I know *your* name," he announced, not budging from his hiding place. "You are Prissie."

"That's right. Have we met?"

The child slipped into the open, and she got a good look at him. Shining raiment, pale green eyes, and straight hair that was easily as long as her own.

Except it was a deep, dark shade of green. His ears came to pronounced points, and his feet were bare. Prissie sank to her knees, for they'd turned to jelly. "You're an angel."

He walked over and gazed down into her eyes. "I am."

As far as Prissie could tell, the boy was in the neighborhood of seven years old, but looks could be deceiving. For all she knew, he'd lived for centuries. Even millennia. Taking in the intricate black stitching that edged his collar, Prissie made another connection. "You're a Caretaker."

"I am," he repeated.

"Hello," she said, a smile sneaking past her surprise. "How do you know my name?"

"From songs."

"Whose?" she pressed, hoping for news of friends who'd gradually faded from her life.

Prissie had once been surrounded by an entire Flight of angels. But as time passed, many of them had been Sent elsewhere. Those who remained only spoke to her in dreams, which faded until the edges were fuzzy. Marcus and Milo stayed by her, though, and she was grateful for their steady presence.

But the boy pursed his lips. "Did you forget Whose you are?"

"Tamaes is my guardian ang–"

He shook his head. "You belong to God."

"Obviously." Prissie tried to make sense of that. "Wait. Do you mean God sings about me?"

One of the boy's eyebrows quirked, and he quoted, "The Lord your God is with you, the Mighty Warrior who saves. He will take great delight in you; in His love He will no longer rebuke you, but will rejoice over you with singing."

Awe crept into her soul and tied a knot in her tongue.

"My mentor says humans are forgetful; however, he said *you* would be different." Touching the tip of Prissie's nose, the young angel asked, "Are you forgetful?"

"Not usually, but nobody's perfect," she replied, searching his face. Skin the color of latte. Eyebrows, lashes, and a dusting of freckles, all in a baffling shade of pine green. Thin lips and a pert nose. He looked so much younger than Koji had been, but his manner of speaking was just as solemn. So different from Prissie's nephew and cousins.

"Are you a member of Jedrick's Flight?"

"I am."

"Does that mean you belong to Padgett?"

The boy straightened slightly. "He is my mentor."

Padgett Prentice lived and worked at nearby Sunderland State Park. Like

Milo and Marcus, he was a Graft, an angel in human disguise. Although they were members of the same Flight, each of them hailed from a different angelic order. Milo was a Messenger. Marcus was a Protector. And Padgett was one of the samayim—storm-bringers, earth-shakers, sea-stirrers. These Caretakers were capable of incredible miracles.

It was news to Prissie that her friend had been granted an apprentice. Not that she was privy to everything that went on in Jedrick's Flight. Far from it. She asked, "Does Padgett know you're here?"

"Soon."

A heartbeat later, the archway in the middle of the room blazed, and Prissie had to close her eyes against the brightness. When she was able to focus again, Padgett stood before her—high cheekbones, black braid, bright bandana. "Pardon my intrusion, miss. I seem to have mislaid my apprentice."

She laughed weakly. "And I seem to be able to see him. This brings back memories."

Padgett offered his hands, helping her to her feet. Then he raised his voice to carry. "Marcus, I found him."

A door in the back room slammed, and Marcus skidded into his workshop. "Where'd the pipsqueak …? *Whoa.*" Marcus glanced between her and the boy before addressing Prissie. "Are you seeing things again, kiddo?"

"Obviously."

Marcus had been Prissie's truest friend for nearly a decade, so she was used to how he looked. But he still teased her for writing him off as a troublemaker back when they were in high school. A wide section of his wavy brown hair looked as if he'd bleached it platinum blond. And from under the edges of his tank top, zig-zag tattoos in cream and gold stood out against brown skin.

"I thought the captain said we *weren't* going to mention …." Marcus pointed between Prissie and the boy, then looked to Padgett for guidance. "You know something I don't?"

The green-haired boy announced, "Milo is here."

Milo Leggett still wore his mailman's uniform when he hurried out of the back room, his blue eyes filled with concern. "Is Miss Priscilla in some kind of …?"

"Trouble?" she finished for him as the young Caretaker slipped his hand into hers.

"Oh, dear." With a chuckle, the Messenger knelt and asked, "What have you done, little man?"

"I was Sent," the child replied loftily.

"So was I." Milo ran a hand through short-cropped ash blond curls. "Though I don't know why. Padgett …?"

The ranger calmly addressed his apprentice. "Your presentation might have benefited from more discretion." Placing his hand on the stone arch, Padgett said, "This is hardly subtle."

"I will take greater care next time," the boy replied.

Padgett dropped to one knee. "Did you remember your first words?"

"No." Bare feet shuffled.

Turning the child to face Prissie, Padgett rested his hands on his shoulders. Gaze warm, voice light, he said, "Miss Prissie Pomeroy, I'm pleased to introduce my apprentice. This is Asher."

"Asher," she echoed, anticipation whirling through her heart. Something was happening. And it felt like something good. Something worth holding onto.

Milo tickled the boy's ribs and nodded significantly.

Standing a little taller, Asher held Prissie's gaze. He kept a straight face, but she caught a twinkle in his eyes that reminded her very much of Zeke. It was just a hint of mischief, but real enough to color her first impression.

"Did you forget?" Padgett asked.

"No."

His mentor's expression grew puzzled. "What are you waiting for?"

"Prissie."

Milo's voice held heavy traces of amusement. "Aren't you supposed to reassure the young lady?"

"No," Asher replied. "First God will answer the prayer of her heart."

And suddenly, Prissie was the center of everyone's attention. She hadn't actually *prayed*. At least, not in any formal way. But the Lord who knew her every thought was generous, and Prissie gladly accepted His gift.

Opening her arms, she asked, "Hug?"

Marcus snorted as Asher slid out of his mentor's grasp and into her embrace.

Asher was warm and soft, and he smelled like fresh air and sunshine. The longer he nestled against Prissie, the more her memories stirred. She recalled the spicy water angels used for washing and the sweetness of manna for meals. When Asher's arms wound tightly around her neck, she closed her eyes to hold back happy tears. His being here unlocked a treasure trove of half-forgotten details, reminding her that forever was never far. Ever near. Endlessly dear.

With a soft giggle, Asher kissed her cheek and finally complied. "Fear not."

CHAPTER 2

THE OPEN INVITATION

In a forest glade where gentle breezes stirred the leaves of slender trees, two Caretakers tended to their flock of yahavim. Tiny angels as bright as sundrops whizzed to and fro on delicate wings, humming along with Padgett's song. Asher smiled at their whimsical dance and whispered greetings to each little manna-maker in turn.

Once they were counted and content, Padgett asked, "Can you tell me why you went to Prissie?"

His apprentice nodded. "I was Sent."

"But why?"

"It is a mystery." Asher scooted closer to his mentor and loudly whispered, "She was not afraid."

"No. Prissie welcomed you with open arms."

The boy asked, "Would she sing with me?"

"Who knows? If you see her again, put the question to her."

"I will."

"Ask? Or see her?" Padgett checked.

"Both!"

"Have you received another Sending?"

"Soon." Asher tugged at the full sleeve of his mentor's raiment. "I love her."

Padgett's gaze held a smile that almost reached his lips. "Many do."

A sudden emotion flickered through the boy's eyes, and he scooted closer. "One who does ... should not."

Prissie didn't look up from her cutting board when the door to the bakery kitchen swung wide. Mr. Pomeroy was due back sooner than later from a rustle-up at the corner store. But when her father didn't greet her as usual, she glanced back ... and blinked in surprise. A young man leaned against the opposite counter, thumbs hooked through his belt loops as he watched her with an expectant expression.

"*You?*"

"Me," he replied, eyebrows waggling.

Shaking free of her astonishment, Prissie hurried forward to welcome him with a hug. But then she remembered and stopped to check if anything was smeared on her apron.

"No need to primp, Miss Priss. You look lovely."

"Don't be ridiculous. I've been up to my elbows in cupcake batter all morning!"

Stepping forward to claim his hug, Ransom asked, "What's a little cocoa powder between friends?"

"But your nice shirt!" she protested.

He rested his chin on top of her hairnet and soothed, "Completely washable."

"I thought you were traipsing across Europe."

"I was."

Prissie poked him accusingly. "No one mentioned that you'd be visiting! Are you on break or something?"

"Nope. I'm variously diploma'd and certified, and I paid my dues in enough bakeries to know which one I prefer. I'm home. To stay."

Finally returning his embrace, Prissie murmured, "Welcome home, then."

Ransom Pavlos had once been her nemesis, the class clown who got on her nerves every time he opened his mouth. But they'd come to a truce around the same time Ransom became a Christian. That was the year everything had changed, mostly for the better. Since he'd worked with her father right through high school, Prissie had ample time to get used to the idea of being friends. Ransom still teased, but she overreacted less.

Easing out of his arms, Prissie dabbed at the smudge she'd left. "Have you been to see Marcus yet?"

"Nope. I came here first." Tweaking a flyaway tendril of her honey-blonde hair, Ransom asked, "Do you see much of him?"

"He lives right across the street." She turned back to her chopping. "We talk every day."

"I talk to him most days, too. But he never mentions you."

"Marcus isn't the gossipy sort."

"So you two are close?"

"As ever." Prissie shot him an exasperated look. "He's missed you, too."

Ransom casually asked, "What about you? Did you miss me?"

"Oh, you know," she replied breezily. "Out of sight, out of mind."

"Ouch."

She laughed. "Did you tell Dad you were coming back?"

"Yes and no. Stuff worked out the last time I turned up on his doorstep asking for a job." With a small shrug, Ransom explained, "I'm taking him up on an open invitation, that there'll always a place for me here."

"Your timing is excellent. With the county fair right around the corner, he'll hardly refuse the extra manpower."

"Thought of that," he mumbled, a sheepish expression in his brown eyes.

She laughed again. "You *know* Daddy will be thrilled to see you. And not just because you can turn out turnovers."

"I *can* do more than that, but I'm willing to do anything." Offering his hands, he said, "Put me to work, Miss Priss."

This was new. Ransom asking to be bossed around? "Hoping to impress someone*?*"

"You've cleverly deduced my masterful plan. Show up, then show off."

"We have sour cherries left over. Make something with those, Mr. Certifiable."

"That's *certified*," he said, tying an apron around his waist. "And what are you in the mood for?"

"Surprise me."

Ransom rolled up his sleeves and set to work, giving her the chance to slyly study him. He dressed better than he used to, and his bushy hair had been trimmed into respectability. Was this the kind of person her school friend had grown into? More polished in his tastes after years abroad. Or was Ransom simply trying to impress her father? Prissie glanced down at her faded sundress and floral apron. She probably looked very unprofessional in the eyes of an honest-to-goodness patisserie.

"You haven't changed much," Ransom remarked.

She wondered at his tone. "Is that good or bad?"

He took a deep breath and released it as a sigh. "Mostly, I'd call it a relief."

"I'm still me." With a roll of her eyes, she asked, "Who else would I be?"

Ransom grinned and reached for a saucepan.

Prissie was glad to see his tension ebb away. He'd probably been nervous about approaching his old boss after so long an absence. But now that he was in familiar territory, he worked quickly and confidently. Which was perfect. Not only was Ransom at ease, her dad would be impressed by whatever confection his former student concocted.

While she finished rough-chopping white chocolate, Prissie hummed lightly to herself. She'd learned the melody years ago from an angelic friend whose songs still circled through her mind whenever she was happy. The notes were always the same, but she'd taken to changing the words to suit her situation. They were her prayer, and the lyrics she applied today celebrated an unexpected reunion. Her dad would be so happy. Marcus's joy would be full. And she was glad, too. Having Ransom around again would mix things up. Not that her life was *dull*. But it would be the three of them again—Ransom, Marcus, and her. Just like before. Only better, because Ransom was home to stay.

"Any news I should know about?"

Prissie shook her head. "I'm sure Daddy covered all the important family news in his emails."

"Yep. I know about little stuff, like babies. And then there's the important stuff. Experimental jam recipes. High school football scores. Weather reports. Baking pan acquisitions." Unwrapping a block of butter, he said, "But he never said much about you, either."

"I emailed!"

"Yep. And copied Neil."

She bristled. "You were both gone."

"And I'm grateful you kept me in the loop," Ransom promised. "But I want to know what 'same old, same old' looks like."

"It's July, so 'same old, same old' looks like berry-stained fingers. It sounds like mowers in the orchard. It smells like dill from the garden. And it means baking all morning and canning until sunset. Like you said, things haven't changed much."

"I know you're leaving out important stuff."

Prissie turned to fully face him. "Like what?"

"Koji, for instance. Hear anything from your Conscience lately?"

When Prissie was fourteen, she'd met an angel, and for nearly a year, she'd kept his secret. Koji was an Observer, one of the archivists of heaven. He'd become her best friend at a time when she needed one. Given everything they'd gone through, maybe they'd needed each other. Prissie said, "Milo puts something in the mailbox from him two or three times a week."

"Mr. Mailman's still in the picture?"

"Where else would he be?"

Ransom studied her face. "So did Koji grow up and marry some island girl?"

She laughed softly. "Wrong on both counts."

"I know it probably sounds crazy, but the whole time I was away, I had the weirdest dreams. Koji was there a lot when I closed my eyes."

Prissie nodded. "I'm sure he misses you, too."

"And you miss him?"

"*Indeed.*" Her smile wobbled. "I love him so much, it hurts."

Ransom cautiously asked, "You're in love with Koji?"

"That's *not* what I said."

After a lengthy pause, he chuckled. "Sorry, sorry. I get it."

Prissie kept her eyes lowered. "You do?"

"Yep. You're not the first person to have a friend, Miss Priss. Nor the first to love someone so much it hurts."

She'd forgotten how quick Ransom was to skip past chit-chat to tackle matters of the heart. Hers was trembling dangerously close to tears, knowing that Koji had visited Ransom in dreams. Even though they were far apart, God allowed them to stay connected.

Thankfully, her father chose that moment to push through the kitchen door laden with bulging grocery sacks. What followed was much back thumping, a gourmet's inquisition, and an inevitable invitation. Ransom would be coming to dinner.

"Can you say stuff in French?" Zeke didn't wait for an answer before asking, "Did they think you had an American accent?"

Ransom's smile wasn't entirely happy. "I know enough to get by, but I pretty much kept my head down and my mouth shut."

"Very un-you."

"It wasn't so bad. Your dad gave me some pointers in case things skewed that way. So I was prepared."

"What kind of pointers?" Zeke demanded, drawing himself up to his full height.

Prissie smothered a smile. Her brother had shown up at his usual time to do dishes only to find his work more than half done. He was entirely impressed by everything from Ransom's new credentials to the custardy cherry tarts cooling on the racks, but he was pressing the one advantage left to him. Zeke had a couple inches on Ransom, who wasn't nearly as muscular as her brother the quarterback.

Ransom explained, "Your dad told me to redeem all the time I'd have on my hands. So I read, studied, memorized a whole pack of Bible verses." Hooking his thumbs into the apron ties at his waist, Ransom added, "I had plenty of time to use my head while I was buttering ramekins or beating egg whites."

Zeke frowned thoughtfully. "You sound like Beau."

Prissie leapt into the opening. Lifting a plate of fresh-baked cookies, she said, "Speaking of Beau, Ransom and I should invite him for dinner. He'd hate to miss out."

"Yeah, I need to get ahold of Marcus, too." Ransom tugged at his apron ties. "Sorry to leave the work half done."

Mr. Pomeroy gripped Zeke's shoulder. "Don't apologize for lightening his load and brightening our day. Dinner's at six."

"I'll be there, sir!" Ransom promised.

Prissie led the way out the bakery's back door and over to a bright red door on the far end of the building. "I'm not sure if anyone's mentioned it, but Beau lives upstairs now. Uncle Lo and Aunt Ida outgrew the apartment, and my brother the scholar needed some quiet. And more shelf space."

"He's interning at the DeeVee, isn't he?"

"*And* teaching Sunday school at our church. Pastor Kern and Pastor Ruggles don't mind sharing … or working around his wonky class schedule." Rapping lightly, Prissie opened the street-level door and called up the stairs. "Anybody home?"

Moments later, Beau Pomeroy leaned through his second-floor apartment door. "Hey, Sis! Where in the world did you find that stray?"

"*Stray*?" protested Ransom as he followed Prissie up the stairs.

She cheerfully said, "He showed up on our doorstep a few hours ago. Daddy didn't have the heart to turn him away."

Looking over his shoulder, Beau loudly announced, "Guys, the prodigal returneth!"

There was a thud of feet, and Marcus rushed out onto the landing above. His expression of amazement melted into a smile. "Yo."

Ransom grinned. "Hey."

Prissie rolled her eyes at everything the best friends were leaving unsaid. But then Ransom jostled her the rest of the way up the stairs, and she found herself in the middle of a group hug. She didn't mind being included in their reunion. Trapped between Marcus's leather jacket and Ransom's smudged shirt, she closed her eyes and thanked God for the unique bonds that flourished in her hometown.

From what she'd been told, Prissie gathered that friendships between humans and angels were rare. Yet she and Koji had been given several precious months together. And Marcus treasured his connection with Ransom, who had no idea he was friends with a cherub.

And then there was Prissie's almost-twin Beau. They'd been born close enough together that for two months each year, they were the same age. The siblings shared a spiritual birthday. And the secret of Prissie's angelic encounters.

"Are those cookies for us?" Beau rescued the plate of goodies and handed them back to Milo, who leaned against the door frame.

The Messenger accepted the plate with a wink for Prissie, who wriggled free and joined him. While she patted at flyaway strands of hair, the off-duty mailman greeted Ransom in flawless French. Chuckling in the face of his astonishment, Milo translated, "You welcomed me as if I were an angel of God, as if I were Christ Jesus Himself."

Ransom grinned. "Galatians."

"Nice," said Marcus.

"Grandpa usually says 'as welcome as flowers in May,' but angels do in a pinch." Beau offered his hand to Ransom, adding, "It's been too long. Welcome back!"

"Thanks."

Milo clasped Ransom's hand next and didn't let go. "Your father notified the post office of his change of address a few years back. Where are you staying?"

Ransom hesitated a little too long. "I didn't have anything *definite* …."

Marcus shot a pleading look at Milo, who said, "You'll stay with us. There's room for one more bachelor with Marcus and me."

"I'd be grateful," Ransom accepted.

Marcus bumped shoulders with him and asked, "You learn everything you needed to?"

"Yep."

"Gonna stick around?" he pressed.

"That's the plan." Ransom locked an arm around his friend's shoulder and quietly promised, "Long haul."

CHAPTER 3

THE FAT ENVELOPE

In the dark of night, a stealthy hand tripped the latch on one of the beehives. The soft drone of insect wings coming from within changed pitch. But uneasy buzzing wasn't enough to ward off their intruder.

"Mustn't linger. Just a finger." Crooning lies, the Fallen exposed a section of comb and thrust in one bony digit. He hooked the wax and tugged, breathing heavily as he dug into raw honey. Pausing long enough to furtively check the sky, he licked his smeared hand, then slid his finger into his mouth. Eyes drifting shut, the demon moaned.

"Good, good. Good bees," he mumbled, cradling his hand to his mouth. "Goodness and mercy. Yours to make. Mine to take."

As a distinctive set of pink wings spiraled low over the nearby farmhouse, the demon studied the gable window over which his old friend settled. He slowly finished his treat, closed the hive, and stole to a better vantage point. Watchful. Wondering.

"Leaving the brother; cleaving to the sister?"

This development opened up appealing possibilities. "Good, good. Good friend." With a hissing laugh, he whispered, "A merciful heart. A good place to start."

Prissie was sitting on the plank fence behind the mailboxes when Milo Leggett rolled up to make his last delivery of the day. "You're home early," he remarked cheerfully.

"It's a special day."

"Is it?"

She wrinkled her nose in the face of his gentle teasing. "I always dream about Koji the night before you bring me one of his postcards. They're never a surprise because he's too excited to wait. And you *know* today's special." The twenty-fifth of July was the day Koji and Prissie met.

"Koji's birthday." Milo turned off his engine and joined her on the fence. "Would you rather be surprised?"

"Things are fine the way they are." Prissie frowned and admitted, "It's strange, though. He was nearly as tall as me the first time he came into my dreams, but he hasn't changed since then. He's like Peter Pan, a forever boy."

"Does that bother you?"

"I understand, but it's a little sad. I feel like I'm outgrowing my best friend."

Milo gazed up through the trees that turned Orchard Lane into a tunnel of greenery. "I don't think age has anything to do with love."

"That's not what you told me when I was nine."

With a groan, the Messenger asked, "Will you *ever* forgive me for turning down your proposal?"

Prissie laughed. "It's funny now. I only wanted to make sure I could keep you."

"I haven't gone anywhere."

"You stayed," she agreed. "And I'm glad. Otherwise, I might start to think I dreamed up the whole thing."

Milo's sidelong look came with a smile. "Taking the miraculous for granted, are we?"

"Maybe just a little."

He didn't criticize. "It's always interesting when that happens."

"What?"

"When one of God's children needs to be refreshed." Pulling a fat envelope from his mail bag, he placed it in her hands. "Things are stirring, Miss Priscilla. Take courage, and know that we're with you."

Much later, Prissie lingered in her bedroom's windowseat, gazing out past the big maple tree in the front yard. "He must save up all year," she whispered to Aquila, who purred contentedly by her hip. "How else could he fill so many pages?"

Koji's annual letter held more precious things than she could count—memories, hopes, praise, promises. And paintings. They depicted little things that Koji saw every day and grand landscapes that couldn't possibly exist on earth. Although he never told her specifically, she knew these were glimpses of forever. Eternity would be beautiful, and he would be waiting there.

"All I do is wait, but it's worth waiting for." Still, Prissie wouldn't lie. She'd have given almost anything to feel Koji's fingers tap her hand. Or to go back to the days when they sat on the porch swing and watched the sun rise. Fumbling for another tissue, Prissie fought off a pang of loneliness. "Soon," she promised herself. Even if it was only in dreams, she'd be seeing Koji later.

A bright flash caught her eye. She turned, fully expecting to see one of her family members with a camera, stealing a candid photo. Instead, small feet pattered along the hallway to her door, and Asher leaned through.

The young Caretaker touched a finger to his lips, then tiptoed away.

Setting aside her gifts from Koji, Prissie hurried after him. A swish of green hair was all she spied before the boy vanished down the back stairs. Mindful of his warning to be quiet, she avoided the creaky stairs and held her breath as she stole into the kitchen. And interrupted Ransom, who was rummaging through their refrigerator.

"What are you doing here?" she asked.

"Your brother invited me over."

"Which one?" she asked, since there was no one else around. Except for Asher. The boy took advantage of a partially open drawer to climb up onto the kitchen counter.

"Jude. He asked me to make him something to eat after school." With a grin, Ransom added, "You never outgrow milk-and-cookie time!"

"We have a cookie jar, and it's full," Prissie pointed out.

"He asked for cake."

"What kind?"

"Something new."

"Can you be more specific?"

"Not until I figure out what I have to work with," he replied, turning toward the cupboard. "Oh, hey! You mostly still keep stuff in the same place."

"Of course. And since this is my dad's kitchen, there's plenty to work with." Prissie was having a hard time focusing on Ransom. Asher strolled along the counter to the refrigerator and clambered up. Clearly pleased with his accomplishment, he sat back to watch. Did he know that's where Koji used to sit? Probably. Prissie wished she could tell Beau they had an angel on top of their fridge again.

Suddenly, Ransom blocked her view. "Have you been crying, Miss Priss?"

She avoided the question. "I hope you weren't planning to make me wash dishes for you. Because I have better things t–"

"Hey," he interrupted. "Spill. Something's wrong."

"It's not. I'm fine."

"Not buying it. First you skip out on work. Now you expect me to ignore damp lashes." Ransom poked her shoulder. "If you can't tell me, I'm calling for reinforcements."

She rolled her eyes and backed up. "I *didn't* skip. Dad gave me some time off."

"Not so fast." He snagged her hand to keep her from bolting. "Something's not right. Or are these tears of joy?"

"Yes. If you must know, they are." Prissie tugged halfheartedly. Hadn't she been wishing for a hand to hold? "I heard from Koji today. It's his birthday."

Ransom relaxed into a smile. "Is that all?"

She shrugged.

"Fair enough. You can blubber into a batter bowl while we bake Koji a birthday cake."

With a quick peek in Asher's direction, Prissie said, "I thought you were baking Jude a cake."

"Changed my mind." He drew her over to sideboard and plucked her apron from its hook. Dropping it over her head, Ransom asked, "What's his favorite?"

"Koji always liked spice cake. And I'm still not doing dishes."

"What have you got against cleanliness all of a sudden?" Lifting a hand, Ransom pledged, "I hereby claim dish duty. You can even boss me around if it'll cheer you up."

"I don't need cheering up," she grumbled.

"Coulda fooled me." Ransom opened the cupboard and twirled through the spice rack. "Do you have a recipe, or should I wing it?"

Atop the fridge, Asher began flapping his arms, and Prissie smiled. "Wing it."

"Sheet cake, loaf cake, roll cake, cupcakes," rattled off Ransom. "Or should we go all out with a towering layer cake?"

"Definitely a tower. At least ten layers. With white icing."

"Decisive!" Ransom crouched in order to rummage through the vast collection of cake pans Mr. Pomeroy stowed in the cupboards. "Are we talking skinny layers, or do I need to locate dowels?"

"Dowels," she replied breezily. "They're in the third drawer down."

"Of course they are. Right next to the blow torch and the potato ricer."

With the shadow of a smile, she said, "Don't be silly. The ricer is with the food mill. We keep safety goggles in the drawer with the dowels and blow torch."

"Sensible."

She hummed noncommittally while tying her apron. It had been a while since Ransom butted into her life and ignored her protests. "You haven't changed much."

"Yep. Still me. For better or for worse."

Asher giggled, and Prissie smiled at their little eavesdropper. Maybe it was time to give him something other than grumbling and complaining to listen to. "You know, I was never able to throw Koji a birthday party."

Ransom muttered, "Him and me both."

That gave her pause. Prissie searched her memory and came up empty. "When's your birthday?"

"Does it matter?"

"I have *no idea* when your birthday is. How is that even possible?"

"Relax, Priss. It's no big deal. Your dad brought it up once, and when I asked him to leave it, he did."

"But why keep it a secret? We would have helped you celebrate!"

"I guess I didn't want to feel like I was asking for anything more than your family already gave." Ransom waved off her chagrin. "And harvesttime is crazy-busy for you Pomeroys. It's not like you could fit in something else."

"Fall? Is it soon?"

"Soonish."

"What day?" Prissie demanded.

"September twenty-sixth."

She checked the calendar. "That's a Sunday. The orchard's closed for a day of rest … and parties."

"I don't really *want* a party."

"That's ridiculous! We should do *something* special."

He looked away, then searched her face. "You really want to do something for my birthday?"

"Didn't I just say that?"

"Anything I want?" he challenged.

"Within reason."

With a cautious tone, Ransom asked, "Spend the day with me?"

"Just me?"

Ransom nodded. "Yeah, just us."

"Doing what?"

"Nothing much." He glanced around, then said, "If the orchard's closed, we can just walk around in there. Call it the grand tour."

"You want to walk around in the orchard," she asked skeptically. "All day."

"If it sounds lame, I'm sorry. I haven't had much practice with stuff like this."

"I suppose we could pack a picnic." Prissie's mouth pressed tight as she thought it over. "Fine. I'll spend the day in the orchard with you, on one condition."

"Let's hear it."

"At dinnertime, we come back here for a *real* birthday dinner. And you'll let Dad bake you a cake."

Ransom offered his hand. "Done deal."

The clasp lingered, and Prissie thought back to all the others who'd asked for her hand at one time or another. Wasn't this the same? *Could* it be the same?

"Who are you thinking about?" asked Ransom.

"Umm … mostly Koji."

"Missing the birthday boy, huh?"

"Obviously."

"You held hands with him a lot."

"He liked to, and I didn't mind." Prissie explained. "It was a friendly thing."

"What about this?"

She blinked. "What?"

He gave her hand a squeeze. "Is this a friendly thing?"

"Yes." With a quick peek at Asher, Prissie admitted, "I think God knew I needed a friend today."

That night, Prissie expected to dream of Koji. She would tell him all her favorite parts of the letter he'd prepared. They'd hold hands. She'd ask questions. He'd coax for songs. That's the way it should have been.

" … under my protection."

"Boys, ploys, blades, maids," chanted a voice in eerie sing-song.

The first voice came again, stern but youthful, like a boy whose voice is still settling. "How long have you been free?"

"Earth quakes, wall shakes, seal breaks." With a hissing laugh, he added, "Free to roam, home sweet home. Aren't you glad to see me, *friend*?"

"Earthquake? But that was nearly a decade ago."

Prissie turned her head to see who was in her bedroom, but the moment she opened her eyes, light assailed her. Her surroundings had changed completely. She was … outside?

A teenaged boy leaned over her—pale with flyaway black hair and bright green eyes. "Verrill, she's here," he announced, speaking to someone behind him. Soft notes sounded, the plucking of a harp's strings.

"Kester?" she gasped, struggling to sit up.

"No, child. Just a humble Messenger." The the musician sat on a stone threshold whose door was missing. "My name is Verrill, and this is my apprentice."

"Raz," offered the other angel with a friendly grin. "Sorry to disappoint. Should I skip the whole 'fear not' spiel?"

"No. I like it." Prissie gazed around, hoping for a glimpse of friends. She recognized the forest glade, a place of refuge that she'd entered many times before through a blue door.

Verrill set aside his harp and stood, offering his hands to help Prissie to her feet. "You have nothing to fear. We are … friends of friends, I suppose."

Raz nodded. "Ethan's part of our Flight."

"Who?"

"The one who's defending you while you sleep."

Prissie looked up into Verrill's face and blinked. Like Asher, this angel had green hair. "I heard someone say something about protecting. Ethan's a cherub?"

"Nope. Guardian," said Raz.

"I don't understand." Prissie scanned the peaceful glade. "Where's Tamaes? Or Taweel for that matter?"

The angels exchanged a look that left her out, and Verrill said, "Never far. But for now, stay with us. Until the unpleasantness is over."

Trusting these two made sense, but Prissie shook her head. "What's going on?"

"We cannot say for certain," Verrill replied apologetically.

"Someone's in my bedroom! Send me back!" She whirled and ran in the direction the blue door used to stand, but no way out appeared.

Raz caught up to her in a swirl of chartreuse wings and grabbed her arm. "It's okay, Prissie. Don't be afraid."

"I'm *not*! How can I help if you leave me ignorant?" she snapped. "Tell me how to pray! Let me do my part!"

Once again, the angels exchanged a long look.

"So be it." Brown wings encircled them, and Verrill added, "Go in peace. And if possible, wake softly."

Then all the lights were doused, and Prissie was back in bed, heart thudding in her chest. The unsettling voice was there, and it raised gooseflesh on her arms.

"Will you Fall into that woman's bed?"

"Enough words," snapped the one called Ethan.

This time when Prissie turned to look, she saw a shadow in the window glass. But then her defender lifted his wings and filled the room with light. She slapped her hands over her eyes with a whimper of protest, and the blaze swiftly dimmed.

Uncovering her eyes, she stared at her angelic visitor.

"Prissie?" The Guardian stared at her, eyes wide, sword drooping.

"Yes, I can see you."

"I am …." He trailed off awkwardly.

"Sent?" she suggested, sitting up and folding her hands atop her quilt.

"Yes." He bit his lip, then turned to face her fully. "My name is Ethan, apprentice to Conrad, and since God placed your name under my hand, my joy is doubled."

CHAPTER 4

THE CHURCH HOPPER

Jedrick swept low on emerald wings, grazing the tops of apple trees in his pursuit. He slashed out at a formless blot, but his blade caught nothing but chill air. In a flash of turquoise, Tycho clipped a turn and unleashed three arrows in quick succession. The bolts sizzled like lightning, but their light revealed nothing in the shadows.

"How did that Fallen get through the Hedge?" asked Jedrick.

"He didn't get *through*. He's been here all along. Sealed away." Tycho's steely gaze briefly met the other captain's. "I don't know how he freed himself, but this complicates matters. He's clever."

"And elusive." Jedrick pulled up to scan the orchard. "Which way did he go?"

"Not sure, but he can't be far. I can smell him." Tycho withdrew another arrow from his quiver and nocked his bow. "Flush him out."

Dropping to the ground, Jedrick strode through the orchard, sword ready. But row upon row, he found no trace of their intruder. His fingers tightened around the hilt of his sword. Close as they were to the battle lines, the Pomeroys' Hedge frequently saw turmoil. Guardians patrolled the property lines, keeping safe their precious charges. What might these hadarim say if they knew a demon lurked in their hard-won haven?

Jedrick's protective nature pushed him to widen his search, but he was rewarded with nothing but the rustle of leaves, the sharp yip of a fox, and the distant hooting of an owl. "Is he gone?"

Tycho landed beside him. "No, he has gone to ground. This demon has learned to hide his tracks."

"He is here," agreed Jedrick. "But where?"

Prissie studied her guest, whose shimmering wings filled her bedroom with rosy light. Compared to the other guardian angels in her acquaintance, Ethan was slim, and there was a boyishness to the curve of his cheek. Although she was curious, she first pointed to her window. "Is he gone?"

"Yes."

"Will he be back?"

Regret flashed across Ethan's face. "Fear not, Prissie. I will be with you."

Tossing aside her blankets, she stood to confront the young angel. "Where's Tamaes?"

"Not far."

"*He's* my guardian angel."

"Yes. He is yours, and you are his."

"Then who are you?" she demanded in exasperation.

"My name is Ethan," he repeated gently. "And I was Sent."

"To me. But *why*?"

He slowly sheathed his sword. "Your safety was my immediate concern."

Prissie's patience was failing. "Ethan, you're going to have to *tell* me what's going on!"

The pink-winged angel hesitated, then asked, "May I invite Verrill and Raz to join us?"

"Please." In her experience, Messengers were much better at explanations. He nodded gratefully, and Prissie ventured, "You seem … young."

"I am the youngest member of this Hedge."

"Guardian angels form Hedges," she recalled. "But doesn't that make you one of ours?"

A smile blossomed on Ethan's face, but before Prissie could pry more specifics from him, a patch of her bedroom ceiling rippled and glowed. An instant later, the two angels from Prissie's dream dropped into the room with a showy swirl of wings.

The one draped in chocolatey folds placed his harp on her windowseat. Stepping forward to take her hands, he said, "Our first meeting was entirely too brief. Let's begin again. I'm Verrill, and this is my apprentice Raz."

With a cheery wave, the angular young Messenger said, "Fear not!"

The more frightening aspects of the night were quickly fading, replaced by a growing sense of wonder. Three new angels stood before Prissie. Real as life. Rare as jewels. She fought to memorize every line of Verrill's kind face. "Thank you. The last few days have been …." She shook her head, helpless to explain, and repeated, "Thank you."

Verrill handed her off to Raz, who beamed down at her. "I'm the one who's grateful. You're my *first* firsthand encounter." He confided, "I didn't like the idea of scaring someone half out of their wits."

"I'm happy to meet you," she promised, looking from face to face. "But can one of you explain to me why Ethan came to my rescue tonight?"

Raz drew her over to the young Guardian, saying, "My good friend is your brother's Guardian."

"Which brother?"

The gentle smile was back on Ethan's face. "Zeke."

Prissie couldn't help it. She giggled. "You've had your hands full."

"My hands and my heart."

Raz said, "Show her, Ethan."

The Guardian turned his palm up, and Prissie could see a row of symbols etched into his skin. "I can't tell what it says." She didn't resist when Raz placed her hand into Ethan's. Even if this angel wasn't exactly hers, opportunities like this were rare and precious to Guardians. "I'm guessing that's my name."

Ethan's lean hands enfolded hers. "My wings will be your shelter."

Once again, Prissie asked, "Can you tell me why?"

His expression hardened. "Blight."

Verrill perched in the windowseat and said, "Please make yourself comfortable, Prissie. Explanations may take some time."

Raz stepped in again, hustling her back to bed and humming happily as he tucked her in. Dropping onto the braided rug, he waved for Ethan to join him. Once everyone was settled, Prissie asked, "What kind of blight are you talking about."

"Not a disease. A person," Verrill replied, settling his harp against his chest and plucking several soft notes. "Blight is the name he took when his former name was lost."

"How does someone lose their name?" But as soon as the question was out of her mouth, Prissie knew the answer. "Oh, of course. When he Fell. Blight is a demon."

Ethan nodded. "And yet Blight considers me a friend."

"Is it *possible* for an angel and a fallen angel to be friends?"

"No!" The young Guardian shifted uneasily under her gaze. "He is full of deceit."

Raz said, "Think of Blight as a creepy stalker who's in violation of a restraining order."

Verrill calmly continued, "For the span of several years, Blight took refuge in your family's orchard. The members of your Hedge didn't notice him because he was as passive as he was secretive. But God in His wisdom Sent Ethan. Blight was lured out of hiding, captured, and imprisoned nearby."

Prissie glanced at the window. "Until now?"

"No," Ethan nibbled at his lower lip. "He claims to have been free for nearly ten years."

"And tonight, he decided to drop in and renew old acquaintances?"

The young guardian angel slowly shook his head. "To make a new one. Blight demanded an introduction."

Her heart lurched. "He wants to meet me?"

"Yes."

Prissie's gaze snapped to Verrill. "Please tell me that's not happening."

Soft notes continued to cascade from the Messenger's harp. "Would you invite him in as you invited us?"

"No!"

"Would you seek him out in order to learn more about his past and your future?"

"Obviously not!"

"Would you believe his words, even if the truths are laced with lies?"

Prissie opened her mouth to protest, but stopped. In much more subdued tones, she asked, "Are you trying to warn me?"

Verrill inclined his head. "He can't sway you with words if you don't listen. He can't touch you if you don't reach out to him."

"And why would I do something so foolish?"

"For the same reason *he* would try something this foolish." Ethan's voice cracked under the enormity of his concern. "Blight is lonely."

On Sunday morning, Ransom showed up in the foyer of Trinity Baptist Church, self-conscious in his shirt and tie. Was he being too obvious?

"I'll be downstairs, setting up my classroom," said Milo. He'd been teaching third and fourth grade boys for years.

Beau, who'd recently taken on kindergarten through second grade, shifted a small cardboard box into the crook of his arm. "Same here."

"You need any help?" offered Ransom.

"No thanks. If our assistants aren't here yet, they will be soon." Briefly touching Ransom's shoulder, Milo whispered, "Incoming."

Ransom turned straight into a warm embrace and mumbled, “Man, I missed getting the Pomeroy treatment while I was away. You have no idea.”

Jayce Pomeroy set him at arm’s length and grinned. “I’m flattered you think so much of me and mine. Is that why you’re church-hopping?”

“Oh, I’m still attending Deo Volente. Thought I’d go for dual citizenship. Marcus and I did the DeeVee’s Saturday service last night, and I hitched a ride with Mr. Mailman this morning.”

Zeke angled across the foyer, a classmate in tow. “Hey, Ransom! Do you remember Jasper?”

Ransom accepted Jasper’s firm handshake. “Gotta admit, the details are a little fuzzy. Weren’t there usually three of you?”

“Yep. We’re two out outta three. Timothy’s the other guy.” Zeke casually hooked his arm through Ransom’s and said, “But this is a bold move.”

“And why’s that?” Mr. Pomeroy asked.

“You don’t get it, do you?” Zeke replied. “After years of Dad’s invitations, Ransom’s finally darkening our door.”

Jasper took Ransom’s other arm in a firm grip. “He’s crossed a line, sir.”

“And why do you suppose that is?” Zeke asked, grinning in the face of Ransom’s discomfiture. “Isn’t it *obvious*?”

“Flat out and bang on,” said Jasper.

Ransom regretted his decision not to invite Marcus. Where was back-up when you needed it? Had these two really figured things out?

“Yep! It’s potluck Sunday. Ransom came to be fed.” Zeke and Jasper took a step backward, dragging Ransom with them. “I claim this patisserie in the name of Pomeroy!”

“Food. The driving force of teenage boys.” Jayce chuckled and waved them off.

As soon as they were in the clear, Zeke whispered, “Relax already. I’m on your side.”

“I didn’t know we were choosing sides.”

With a guileless smile, Zeke said, “Work with me, and I can make sure you have the best seat in the house for this morning’s service.”

“And if I don’t?”

“I’m willing to bet you’d be stuck in the third row, left-hand side, right between Dad and Uncle Loren.”

Ransom glanced at Jasper, whose grip hadn’t loosened. “Insider information. We have it. You’ll need it.”

They ushered Ransom downstairs, steering him into the church’s crowded kitchen. Potluck preparations took place under the watchful eyes of Zeke’s and Jasper’s grandmothers. Which is probably why they weren’t immediately chased out. Zeke took on the role of tour guide. "I recommend the potato salad on account of it's Grandma Nell's. Be sure to try the spiced apple slices. Priss made them … *and* that crock of pickled vegetables. Good stuff."

Peeking under the ceramic lid, Ransom sniffed curiously. "What about you, Zeke?"

"Baked a cake. You'll see."

Prissie sailed through the door with a double-wide pan of scalloped potatoes and did a double-take. "Ransom! I didn't expect to see you here."

He waved weakly. "Hey."

Zeke jumped in to make space on the counter. "Nice surprise, right Sis?"

"Of course," she said distractedly.

"Is it okay if he sticks with you this morning?"

Prissie shook her head. "Probably not. I won't be sitting with the family today."

With a snap of his fingers, Zeke said, "That's *right*! Musta slipped my mind!"

Jasper poked Ransom in the ribs, and he took his cue. "What are you up to, Miss Priss? Nursery duty?"

"Unofficially. I have dibs on Essie this morning. Cuddle time with my newest cousin means a short break for Aunt Ida." She smiled apologetically. "I'll be in the cry room."

"I'll show him the way," Zeke offered, hauling Ransom back out the kitchen door. "He doesn't mind."

Ransom dutifully echoed, "I don't mind."

Prissie waved vaguely and headed for the refrigerator. Meanwhile, Zeke and Jasper herded him into the far corner of the fellowship hall. "There," Zeke said. "You're all set. Now it's our turn."

"Guys. As much as I appreciate your … *support* …."

Zeke interrupted. "Don't mention it. Only we want your help with Timothy."

"Your third musketeer?"

Jasper said, "We've been friends with him since kindergarten. And we'd like to keep on being friends, straight into forever."

"And you're an evangelism kind of guy," Zeke added.

"He's not saved?"

Zeke shook his head. "I've asked him to come to church, but nothing doing. He doesn't want to give up his day to be lazy. Not even to spend more time with me and Jasper."

"You want me to talk to him?" Ransom asked.

"Kinda. But not about church. And not here at church." Zeke waved his hands. "I figure just spending time with you is enough."

"How's that?"

"You ooze Christianity."

"I do?"

Jasper backed up his friend. "You're dribblin' all over the place. Can't help yourself."

Zeke nodded eagerly. "If Timothy gets to know you, it'll be the next best thing to church."

Ransom shrugged. "I'm game, but what's he going to think about me being the infamous trio's new best friend?"

"Already thought about that, and some of it's easy." Zeke explained, "We camp, and you could come along on our next trip. Cook for us."

Jasper added, "And maybe you could come to our games. Become a pep band groupie. Say hey to your favorite trombone player."

"Sure, sure, that could work out." Ransom flipped to the back of his Bible and found an opening. "I'll add him to my prayer list. You guys been praying?"

"Since forever. Milo can vouch."

Jasper explained, "When we were in his class, every Sunday he took prayer requests. Every Sunday, Timothy was ours."

"Talk about long haul," Ransom murmured, jotting fast. After they finished the info-swap, he glanced back toward the kitchen. "Hey, Zeke, did Prissie seem distracted to you?"

Zeke followed his gaze. "A little, yeah. Sis started watching the sky again. And talking to herself. I was gonna mention it to Beau. He gets her better'n me."

"But first, we need to sneak Mr. Obvious into the cry room." Jasper cuffed Ransom's shoulder. "If you're lucky, Miss Oblivious will notice you're there."

Ransom's brows lifted, and he relaxed into a smile. "Maybe you boys don't know as much as you think. Not once—not ever—has Miss Priss been able to ignore me."

Church started, and Prissie swayed in time to the muffled opening hymn. Since no one else was using the cry room, Ransom had Prissie to himself. Mostly.

"Essie, meet Mr. Pavlos. He's your auntie's friend." Tilting the month-old baby so Ransom could see, she completed the introductions. "This is Essie, short for Esther."

"Auntie, huh?" Ransom slipped his finger under the baby's tiny hand. "I thought this was your Aunt Ida's new baby."

"That's right. Essie and I are actually first cousins, but the whole family agreed it would be easier for my brothers and me to go by *uncle* and *auntie*."

"Uncle-hood is a stretch for someone like me." At her puzzled look, he shrugged. "Only child."

"Well then, we'll just have to make you an honorary uncle." She crooned, "Did you hear, Essie? This is your Uncle Ransom."

They lapsed into silence as the pastor prayed, and Prissie hummed along with the next hymn. A thick pane of mirrored glass shielded them from the rest of the congregation, but it might as well have been a brick wall for all the attention Ransom paid. His attention was riveted on Prissie. She was sweet to the baby, but something was off. What had Zeke said about talking to herself? Maybe it was time to give her someone to talk to.

When everyone sat, and announcements filtered through the speaker mounted in the corner, Ransom offered an opening. "Hey, Miss Priss. You look like you have more on your mind than Miss Essie there."

For a moment, Prissie looked torn between a polite lie and an uncomfortable truth. She glanced around, then leaned close to whisper, "Can I ask you a question?"

"Yeah. Of course. Anytime."

"Do I seem lonely to you?"

Ransom fought the urge to steer the conversation straight at his own lonely heart. "Not at first glance, but knowing lots of people doesn't always mean you have everything you need. For instance, you've been missing Koji lately."

"That's true."

"When something's missing, we feel it. Doesn't matter how full our days are." Ransom ran his thumb along the spine of his Bible. "That's how I felt back before we were friends. Lonely for something. In my case, that turned out to be God."

Prissie sighed. "Someone told me I'm in danger of doing something truly stupid. And the reason I'm at risk is because I'm lonely."

"Does their opinion carry weight with you?"

"Yes."

"Do they know you well?"

"Better than anyone."

"Then it'd be foolish to ignore them."

She sighed. "I wonder if this is how Peter felt when Jesus told him there were three denials in his near future."

Ransom hated it when Prissie's smile went missing. Draping his arm over the back of the pew, he said, "I'd be happy to form an alliance to keep you from wallowing in loneliness."

"We're already friends."

"Then we'll call it a campaign. I'll find all kinds of ways to remind you that you're not alone."

"Like what?"

"Not sure. But I don't like the way loneliness creeps in and steals the good stuff."

Prissie's expression shifted, and she focused on him for the first time all morning. "Ransom, are you lonely?"

"Absolutely *starved* for affection."

She rolled her eyes, but she also took him at his word. "Would you like to come home with us after church? You could peel apples or play checkers or doze on the couch."

"Is that your idea of affection?"

"More like my idea of a lazy Sunday afternoon," she countered. "Add a purring cat, a mug of tea, and a starving friend … and neither of us will be lonely."

"Count me in."

"And you can invite Marcus."

Ransom tried not to sound disappointed. "Sure. I'll do that."

Chapter 5

The Shared Umbrella

With a practiced flick, Milo opened the mailbox with *Jayce and Naomi Pomeroy* printed on the side … and slowly drew back his hand. A tattered blue ribbon secured a bouquet of golden flowers. The note tucked amidst their stems made the recipient clear; they were for Miss Priscilla. But Milo's expression hardened, for the spidery calligraphy betrayed the sender. As did the stench.

Did Blight really expect a Messenger to play delivery boy?

Milo hopped out of his car. Whisking out the unwanted gift, he carried the flowers across the road and tossed them into the tall grass in the opposite ditch. The bundle joined three other wilted bouquets. "Your attentions are unwanted," Milo announced.

Ping!

Blue wings exploded around the mailman's shoulders, too late to do much good. Milo pivoted as the rock hit the ground at Taweel's feet, deflected off his sword.

"Thank you," Milo said, his gaze sweeping the thick greenery. "That would have hurt."

The big Guardian grunted.

Returning to his car, the mailman groaned. All the purple coneflowers under the Pomeroys' twin mailboxes had been ripped from their stems and piled onto his driver's seat. "That's just petty." In a tight undertone, Milo asked, "I don't see him. Is he that close?"

Taweel signaled to the next-closest Guardian, who sat in the branches of a big oak. "Too close."

Then light flashed, and two more angels appeared.

Asher made a soft noise of dismay and hurried to gather up the spoiled flowers. "Hush, lovelies. We are Sent."

Padgett's eyes raked the nearby trees. "Is this the first time he's reacted violently?"

"It is," Taweel said gruffly.

"This makes no sense." Milo watched Asher for a few moments as the boy mended the torn flowerbed. By the time he was done, not a single purple petal would be out of place. "Why does he keep trying?"

"Who can say?" Padgett frowned deeply. "Furl your wings and finish your delivery, Milo. And tell Jedrick."

Milo ran a hand through his hair, which felt as if it was standing on end. "What should I say?"

"Tell him … the enemy knows we cannot find him. And this will make him bold."

"Lemon poppy seed is all done." Prissie pulled the final pan of muffins out of the oven and slid them onto cooling racks. "Are you sure you can do without me for a couple hours?"

"Pearl and I can manage until Ransom clocks in." Her father stopped kneading long enough to wave her toward the back door. "Tuesdays are a tradition. Don't disappoint our young'uns!"

Ever since graduating from high school, Prissie had been taking her young cousins, niece, and nephew to the library for storytime. "If you're sure," she said, already untying her apron. "Where *is* Ransom anyhow?"

"Oh, some appointment or other."

Prissie gave him a hard look. "You know something."

"As his employer, I *may* be privy to certain information."

"There's a loop here, and I'm not in it." She propped her hand on her hip. "Is he up to something?"

"Aren't we all?" With a shooing motion, her father said, "If you're curious, pin him down later, but Ransom's news is his to tell."

"News. So you *admit* there's news." She hung her apron and picked up her book bag.

"Patience, my girl." Her dad gave his bread dough an affectionate pat, then draped a towel over it. "And grab the umbrella. The forecast and the sky are in agreement for once."

Prissie hooked the handle of an oversized green umbrella over her arm, called one last goodbye, and slipped out the kitchen door. Lightning lent the dull gray sky a brief silver lining, and gusts rustled fitfully through the ivy that grew up the adjacent brick walls. Rain looked ready to cut loose at any moment, so Prissie prepared to make a run for it. But that's when she spotted the stone arch, smack dab in the middle of the access road.

She peered around, then tentatively called, "Asher?"

"I am here."

Prissie jumped and turned to find the young Caretaker seated on the step, picking leaves out of a ceramic cat dish. She asked, "What are you doing here?"

"Speaking with you."

With a small smile, she said, "I'm on my way to the gazebo. Members of my family will be meeting me there any minute."

The green-haired boy asked, "Have you been inside Town Hall?"

"Of course. The library's on the first floor."

Asher shook his head. Fitting his hand into hers, he led her around the corner of the bakery. Town Hall was a West Edinton landmark, kitty-corner across Main Street from Loafing Around. Set back from the road, the gray stone building had a wide front lawn overshadowed by trees that had been planted more than a century ago.

Pointing to the clock tower, Asher repeated, "Have you been inside?"

"Aunt Ida took my older brothers up once when we were little, but no. I don't do heights." Prissie added, "Even if I wanted to climb all those stairs, they keep the door chained."

"This way," Asher said, tugging her back into the alley.

Prissie dragged her feet, but the angelic boy didn't slow down. He pulled her straight through the stone arch. One moment she was at street level, and the next she was gasping for breath in the tower.

He'd brought her to the room just below the clockworks, where the town bell used to hang. Although there was a low wall, Prissie was surrounded by sky. She shrank down, putting her back to thick gray stone and hugging herself. "Asher, I don't *like* high places!"

"Fear not, for I am with you." He wrapped his arms around her and promised, "You are safe with me."

"You're right. I know you're right," Prissie said through clenched teeth. "But just the same, I'd rather not look down."

"Asher!" They both looked up as pink blazed against heavy clouds. Ethan landed in one of the openings, his boots scraping softly against stone. "Tamaes would be furious if he knew what you have done."

The boy blinked. "I was Sent."

Ethan dropped into the cramped room and knelt beside Prissie. "I apologize. I am here. You will not fall."

"I know," she sighed. "But that doesn't explain *why* I'm here."

Turning to Asher, Ethan asked, "Does Padgett know you are here?"

The boy shook his head. "He was not Sent."

"I see." Ethan bit his lip, then said, "There must be a reason."

"Yes." Asher stood on tiptoe in order to see over the wall. Pointing to something far below, he said, "That."

Ethan leaned out over the wall and groaned. "How long has that been there?"

"Since before dawn, when Prissie and her father were the only ones awake."

"What is it?" Prissie asked.

Holding out his hand, Ethan said, "See for yourself."

Prissie accepted his help in standing. When he tucked her arm through his, she got a grip and eased forward. Through a gap between trees, she had a clear view of the street below, and though her every instinct shied away, something caught her eye.

Scratches and smudges. Darkened patches. Scattered twigs and leaves. Smears of mud. Lines of pebbles. No one on the sidewalk would have noticed that they formed a pattern. "Those are words," she whispered. "Koji used to write using letters like that."

"Every archivist of heaven uses that language," said Ethan.

"An angel wrote that?" Prissie glanced between her companions. "What does it say?"

Ethan shook his head. "Not an angel, although he once dwelt in white towers."

"There is a play on words." Asher translated, "May Prissie Mae Prosper."

Her confusion mounted along with her dread. "But that sounds like a prayer. Or a blessing."

"Ethan should treat this as a threat," said Asher. "Your name and his are entwined. You are his choice. He has marked you."

"His? Who's he?" Prissie scanned the mess on the pavement. "There's no other name."

"Prosper." Asher said, "I have been holding back the rains so you could see."

Prissie glanced between the dark sky and the words scrawled across Main Street. While she watched, a car drove over the letters, sending a few leaves scattering. "Are you saying that's some kind of … love note?"

"One he did not plan for us to notice." Asher wiggled his fingers as if he was waving to the clouds. Immediately, fat drops began to fall. Messy splats quickly turned into a downpour that washed away the unwanted message.

"So there's a demon named Prosper?" Prissie sighed and asked, "Wasn't Blight bad enough?"

"They are also entwined." Asher took Prissie's hand, then Ethan's. In an instant, the three of them stood in the gazebo. Rain sheeted off its roof on all sides, temporarily surrounding them with eight waterfalls. "When the angel known as Prosper was newfallen, he took the name Blight."

"That changes nothing." Ethan drew his wings up around his companions. "Even so, I am here."

Asher's forehead creased. "There is a change. Something you must learn."

Prissie asked, "What could possibly be worse than receiving a love letter from a demon?"

"When your precious friend Koji was newfound, he made a friend."

"By any chance." Prissie gripped the umbrella handle with hands gone cold. She glanced uneasily at Ethan, who looked stunned. "Are you telling us that Blight used to be …?"

Asher nodded. "Koji's friend."

After storytime, Prissie and her young charges braved the wet. Heavy rains had slowed to a steady drizzle, and water dripped from overhead branches, plopping noisily onto their umbrellas.

"We didn't hafta go inside!" exclaimed seven-year-old Josiah. He abandoned the shelter of his older brother's umbrella to thump up the steps of the gazebo. "See, Nat? Our regular place has a roof."

"But the floor's wet." Nine-year-old Nathaniel tilted back his red umbrella to survey the situation. "If we made grass mats for the sides, that might work."

Prissie said, "I don't think the mayor would like it if you turned the town's gazebo into a grass hut."

"We're gonna make one when we're camping, though," Josiah said. "Uncle Zeke promised!"

Four-year-old Juliette slipped her hand into Prissie's. "Not me. Can I stay with you, Auntie?"

"Since Essie's too little, it'll be just you and me in the girls' tent."

"A pink tent?"

"Of course it's pink! Won't that be nice?"

"Is tents nice?" Juliette asked nervously. "I don't know how."

"Tents *are* nice. Trust your Auntie. We'll make your first camping trip *so* special." Turning to check on their straggler, Prissie called, "Come on, Bennett. Uncle Grandpa's expecting us."

Bennett was testing the mettle of his yellow rain boots by wading through the deepest puddles. Sloshing over, he joined Prissie and his little sister under the green umbrella. "Can I have a cookie?"

"Let's go see if your Uncle Zeke is on cookie duty," Prissie said.

Zeke was the one who'd started the whole "Uncle Grandpa" thing for their dad. It was part shortcut, part nickname, and quite practical. Mr. Pomeroy was uncle to Nathaniel, Josiah, and Essie Morrell, but Tad's children—Bennett and Juliette—overlapped them. Josiah and Bennett were the same age and showed up on their Uncle Grandpa's front step as often as possible.

The whole troupe filed through Loafing Around's front door, jangling the bell and chorusing, "Uncle Zeke! Uncle Zeke!"

He grinned broadly and draped his arms over the display case. "What'll it be, young'uns?"

Bennett hustled to the front counter and asked, "Didja bake me a cookie?"

Zeke wrinkled his nose. "Not exactly."

"How come?" Josiah asked, the picture of disappointment.

Nat poked him. "Maybe because you didn't say please."

Josiah tried again in wheedling tones. "Didja *please* bake me a cookie?"

"*Please*?" added Bennett

While her brother teased, Prissie quietly collected umbrellas and wet jackets. But her mind was elsewhere. Peering at the rain-washed street beyond the bakery's front window, she pondered this seemingly providential twist. Koji had been friends with an angel who Fell. And this particular Fallen was lurking nearby. "It's a small world?" She shook herself and checked to see if her brother was still holding out.

Zeke said, "I didn't do any cookies. But Mr. Pavlos went a little crazy, so we have twice as many as usual."

Right on cue, Ransom came through the kitchen door with a loaded tray. "Did you just call me Mister, because … oh! Hey, Miss Priss! Wanna taste test?"

"No thanks. I haven't had lunch yet."

Ransom's eyebrows shot up. "You don't approve of cookies for lunch?"

"Don't be ridiculous."

"Well that's a problem. I'm pretty sure the boss asked me to sneak these guys an appetizer."

Josiah and Bennett snickered, and Juliette plucked at Prissie's skirt. "He's funny," she whispered.

Prissie asked, "Don't you remember him from dinner at our house?"

The little girl nodded but stuck close.

Zeke caught his sister's eye and said, "I can cover this if you want to take lunch, Ransom."

"It's only been a couple hours since I got here. Not really needing a break."

"Prissie, you should take him over to that new place." With a sweet smile, Zeke added, "And bring me back a sammich."

Mr. Pomeroy emerged from the kitchen with stacks of plates and bowls, and Prissie helped everyone find seats. Lunch with Uncle Grandpa was part of the whole library day tradition. One she wasn't in the mood to enjoy. Maybe she should sneak upstairs for a chat with Beau. However, when she turned, Ransom was already pulling on his jacket.

"I'm game if you are, Miss Priss. Let's go find Zeke that 'sammich.'"

"I guess."

"Hardly the enthusiastic response I was hoping for, but I'll take what I can get."

Prissie closed her eyes and begged, "Don't."

Ransom was at her elbow, steering her toward the door. "Won't," he quietly promised. "Come on."

They walked in silence, sharing the green umbrella. Drizzle drifted into the little rivulets filling the gutters. And passing cars made wet noises as they kicked water into their wheel wells. Prissie's pace slowed to a meander, and Ransom finally cracked.

"If there's someplace else you'd rather be, I'll get you there," he said.

"This is fine."

"By which I hope you mean we're headed in the right direction."

She glanced up and said, "It's a little further this way, but a block off Main."

"Anything you want to talk about?"

It wasn't as if Prissie could tell Ransom that she had a demonic stalker. Again. She pulled her hands inside her sleeves and wished for Tamaes. Hadn't he been her place of refuge the last time hell broke loose in West Edinton? But all God was letting her have this time around was a pint-sized Caretaker, a pink-winged teen angel, and Ransom. Which really wasn't so bad.

"O, ye of little faith," she murmured, smiling at her own foolishness.

"What was that?"

Prissie stopped in her tracks and waved a finger under her friend's nose. "*Yes*, there's something I want to talk about. Where *were* you this morning?"

Ransom straightened. "Job interview."

"You *have* a job."

"One I love," he agreed. "But I have plans that'll cost a bunch. So I figured I'd work two jobs for a while."

"What kind of plans?" Prissie asked.

"I'm going to buy a house."

"Really?"

"Yep. Marcus would probably let me stay on with him and Mr. Mailman, but … like I said, I have plans."

He started walking again and she followed in order to stay under the umbrella. "Where will you work?"

"Derick Matthews recommended me to the owners of Porter's Farm and Home. I start next week. Afternoons and evenings. Weekends. Whatever I can get."

Prissie bit her lip. This was all very sudden, but it made sense. Daddy had given Ransom as many hours as he could, but it wasn't full time. And probably wouldn't be unless or until Zeke went off to earn his own culinary degree.

Ransom interrupted her line of thought. "This looks promising."

They'd arrived at Dill Brickle's, the quirky new sandwich shop and ice cream parlor on Poplar Street.

With a half-smile, he added, "Should I be wondering why your little brother craves pickles and ice cream?

Prissie laughed. "Zeke hangs out over here a lot because one of his friends is an employee. Do you remember Jasper?"

"Zeke renewed our acquaintance on Sunday." Holding the door for her, Ransom said, "Have to admit, I didn't pay much attention to your younger brother's friends back when they were shorter than me."

"Jasper's older brother is the owner. Daddy gave him lots of advice when he was starting up. They get their bread and sandwich rolls from our bakery, and we get the family discount." She stepped inside and immediately collided with a running child.

A woman turned from the counter. "Colin, I swear. One more time, and I'm going to … *Prissie*?"

"So you two?" Margery's voice dropped to gossipy tones. "I thought you were with Marcus."

Prissie forced a smile. "Marcus is a friend, and Ransom and I work together at the bakery. We're here to pick up lunch for the others."

"How boring," her old classmate sighed. "Aren't you seeing anyone?"

"No."

"If he didn't come back for *you*, then why bother?" Ransom's back was turned, so he didn't see the way Margery's gaze raked him. "Omigosh. Don't tell me he and Marcus have a thing?"

"No!"

Ransom glanced their way, eyebrows lifting at Prissie's sharp tone. She waved him back to his conversation with Jasper, and Margery smirked. "Didn't think so. You three always did stick to the straight and narrow."

Unlike Margery. But Prissie was too kind to say as much.

She and Margery had been close all the way up until high school, when their friendship fell apart. While Prissie grew closer to faithful friends and family, Margery had started dating. And never just one boy. Prissie had given up keeping track of her former friend's latest boyfriend … until senior year, when Margery's mom fought tooth and nail so her daughter could finish up with her classmates. Graduation robes had done a good job of hiding Margery's baby bump.

"If I was you, I'd have gone for that cello player. Tall, dark, handsome, and a foreign accent. *Scrumptious*!"

Prissie smiled faintly. "He's a little old for me."

"Don't tell me you're still pining for the mailman?" Margery asked with a laugh.

"Milo and I are good friends, the same as ever." In an effort to distract Margery from her non-existent love life, Prissie addressed her son. "Are you having fun at your grandma's house?"

Colin had inherited his mother's delicate features, fair curls, and green eyes. And her sigh. "It's *boring*!"

"The fair's next week. Will you stay for that?"

Margery answered for him. "We're here so I can go back to school. I'm supposed to make something of myself by earning an online degree while Mom spoils her grandbaby."

"Colin's father …?"

"Long gone. I'm using my maiden name again."

"I see." Prissie had never known how to react to people who were so quick to cast off something she'd been raised to think of as a lifelong commitment. In her awkwardness, she switched back to Colin, who'd been subtly trying to escape his mother's grip. "Are you looking forward to the fair?"

"Maybe. If Mom lets me go in the barns."

Margery wrinkled her nose. "Roller coasters I like. Pigs and chickens, not so much."

Prissie said, "If you want to learn about farms, I could introduce you to my brother."

"Which one?" Margery's laugh had an edge of mockery to it. To Colin, she added, "Prissie has five."

A look of longing flitted across Colin's face. "I've only got me. Are all your brothers farmers?

"Two farmers, a medical student, a pastor-in-training, and a patisserie wannabe."

Colin's forehead creased. "What's a … pat-tiss-yay?"

"You're looking at one," Ransom interjected as he joined them. "That's fancy-talk for a baker. We make cakes and cookies and stuff."

The boy asked, "You're her brother?"

"Nope. Friend of the family. I was in your mom's class, too. Hey, Margery."

"Hi, Ransom," she replied, giving him a smile that set Prissie's teeth on edge.

Touching Colin's shoulder, Prissie said, "My brother Tad's a farmer, and his son's about your age. And my other brother Jude would live in our barn if Momma let him. Any of us would be happy to show you around."

Colin leaned into his mother. "Can I?"

"We'll see."

"Pleeease?"

Margery gave in with a tight little smile. "We'll see you at the fair."

CHAPTER 6

THE ALLEY CAT

Tamaes sagged to a seat beside Jedrick, who smiled sympathetically. "How fares your new charge?"

"I used to *laugh* at the stories Ethan shared."

"Zeke lives up to his reputation?"

"Several times a day."

Jedrick clapped his shoulder. "Would you like my support?"

"No, thank you, Captain." Tamaes slowly admitted, "I will stand steadier knowing you are near Prissie."

"Tycho's Flight boasts eight cherubim, all capable warriors. Ethan has their support."

"I know it. And I *am* grateful."

"But ...?"

Tamaes touched his breastplate. "My heart still beats for her."

The cherub calmly said, "All the more reason for you to withdraw for a season."

Reddish-brown eyes slowly widened. "Captain, I cherish her as one of God's Beloved! I would never ...!"

"Peace, friend," Jedrick soothed. "You are above reproach. But Prissie's heart grows restless. While this Blight is a danger to her, you are an even greater threat."

The Guardian's jaw dropped. "I fail to see h–"

Jedrick cut him off. "How you could cause Prissie to fall?"

Tamaes's wounded look shifted into utter confusion. "*Fall*?"

"How could she not, when your feelings are so transparent." With a bemused shake of his head, Jedrick explained, "At this juncture in her life, Prissie could easily fall in love. With you."

When Ransom arrived at the bakery before sunup the next morning, the whole place smelled like lemons. Prissie was alone at the stove, whisking the contents of a saucepan. He asked, "Where is everyone?"

"Fairgrounds. Dad and Zeke are meeting Tad at the family booth, paintbrushes at the ready. Grandpa Pete says it's due for a fresh coat."

"So it's just us today?"

Prissie hummed and affirmative. "Pearl will be here at opening to run the register, but we're it for the kitchen. As soon as we sell out, we're closing up for the week."

Ransom eased up behind her for a better look. Neat cubes of butter dropped into silky yellow custard. "What's this for?"

"Test run on this year's pie."

"You're entering one at the county fair?"

"It's tradition!"

His attention strayed to the curve of her cheek. "Not apple?"

"Obviously." She checked the oven timer, then turned off the burner. "Grandma Nell and I always do a classic. Or a twist on a classic."

"Lemon meringue?" Ransom guessed. Prissie's quick glance and coy smile made him realize he was probably standing a little too close. But the smile wasn't for him. It was for a pie.

"Buttermilk pie with a layer of lemon curd on top. Tart and tangy, with plenty of pucker!"

Ransom's gaze locked on her pout, and he dragged himself back a step. "Sounds like a winner. Do I get a taste?"

She moved to the oven and peered through the glass. "It should be chilled by lunchtime."

"Great. Looking forward to it," he managed, retreating to the other side of the kitchen. Prissie had been confusing him since junior high. Her uppity attitudes and little inconsistencies had made her easy to tease when they were teens. But her faith had piqued his curiosity, and her father had unraveled its mysteries.

The strangest upshot of becoming friends with Prissie had been watching her give her trust so completely to Marcus. Ransom could still remember the day he'd decided to be happy for his best friend because Prissie was exactly the kind of young woman he'd have chosen for himself.

Not the kindest of epiphanies. What kind of idiot fell in love with his best friend's girl?

"I'll start pastry for turnovers." Ransom tied into his apron and crossed to the refrigerator. During the county fair, Loafing Around cranked out nothing but turnovers and caramel apples, which the Pomeroys sold in their booth at the fairgrounds.

He stepped inside the walk-in refrigerator, letting the door *thud* shut behind him. Bowing his head, he took a slow breath. Ransom had assumed that by the time he conquered culinary school, international courses, and assorted internships, there'd be wedding bells and baby booties happening for the Truman family. But Marcus moved slower than double fudge brownie batter.

Rolling his eyes toward the ceiling, Ransom asked God if this was comeuppance. "Back when I wanted her friendship, that's all I wanted. Now it's all I've got."

Was it crazy to hope? She'd waited. Maybe not for him *specifically*, but he had a decent chance. Probably. Getting a read on Prissie's feelings was harder than he'd expected. Ransom found himself over-thinking every little thing she said or did, searching for proof that she cared. Which was stupid because she'd cared about him for a long time. As a friend. And always would. As a friend.

The refrigerator door opened and Prissie gave him a flat look. "What do you think you're doing, locking yourself in the fridge?"

Oh. Right. The broken door handle. With a lopsided smile, he said, "Improvising a prayer closet."

She glanced around at the wire shelves of fruit, butter, cream, and eggs. "What are you praying for?"

"Courage."

Her eyebrows arched. "Since when? You're one of the most audacious people I know."

She had a point. Grabbing several pounds of butter, he followed her back into the kitchen. "In that case, can I ask you a personal question?"

"If you must."

"How do you feel about Marcus?"

"That all depends on who you ask." Prissie shrugged. "People still make the most ridiculous assumptions."

Ransom stood a little straighter. "I'm not asking *people*. I'm asking you."

"Marcus is a dear friend. Something you of all people should understand. Aren't you his best friend?"

"Well, yeah. But I've been away, and you two have always been close." With a sidelong look, he dared to say. "All signs point to love."

"Of course he loves me," Prissie said. "That's what friends do. Or don't you love Marcus?"

This was *not* the direction he'd expected this conversation to take, and Ransom floundered. "I don't exactly spout off, but yeah. He's the brother I never had."

"He'd probably like hearing that from you."

"I'm pretty sure he knows."

Prissie shook her head. "Hearing those words will give him more joy than he'll ever admit. Tell him."

"Uh-huh." Ransom unwrapped butter and pulled the scale closer. How had this turned into a discussion of his feelings for Marcus?

"Some things go without saying," she continued. "But some things really should be said. Otherwise, you're left guessing."

Exactly why he was stuck in limbo! But something in Prissie's tone made him suspicious. "Is someone leaving *you* guessing?"

Prissie turned to face him, but she didn't meet his gaze. "Koji sends me mail all the time, but it can be frustrating how little he actually *tells* me. I'm not very good at reading between the lines."

"He wouldn't keep in touch if he didn't still care."

"In which case, I have boxes of proof Koji loves and misses me." She sighed and tried for a smile. "I'm being selfish."

"I'm sure he's doing the best he can." There were so many things Ransom wanted to say, but they definitely weren't what she needed to hear right now. "It's just like you said, Miss Priss. He loves you. He misses you. That's what friends do."

"I know."

"So … *boxes* of proof?" Ransom asked lightly. "Makes my emails sound few and far between."

Prissie smiled softly. "Koji's always been faithful, even in his correspondence."

He couldn't resist prying. "What does he find to say if he's not telling you anything?"

"It's mostly art. And if he writes anything, it's usually Bible verses."

"Could I see?"

The back door burst open, and Beau stumbled in. "Sis! Do you s–" he exclaimed before cutting himself short. Gulping for air, he closed and locked the door, then tried for a casual tone. "Hey, Ransom."

"Hey. What's up?"

With a pleading look at his sister, Beau asked, "Any chance Marcus is here, too?"

Prissie shook her head. "Just us. Why?"

"I was working on my paper, so I didn't really notice when it started." With a quick glance Ransom's way, Beau said, "There was this *smell* in the alley."

"Skunk?" ventured Ransom.

"No, but it was definitely from the stench end of the spectrum. Sis, do you mind if I give Marcus a call?"

Trying not to feel left out of the siblings' silent communication, Ransom pretended to be more interested in exact measurements. Still, he saw the way they both jumped when the back door's knob rattled.

Prissie paled at the sharp rap that followed, and Beau's voice deepened threateningly when he called, "Who's there?"

"Relax, Boaz. It's me."

"Thank God," he muttered, hurrying to let Marcus in. "We were about to call you."

"No kidding?" Leaning against the closed door, he nodded to Prissie and offered Ransom a calm, "Yo."

"Didn't realize you were on call," Ransom said. "Or were you hoping I'd make you breakfast."

"As a member of West Edinton's Main Street Business Association, I've been known to lend a hand." Marcus smirked and added, "But I could eat."

Ransom immediately brightened. Baking in general was great, but feeding friends was his favorite. It was one of the reasons he loved the whole small-town-bakery vibe.

Beau quietly asked, "Can we check the alley?"

Marcus nodded and opened the back door. When Prissie and Beau moved to join him, Ransom abandoned his pastry and followed. The sun was barely up, so the narrow street behind the bakery was deep in shadow. But there was enough light to see by. Ransom asked, "What is it you're expecting to find?"

"Nothing," Beau replied earnestly. "I hope we find nothing."

Prissie was staring into the sky overhead, which made no sense. But it made Ransom scan the vicinity with more care than usual. The access road behind the Main Street shopfronts wasn't too interesting. Brick walls with some kind of vines tracking up toward gutters. Garbage bins and dumpsters. Cement ramps or stairs leading to back doors. Parking spaces marked off by faded paint. "If something stinks, I don't smell it."

Beau rubbed at his nose and grimaced. "Maybe it's gone. Whatever it was."

In the gap between the bakery and the neighboring building, Marcus stopped and groaned. "You still feeding alley cats, Prissie?"

Ransom crowded in behind his best friend and muttered, "Aw, man. Poor thing."

Marcus gently lifted a limp body and slowly backed out. The gray-striped tabby's lips were pulled back in a snarl, but there was no life in its half-lidded green eyes. He asked, "Is this one of your regulars?"

"Yes," she whispered, gently stroking matted fur. "But what happened to her?"

"I should have a shovel in the shed behind my place." Marcus steered Prissie out of the narrow alley. "Do me a favor. For the next little while, I don't want you picking up or petting any more strays."

She looked ready to argue, but then she nodded. "I'll make sure Zeke knows, too."

"I'd be grateful."

"And come right back after you're done," Prissie invited. "Keep us company and try my new pie."

"Sure," Marcus agreed. "And later, Beau and I can go for sandwiches."

Ransom stood silent, watching the people he cared about most. Maybe they weren't used to having him back, and that's why their plans didn't include him. Or maybe this was consideration. He'd be folding pastry for hours, so they'd bring the party to him. And now he was over-thinking things again. "Pastry's waiting on me," he said, backing toward the bakery door. "Sorry about your kitty, Miss Priss."

"Thanks."

As he retreated into the kitchen, Ransom had the uncomfortable feeling that they were glad he left.

Marcus wore a clean shirt when he let himself in the back door almost an hour later. "Yo."

"Hey." Ransom kept right on folding and rolling. "She's upstairs with Beau. Guess they had stuff to talk about."

Leaning against the counter next to him, Marcus bluntly asked, "What's wrong?"

Ransom slapped his hands on the floury board and let his head hang down. "Prissie thinks it's about time I bare my soul."

"Not sure I follow."

"Not sure I do either, but she's probably right." He peeked at his friend out of the corner of his eye.

Marcus's brows furrowed. "About what?"

"That I should confess my deep and abiding affection."

"For what … fondant?"

Ransom faced his friend more fully and offered a crooked smile. "For you."

"Oh."

"You okay with that?"

"Not a problem."

"Good enough for me!" Ransom wielded his rolling pin like a pro. *Thump.* Roll. Turn. Fold. After a lengthy silence, he muttered, "I mean it, you know."

"Got it. But are you sure I'm the one you should be saying this to?"

Ransom straightened, then sighed. "That's what Prissie thinks."

"Oh. You okay with that?"

"Not even close."

A soft *ping* from the direction of Prissie's things interrupted the rhythm of pastry-making moments before the back door swung open and she stepped inside. Ransom tried not to sound as sour as he felt. "Your phone wants you."

"If it's not one thing, it's another," she murmured, fishing a petal pink phone out of her bag.

At her soft gasp, he glanced over in time to see the prettiest smile of the morning spent on a tiny phone screen. But before his mood could plummet any further, she hurried to his side.

"It's Baird!"

Ransom's eyebrows shot up. "No kidding? I haven't heard from him in ages."

She offered her phone, saying, "He wants to talk to you."

Under a selfie of an exuberant redhead, Ransom read what Prissie had already typed. *Ransom's back in town.*

Baird had replied, *Knew it! A little bird told me. Glad?*

So much.

Put him on!

Ransom cradled the pink phone close. God was pretty amazing, giving encouragement when it was needed most. "*So much* is better than so-so," he remarked.

Prissie flapped her hands at him. "He doesn't get to check in very often. Don't waste this chance!"

Baird's next text pinged onto the screen. *U there, doozy-level mentoree of mine?*

Ransom grinned and tapped in, *Speak, for your servant heareth.*

Still quoting in worthwhile ways! ^ __ ^ d

DV's not the same without you and Mr. Peverell.

*U *really* want things to stay the same?*

With a swift glance at Prissie, he admitted, *Change can be good. I miss our talks.*

Ditto. I want to give something to Prissie, but I'm too far away right now. Help me out?

"What's he saying?" Prissie asked, tugging at his sleeve.

"Hang on. He asked for my help." Ransom typed, *You got it.*

"With what?" she demanded.

Baird responded, *Awesome. First, ask if she's braced.*

Ransom's eyebrows rose, and he said, "Prissie, Baird wants to know if you're braced."

Her expression crumpled, and she hid her face in her hands.

With a helpless look at Marcus, Ransom asked, "What just happened?"

The phone pinged again. *Stop holding back. Hold her.*

Pulling Prissie close was surprisingly easy. She melted against him and sniffled softly. Ransom rested his chin on top of her head. "You hugging me or Baird?" he asked in teasing tones.

"A little of both."

Marcus rescued the phone and texted something, then held it up so Ransom could see. *Hug happened. You're a meddler of the first order.*

Baird's response came through quickly. *Don't be stingy, Marcus. Send up a pic!*

"How'd he know it was you?" Ransom asked.

Marcus just shrugged and took a step back. Aiming the pink phone their way, he gestured insistently. Prissie hid her face, but Ransom relaxed into a smile that was all for her.

CHAPTER 7

THE ABANDONED ROOM

Marcus and Ethan sat side by side on the back step of the bakery, the fullness of their unfurled wings bunched behind them in a coral blur. Verrill was saying, "Possession. Without a doubt."

Picking up the glazed ceramic dish Prissie used to put out food for strays, Marcus turned it over in his hands. "I didn't even know possession was an option. Aren't former Messengers the only ones who can mess with people's heads?"

Verrill laced his fingers together. "The vast majority of demons who intrude and infest were once malakim. But the clever, the ambitious, and the bored have learned how to eavesdrop on dreams. Or in this Fallen's case, to make the most of flora and fauna."

"Camouflage," Ethan sighed. "He's using animals to get closer to Prissie."

"And burrowing into trees and things before we can make a grab," Marcus added, eyeing the adjacent wall of ivy.

Raz spoke up. "Now that they know what to look for, our Flights are finding plenty of evidence. Dead animals. Dying trees."

Verrill said, "Blight hinted at this *talent* when he chose his name. Six wasted apple trees. Two pines with rusty needles."

"Do we know how to pin this guy down?" Marcus asked. "Because Prissie lives in an orchard. And in a little over a week, she'll be camping in the woods."

"He talks to me," Ethan said. "I may be able to lure Blight into the open."

"That worked once." Marcus said. "If he's as clever as you say, I doubt it'd work again."

With a small shake of his head, Verrill said, "You may not be able to keep Prissie away from trees, but you can surround her with a Hedge."

Ethan touched Marcus's arm. "As Naomi Pomeroy says, 'The more the merrier.'"

Prissie dreamed she was running through the orchard, ducking under branches, trying to get a better look, but leaves only allowed her brief glimpses of the boy. She wanted to call him back, but desperate hope choked her voice. Was it possible? Straight, black hair brushed his shoulders, and when he reached up to touch a branch before darting around the tree, she saw gold and silver threads glinting on his cuff. *Koji?*

But then several yahavim were there, squeaking and humming as they pulled at her clothes and hair. And when she stumbled to a halt, she noticed that the spot where the boy touched the tree branch had darkened. The stain crept outward, leeching the life from all the limbs. Within moments, Prissie was standing in a musty fall of dead leaves.

"Prissie, wake up!"

Another person spoke her name, and this time she knew who it was. Turning toward his voice, she whispered, "Koji?"

"Don't believe him!" came a sharp retort.

She woke with a start and staggered. Why were her feet wet? Her heart hammered crazily as she tried to make sense of her surroundings. It was dark, and chilly water lapped around her ankles. There were stars overhead and ... was that the bridge?

Picking up the sopping hem of her nightgown, Prissie waded out of the duck pond behind their barn. Had she been sleepwalking? Nothing like this had ever happened to her before. The silence was so heavy, she jumped when the frogs in the pond suddenly started their usual summer racket.

Hurrying up the path toward the house, she paused with her hand on the gate. Words reached her, soft and light. "Is that you?"

Prissie's voice shook when she asked, "Who's there?"

"It is me."

She swallowed hard. "It can't be. You're half a world away."

The boyish voice answered, "Nothing is impossible."

"This is." Turning around, she searched for some sign of her Guardian. "This is definitely impossible. You can't be Koji."

"Why do you doubt me?" he asked, perfect to the last inflection.

"Because Koji would never lead me into danger."

"Prissie!" Ethan shouted, tearing around the side of the barn. "He got away from me. Be careful!"

Her knees nearly buckled in relief, but a hissing laugh sent chills up her spine.

"You hear me. You are near me. That is enough. For now."

Ethan didn't slow for the fence. Planting one hand on the topmost rung, he sailed over the top. The instant his feet hit the ground on her side, he closed the distance between them. Pulling her into his arms, he brought up his wings, shielding her in a shushing cocoon of rosy light.

He was trembling. Or maybe it was her. She rested her forehead against his breastplate and fought for calm. "I was dreaming. It was a bad dream."

Strong arms tightened around her, and Ethan whispered, "Forgive me."

"Where *were* you?"

"My teammates discovered Blight's lair. We were distracted by what we found there, and Blight took advantage of my inattentiveness." Easing back in order to meet her gaze, the young Guardian said, "I should not have left your side."

Prissie grimaced. "*Lair* sounds ominous."

"I wish to study it further." Ethan bit his lip, then asked, "Are you willing to join me?"

"Is it far?"

Ethan's wings parted enough for her to see out. "There."

"In the apple barn?" she gasped.

The young Guardian shook his head. "His room is part of its foundations. He was underground."

The apple barn had been the orchard's shop and showroom for so long, Prissie never remembered it being used for anything else. "This is the older of the two barns. The original one," she said, plucking at her nightgown. The sodden hem kept clinging to her legs. "Have you been down here before?"

"Yes." Ethan's smile was sheepish. "Zeke enjoys exploration."

They were in the barn's basement, where rusted stanchions reared up out of the uneven cement floor. On either side of an elevated aisle, there was room for at least twelve animals. Troughs on one end for feed. A pit on the other for manure. "My dad tells stories about keeping a milk cow named Corabelle. But that must have been forty years ago. And in the newer barn."

Ethan lifted his wings, illuminating flaking paint on old boards. "Your grandfather's Guardian has been here longest. He remembers when this room was in use."

If there was a door, Prissie couldn't see it. Whitewashed boards were nailed across the entire wall. She checked her bearings. All the windows were on the downhill side of the barn, which faced the pond. The opposite wall was built of uneven blocks of heavy gray stone. That part of the building faced the driveway up above. But they were at the narrow end of the building. Prissie said, "If there's a room behind here, it's under the corn crib."

"Yes."

"How are we supposed to get in?"

"The way is before us. But I would prefer to carry you."

Prissie looked between him and the barricade of boards. "Is it dangerous?"

"No. But it is unpleasant."

She lifted her arms, and he picked her up. Tucking his wings around her, Ethan turned sideways and eased right through the wall. Prissie wanted to ask how he'd know where the break was, but one glimpse inside the room beyond robbed her of words.

Although she'd known that the corn crib straight above had a circular base, no one had ever mentioned that there was a basement beneath it. The round room was spacious enough for the two angels already present to stand with wings upraised as they scrutinized curving stone walls.

"Is there any point in reading this record?" The angel with deep green wings touched the wall, which was covered in filth. "A decade of obsession."

"Jedrick!" she exclaimed, reaching for him.

"Prissie Pomeroy." As his huge hand enveloped hers, Jedrick's stern features softened. "Marcus speaks of you with great fondness."

Marcus was Jedrick's apprentice, so the two cherubim probably compared notes every day. But Prissie hadn't seen the Flight captain in a few years. She'd forgotten how imposing these giant warriors could be. In a small voice, she said, "I couldn't ask for a more faithful friend."

The other cherub, whose sharp features and wheat-colored ponytail seemed vaguely familiar, looked to Ethan. "Why did you bring her here?"

Ethan's wings drew up around Prissie as if to shelter her from criticism. "Zeke's mischief pales in comparison to Prissie's circumstances. I will not leave her alone."

"I approve." Stepping forward to offer his hand, the turquoise-winged angel said, "I am Tycho. Ethan's name is under my hand."

Prissie double-checked the stitching at Tycho's collar, which was the sea-green of a Protector. "His Flight captain?"

"You are well-versed in our ways." Tycho leaned closer and gravely inquired, "What do you think of our Ethan?"

"He's ... cute." When a slow smile spread across the cherub's face, she hastily added, "And very capable!"

"A neat summation." Tycho said, "Thank you for accepting Ethan's unexpected Sending with such grace. He'll undoubtedly benefit from your support."

Prissie glanced up into Ethan's face. It was hard to tell, what with his wings throwing off so much pink light, but he might have been blushing. "Aren't you meant to be *my* support?"

"You're *both* in danger." Tycho expression hardened. "Ethan, this Fallen has not given up on you. Blight wants to bind you to his side."

Jedrick said, "Look here."

The walls. Prissie had assumed that the stone walls were simply dirty, but on closer inspection, a pattern emerged. With surprising delicacy, letters marched their way around the room. Swoops and flourishes. Asides and illustrations. Blight had spent his years of captivity illuminating his prison cell.

Ethan stepped closer to the nearest section, and something crunched under his foot. Prissie glanced down and recoiled. No wonder the Guardian had insisted on carrying her. The entire floor was littered—sharpened twigs, twists of wire, animal skulls with empty sockets, moldering feathers, and egg shells with blackened interiors. Makeshift tools of an archivist's trade.

She spotted a cat's skeleton in the mess, and an uncomfortable idea sent a shiver up her spine. "Did he kill animals to use their blood for ink?"

"Nothing so temporary," Jedrick said grimly. "This record will stand for as long as these stones remain one upon another."

Prissie looked closer. It was true. Blood would have turned to brown and rust before flaking away. The calligraphy gleamed darkly, as if the ink was still wet. "Shimron painted with light. Did Blight paint with darkness?"

"In a way. This is his blood." Jedrick's frown deepened. "This is the outcry of a blackened heart."

"Like other Fallen, he has set himself up as an accuser," said Tycho. "When he chose this space for his cell, I assumed it was because of the shape. However, I believe he wished to remain near Ethan."

The angel Prosper had been made for towers, but Blight only rated a pit. A life laid waste. All his skills buried and boarded over. Nothing left but regrets and loneliness. Prissie shrank into Ethan's protecting wings and asked, "What does it say?"

"Terrible things," Ethan answered, turning his back on the demon's record. "Nothing good has ever come from listening to his ravings."

"Except this," said Jedrick.

Prissie saw dread flit across Ethan's face, and she touched his shoulder. "Fear not," she breathed, for his ears only.

His glance was all surprise, followed by gratitude. "Show us."

At the far end of the old creamery, words spun outward from an open space on the wall. Within this frame, bent pins and rusty nails had been forced into cracks and crevices, tacking brittle flowers and dead bees to the wall. If this lifeless swarm wasn't bad enough, there were small tokens—an earring, a plastic teacup, an old key, a cereal box toy, the wrapper from a sucker, a bottle cap. Stolen trinkets. Lost baubles. Proof that a demon had been ever near.

"Many of these things are Zeke's," Ethan said in a tense voice.

Prissie nodded. "The rest are mine. Except … this one." She touched a small blue plastic flashlight dangling from its strap. "It looks just like the one I gave to Lavi back when Ephron was lost. I wondered what happened to it, but this *can't* be the same one. Can it?"

"I would not be surprised." Ethan gestured to the walls around them. "Blight has shown himself to be both patient and thorough. Seven years he eluded me. Another nine he has been free."

"Thorough?" she echoed.

Ethan sighed. "He has been observing your family for nearly two decades. Blight knows your routines, your traditions, your secrets, your mistakes. This is a faithless, graceless record of lies and shortcomings, disobedience and lapses in judgment."

A whole room filled with evidence that the Pomeroy family wasn't perfect. Prissie's face heated at the thought of how often she must have disappointed God. How much sin had this demon exposed? When she checked to see if Jedrick was still reading, she found the cherub's gaze waiting for hers.

"Blight's blood cries out against you, but sin's wage has been paid. Fear not."

"Then why did he bother?" she asked, trying very hard not to look at the fallen Observer's wretched archive. "It must have hurt."

Jedrick brought up his wings, obscuring much of her view, forcing her to focus on him. "Blight rails against the Creator who cast him out for a single, terrible choice. His fury is for the Father who forgives and forgets."

Tycho spoke. "*He* forgets that for a single, terrible choice, humankind learned death's sting. But this argument is older than Time … and changes nothing."

"What good can come of this?" asked Ethan. He searched Jedrick's face. "You spoke of an exception."

With a sweep of emerald wings, Jedrick drew their attention back to the skewered wall. "Most of these words were meant for God. Many are addressed to you, Ethan. But he must have expected Prissie to see this for herself."

She leaned forward, trying to make sense of the letters. "It's no use. I can't read your language."

Jedrick waved to Ethan. "Back up."

As the young Guardian shuffled back until he stood against the room's door, Jedrick and Tycho took up positions on either side of the focal point Blight had created. Kicking aside the clutter, they knelt and lifted their wings, stretching them forward so that they touched. Ever so slowly, they increased the amount of light they were giving off.

Ethan muttered something about the ark of the covenant, but Prissie gasped. Now that the walls and ceiling were illuminated, she could see the method underlying Blight's madness. Some letters were heavier. Some sections more closely written. Some places left blank. And having stepped back to the threshold, a picture emerged.

Prissie's voice shook. "That's Koji."

"Yes," said Jedrick. "Look at his collar."

Every angel's raiment was decorated with rows of embroidery in colors that indicated their order. In this surreal portrait of her best friend, the embellishments along the collar were rendered in looping letters in her own language. Tilting her head to one side, she read them aloud. "Newfound friend, newfallen be. With you and she, we could be three." Then in ragged capitals, a bitter postscript. "Why can't you hear me?"

"He knew Koji. And he knew Koji was here." Prissie glanced at Jedrick. "But Koji never realized?"

Her friend's former Flight captain nodded. "Blight's plan was frustrated by God's purposes. Koji's ears were tuned to Ephron's call."

Ethan said, "He devised a plan. One that included Koji and Prissie."

Tycho warned, "Plans can be adapted. And the former obstacle is gone."

"I can hear him," Ethan acknowledged.

Prissie shivered. "So can I."

"Cornered demons are doubly dangerous. But a demon who grasps at hope …?" Jedrick's wings snapped back, and he stood. "Step carefully, Ethan. A snare has been laid for your feet."

Ethan carried Prissie out the way they'd come, but he didn't set her down when they emerged from the barn.

She grumbled, "I can walk."

"Please?"

Prissie searched the young Guardian's face, then bit her tongue. Holding her had been a comfort to Tamaes at one time. So what if it made her feel like a child. She pulled the trailing edge of his wing more snugly around her shoulder. "Fine."

Ethan's arms tightened around her. "Thank you."

"Can I ask you something?" At his inquiring glance, Prissie asked, "Is Tamaes close by?"

The young Guardian stopped in the middle of the driveway. "He is here."

"*Here* here, or somewhere nearby?"

With a telltale glance, Ethan repeated, "He is here. When I was delayed, Tamaes was the one who stood between you and Blight. He called you by name, and you woke." His husky, adolescent tones cracked. "He has been with us all along."

Prissie's eyes stung. "Why can't I see him?"

"Who can fathom the wisdom of God? But I can offer a guess."

She repeated, "Why?"

Ethan smiled faintly. "Because I need you more."

CHAPTER 8

THE FAIR LADY

"Perhaps you should not enter." Padgett gazed at the creamery walls without expression. "This is a faithless record."

"These words have no meaning." Asher picked his way across the littered floor. "They are empty; they are an offense."

His mentor turned and pointed toward the door. "Truly, Asher. These walls hold nothing but spite and despair. Avert your eyes."

"You are right, and you are wise."

"But …?"

"But I am Sent."

Padgett peered around Blight's prison cell, then back at his young apprentice. "To do what?"

Asher lifted both hands and said, "This." Immediately, the curving walls shed their stains as the terrible record fell like black sand, hissing as it hit the floor. By the time silence returned to the filthy chamber, every speck had vanished. No record of wrongs remained. With a pleased smile, the boy said, "They have been removed as far as the east is from the west."

"Amen and amen."

When Ransom arrived at the fairgrounds with Mr. Pomeroy, reinforcements met them in the unloading zone.

"Mornin', Ransom," said Tad. Prissie's oldest brother had two tousle-haired tagalongs.

"Mornin', Uncle Ransom," said his son Bennett. The boy stared up at him with serious gray eyes that made him look a whole lot like his dad.

"Uncle Ransom, didja bring breakfast?" asked Josiah. "What can I carry, Uncle Grandpa?"

While Jayce found things light enough for his nephew and grandson to manhandle, Zeke elbowed Ransom. "Sounds like you're already family. Did Prissie make an uncle of you?"

"I figured that was your doing."

"Nuh-uh. Hey, Bennie-boy. Since when is Ransom an uncle?"

"Marmee said Auntie said Essie said so," replied the seven-year-old.

"And there you have it. Momma's big on respectful handles." Zeke grabbed more pastries, then paused. "Oh, that's just plain sly."

"What?"

"Ponder this, Mr. Pavlos." Zeke's eyes sparkled. "How come you're Uncle Ransom, but Marcus is, was, and always will be Mr. Truman?"

Ransom's heart was a little lighter as they made their way over to the Pomeroys' booth. The building sported a fresh coat of red paint, and sometime in the years while Ransom was away, they'd added striped awnings. "Looks good. Smells good."

Grandma Nell already had the coffee perking, and Grandpa Pete was tinkering with the burner on his kettle corn machine. Once the turnovers were safely ensconced in the display cases next to rows of caramel apples, Tad gave Ransom a quick tour. Behind the scenes, amidst coiled power cords and huge ice chests, the Pomeroys had added a second, larger awning. "Home away from home?" Ransom asked.

"The year Bennett and Josiah were born, Ida suggested adding this space. We call it the nap room. Makes it easier to keep our families together during the fair."

Ransom gave the hammock a push and peeked into the playpen. "You're expecting another one, right?"

"Mel's expecting our next in February."

"You're pretty good at this whole family thing."

Tad shrugged. "Just doing what I can for my lot."

Left to himself, Ransom nabbed water from one of the ice chests, then snooped. But despite peeking around every corner, he saw no sign of Prissie. Sidling up to the register, he checked the schedule posted next to it. His heart sank.

Just then, Naomi Pomeroy came up behind him. “Do you have a schedule conflict?”

“No, ma’am. Not exactly.” When Mrs. Pomeroy’s eyebrows arched in a way that made the mother-daughter resemblance obvious, Ransom blurted, “I was just checking to see if Prissie and I share any free days.”

“And you don’t?”

“No, ma’am.”

She hummed. “If you don’t mind, I’ll bring Tad up to speed. I’m afraid he’s a lot like my brother Abel. Slow on the uptake where matters of the heart are concerned.” With a light laugh, she said, “It’s a miracle that man married.”

Ransom tried not to gawk. “You knew?”

“You’re surprised? When my daughter started keeping company with an entire roomful of men and boys, I watched *very* closely.”

“I thought I was careful.”

“You certainly are,” she said amiably. “Probably a little too careful since Priscilla is also like her Uncle Abel. Subtle hints won’t get you anywhere.”

“Does *everyone* know?”

“Not yet.” She patted his arm. “But don’t let that fluster you. You know what my girl’s like, and you know what she needs.”

“Time.” Ransom quietly asked, “You … don’t mind?”

Mrs. Pomeroy laughed again. “My opinion should be the last of your worries. Now! I’ll have that little chat with Tad. You go find Prissie. She’ll be with Jude in the animal barns, waiting to meet up with Margery and her son.”

Leaning over the low fence surrounding the goat pen with the Pomeroy Farm banner on the gate, Ransom said, “I remember your older brother sleeping wherever he dropped. Is this a family trait?”

“Nah.” Jude Pomeroy opened his eyes and smiled. At sixteen, he was the youngest, tallest, and quietest of Prissie’s brothers. “These guys have been skittish all morning, but if I relax, they relax.”

“So what exactly do you do with goats?” Ransom reached down to tug at the ears of a brown and white kid. “Going into the cheese-making business?”

“Maybe. Tad and I thought it would be nice to add a petting zoo for kids who visit the farm.”

“Can I meet them?” Jude waved him over, so Ransom climbed into the pen and sat in the straw. It was fresh stuff that smelled good, so he settled back, enjoying the way it rustled. Snagging a piece with its delicate seed-end intact, he stuck it between his teeth. “How’s this? Do I look authentic?”

“Not really. Where’d you find that shirt?”

"Paris."

With a soft laugh, Jude said, "It shows."

"Yeesh. They said the same thing at the hardware store. Guess I'll have to find myself some plaid flannel for when I'm not wearing chef's whites."

"Nothin' wrong with Paris shirts if that's what you like." Jude slipped a hand into one of his jacket's oversized front pockets.

"And you like goats."

"Yes."

"Do you do other stuff? Hobbies. Sports. Music."

Jude's gray eyes betrayed embarrassment. "Not really."

Ransom held up his hands. "Hey, I get it. Farming is a whole big lifestyle kind of thing. It's just that I don't know you very well. So it's awkward small talk time."

Relaxing into a shy smile, Jude said, "There's not much to tell. I go to high school, drive tractors, and raise chickens."

"And goats."

With a thoughtful nod, he said, "And maybe a donkey. Or a pony."

"Or both?"

Jude's smile came easier. "Maybe. You okay with critters?"

Ransom indicated the little goat who was butting his leg, demanding more attention. "So far, so good."

"Hold out your hands." In one smooth motion, Jude pulled a rabbit out of his pocket and placed it on Ransom's outstretched palms.

"Aw, man!" Ransom's hands closed protectively around the bundle of black fur. "Why am I not surprised you keep bunnies in your pockets? What's your next trick?"

With a wink, Jude brought out a tiny, bristling piglet. "You think Margery's little boy will like them?"

"I know I'm wowed!"

"You and your pocket pets," came Prissie's exasperated voice. "I can't believe you brought Charlotte to the fair."

Jude cuddled the piglet close. "I won't let anything bad happen to her."

Prissie's expression immediately softened. "I know, Judicious. You're an excellent guardian."

Ransom tried not to be too obvious in his admiration. Prissie's blue dress wasn't one he remembered, and she'd done something twisty with her hair to keep it up and out of the way. But when she met his gaze, concern lanced through his heart. The first day of the fair had always made Prissie sparkle with excitement, but she was tense and subdued.

Thumping the straw, he said, "Sit, Miss Priss. Help me fend off your brother's menagerie."

With a swish of full skirts, she let herself through the gate. Jude scooted over, and she sat between them. Poking her brother's chest, Prissie asked, "Who's in your inside pocket?"

"That's a surprise," mumbled Jude.

She leaned close and smiled knowingly. "You're purring."

"Maybe I'm happy."

There was no denying Jude's aura of contentment, surrounded by animals and sure of his future. Ransom considered his own happiness, which currently hinged upon Prissie's. It didn't take a genius to see that something had stolen hers, so he tapped her shoulder. "Hey, Miss Priss."

"Hmm?"

"I like that dress."

She glanced down, then smiled wryly. "I try to make a good impression, then ruin my own efforts by sitting in a goat pen cuddling a pig."

Ransom attempted to follow Prissie's way of reasoning. "You want Colin to like you?"

"Obviously."

That couldn't be all. She was holding something back. "What else?"

With an unhappy shrug, she asked, "Do I look like a lonely, miserable failure?"

"I'm going with *no*. Was that the goal?"

Prissie sighed. "Margery makes me feel like I'm falling behind."

She was comparing herself to an unsaved, unhappy, unemployed, unwed mother … and feeling like a failure? Glancing over to include Jude in the conversation, Ransom said, "Women mystify me."

Jude leaned into his sister. "Are you miserable, Sis?"

"No," she sighed.

"Lonely?"

"Less and less."

Ransom crowded closer on the other side. "Then how do we convince Miss Priss that she is beyond compare?"

Jude met his gaze over the top of Prissie's head and innocently said, "Maybe instead of complimenting her dress, you should compliment *her*."

"Ya think?"

"Worth a try," Jude replied. "If that doesn't work, I have a kitten."

She was already smiling, but Jude gave him a look. So Ransom followed through. "Hey, Prissie?"

"Hmm?"

"You're beautiful."

She rolled her eyes. "And you're ridiculous."

"I'm not kidding, Miss Priss." Ransom risked a little more. "I've always thought so."

Just when his words seemed to sink in, Jude nudged Prissie. "We've got company."

"Omigosh!" Colin was standing on the bottom run of the pen's low fence, hanging over as far as he could. Eyes wide, he asked, "Is that a baby pig?"

Ransom held up his critter, "Nope, baby rabbit."

"For real?" Without asking first, the boy swarmed over the fence and stuck his hand out to the brown and white nanny goat. "Will it bite me?"

"No, she won't," replied Jude. "But her kids might try to suck your fingers."

"She's got twins?" Colin asked, kneeling in the straw and crawling closer to the pair of youngsters curled together in the corner. Without waiting for an answer, he asked, "Are you one of the farmer brothers?"

"Yes. Do you like farms?"

"Mom says they smell bad."

"Some parts do. Others don't," said Jude. "Do you like apples?"

"Yup."

"How about cats?"

While Jude introduced Colin to a kitten with orange fur, Prissie stood to greet his mother. "Good morning, Margery. I'm glad you made it."

Margery glanced up from her phone. "Look, I can only stay for a little while." Her gaze veered Ransom's way and turned speculative. "Just long enough to be neighborly. Hey there, Ransom."

"Mornin'." Ransom turned the rabbit back over to Jude and stood, brushing off his pants.

"Aren't you a pleasant surprise!" Margery reached up and smoothed the collar of his shirt. "You barely fit in around here anymore."

"Jude assures me I fall short of the rural ideal."

"You don't fall short. This is overshot. How much European finery is stashed in your closet?"

"None, since I don't own a closet." Ransom glanced Prissie's way. Her back was straight. Her jaw was set. Easing out of Margery's reach, he quietly added, "Yet."

In careful tones, Prissie said, "I thought we were going to spend the whole d–"

Margery interrupted. "Look, I wouldn't have come at all, but Colin wouldn't stop whining that I'd promised. Which I guess I did, but geez. This is a total waste of money. Plus, he'll smell like *cow* all the way back to the city."

Ransom asked, "Why the sudden trip?"

"Stuff happened." With a sigh, she jammed phone into her back pocket. "And Mom's got a thing, so I can't leave him with her."

Prissie glanced down at the boy. Jude was coaching him on the best way to be gentle with bunnies. Something in her expression shifted, and she said, "If you're comfortable with it, you could leave him with us for the day. Josiah and Bennett are here, so he'd have friends. Zeke and I planned to show them everything."

"Be careful what you ask for. If I dumped him on you now, you'd be stuck for two weeks." Margery gave a short, bitter laugh. "The perfect vacation for both of us."

Letting herself out of the gate, Prissie quickly said, "Stay right here. I'll go get the boys and bring them over."

Margery smiled at Ransom. "I don't mind."

With a stiff nod for Margery, Prissie said, "Thanks. I'll hurry back." Then to Ransom's surprise, she gave him a look. "And you, come with me."

He had no trouble keeping up with Prissie's pace, but the opening day crowds were already making it tough to maneuver. Lengthening his strides, he rested his fingertips on her back to keep her close. Would she mind? A glance showed that her lips were pressed in a thin line. Not a good sign. "Slow down, Prissie. What's gotten into you?"

"I need to talk to Momma."

"You look angry."

"I *am* angry. At myself."

Taking her arm, Ransom pulled her aside into the relative privacy of an empty picnic area. "I'm having a hard time keeping up with you this morning. Help a friend out?"

Her cheeks stained pink, but conviction colored her tones. "Margery and her son need us to be friends, and here I am treating her like an enemy. Which she's not." Taking a deep breath, she explained. "I want to talk to Momma about taking Colin. I get the feeling that Margery honestly needs a break, and I don't know if I can be there for her in any other way. So … so … so there," she finished, glaring at him.

Ransom took her by the shoulders and leaned close. "Before we go a step further, there are two things you need to know."

"What?"

"First, I expect a rematch on the bumper cars later tonight."

Prissie blinked, then calmed down considerably. "Of course. It's tradition."

He nodded. "And second, you're still carrying a pig."

Ransom was just finishing up his shift in the kettle corn line when Prissie and Zeke returned to the family booth. Margery must have agreed to the Pomeroys' offer because Colin trooped in with Bennett and Josiah. Within minutes, Zeke had given all three a leg up into the hammock, where they woke Tad with noisy introductions.

"*Another* brother!" exclaimed Colin. "Can brothers be this old?"

"This one's Tad," Zeke confirmed. "He's my big-big-big brother, and the oldest of us all."

Bennett chimed in, "Except he's my dad, so I don't call him Tad."

"What do you call him?"

"Dad."

Angling over for a better look, Ransom caught sight of Prissie. She'd perched on the ice-chest, ankles primly crossed as she sipped at a water bottle. Her hair was escaping its coil, creating pretty little tendrils around her face, and her smile seemed weary. The day had been hot, and her nose was showing signs of sunburn.

Josiah announced, "I get to call him Uncle Tad. Only except he's my cousin. Nat told me so."

Colin made a funny face. "Who's Nat?"

"My big brother."

"You got a brother?"

Clearly the boys hadn't gotten around to discussing family ties. Ransom felt for Margery's little guy. Being an only child could be a drag.

"*And* a sister," boasted Josiah. "She's new."

Not to be outdone, Bennett said, "I have a sister, too. Don't you?"

"Mom says babies are too much trouble."

Zeke quickly said, "Well we have plenty to share. Right, boys?"

After the chorus of affirmatives, Tad asked, "Did you enjoy your day, Colin?"

"Omigosh! Farmer Jude let me hold the pig. And I got to get eggs out of chicken cages."

"We have pigs and chickens at home, too," Prissie said. "You can help us take care of them."

"I get to live with Farmer Tad?"

"Not exactly," she replied. "But Farmer Jude lives in our house. And so do Zeke and I. And Josiah and Bennett are both going to sleep over."

Colin seemed to be counting on his fingers behind his back. "How do you fit?"

Zeke cheerfully replied, "They stack us up in bunk beds."

"For real?"

Prissie was trying not to laugh, which made Ransom's smile widen. He didn't realize he'd given himself away, but Tad was watching. Thoughtful gray eyes crinkled a little at the corners. "Better re-check the schedule, Ransom. I needed to rejig some of your hours."

"Will do," Ransom said awkwardly. He beat a hasty retreat, but not alone.

Zeke followed and jostled to see the changes his brother had made in red ink. "Would you look at that? Three overlapping blocks of free time. What'll you do with all those possibilities?"

"Something tells me I'll be escorting three seven-year-olds around the fairgrounds."

"Yep. Good practice for in case you and Sis have triplets." Zeke checked the clock, then leaned way out the booth window. Waving excitedly, he called "Right on time!"

"Hey, Zeke!" called Jasper.

Hustling outside, Zeke quickly returned, dragging another teen up to the window. "You guys need official re-introductions. Ransom, this is Timothy."

"Hey," Ransom said, offering a hand through the window.

Timothy accepted his greeting with a wary expression. "Hey."

Jasper thumped the counter and bellowed, "Hello, Pomeroys!"

From all directions, assorted family members chorused back, "Hello, Jasper!"

"And Timothy!" Zeke called.

Again, the family chorused, "And Timothy!"

Ransom chuckled. "Nice."

Jasper grinned. "We're grabbing grub. Meet you around back in fifteen."

"Fair enough." He waved them off and nearly collided with Prissie when he turned around. She was reading the updated schedule. And yawning. Ransom said, "Zeke asked me to hang out with them for a while. Not sure how long that will take. Do you still want to do bumper cars tonight?"

"Wouldn't miss it."

By the time he worked his way around the back of the booth, Zeke and his friends had laid claim to a battered metal picnic table. A mountain of spiral-cut fries was heaped onto sheets of newspaper, and two paper plates contained puddles of ketchup. They'd rounded out the meal with four chocolate milkshakes.

"Saved you a spot," said Zeke, who was dipping his fries in the ice cream. "C'mon and try it. Best invention since s'mores."

Ransom slid into the seat across from Timothy, who had spiked brown hair and lots of freckles. The wariness was still there, and he focused on eating, letting Zeke and Jasper handle all the talking.

Finally Zeke set aside is empty cup and announced, "Ice-breaker time."

"Why?" moaned Timothy in a high, nasally voice.

Zeke said, "Basics version. We'll save the advanced version for the camping trip."

Timothy frowned. "He's going?"

"Relax, man. Ransom's got his own trio," said Jasper. "Zeke just wants to stay on his good side so we can eat his cooking."

"Assuming a patisserie can function in the wild. Can you go retro?"

Ransom waggled his eyebrows. "Impress me with your fishing skills, and we'll find out."

"So … basics!" Zeke said. Pointing to Timothy, he rattled off, "Mr. Grable is the short one, the musical one, the freckled one, and the one you should never—*ever*—underestimate in games of chance or strategy."

Timothy rolled his eyes.

Jasper pointed to Ransom and followed up, "Mr. Pavlos is way older than us, bakes better cookies than my Grandmama, and has it bad for someone's sister. Not that we judge."

Ransom sighed. "*This* is what you think of me?"

Zeke snickered. "We're too polite to mention the other stuff. Trust me, it's worse in the advanced version."

Timothy fingered Jasper and said, "Sleeps with a stuffed frog, gets manicures every week, and breezes through advanced math like a boss."

"Hey, my sister-in-law's a cosmetologist," protested Jasper.

Singling out Zeke, Timothy offered another list. "Can juggle ten apples at a time, only plays the piano when he thinks no one's around, and has a pet name for the mailman."

"So there ya go," Zeke said. "This is us."

Jasper raised a hand. "Anyone else thirsty? I'll grab water."

Zeke shot to his feet and crumpled up the newspaper. "Lemme get rid of this, and I'll help you."

Ransom was appalled by their lack of subtlety. A quick check confirmed that Timothy was staring at him with an expression of hostile resignation. Stifling a sigh, Ransom said, "Sorry. They mean well."

"So … you and Prissie?"

"I'm beginning to think she's the only one who doesn't realize."

"Either she's dense or she's pretending not to notice." Timothy asked, "You're not actually going to let Zeke help you, right? Because that would be catastrophic."

"I've never asked for help." Ransom glanced over his shoulder. Prissie was quite possibly within earshot. "This is between me and her."

"So you're going to tell her?"

"That's the idea."

Timothy asked, "So when's that going down?"

"Not sure. Still praying on it."

"If she doesn't want you, what will you do?"

Ransom swallowed hard. This was not a conversation he wanted to have, least of all with a guy he hardly knew. "I don't know. All I can do is keep trusting and trying."

"Uh-huh."

"Why are you so interested in my plans?"

"I'm not," Timothy replied. "But any minute now, you're going to launch into a conversation *I* don't want to have."

Cracking a smile, Ransom said, "You knew."

Timothy snorted. "You're the latest in a long line of useless strategies. Well, fine. If you want to talk about my soul, I'm going to pry into your love life."

"Deal."

"Huh?"

"I'll tell you anything you want to know if it means you'll listen to what I have to say."

"You'll be sorry."

Ransom countered, "It can't possibly be worse than Zeke's advanced version ice-breaker."

With a confident smile, Timothy said, "Try me."

CHAPTER 9

The Upstairs Boy

Jude eavesdropped on his three helpers while they headed back to the house after gathering eggs. Their conversation had taken an interesting turn. One that made it clear that the previous night's bedtime stories had been Bible-based.

"Okay, then how come talking donkeys are real, but not green ogres?" Colin challenged.

Josiah wasn't fazed. "Because Balaam's donkey didn't always talk. Just that once, when the angel was there."

"So angels are real?"

"Course!"

"But not elves."

"Nah. Those are for fairy tales," Josiah said, glancing at Bennett for support. The other boy nodded.

"I don't get it." Colin shook his head. "Like how come giants are real, but not magic beans?"

Bennett said, "Them other stories are just for fun. My dad says it's okay to have fun if you remember which parts are real. And the Bible's real."

"Every part's true?" Colin's face was a picture of perplexity. "Is he right, Farmer Jude?"

"Yes." Jude turned up the farmhouse's sidewalk. Bennett and Josiah ran up the porch steps, eager for breakfast and already bragging about how many eggs they'd found. But their guest hung back. Jude asked, "Okay there, Colin?"

"Is the only son part real?"

Jude's mouth went dry. He was perfectly comfortable talking about apples and chickens, but faith was a whole different matter. Zeke was much better and bolder about stuff like this. Too bad he was already at the bakery. "Umm … do you mean Jesus?"

"Yeah. Mr. Uncle Grandpa read lots of stuff about Him." With an odd expression, Colin whispered, "How come that guy's named after a cuss word?"

"He's not. People who use His name like that are being impolite to God."

"Omigosh! They're disrespecting the Bible guy?"

Jude's lips twitched. "Pretty much. It makes us sad."

"Really? Does that mean you're like Mr. Uncle Grandpa? He says he *loves* Jesus."

"Yes."

"How come you love someone from a book?"

Sitting on the porch steps to remove his boots, Jude tried to find words. Dad was so good at this kind of thing, and so was Beau. Any other member of his family could have put their faith in terms Colin would understand. Jude's face felt hot, and he mumbled, "It's been that way ever since I can remember. Our whole family is Christian."

Colin's face scrunched. "So it's a family rule? You gotta?"

"No." Jude knew he was failing hard. "When I heard the same stories Uncle Grandpa told you last night, I wanted to be like Jesus. He was good and kind. And so brave."

"The bad guys hated him."

"Yes."

"They were way worse than bullies."

"That part of His story always makes me sad," Jude said softly. "I don't like to see anyone or anything suffer."

"There was nails and thorns and a bad whippin'," Colin continued, as if sharing a great secret. "And they killed him dead."

"Yes, but only because Jesus let them. And He didn't stay dead."

The boy followed him inside, padding after Jude in stocking feet. "Are you sure that part's real?"

"Yes." Jude managed a smile. "I'm sure."

At the laundry room sink where they washed up for breakfast, Colin asked, "So where's Jesus now?"

"Heaven. He's building a city for everyone who loves Him."

"Why?"

"Because people who believe Jesus become part of His family."

Colin's eyes lit up. "Oh, yeah! I get it."

He did? As the boy hurried out to join Josiah and Bennett at the table, Jude followed with dragging steps. Believers were supposed to jump at chances to share the gospel, but he was terrible at it. Too bad Ransom wasn't around. He was so comfortable with saying what was on his heart.

Jude sat across from Colin at the big kitchen table and murmured thanks when Momma placed a bowl of oatmeal before him. Maybe if the kid kept up with his questions, she could jump in. But Colin seemed to have left any thought of Bible stories behind him.

"How come you don't eat cereal for breakfast?"

"Oatmeal's a kind of cereal," said Bennett. "Hot cereal."

Colin jabbed his spoon into his serving of mush. "I like fruity crunchy stuff better."

"There's fruit," Josiah said, pointing to the array of small serving bowls on the table. "And nuts are crunchy. Watch how I do it."

Following his new friends' example, Colin doctored his oatmeal with blueberries, banana slices, and slivered almonds."

"Then honey!" Bennett held a spoonful of the golden stuff high over his bowl. As he drizzled threads, he bragged, "From our own hives."

"You grow your own honey?"

Josiah snorted. "You can't *grow* it. It's bee spit!"

"For real? Lemme try."

After his own bowl was ready, Josiah clapped his hands together and prayed right out loud. Jude was so used to the Morrell family's mealtime routine, he didn't think anything of it. But Colin goggled at him.

"What did you do that for?"

"'Cause I'm thankful."

"To your grandma?" Colin asked, sneaking a look at Mrs. Pomeroy.

Josiah shook his head. "To God."

"God didn't make breakfast."

Bennett jumped in, saying, "He made oats and berries and bees when He created the world. And even though that was a long time ago, He still likes it when people remember to say thanks."

Colin scanned all their faces before announcing, "You people are weird."

Jude chuckled. Taken out of context, the boy's remark was insulting, but Colin sounded envious.

Mimicking Josiah's clasped hands, Colin asked, "Can I be weird, too?"

"Please do," Jude said, giving the boy an encouraging nod.

"Thanks, God, for making oatmeal and for writing good bedtime stories."

Colin puffed out his cheeks for a moment, then added, "And for being real because Farmer Jude says so. So You should let me be part of Your family like these guys. Because being the only kid stinks. Jesus musta figured that out, too. So, yeah. That's all."

Everyone at the table stared at Colin.

Josiah spoke up first. "Hey! Did you just pray to become a Christian?"

"Duh." Colin shoved a spoonful of oatmeal into his mouth before cheerfully mumbling, "Weird, huh?"

A few days after the county fair, a line of thunderstorms rolled in with a rumble and crash, leaving steady rain in its wake. Although Prissie expected any number of people to trundle in through the kitchen door, tracking mud, Ransom wasn't one of them. She asked, "Wasn't today supposed to be your big chance to relax?"

"Sure," he said, shedding a dripping jacket and kicking off his shoes. "I slept past three for the first time in recorded history and ran out of things to do by six. So I took a walk."

"You *walked* here? In this rain?"

"That was the plan, but Tad spotted me before I got very far and offered a ride."

"You have a talent for wrangling invitations from my brothers." She hustled into the laundry room and came back with a towel. "Though there's really no need to stand on ceremony. Everyone thinks of you as family."

He stopped roughing up his hair and peeked out from under the towel. "You do?"

"Hmm?"

Ransom stood awkwardly in stocking feet, pushing damp hair into a semblance of order. "Do you think of me as one of your brothers?"

"No, but if you were a girl, I might take you for a sister." She laughed at his agonized expression. "I could tell you my secrets, paint your toenails pink, and make teensy cookies for tea parties."

"I don't have to be a girl to do all that." Ambling over to see what recipe she was considering, he asked, "What are we baking?"

Maybe it was childish, but she hid the recipe with her hand. "Nope. If you want to help, you'll have to let me paint your toenails."

"Sure."

"Really?"

"Why not?" Glancing around the empty kitchen, Ransom said, "Especially since there's no one around to witness my induction into your sisterhood.

Where is everyone?"

"Momma and my grandparents are hanging out in the apple barn in case anyone drops in for a bushel, doughnuts, or hot cider. Tad and Jude are entertaining the kids in the animal barn. Rainy days mean rope swings." Moving to the back stairway, she ordered, "Off with the socks. I'll go get the polish."

When she returned with three bottles to choose from, Ransom remarked, "I've never seen you use this stuff."

Prissie nodded. "It's a waste of time on my fingernails since I'm always washing dishes or gardening, but I paint my toenails. Pick."

He considered his options—a pearly shade of pink, soft coral, and vibrant bubblegum. "Guess if I'm going to go for it, I should go all out."

"The zealous type," Prissie said, shaking the brightest bottle in the batch.

"No sense being wishy-washy."

Prissie couldn't believe Ransom was submitting to something as foolish as a pink pedicure. He could have gone swinging in the barn with the rest of the boys, but here he was. "I'm glad you came over," she confessed. "The house feels empty today."

"If you need me, you can always call."

"I was going to call Aunt Ida, but you'll do." Her teasing glance was met by a relaxed smile that was easy to match. "I've hardly seen you since the fair. Have you been busy with your other job?"

"Actually, Marcus and I spent most of yesterday snooping through houses. There's quite a few available in the area, but I'm not sure what to do. It'll have to be something small."

"There's just you."

"Sure, but I need to plan ahead some." Ransom's expression turned tentative. "I want to give the whole family thing a whirl."

She paused mid-brush and had to sweep up a dribble with her finger. "Oh. I didn't realize."

"Is it so hard to imagine me wanting that stuff?"

It was in a way, but Prissie shook her head.

"I was hoping you could give me some advice. About houses." Ransom gestured broadly. "There are these little places in town, sort of like cottages with picket fences. But they're kind of cramped. I found more properties down by Harper, but I wanted to stay local. Which means poking around the back roads some more."

Prissie slowly started a second coat. "Oh. That makes sense."

Ransom sighed gustily. "Miss Priss, look at me."

"Hmm?"

"I want to know what I should be looking for. What kind of stuff do you think a home should have?"

"Indoor plumbing. A leak-free roof. Adequate counter space."

He chuckled. "I'll have the inspector check for that. But I was thinking more like … wish list stuff. If you could choose details, what would they be?"

She gave a more honest answer this time. "I'd want a big garden, an old-fashioned pantry, and lilac bushes."

"And an apple orchard?"

"Obviously."

Ransom shook his head. "You're gonna be a tough girl to please."

"Don't be ridiculous. I'm already happy."

"My point exactly!"

With a small sigh, she said, "Don't you start. People are always trying to pair me off with some nice boy they know. Or send me off to college so I can broaden my horizons, which is just another way of saying meet some nice boy."

"I'm not asking you to change," Ransom promised. "And I'm not sure *this* change is good for me."

She brushed her fingertips over the small tufts of curly hair on his toes. "You have beautiful arches, but this definitely takes away from the overall presentation."

He wriggled his toes.

"Careful! You'll smudge them before they dry."

"Guess I'm stuck barefoot for a while."

"Heaven help you if Zeke notices."

Ransom grinned. "A deal's a deal. Unless … say, Miss Priss. There's something else I've been wanting to do, and a rainy day seems like a good excuse."

"What's that?" she asked, crossing to the sink to wash her hands.

"I've never seen your room."

"So?"

"I'm curious."

Prissie pointed to the back stairs. "Mine's the first room. You're welcome to take a look."

He sighed. "I was hoping for a guided tour."

"It would be a short tour. My room is smaller than this table."

"And … I was hoping you'd show me some of those boxes of stuff that Koji sends."

"Oh." Sharing Koji's gifts with Ransom did sound like a pleasant way to pass the day. In fact, the more she thought about it, the more she wanted to. But there was a hitch. "I'll need to check with Momma first."

"Why?"

"We have a family rule about guests in bedrooms." Prissie sighed. "I'm hardly a teen anymore, but I'm still part of this household. Safe to assume the rule's still in place."

Ransom smirked. "You won't just smuggle me in?"

"Wait here."

She stepped into shoes and grabbed an umbrella, then hurried along the sidewalk to the apple barn. Pulling Momma aside, Prissie relayed Ransom's request.

"Thank you for letting me know, Priscilla."

"Do you think it's okay?"

Mrs. Pomeroy asked, "Are you worried about his intentions?"

"No!"

With a laugh, she said, "Gracious, dear. Indulge the boy's curiosity. Bring Aquila if you feel you need a chaperone. And leave the door open."

"Obviously." Prissie hesitated, then said, "If we go through every box, it'll probably take all day."

"He's welcome to stay for dinner. Your grandmother and I will call when it's ready."

Prissie was blushing when she returned to the porch where Ransom waited. "I feel silly, but rules are rules."

"Did I gain parental approval?"

"They don't seem overly alarmed," Prissie replied, giving her umbrella a shake before stowing it. "One guided tour, coming up."

Ransom followed her up the back stairs. "So I'm not considered a threat to your virtue?"

"Don't be ridiculous."

"Am I supposed to be flattered or insulted?"

Prissie turned to face him. "What's that supposed to mean?"

"No one thinks I'll try something." Eyebrows arching, Ransom said, "I could be capable of something fiendish."

Propping her hand on her hip, she asked, "What are you going to do, tie my hair in a knot?"

"Nah. But a guy doesn't like to be written off. My pride's injured."

She resumed climbing the creaking staircase. "I'll manage a few palpitations of the heart if you like."

"Very generous."

Prissie's bedroom was tucked up under one of the big farmhouse's gables. The tiny room's ceiling was angled so sharply that the top corner of the door was cut off.

"Old houses have the best quirks!" exclaimed Ransom.

"I know. I love this door. It's my second favorite part of this room."

"What's the first?"

She hesitated, then answered, "Good memories."

"I like it." He stepped further into the room, which held little more than her bed, a wardrobe, and a small dresser. The walls were different colors—soft pink, peach, and yellow—with fat roses and peonies showing up here and there. "These look hand-painted."

"They were a gift from Zeke."

"Impressive." Indicating the stained glass diamonds hanging in the corner of the window, he asked, "Marcus's handiwork?"

"Yes. I think they were the first glass things he ever made." Prissie explained, "I used to have a stained glass window here, all in diamond patterns. It was beautiful."

"Your favorite part?"

"My special treasure. But there was that big accident, and it shattered."

Ransom walked over to the wide windowseat, with its heap of pillows. He peered past the rain-spattered windowpanes. "Yeah, I remember."

"Marcus made these to cheer me up."

"Do they?"

"They're an excellent reminder that I have good friends."

Ransom patted the cushioned seat. "May I?"

"Make yourself at home," she said, kneeling on the braided rug in order to reach the boxes under her bed. After more than nine years of correspondence, she had five. "Do you want to start with the oldest or the newest?"

"Beginning stuff. So he can impress me with his growing prowess." When she joined him in the windowseat, he asked, "Should I be alarmed that you brought tissues."

"Just in case," Prissie replied, tucking up her feet. "These usually stir up a few tears, so don't tease."

"Not a chance."

They had some trouble finding a comfortable position, but Ransom generously offered his shoulder. Leaning against him, Prissie was able to hold the cards so they could both see. Voices pitched low. Emotions running high. Minutes became an hour, and moments stretched into eternity, where Koji waited for them both.

"What's with the princess crown," Ransom asked, snagging a small painting featuring a delicate tiara covered in pearls.

"It's something from the attic," Prissie explained. "We have several generations' worth of memorabilia up there. Our personal archive. Momma wore this on her wedding day, and Koji took special interest in it."

"Sounds like another opportunity for rainy day exploration," Ransom hinted.

Prissie shook her head. "More like winter day. It's stifling up there in summer."

"Gotcha. Guess I can wait until the snow flies." Taking another postcard, which featured a solitary white tower standing in a field of yellow flowers, Ransom said, "If a picture's worth a thousand words, these are whole books. I can't believe he'd trust something like this to the post office."

"He has a lot of faith in my mailman."

Ransom was the best kind of audience for an afternoon of show-and-tell. He exclaimed over Koji's art, read all the Scripture verses aloud, tried to sing when there were lyrics, and passed her tissues whenever she sniffled. After hearing her stories about letters that arrived just when she most needed their encouragement, Ransom mumbled, "I wish I could have been there for you like he was."

"You were." She tipped her head back to meet his gaze. "You and Marcus stayed when Koji couldn't."

He looked between her and the sheaves of art. "Miss Priss, this guy loves you."

"Yes, I know."

His brows drew together, and he muttered, "He's not the only one."

Prissie searched Ransom's face and wondered why he kept telling her things she already knew. Maybe to encourage her? Or maybe because of what she'd told him the other day … about some things needing to be said out loud. "That's how it's supposed to be. You, me, Marcus, and Koji—we all love each other."

"That's us." Ransom's smile had an ironic twist. "Study buddies forever."

"That's a nice thought."

Ransom's arms wrapped around her from behind. "Thank you for showing me your treasures. Wish I could return the favor, but I don't have much."

She closed her eyes and thanked God all over again for Ransom's return. "There must be something," she murmured. "Everyone has something."

"I'm pretty attached to my Bible. It was a gift from your Dad. And there's you and Marcus. Everything else is faith and hopes."

"And love," she added. "To have the full set, you need faith, hope, and love."

In a small voice, Ransom confessed, "Love you, Miss Priss."

She laughed and asked, "Was that so hard?"

"Insanely difficult." Tightening his grasp, he said, "And now I'm sorely tempted to do something fiendish."

"And ruin this cozy moment?"

"You promised palpitations."

Prissie laughed again. How many times had she found shelter in the safety of an angel's wings? Wasn't this the same as that? Ransom wasn't as heroic as Tamaes or as princely as Milo. He lacked Jedrick's musculature and Ethan's shimmering wings. But he'd reached for her when she needed holding. Listening to her rambles. Smelling like bakery spices. Giving her reasons to smile.

Peering out the window at the rain, Prissie's focus shifted, and she realized she could see Ransom's reflection in the glass. His head was bowed, and his cheek rested against her hair. Soft as a sigh, he asked, "Do you even see me?"

Her heart lurched because he sounded so lonesome. Of course she could see him. As clearly as if he were an angel.

Just as Grandma Nell and Mrs. Pomeroy were putting the finishing touches on supper, Prissie hurried to the kitchen door. "You made it!"

"Yo."

Ransom turned from the counter, where he was trying to make sure his three young helpers didn't toss the salad straight onto the floor. "Hey, Marcus. I didn't know you were planning to be here today."

"Neither did I. Prissie called."

She laughed. "Poor Ransom's been stuck with no one but me for company all day."

"Uncle Beau!" cheered Bennett and Josiah.

"He's the pastor brother," Colin said wisely. When he spotted the third guest, he hopped down from his step stool and ran forward. "Teacher!"

Zeke easily matched the boy's enthusiasm. "My 'Lo!"

As Milo eased out of his jacket, Ransom said, "Hey, Mr. Mailman."

"Good evening, one and all." With a smile that included three generations of Pomeroy women, he added, "Thank you for your hospitality."

Beau asked, "What happened, Zeke? Isn't it a little early in the day for pajamas?"

Zeke said, "It's kinda a long story … involving a fence post, eleven apples, and the pig sty."

While the trio of boys loudly filled in more details, Marcus eased through the clamoring youngsters, Prissie close on his heels. He smirked at his best friend. "*Poor* Ransom?"

"I'm a suffering saint," he said, crunching into a pickle.

Prissie shook her head at their nonsense. "Admit it. You're glad for the reinforcements."

"If you say so, Miss Priss."

A faint warbling caught her attention, and she excused herself to the little office nook off the kitchen to grab her phone. Checking the display, she answered, "Margery! Did you want to talk to Colin?"

"Are you actually out somewhere? What's all that noise?"

Prissie laughed. "I'm home, but the guys just arrived. Everyone's still saying hello. Hang on a sec." She escaped the hubbub by going halfway up the back stairway. "Better?"

"Which guys?"

Sitting down, Prissie said, "Milo, Marcus, and Beau. Zeke's here. And Ransom."

"Aha! I knew he'd be sniffing around!"

"Who's doing what?"

Margery sounded exasperated. "Ransom is on the prowl!"

"Don't be ridiculous. He and I have been friends for years."

"I swear, you live your life with rose-colored blinders. Don't you date?"

"I've been out with friends plenty of times."

"Group dates don't count. Grab the guy. Betcha he grabs back."

Margery's laughter put Prissie's teeth on edge. "Don't be ridiculous. Besides, this week, I'm watching the kids …."

"Excuses, excuses! You're not going to get anywhere if you're always watching other people's kids so they can have a life!"

Prissie refrained from pointing out that one of those children was Margery's. Taking a deep breath, she calmly explained, "Ransom doesn't think of me that way."

"Omigosh, you are so frustrating!" Her voice turned saccharine sweet. *"Mark my words. Ransom has his eye on the future, and you're in his plans. He wants marry into the family business."*

"Impossible." Ransom wouldn't use her like that. That's not how friends treated one another. "You're wrong."

"You'll see. And then I'll get to say 'I told you so.'"

Margery hung up without taking the time to say hello to her son. Prissie sagged against the wall with a groan of frustration. Why did people have to stomp all over her life with their assumptions?

Marcus appeared at the base of the stairs, then quickly climbed them. Joining her on the stair, he asked, "Trouble?"

Prissie grumbled, "First you and me, now me and Ransom. Why would people even begin to think we're a couple?"

He searched her face, then addressed the ceiling. "I don't have the delicacy for this."

"For what?" she asked sharply.

"Heaven help us all. Fine." Holding out his hand, Marcus said, "Give me your phone."

She surrendered it and watched him flick to her picture album. "What are you looking for?"

He placed the pink phone back in her hands. "This is what I see. Take a good look, kiddo."

Prissie stared at the snapshot, taken on the day Baird had texted to ask if she was braced. She wasn't. Not for this. Marcus wrapped his arm protectively around her shoulders, and she leaned into his support as she faced the possibility that Ransom had a hidden agenda. Or was it hidden? He'd hinted at plans. Didn't this confirm Margery's suspicions?

"That's everything, but not everyone," came Momma's voice from below. "Maybe someone should ring the dinner bell."

"My turn!" exclaimed Colin, and the kitchen door slammed. A moment later, the din of the dinner bell made it impossible to hear.

Prissie allowed Marcus to lead her into the kitchen, where Ransom met their arrival with quirking eyebrows. "Phone call. Stairway," Marcus said shortly, steering Prissie toward the chair next to Ransom's.

But then bell's clanging cut off, and the kitchen door burst open with a gust of damp air. Colin ran up to Prissie with an enormous armful of golden flowers and proudly presented them. "He said they're for you!"

"*Who* said?" Marcus asked gruffly, his grip tightening on Prissie's arm.

"A guy." The boy's smile widened. "Does Aunt Prissie have a boyfriend?"

"I … no." Prissie noticed that Milo was on his feet, and Beau was covering his nose. Ransom's expression was more difficult to read. Marcus hissed softly as Ethan limped into the kitchen, face pale and blood seeping between his fingers where he clutched at a thorn-like dart buried in his upper arm.

The battered Guardian locked eyes with Marcus, nodded shakily, then collapsed onto the kitchen floor.

CHAPTER 10

THE PUP TENT

Ethan mumbled, "Go back downstairs."

"No."

"Prissie, your friends are worried about you."

"Maybe I'm more worried about the friend who collapsed in our kitchen and had to be carried out by two cherubim."

Tycho and Jedrick knelt in either side of the wounded Guardian, their wings turning Prissie's tiny bedroom into an impenetrable refuge. Ethan's captain asked, "Ready?"

He gritted his teeth and nodded. In one swift motion, Tycho pulled the wicked dart from his upper arm. Eyes crossing, Ethan groaned, then immediately felt bad. Had he not frightened Prissie enough?

Jedrick's hands locked around the wound, staunching the flow of blood. He said, "Ethan is right, Prissie. You should return to your guests."

She shook her head, and that wasn't all that was shaking.

Ethan clumsily took her trembling hand in his. "Fear not. This injury is not my first, nor will it be my last. I will mend." To his surprise, she kissed his knuckles.

"Thank you. For every wound you've ever taken for our sakes, thank you." Prissie met his gaze with utter calm. "But I'm not scared. If anything I'm angry. How could that demon use a child? Was Colin hurt?"

Jedrick's expression softened into a smile, and Tycho studied her with interest.

She didn't know. But how could she? Fighting to keep his voice steady, Ethan repeated, "Fear not. The enemy cannot touch Colin."

"Cannot? But why?"

Tycho said, "Ask your brother. Jude bore witness to Colin's first prayer."

In a twinkling, joy suffused Prissie's face. With a shaky giggle, she murmured, "That little sneak! When? He never said a thing."

Ethan wished she could hear the boy's Guardians, who had not ceased to sing for days. But perhaps Prissie understood, even without hearing their booming voices. And someday they would certainly thank the young woman whose generosity had opened the door to joy.

Ransom caught a ride to the Pomeroys' farm with Zeke, who craned his neck and grinned. "Perfect! Sis is in the garden. I'll meet you in the barn in twenty minutes or so. That's where we stow the cast iron for camping."

"Twenty minutes," he agreed. Which wasn't long to do what needed to be done. Especially since he didn't have a clue what that was.

While Zeke jogged to the house, Ransom cut across the lawn, racking his brain for something to say. Ever since she'd received all those golden flowers from her mysterious admirer, Prissie had been doing a masterful job of avoiding him. No easy task when you saw someone every day. It was like junior high all over again. At work, she carried on the pretense of small talk, but he'd lived at arm's length long enough.

"Doesn't look like your day off was much of one," he said. "How's it going?"

Prissie glanced up, then ducked her head so the brim of her floppy straw hat hid her face. "You moonlight in a lumber yard. I put my extra hours into a kitchen garden. The only difference is I'm paid in pickles."

"Sounds worthwhile."

"When Grandma Nell's knees started acting up, she entrusted this to me." Sitting back on her heels, she gestured broadly. "Momma calls it my family inheritance."

Ransom crouched and prodded at a tuft of chives. "The best worldly riches, assuming you have the green thumb to make the most of it."

"I can feed a family of seventeen with zucchini to spare, year in and year out, world without end."

"Prissie?" He waited for her to raise her head and meet his gaze. "Are we okay? Because something's not right, and I need to know if I messed up."

"No. It's nothing."

He poked his finger into the soil. "That's not like you, Miss Priss … lying to a friend."

She flinched.

Ransom kept talking. "We had a good day. Best I've had since *ever*. But everything went wonky at dinnertime, and it wasn't just the flowers. When I touched your arm, you jumped a mile and bolted. And I'm starting to miss little things like eye contact."

Prissie glanced up.

"Can I fix this?"

"No, you can't," she said quietly. "Except maybe to pray. That's all I know how to do when things get this confusing."

"You got it. Stand up," he ordered.

She did, brushing vaguely at her knees before smoothing her skirt. "I'm sorry if I've been worrying you."

"You have *no* idea. So c'mere." Prissie looked ready to run, so he caught her arm and tugged. "If praying's all I can do, let's pray."

"Now?" With a wariness that was new to their relationship, she eased into the circle of his arms. The hat wasn't cooperating, and she pulled it off, revealing hair left loose for once.

Ransom fixed his gaze on the treetops to avoid letting all those honey-colored waves distract him. "God, I don't know what all's going on, but it can't be good since it's pulling friends apart. If Prissie needs me, let me be there. And vice versa. Because that's what friends do."

Prissie quietly added her own prayer. "We need each other, but we need You more. So here we are, trusting. Everything is in Your hands. Especially us. Help me to remember that."

Ransom whispered his amen, then gave her a quick squeeze. "So we're okay?"

"Obviously." Her smile tilted toward teasing. "You're the same as ever."

"You say that like it's a bad thing!"

"No. Keep it up."

"Sure. So … after I finish inspecting cast iron skillets in the barn with Zeke, can I come back to the house and see you?"

Prissie hesitated. "What for?"

"Camping starts tomorrow, which means a whole lot of manly bonding in a pup tent. And I'd really rather not show up with bubblegum pink toenails."

On his first full day as camp chef, Ransom overcooked the eggs, served a thick rice pudding that tasted faintly of smoke and spice, and earned the nickname Cookie. Mixed blessings. But the weather was good, and the company was better.

Ransom wasn't sure how he felt about being the oldest member of their group. Thankfully, he was spared from being the most responsible by Beau, who'd decided to come along at the last minute.

Uncle Beau and his small stack of books and journals had been given a place in the enormous blue tent with Zeke and the three seven-year-olds. The rest of them were paired off in three pup tents. Jasper and Timothy shared the red one. Marcus and Ransom were in the yellow one. And Prissie and Juliette had the pink tent. Two screened canopies, a campfire pit, and a charcoal grill completed the short list of amenities.

"You still in the kitchen, *Cookie*?"

"Aren't you supposed to be fishing for lunch?

"You wish." Timothy dropped onto a folding chair. "If Zeke and Jasper want to play camp counselor, that's their prerogative. I'm no good with kids."

"So you're here to heckle the help?"

Timothy rubbed his nose, hiding a lopsided smile. "I'll go easy on you if you feed me."

"Fair enough." Ransom popped open a cooler and rummaged in one of the bakery boxes. Holding up an iced turnover, he said, "These were back-up. In case I burned everything this morning."

"I'll take two." Waving with both hands, Timothy said, "Knowing people in the fancy-schmancy bakery business has its perks."

"What are you aiming for?"

"College."

"What major."

"I don't really care." Timothy took a big bite of pastry and used the tip of his tongue to catch delicate flakes. "Mom's the one hell-bent on a university degree. As long as they have a good music program, I'll be okay."

"Trombone, right?"

"So?"

Ransom wasn't sure what was behind Timothy's defensive tone. "*So* … you must like it about as much as I like batching cookies."

"More. It's the one thing I'm good at."

"Do you do classical stuff … or the seventy-six trombone marching stuff?"

"All of the above. I'm in orchestra, pep band, *and* jazz band.

"If you're that into it, maybe you should teach music."

"Maybe." The brief flicker of interest in his eyes was quickly replaced by suspicion. "Here's a question. Are you actually into music, or are you trying to figure out how to haul my heathen ass into heaven?"

"Both."

"Well you're doing a lousy job at reconnaissance," Timothy said, licking his fingers. "Because I just told you I don't like kids. You couldn't pay me to be a teacher."

Ransom was all set with a retort, but he caught a bright flutter of pink out of the corner of his eye and glanced out past the canopy. Then did a double-take. Prissie was obviously headed for water. Her swimsuit and flippy skirt cover-up thingie were certainly modest by most standards, but … wow.

Timothy's laugh was a goofy, snorting thing. "Oh, *that* wasn't obvious."

Ignoring him, Ransom stepped out from under the canopy to get a second look. He wasn't about to explain to some high school kid that he could count on one hand the number of times he'd seen Prissie's knees.

"Hey, Prissie!" Timothy called. "Where are you two headed?"

Ransom froze as she left off talking to Juliette and turned. He really shouldn't have gone for the second look.

Timothy whispered, "*Busted.*"

She said, "We're going to catch crayfish. Are you coming?"

"Dunno." Timothy asked, "Do I need any special equipment?"

It was a fair question. Juliette was holding a tiny net, like kind you use for scooping fish out of tanks.

Prissie laughed. "Bring a pail, your courage, and our chef. This is no time to be loitering in tents. The creek is calling!"

Ransom found his tongue. "We're right behind you!"

When she waved and led Juliette on, Ransom dove into the tent, hastily stowing the last of his gear. Grabbing a plastic basin, he zipped shut the screen. "Ready?"

Timothy fell in step beside him. "All except the courage part. Have you *seen* crayfish?" He executed a full-body shudder.

"Not for a lot of summers. Marcus and I would sometimes come on our bikes and meet Prissie, but she always wanted to look for tadpoles."

"We don't bike over here so much anymore. Football practice, music lessons, jobs." Timothy wrinkled his nose as he squinted toward the river where his friends were fishing. "This is our last year, then we split up. Maybe for good."

Ransom paused at the top of the bank leading down to a wide, shallow creek overhung with trees. Clear water rippled lazily over smooth stones, and overhanging tree branches formed a cool, green tunnel. Prissie had waded out and was showing her four-year-old niece how to float leaf boats on the current.

Dragging his thoughts mostly back on track, Ransom said, "I didn't really want to leave this. I didn't know if I'd be back."

"You lucked out." With a speculative air, Timothy added, "Or she did."

"Not luck," Ransom said quietly. He'd ached and prayed too much over Prissie for this to be anything but God. "She'd probably call it providence … or a catastrophe. Hard to tell which way things will swing."

Timothy frowned. "Don't you date?"

"Unless you count group stuff …."

"I meant Christians. Because Zeke and Jasper don't have girls either."

"Gotcha. Christians date." Ransom shrugged. "Zeke and Jasper probably have their reasons. I know I put it off because I was still struggling to sort out this and that … and saving every penny so I could travel to Europe."

Timothy's frown deepened. "What about while you were overseas. You could have found someone and messed around, and no one here would know."

Ransom could feel his eyebrows on the rise and tried not to be insulted. Maybe this guy didn't have someone to ask about this kind of thing. So he was blunt. "While I was in Europe, a few women made offers along those lines. I always told them I had a girl back home. After that, they either lost interest or my respect."

"Harsh."

"My folks messed up. I want to get it right. School came first, but marriage is next on my agenda." No sense denying something everyone—except Prissie—had figured out.

"You're gonna skip dating and propose?"

Ransom rolled his eyes and turned the tables. "What's the purpose of dating?"

The wariness was back in Timothy's expression. "Most guys want a good time."

"And this is where I have to bring up my faith. Because I want good things, too. But in the right order." He gestured toward Prissie. "So I'm waiting until she's ready. And working at making sure everything's ready when she is."

"Kinda presumptuous," Timothy remarked. "She might be playing dumb because she's afraid to hurt your feelings. This could be her way of saying let's be friends."

"You think I haven't thought of that?"

Timothy shook his head. "Nope. You're smart. But even smart guys do stupid stuff when there's a girl involved."

Ransom got the impression Timothy was speaking from experience, but this didn't seem like the right time to pry. Instead, he said, "You know, I thought you'd be avoiding me."

"Zeke asked me to make the new guy feel welcome."

"Subtle."

"Zeke doesn't *do* subtle, but I'm used to it." The freckled teen picked his way down to the water's edge and kicked off his shoes. "He and Jasper have been pushing and pulling me along my whole life."

"About Christianity?"

"About *everything*. Not sure I'd have passed any tests if they didn't help me study. They're the ones who convinced my mom I should have a bike … and therefore a life. And it's not every short, skinny band geek who's got two popular jocks for backup."

Ransom stuffed balled up socks into his sneakers and waded out after Timothy. The water was so clear, he could pick out the darting shadows. Would catching a minnow impress Juliette … and therefore Prissie? Bending over, he slipped his fingertips into the water and watched for his chance.

Timothy found a stick and poked around, but stuck close. Ransom figured they'd pried into his love life enough to warrant an opening foray. "So what's the deal? Do you have a problem with Christianity?"

"You really haven't been paying attention to anything but Prissie's legs."

Caught mid-peek, Ransom straightened and turned his back on the girls. "Leave off," he grumbled.

"Not a chance." Timothy propped his stick against his shoulder and smirked. "My two best friends are Christians. Clearly, I don't have a problem with them believing in Jesus."

"But *you*?"

Timothy's expression wavered. "Just one more way I don't fit in. Only this time, they're holding it against me."

"I wouldn't go *that* f– "

"Speak of the devil," Timothy interrupted, lifting a hand.

Zeke jogged along the edge of creek, skipping over every root and stone as easy as strolling along a sidewalk. Like he knew the way so well, he didn't have to look down. "Hey, Timothy! I hope you know I was kidding about tossing you in the river."

"Uh-huh."

"Timothy coulda handled it," Zeke said to Ransom. "He used to be on the swim team, only he quit."

Ransom glanced at Timothy, whose lip curled. "I like swimming. I don't like swimming back and forth between two lines while a has-been coach yells from the sideline … and imposes rules he doesn't follow."

Zeke grimaced. "Your coach let himself go some. Gotta respect Coach Hobbes, though. He works out with the football team and can put any one of us on our backs." He switched to Ransom, saying, "Swimming is what brought me and Timothy together. Our moms enrolled us in lessons. What were we … guppies?"

"Yeah, and Zeke was the first guppy to jump off the high-dive board," Timothy said, traces of pride in his tone.

"Momma's got the pictures to prove it." Zeke pointed downstream, toward the river. "Anyhow, I came back to invite you to fish with us, if you want to try your hand. Or were you hoping to reel in Sis?"

"He acts like he's never seen a girl's legs before," Timothy reported.

Zeke leaned forward and lowered his voice. "Girls, plenty. Sis, not so much. She does that whole long skirt thing, so her legs are like … a myth."

Timothy snickered, and Ransom glanced upstream to see if Prissie could hear them. But he stopped hearing the boys' banter. Something was wrong.

Tense and pale, Prissie was pushing Juliette toward the homeward bank, but the little girl clung to her leg. Following Prissie's line of sight, Ransom punched Zeke's shoulder.

"Kidding, kidding!" he laughed.

Prissie raised her voice then, deathly calm, but with a tremulous edge. "Zeke, come get Juliette." Her attention fixed on the forest as she eased backward. "And if the boys are close by, get them out of here."

"I'm coming! Did you spot a snake?" Zeke hustled along the creek's edge. Scooping up Juliette, he gawked. "Whoa … anyone have a camera?"

A big stag with impressive antlers emerged from the shadows, facing off with the Pomeroys. The haughty tilt of his head defied the campers who were standing in his watering hole. Ransom quickly sloshed over to Prissie, who stood transfixed. Taking her by the shoulders, he muttered, "Nice and easy, Miss Priss. We'll give Mr. Deer a turn at the creek. He could be thirsty."

She whispered. "Do you see that?"

Prissie wasn't moving, so Ransom wrapped his arms around her waist and half-carried, half-dragged her backward. "Plain as day, and territorial as all get out. So let's get out of that bad boy's way," he said, keeping his voice low.

"His eyes," she said, wrapping cold fingers around his forearms. "Do you see his eyes?"

Ransom looked more closely at the stag. "I didn't know deer could have blue eyes. Kind of spooky."

Prissie slapped her hands over her ears and begged, "Make him stop!"

The deer lowered its head and shook its antlers, and Ransom hastened their retreat, backing straight into a uniform. "Oops, sorry, Mr. Ranger."

"Hello, Mr. Pavlos."

"Padgett!" Prissie gasped, whipping around so fast, she almost toppled Ransom over.

"Fear not, miss. We'll take it from here."

Ransom had enough wits to wonder who *we* was since there were no other park employees in sight. But he was mostly preoccupied with Prissie, who'd turned his practical necessity into an awkward position. He was trapped between the two of them. Ranger Prentice must have been stronger than he looked, because he was supporting both of them.

Zeke gave him a thumbs-up.

Timothy, who'd just snapped several pictures of the stag, turned his phone's camera on them.

Padgett calmly intervened. "Miss, let Ransom find his balance. Ransom, would you please escort her back to camp."

Prissie's wide eyes suddenly locked onto Ransom's face. On the up-side, she regained a little color. On the down-side, she pushed off and fled.

Zeke chuckled. "Kicked to the curb."

"Crash and burn," agreed Timothy.

Ransom excused himself and chased after Prissie, even though he was becoming increasingly sure she had no intention of letting him catch her.

The sound of the tent zipper pulled Ransom out of a light doze as Marcus crawled inside, bringing along a whiff of wood smoke and bug spray.

"You gave up early."

"Did you have to put it like *that*?" Ransom groaned.

"Nope. Sorry." His best friend unlaced his boots, then ditched his socks. Crawling onto his sleeping bag, he dropped face-first onto his pillow, then bunched it up under his chin. Rapping his knuckle on the cover of Ransom's Bible, he asked, "Feeling better?"

"Some." He flung an arm over his eyes. "I don't know why I thought I'd get to spend time with Prissie on this trip. When she isn't with Juliette, she's with Juliette and the boys. And I could do without three *other* boys who insist on butting in with broad hints and bad advice."

"You and Timothy seem to get along."

"Guess so. But I can see why Zeke and Jasper don't know how to deal with him. The kid has things messed up in his head. Like his friends won't accept him unless he accepts Jesus. Which isn't much of a foundation for faith. It's gotta be for the right reasons."

"Amen and amen."

Ransom sighed. "Then why does it feel like I'm doing something wrong?"

"Maybe you are."

"Wish I knew what," he muttered.

"Sleep. You need sleep."

Marcus's hand found Ransom's forehead, and it was like someone flipped a switch.

Instead of a pup tent and a sleeping bag, Ransom was standing in a room full of books. Everything about the space was bright and beautiful, and he was sure he'd been here before. A recurring dream. Turning to check if the foot of a spiral staircase was still where he remembered it should be, he blinked. On the bottom step stood a boy with straight dark hair, pointed ears, and radioactive pajamas. "Koji?"

CHAPTER 11

THE SHORT VERSION

"Koji," Ransom repeated, frowning in concentration. "We've done this before. This dream."

"Indeed." Koji's solemn expression warmed into a smile. "A way has been made for us to meet. The memory will fade, but we have *now*."

"Now's good." Ransom found he was wearing a pure white tunic that shimmered in the abundance of ambient light. "So how often do I ask why you haven't grown?"

"Every time." Koji hopped off the bottom step and walked over. Even when he stood tall, he didn't quite reach Ransom's shoulder. "Just as I always ask if she is still precious to you?"

"*You* know?"

"God knows."

"You, God, and everyone knows. Everyone *except* Prissie."

Koji's fingers brushed the back of Ransom's hand. "Have you told her?"

"Working on that. I guess I was hoping she'd catch on, but nothing's ever been that easy where she's concerned." His shoulders drooped. "Besides, too many other people have her attention right now."

The angelic boy nodded solemnly. "Your hopes require her cooperation."

"And she isn't cooperating."

Taking his hand, Koji led Ransom under the winding staircase that hugged the white stone wall and into a book-lined alcove. The space was papered with partially-completed paintings. Most of them were just the right size to fit in a mailbox. Koji dropped Ransom's hand and shyly announced, "This is where I paint. My room."

"You're an amazing artist."

"I am an apprentice with much to learn. But I am Sent to you. I bring a message." Koji's toes scrunched up on the patterned rug beneath their feet. "This is for your good."

"You're an angel."

"Yes."

"Which means this message is from God …?"

"Indeed."

Ransom's knees buckled, and he sank to the floor. "Umm … sorry. I don't think I can take this standing up." With a shaking hand, he covered his mouth, which had begun to tremble. "Koji, I'm scared."

The boy stepped closer and asked, "Will you hear my words, even if they are not easy?"

"Yes. Always. Please." To Ransom's embarrassment, his eyes began to water. "You may have to pick up the pieces afterward, though."

"Fear not." Koji took a deep breath, then said, "You have been faithful in your devotion to the woman you have chosen, and you have been faithful to your Lord. Well done."

Ransom's heart soared, then faltered. He could feel it coming. "But …?"

"You see her, but she is like this." Koji turned his back on Ransom and gestured broadly. "Many need her help, her time, her attention. She is merciful as God is merciful. This is her gift: compassion."

Ransom nodded. One of the things he admired most about Prissie was her kindness.

"You are being tempted."

"I'd never do anything inappropriate. You gotta know I respect her and her family and God too much t– "

"Listen," Koji sighed, and the formality left his tone, as if his next words were an aside. "Prissie was similarly tempted when I was called away. She wished to keep me for herself. If I had fulfilled her desire, my service to God would have ended."

"Are you going to ask me to say goodbye to Prissie?" Ransom whispered.

Koji didn't answer directly. He faced Ransom and said, "You desire *this*. That she turn her back on the people God has set in her path. That she choose you above all others, even if it calls a halt to her service."

Ransom flushed, then paled. Here, he'd been thinking of himself as patient.

But in God's eyes, his motives were off-kilter. So selfish. So jealous. So greedy. "I *do* want her to love me back. Desperately."

A slim hand patted his shoulder. "Instead of standing behind Prissie, looking over her shoulder at those you feel are rivals, do *this*." Koji walked around behind him. "Place your back to hers, and see what awaits. God has things for *you* to do. They will surely be before you."

Ransom heaved a shuddering sigh. "You're not asking me to give up on her?"

Koji blinked. "That was neither said nor implied."

"Does that mean I can get my hopes up?"

"I cannot tell you what only God knows."

"Figures. Can't blame a guy for trying."

Koji circled around and dropped to his knees in front of Ransom. "Above all else, Prissie values faithfulness. Stay faithful."

"I can do that much." Sensing that the message had been delivered in its entirety, Ransom relaxed into a smile. "Does this count as meddling? Seems like a lot of people have been playing matchmaker."

Tipping his head, Koji said, "My friend is lonely in ways I cannot understand."

"Are you talking about Prissie … or me?"

"Yes."

Recalling something Prissie had told him not long ago, he said, "She loves you, you know."

"Indeed."

"Can I give you something in her place? Because if she was here, she'd be hugging you." When he opened his arms, Koji jumped into them, clinging so tightly that Ransom wished he'd asked sooner. "Hey, Koji. You know I love you, right?"

A soft laugh bubbled up, and when Koji finally let go, his eyes were bright. "It is difficult to find words to express the joy your friendship inspires."

"One thing. I'm clued in *now*. But when I wake up, most of the details slip away. What's the use in giving me advice I won't remember?"

Koji touched Ransom's chest with his fingertips. "Your heart will hang onto what is important. This is wisdom, and it will guide your steps."

"Sounds promising, but still vaguer than I'd like."

"Do you wish to hear my opinion?"

Ransom's chuckle ended as a sigh. "Tell me, Koji the angel, my strange and wonderful friend, what do *you* think I should do about Prissie?"

"I think you should tell her."

Prissie woke to snuffling. Like a dog sniffing for crumbs, only much, much bigger. A gusty *whuff* set the hair at the back of her neck on end. First a stag, now a bear? Her prayers were already flying heavenward when she thought to check on Juliette. But the impulse was forgotten the moment she realized that a fragile pink wall wasn't the only thing lying between her and danger.

Asher lifted a finger to his lips, then pressed his hands together and tucked them under his cheek.

His presence eased Prissie's fears. No matter what might be outside the tent, she and Juliette were safe, for God had Sent one of His angels to watch over them. Or if Asher's exaggerated pose was any indication … to play at camping.

"Is this your first time inside a tent?" she whispered, offering him half of her pillow.

He scooted closer. "Heaven's encampments are filled with tents."

"We could use an encampment right about now." Shuffling steps came closer again, as if their intruder was pacing back and forth. Prissie looped and arm around Asher, pulling him away from the bear sounds.

"Are you protecting me?" he asked.

She felt a little silly. "It's probably the other way around."

Asher snuggled close, laying his head on her shoulder. "Fear not. I cannot give you an encampment, but I have brought a tent."

Light bloomed as if night had turned to day. For a moment, the dark, shaggy outline of an animal was silhouetted against pink fabric, but with a rustle of grass and rattle of leaves, the bear crashed away through the woods. Prissie slowly sat up and whispered, "What did you do?"

Asher popped up and repeated, "Brought a tent."

"But it's light outside." The walls of her pup tent glowed as if someone had turned on a floodlight. "Is it morning?"

The boy shook his head. "It is night."

Ethan's voice came from outside. "Asher, is this your doing?"

"Yes."

Beyond the tent wall, the Guardian sighed. "Did he wake you, Prissie?"

"The bear did. Is it safe?"

After a lengthy pause, Ethan answered, "Very safe. Come and see for yourself."

Prissie glanced uncertainly at Juliette. Asher sat beside the little girl, his hair pooling on the blankets and sleeping bags. Hugging his knees to his chest, he said, "I will be with her. She will not wake before you return."

Whispering her thanks, Prissie grabbed a shawl and slip-ons, then slowly unzipped the tent.

Ethan was waiting for her, hand extended. "Do not be alarmed. We are with you."

While he helped her to her feet, she looked up, but the night sky was missing. Replaced by loose folds of creamy fabric that shimmered like raiment. Shaking her head in disbelief, Prissie whispered, "He brought a tent."

"Yes. Our tent," said Ethan. "It belongs to Tycho's Flight."

"And so we are here as well," said Tycho. The turquoise-winged archer stepped forward. "Encamped around you."

Which was entirely true. The structure was both tall enough and wide enough to surround the entire campsite. All four tents, the campfire, their canopies—everything was walled in by luminous cloth that flowed freely in a breeze Prissie couldn't feel.

An angel Prissie didn't know seemed to be waiting for something. Sharp features. Wiry hair. Wondering eyes. "Hello," she said.

"Oh!" Ethan took Prissie's elbow, then touched this newcomer's arm, forming a bridge. "This is Conrad. He is my mentor."

Conrad was shorter than Ethan, but Prissie still had to look up; he was easily as tall as Prissie's father. And clearly flustered. She offered her hand. "I'm glad you're here. Thank you for scaring off that bear."

He gently took her hands between his. "Hello, Prissie."

"Don't forget *fear not*!" Raz strolled into the tent just ahead of his mentor. "She likes that part."

Verrill backed him up with a wave of hands. "These opportunities don't come often."

Prissie doubted Conrad needed the extra encouragement. Her own Guardians had been terrible about making eye contact, but this warrior held her gaze with quiet intensity. He knew how rare this meeting was. That's why he was letting the moment stretch.

Conrad smile was more of a smirk when he finally said, "Fear not."

Ethan asked, "May I show her around?"

"Worth a try, right?" Raz said, glancing between their mentors.

Verrill frowned thoughtfully. "There should be time, but keep it quick."

"Are we on some kind of schedule?" Prissie asked.

Releasing her hand, Conrad said, "Ethan is eager to begin."

Turning to the younger Guardian, Prissie asked, "What did you want to show me?"

"You can see my mentor, my captain, and my tent. Perhaps you can see my teammates as well. I want to share this joy with them."

Prissie blinked, then laughed a little. "Like Raz said, it's worth a try. Let's find out how much God wants me to see."

Ethan guided her through the tent's open flap. Raz rushed to take her other arm, looping it through his. Their manners reminded Prissie of those times when Zeke and Jasper dragged her into some new mischief. A moment later, she was grateful for their support.

She didn't mean to squeak, but the cherub standing just outside the tent took her by surprise. He towered at least ten feet, possibly twelve. The arrow resting against his bow had to be taller than she was, and the spear strapped to his back was like a small tree.

One look into her face, and the archer dropped his weapon and raised both hands. "Fear not!" he gasped. "Ethan, Raz, didn't you warn her? Tell her it's okay!"

"Calm down, Garrick. She knows." Raz turned to Prissie and whispered, "Big softie. Tell him it's okay."

"I'm fine, I promise." She mimicked the dissembling warrior, raising both hands. "My name's Prissie … but I suppose you already knew that part."

Garrick offered his palm. "Ethan sings of you at evensong."

"And he's in my prayers," she said, pressing her hand to his. It was reassuringly warm. "You will be, too, assuming I remember all this. It's beginning to feel like a dream."

The archer's hand closed around hers. "Waking or dreaming, we're here."

"Next is Yannis, he is Garrick's apprentice." Ethan led her around the corner of the tent, to where another cherub stood guard. Prissie did a double-take and leaned back to see if Garrick had moved. But the archer was still there, reclaiming his cast-off bow and arrow.

"Twins?" she asked.

Garrick smiled impishly. "Almost."

Prissie knew something about being an almost-twin. As fresh amazement dawned on a face she already knew, she looked for some way to tell the two apart. Brown skin, purple wings, heavy braids, full quivers. Even Yannis's and Garrick's dimples were in the same place. This archer carried no spear, but otherwise, he seemed identical to his mentor. Giving up with a smile, she extended her hand. "I'm Prissie. Thank you for watching over my family."

Introductions continued right around the perimeter, and by the end Ethan was aglow. Prissie understood his happiness, but all the attention worried her a little. This wasn't her first time being ushered into the midst of a Flight. Yes, she was glad to encourage these angels, to cherish their names, to thank them personally, but didn't this mean there was something terrible ahead? Why else would God allow them to meet?

Putting the miraculous tent at her back, Prissie gazed toward the stars. Frogs peeped and croaked. An owl hooted. Crickets added to the chorus.

Everything was so peaceful, but she doubted this was a quiet night. "There's a battle all around us, isn't there."

Ethan extended a wing behind her. "Yes."

"And Blight followed us here."

"Yes."

Prissie was about to ask what she was supposed to do, but the sound of a zipper tore through the campsite. She whirled in time to see Garrick and Yannis pull apart loose sections of their tent's wall, revealing the yellow pup tent. For a moment, she thought Marcus had decided to join them, but Ransom straightened and stretched.

Peering around vaguely, he said, "Hey, Miss Priss. How come you're standing out here, all alone in the dark?"

She opened her mouth, but how was she supposed to answer him?

Ethan touched her shoulder and said, "Fear not. We are still here."

And the wash of light winked out, simplifying matters. Tugging her shawl more tightly around her shoulders, she said, "I'm not alone. You're here."

"Need an escort?" he asked, indicating the path to the park's restrooms.

Since it was a reasonable excuse for her to be out and about, Prissie said, "Thanks."

Ransom fished in his pocket and pulled out a small flashlight. Hitting the on switch, he asked, "Wanna share?"

Prissie stared. "You kept it?"

"Sure." He trained the pink flashlight on the trail as they walked. "This was a gift from a friend. I take special care of it."

Prissie remembered the day she'd bought it. "We weren't friends then."

"Oh, I dunno." Ransom yawned noisily before adding, "I think we were already friends back then. It just took you a little longer to notice."

She tensed.

He sighed. "Prissie?"

"Hmm?"

"Don't worry so much."

They passed under one of the lampposts that lined the park trail, and she stole a look. Messy hair. Sleepy gaze. Relaxed smile. Why did Margery have to go and put strange ideas in her head? Ransom couldn't have ulterior motives. "Who says I'm worried?"

He shrugged. "Just seems that way. But me and Marcus will be here for you. Whatever you need. Same as always."

"Thanks."

Ransom's steps slowed. "I think I dreamed about Koji again. It's all blurred, but … yeah."

So they'd both been visited by angels? Her in person. Him in dreams.

"Say, Prissie. How do you like your marshmallows? I turned in before I could find out."

"Is that what they call a burning question?"

He chuckled. "All depends on your answer. So?"

She said, "The perfect marshmallow is toasted slowly, so it blushes beige. And once it's all melty on the inside, I torch it for a few seconds because I love that blackened sugar flavor."

"Good to know." They strolled slowly past picnic shelters and darkened campers. "Timothy's doing this thing lately, trading questions. I can only ask him personal stuff if he can play inquisitor."

Prissie shook her head. "He's a good kid, but he can be such a brat."

"So I was thinking. Now that you've revealed the intimate details of your marshmallow preferences, is there anything you want to know about me?"

Oh. Was he giving her the chance to clear the air? Maybe that was best. Get it out. Get it over with. "There was this *one* thing," she said slowly. "It's ridiculous, I know. But Margery said …."

"What did Margery say?" he prompted.

"She told me you … umm." Taking a deep breath, she said it all in a rush. "Margery thinks you want to marry into the family business. But you don't have to go *that* far to work for Dad. He already loves you like a son. So you don't have to try to get on my good side."

Ransom stopped walking. "I thought I was on your good side."

"You are. And you *already* have a place at the bakery. Which is why this is so frustrating." Tugging unhappily at the end of her braid, she admitted, "Ever since she said those things, it's been bothering me."

"Calm down, Miss Priss."

She shook her head. "I don't *like* misunderstandings."

"You're right, and I'm sorry. This is my fault." Ransom rolled the little flashlight between his fingers. "The reason you don't understand is because I didn't explain. Looks like I should do that."

Prissie hadn't expected an apology, let alone an explanation. "Yes, I think you should."

"Do you want the short version or the long version?"

"Better keep it short."

"Sure." Stepping closer, he dipped down and brushed her cheek with his lips. "Love you."

"No, you don't."

Ransom smiled crookedly. "Figures you'd argue the point."

"Maybe you'd better give me the long version."

"I love you, and I want to marry you."

Prissie's bewilderment doubled. "You're *proposing*?"

"Not precisely. But now you know exactly how I feel and what my intentions are." When silence stretched between them, Ransom added, "I didn't want to rush you."

"How is this not rushing?"

"I've been right here for almost a decade. But you never really noticed."

That felt like an accusation, and she bristled. "So this is *my* fault?"

"No, Prissie. I already told you. Any misunderstanding is my fault."

"Is *this* what you meant when you said I don't see you?" She floundered in the face of his calm. "Because I see you every day."

Ransom squared his shoulders. "Sure. But now you'll see me differently."

Prissie spent the following morning watching Ransom and trying not to be obvious about it. That's how she knew that he wasn't paying her any attention. And for reasons she couldn't fathom, that left her feeling slighted. Or annoyed. Actually, *both*.

The whole situation was unreal, like being twelve years old all over again. Back when Ransom first showed up at her school, she'd kept an eye on him because she knew he was trouble. But since becoming friends, he'd faded comfortably into the background, a part of the new normal.

Even that upset her on several levels. Maybe Ransom's secret wasn't as terrible as Margery had suggested, but he *had* been keeping one. And Prissie felt stupid for missing something so huge. He'd been one of her best friends all through high school, yet she'd never noticed anything out of the ordinary. Was it because she wasn't paying attention? That idea made her uneasy with herself, and she interrupted her inner dialogue with the Lord to whisper, "What kind of friend does that make me?"

"Sis?"

She started guiltily as Jude crouched beside her chair.

"I get the idea you didn't really hear Beau."

"Umm … no. Did I miss something?"

"He and Marcus took the kids to the nature center. If you wanted to catch the rangers' bird migration spiel, you'll need to hurry." Jude searched her face and added, "But it might be good to rest up while it's quiet."

Prissie glanced around. Only Jude, Timothy, and Ransom were in view. "Where did Zeke and Jasper go?"

"We needed ice." Jude patiently rehearsed the day's schedule. "Nature center this morning with Beau. Zeke's doing the supply run. I'll take the kids over to the pond this afternoon. And Ranger Prentice is doing a thing about bats by the cave entrance at sunset. Colin's really excited about that one."

"Of course. And you're right. I *am* a little short on sleep."

She welcomed the excuse to retreat into her pink tent. From its open flap, she could still see Ransom, who seemed to be telling Timothy about life in Paris. Normally, she would have loved to hear more about his travels, but after last night, she didn't want to give him the wrong idea. So she'd given a false pretense instead. Because in the end, Ransom was right. Her perspective was changing.

Ransom gestured broadly as he talked. Timothy's snicker turned into a squeaky laugh. Jude pulled up a chair and joined the conversation by asking a question Prissie couldn't quite hear. And Prissie felt very alone in her discomfort. How could Ransom go on acting like normal? Why could he still joke and smile as if nothing had happened?

Propping her chin on her hands, she tried to see Ransom in a romantic light. But no matter how long she stared, he was … Ransom. Nice guy, yes. Good friend, always. He was someone she was glad to see. Someone she enjoyed talking to. But not exactly knight-in-shining-armor material. That role belonged to Tamaes, Ethan, Jedrick, and the rest. Prissie's conscience twinged. It wasn't fair to compare. Ransom was just a man. One she respected and loved in a friendly way. The same as always.

The guys' heads turned, and Jude stood to welcome someone. Prissie leaned to one side and frowned. Milo? Why wasn't he at work? She was halfway out of her tent before she remembered that she was supposed to be napping.

Ransom spotted her first, and his eyebrows lifted ever so slightly. She could almost hear him ask, *"Are you okay? Are we okay?"*

And she didn't have an answer for that. Not yet.

Even as she shied away, he shook his head and smiled, as if to say, *"Relax, Miss Priss. Everything's fine."*

But was it? Something felt off.

"Miss Priscilla."

She managed a small smile for Milo, who'd come over to her side of the camp. "Shouldn't you be on your route?" she asked.

"My vacation time's been piling up, so my boss encouraged me to take the day off."

Her smile faded. Did that mean God had Sent him?

Milo stepped closer, and his tone shifted. "You seem distracted."

"You know I am." She winced at how snippy she sounded. "Sorry. How much do you know about what happened last night?"

He held up a finger and glanced toward the dirt road that ran through the campground. A moment later, Zeke's pickup rounded the bend. Ransom, Timothy, and Jude ambled over to help unload. Milo waved to Zeke and Jasper, but he stayed at Prissie's side and said, "I'm standing inside a tent under the guard of eight Protectors, which is in turn surrounded by a formidable Hedge. What's more, two Caretakers are close enough to cause the enemy great dismay."

"I *know* we're safe," Prissie sighed.

"Which means something *else* is bothering you."

"Only Ransom."

The mailman chuckled. "What's new?"

Prissie rubbed at the cheek where Ransom had kissed her. God certainly had a strange way of doing things. Why would He send her first love into the middle of this predicament? Only one answer fit, but she didn't know if it was divine inspiration or her own overwrought imagination. But maybe it didn't matter. Either way, she finally had a handle on the situation. Because she knew what it was like to love someone who didn't love you back. At least, not in the same way she'd wanted to be loved.

"Do you love me, Milo?"

"Yes."

An old ache tugged at Prissie's heart, and its strength surprised her. Even though it was mostly a memory, her childhood crush on Milo was still a part of her. Maybe this was God's answer to her plea for help? Saying things out loud had always helped her sort out her ideas, so she kept talking. "You never ignored me or avoided me."

"How could I?" he asked. "That's not love."

"I was ridiculous, but you were patient and kind."

"Love is," Milo said with a smile.

Yes, she definitely had a plan. She'd face Ransom and his feelings because they were friends. And friends loved at all times, even mixed up ones. And if she was as good and kind and honest, maybe her friendship with Ransom could be saved. And everything would go back to normal.

With her eyes fixed on Ransom, she said, "Milo, tell me not to be afraid."

But instead of the *fear not* she so desperately wanted, Milo said, "Perfect love casts out fear, Miss Priscilla. Now, if you'll excuse me, I have a message to deliver."

And then he walked over to Ransom.

Prissie stood rooted to the spot. Wasn't Milo here for her?

But the Messenger drew Ransom aside and said a few words. Hardly more than a sentence or two. But it was enough to send a whole range of emotions across Ransom's face. And then he said, "Hey, Zeke. You mind if I take off for a couple hours?"

"You need the truck?" Zeke asked.

"Nope. I'll catch a ride with Mr. Mailman."

When Milo and Ransom left together, Prissie knew she should be relieved that the rest of her afternoon was complication-free. Instead, she was left with the maddening feeling that God was up to something, and she was out of the loop.

CHAPTER 12

THE ANSWERED PRAYER

Bennett and Josiah ran ahead, leading Colin in the direction of their campsite. They knew the way, so Beau dropped back to walk with Marcus, who'd matched Juliette's pace. She dawdled along, singing a nonsense song as she watched for interesting pebbles on the gravel road.

In a low voice, Beau said, "Tell me there's something I can do."

Marcus spared him a glance. "Last I checked, our job was to escort these kids to and from the nature center."

"You know what I mean." Beau kept his tone even.

"This isn't your battle, Boaz."

He wrinkled his nose. Marcus had been using his full name ever since the memorable day that Beau found out his sister's classmate wasn't human. "Is it yours?"

"You know how this works," Marcus countered. "The battle belongs to the Lord."

"Spake the cherub," murmured Beau.

Marcus smirked. "I know you're praying. That's good enough."

"But Sis is acting strange," Beau protested. "She's been uneasy ever since that stag showed up down by the creek."

"I noticed."

"Is she in danger?"

When Juliette pounced on a green pebble, Marcus stopped and hooked his thumbs in the back pockets of his jeans. "You know Prissie. You've been the brother that sticks closer than a friend."

"Well, sure. We have a lot in common."

"Her brushes with spiritual warfare have given her perspective. And courage."

Beau nodded thoughtfully. "Sis trusts God. And friends like you."

"Yep."

"Then why …?"

"Ransom."

"Oh?" Beau held Marcus's gaze for several beats, then blinked. "*Oooh*!"

"Yep."

Ransom slid into the passenger seat of Milo's car. "Marcus and I checked out every house in the area that's up for sale. Nothing was quite right. I either have to start looking outside West Edinton … or start from scratch with land."

"You'd prefer a house?"

He nodded. "Old houses have personality. And hedges."

Milo exited the campground and aimed for the highway. "You have a special fondness for hedges?"

"Something like that. Especially if they're lilac hedges."

"Then you'll definitely want to see this place."

Ransom turned in the seat. "So is this house on the market?"

"Nope, but the owner has been quietly packing up for months. She asked me for advice yesterday, and I offered to introduce you." Milo hit his turn signal and added, "If you like the place, I'm confident you can work something out between the two of you."

"Maybe. Though at this point, I'd be grateful for anything. Beggars can't be ch–" Ransom suddenly noticed where they were and gripped his armrest. "Milo, this is Orchard Lane."

"Is that a problem?"

"Are you kidding?"

Milo's eyes sparkled. "I thought you'd be pleased."

Up until this moment, Ransom hadn't given any thought to the other houses on the road leading to the Pomeroys' farm, but he was paying attention now. Half a dozen houses were tucked into the woods along the south side of the road. Then came a rolling green pasture with a pond. On the opposite side of the road, field corn gave way to apple trees. "That's Pomeroy property."

"Yep." Milo slowed to a snail's pace and pointed. "Their land extends all the way to the highway. Mrs. Pierce tells me that her place was once a part of Pomeroy holdings, but that was a hundred-fifty years ago, give or take."

Ransom leaned forward as Milo pulled to a stop in front of a narrow driveway that disappeared into a thick wall of greenery. "Is this the only other house on the north side of the road?"

"That's right." Milo parked and opened his door. "I'll give you a quick tour of the yard, then introduce you to the owner. She knows we're dropping by."

Staring farther down the road, Ransom tried to get ahold of himself. "Their place can't be more than half a mile away."

"Less, actually." Milo patted a small silver mailbox in a friendly way, then snapped a heart-shaped leaf from the enormous hedge that hid the property from view. Handing it to Ransom, he said, "There's your lilac hedge."

Ransom's hopes were up so high, he was experiencing vertigo. "Is this going to be more than I can afford?"

"I think it'll be in your range," Milo said. "The house is a little on the shabby side. A fixer-upper. But with love and attention, you could bring out its best."

Past the lilac hedge, the driveway curved toward a brick building with tall, narrow windows, a steep roof with a cupola, a deep porch overhung with climbing vines, and two front doors. But the thing that brought Ransom to a standstill was the abundance of pink. Instead of a grass lawn, the house was surrounded by flowers.

Milo said, "Once upon a time, this was a schoolhouse. It's on two acres and has its own well. There are a few outbuildings."

Ransom dragged his gaze from the small house and scanned the area. The driveway ended in front of a detached garage, and he spotted a small shed and what had probably once been a chicken coop. Taking in a fenced-off square, he asked, "Would you call that a *big* vegetable garden?"

"Too big for an old granny like me."

Ransom turned to find a bent woman watching them from the porch. She had wooly white hair and wore a yellow cardigan over a floral house dress.

She continued, "But it's a good plot. I used to feed my family out of that garden all summer long."

Milo said, "Mrs. Pierce, this is Ransom Pavlos, and he was favorably impressed by your lilac bushes."

The old lady brightened. "Do you like flowers, young man?"

"Yeah. Especially these."

Milo plucked one delicate flower from the waist-deep moat of pink. He offered it to Mrs. Pierce. "I remember when your husband planted these. He insisted it was because he hated to mow, but I think they were a gift for you."

"Oh, I don't know," the woman murmured.

"They're cosmos, which is Greek for *beautiful*," said Milo. "A compliment if ever I saw one."

Mrs. Pierce smiled fondly at Milo, then turned her attention back to Ransom. "My mister is with the Lord now, and I can't take care of our home." Knotting her gnarled fingers together, she asked, "Do you think you could love this place like we did?"

"*Could*? Ma'am, I already *do*." Ransom stepped forward and offered his hand. "Will you sell it to me?"

She laughed. "You haven't even been inside. And you should know that the pipes creak and the roof needs replacing."

Still reeling from God's attention to detail, Ransom said, "Doesn't matter. This is the answer to at least a thousand prayers. Maybe ten thousand. You have no idea."

"Thank you, Jesus." Mrs. Pierce's wizened hands surrounded his, and she gave a small squeeze. "Sold."

Buying a house would take more than a handshake, but Milo knew exactly who to talk to in order to make things happen—banker, city clerk, inspector. When Ransom returned to campsite, he had three business cards in his back pocket and a big reason to smile. Milo promised to keep quiet, but Ransom wasn't sure he could do the same.

He found Marcus hanging out under one of the canopies, keeping Prissie company. Dinner prep was more than half done, and Ransom exclaimed, "Thanks for stepping in!"

Prissie eyed him warily. "Where've you been?"

"Out and about."

"Can you be more specific?" She zeroed in on Milo. "You guys are up to something."

The mailman raised his hands, silently proclaiming his innocence. "I'll just go say hello to Zeke," he said, retreating toward the nearest trail.

Prissie rounded on Ransom again, hands on hips, eyes flashing. "Is this any way to treat your friends?"

He joined them inside the canopy and took his time inspecting progress. Reaching for his apron, he stole a look at Prissie. She was annoyed with him, but as curious as kittens. And she seemed to be using Marcus as a shield, which also wasn't any way to treat a friend.

In one long step to close the distance, Ransom hauled Marcus into a headlock that quickly turned into a lopsided hug. "If you must know, Miss

Priss, I'm happy. So rejoice with the one who's rejoicing. C'mere."

She'd never minded group hugs before, but she hung back until Marcus held out a hand. "You heard him. C'mere."

And Prissie took her rightful place in the huddle.

Ransom asked, "How do you *do* that?"

Marcus just shrugged and said, "She has a point. You're in the exceedingly-abundant stage of great joy. And you're usually better at keeping secrets."

Prissie stiffened, and Ransom patted her back. "Of course I'm telling you guys. But just you two. So you can pray with me." To Ransom's relief, he felt a light touch on his back.

"Pray for what?" asked Prissie.

"Mr. Mailman found me a house," Ransom explained. "I'm blissed out and blessed, and it's more than I could ever ask or think. I've never had a personal miracle on this scale, and I just feel so … loved."

Marcus said, "Because you are."

"Hope so. Lots of paperwork needs to happen. And the place needs work."

"I'll help."

"I'm gonna accept that offer," Ransom said. "You're way handier than I am."

"Good for you." Prissie tried to pull back. "I'll leave you guys to it."

Ransom tightened his hold. "Nope. Not done."

"Why not?"

"Still happy."

Marcus muttered, "I bet."

Prissie asked, "Any chance of this happiness abating before dinnertime?"

"Nope. You're stuck with me."

"Long haul," Marcus said, pulling them both closer. "God's lookin' out for you."

"Yeah, He's good at that. Impressively so." Ransom closed his eyes and leaned into his best friend. "I might need someone to pinch me."

Ransom yelped when both his friends offered their enthusiastic support.

Sunset found their whole crew at the entrance to one of the smaller caves. Prissie had staked their claim on a grassy vantage point with a plaid blanket, but none of the kids seemed interested in sitting still. Even Prissie was off chatting with her ranger friend. Beau finally resorted to the buddy system to keep tabs on everyone.

Since Ransom didn't have any kid-sized obligations for the evening, he sprawled on the blanket and closed his eyes. Daydreams about a home of his own turned into prayers for the future, but it wasn't long before his thoughts turned to mush.

Prissie interrupted his doze with a hand on his shoulder. "It's almost time."

Ransom cracked an eye at a sky painted in evening hues. Then he turned his head to contemplate Prissie, who was voluntarily sitting at his side. "You came back."

She arched her brows. "According to Zeke, you're my buddy."

"What about Juliette?" he asked, sitting up and peering around. Over by the cave entrance, Padgett and another park ranger were calling the milling group to attention.

"I'm not going into the caves tonight. But Juliette said she'd go if Uncle Zeke carries her."

Ransom lowered his voice, not wanting to interrupt Padgett. "Are you afraid of the caves because of that one time you got lost in them?"

Her lips formed a thin line. "A little, yes."

"Prissie, Are you okay?"

"Shh."

Everyone else was staring into the sky, waiting for the bat colony to show itself. Moments later, a dark silhouette darted into the open. A corporate sigh. Excited whispers. Then a relative uproar of awe as the trickle became a river and hundreds of bats rushed into the darkening sky.

Ranger Prentice answered questions from the crowd, then organized the special evening tour of the cave. Prissie didn't budge, and Ransom said, "I'll help you guard the gear."

"Thanks."

Stars winked into existence, and the air cooled. It didn't take long for Ransom to realize that there weren't any lights up here. Although his eyes were adjusting, it was dark. And they were alone. Even though they weren't touching, he could feel Prissie's presence … and her silence.

He cleared his throat. "Hey, Prissie?"

"Hmm?"

"Please don't hate me."

"I don't hate you," she replied evenly.

"Don't dislike me."

She huffed and said, "I'm here, aren't I?"

"Guess that's a good sign." Ransom scooted closer, and their arms brushed. Nudging her with his elbow, he asked, "Can I tell you something?"

"We're friends, Ransom," she replied softly. "You can tell me anything."

"But some stuff's hard to say. And you might not like it."

"Anything," she repeated.

"Prissie, I'm scared."

He could feel her turn toward him. "Of what?"

"Of how much I want my own way. Of what that means about me as a person. Of taking stuff for granted. Of working toward the wrong goal. Of losing your friendship."

"We'll always be friends."

After a lengthy pause, Ransom asked, "Was that your version of 'lets just be friends'?"

"All I meant is that I'd hate to lose your friendship."

"I'm good with that."

Prissie shifted, making herself comfortable beside him, then changed the subject. "If you want someone praying for your house stuff, you should talk to Beau. He can keep a secret."

"Might do that."

"And … could you pray for me, too?"

"About what?"

Prissie sighed and said, "It's ridiculous."

She was going to confide in him? Even after what happened last night? Ransom had to swat down a dizzy swirl of hopes to focus on what she was saying.

"I'm supposed to give Colin back to Margery on Sunday."

"Supposed to?" He could feel his eyebrows slowly rising. "Were you thinking of keeping him?"

"I wish I could."

Ransom shook his head. "Margery wouldn't go for it."

"I know."

"Then why …?"

"Because Colin's faith is new and fragile. I don't want Margery to stomp all over it."

"Faith?" he exclaimed. "Since when?"

"Since Jude," she replied, a smile warming her voice. "Colin had questions, and Judicious was around to answer them. When I asked, Colin said he prayed with my brother at breakfast. Thank you, God, for this oatmeal and let me into your family … all in one fell swoop."

Another kid from a broken home finding faith because of the Pomeroys faithfulness. Amazing. Ransom wrapped an arm around her shoulders and started to pray. "God, I didn't know I was supposed to be celebrating a new little brother in faith. Thank you for Prissie, who felt so strongly that Colin should stay over. And thanks for Jude and his crazy pocket pets. And for Jayce and Naomi who opened their home. All so a lost boy could be found."

He could feel Prissie nod.

Staring up at the stars, Ransom said, "I know what that's like, and I know how much it means."

To Ransom's surprise, Prissie sniffled.

Tugging her closer, he tucked her head under his chin. "You found a way into his life, and we know You take care of Your own. Show us what we can do to help. And maybe Colin can do better than I've done. Let that boy's life shine in a way that his mom and grandma will find You, too."

Prissie whispered her agreement.

Ransom went right on praying. "And while I'm here, and it's just us … help me be wise with this woman. Because I don't want to make a mess of something that's always mattered." His breath hitched, and he was glad she couldn't see his face, because his emotions were all over the place. He was about to tack on an *amen* when Prissie took over.

"Heavenly Father, I know we're safe in Your keeping, but that doesn't mean I don't get scared. And I know You're wise in all Your ways, but I'm easily confused. Your plans are good, but I don't usually understand why until later. Let your faithfulness in the past strengthen my faith in the moment." Prissie took a deep breath, then added, "And since it *is* just us … do something about Ransom. He's apparently lost his mind."

"More like my heart."

She grumbled, "He's being impossible."

"With God, anything's possible."

Prissie snorted. "I highly doubt Gabriel was talking about you."

Ransom had a zingy come-back all ready, but Prissie turned her head, probably to glare at him, and her nose bumped his chin. And when he lowered his head, their cheeks brushed. She froze, and he knew he was about to cross a line he shouldn't. "Hey, Miss Priss."

"Hmm?"

"Is it bad that I prayed to be wise, but I still want to do something unwise?"

"Definitely a bad sign," she whispered.

"Then this would be a good time to run."

"Amen." She eased out of his arms. "Let me know how it goes with that house."

"Sure, sure," Ransom promised. "You'll be the first to know."

After the camping trip, Ransom hardly saw Zeke anymore. School was back in session, and football practice kept him from the bakery. Jasper was in the same boat, so Ransom's connection with Timothy vanished. "How am I supposed to witness to someone I never see?"

"Praying to your pastries?"

Ransom smiled crookedly at Beau. "You're half right. What brings you down from the heights of academia?"

"A Pomeroy never outgrows milk and cookie time!"

"Man, your folks raised you right. Pull up a stool?"

"Gladly."

Beau helped himself to milk, and Ransom handed him a plate. "Raid the bakery case. If you're into warm cookies, go for the peanut butter chocolate chip ones. They're fresh."

"I know. I could smell them," Beau said. "Very distracting."

Ransom could hear him swap pleasantries with Pearl, but it wasn't long before Beau returned. Snagging a stool, he sat at the end of the counter. "So who are you trying to witness to?"

"Timothy."

Beau mumbled around a bite of cookie. "Zeke put you up to it?"

"Yep. And Timothy knows it."

"He's a smart guy."

"He's a lost guy," Ransom used his thumb to smooth dough bits off his rolling pin. "And he knows that, too. Wish I knew what was holding him back."

Beau slipped a notebook from his back pocket and flipped through its pages. "I've been praying for Timothy on and off since middle school, but I'll bump him to the top of my list."

"That'd be good."

Shoving the rest of a cookie into his mouth, Beau chewed thoughtfully. Then pointed between them. "Wanna pray?"

Ransom's eyebrows shot up. "You kinda cut to the chase."

Beau chuckled. "I learned it from you."

"Fair enough!" Ransom started, "Thank you, God, for dropping me into a thicket of cookie-munching, God-fearing, people-loving Pomeroys."

Beau smoothly followed. "You dropped Timothy into our lives, too. We all care about him, and I know Zeke loves him. But that can be hard to say."

"No kidding."

"He has our love, and he has Your love. Open Timothy's eyes to eternal things."

Ransom kept right on folding and rolling pastry for turnovers. This was normal for Ransom, whose prayers had turned much more conversational while he was away from the States. Loneliness and language barriers had pushed him closer to the One who knew his heart.

Back and forth, they prayed. A sentence or two. Short and simple.

Straightforward and honest. Beau finished his cookies and switched to washing dishes, and still they prayed.

"Something's holding Timothy back, and I don't have a clue what it is." Ransom shook his head. "I think he wants me to figure it out though."

"So help Ransom listen carefully, see clearly, grasp quickly," prayed Beau. "Show him what Timothy needs."

"He's been fending me off with questions that are so personal, it's embarrassing. If it's my vulnerability he needs, You've got it."

Beau reached for a dish towel. "Give Ransom the right words when his chances come."

"It doesn't have to be me, God. Any one of us knows the way to You."

"Heaven aches to celebrate a life made new," said Beau. "Let it be soon. Amen."

"And amen," finished Ransom.

Peace filled the lull in the bakery kitchen. And Ransom breathed a silent prayer of thanks. It was as if God had swept out all his worries, chased away all his doubts. Everything was in His hands. Even this.

Beau leaned against the counter and asked, "Are you coming to the football game on Friday?"

"I was going to, but my shift at the lumber yard conflicts. I wouldn't be able to get over there until halftime."

"Just in time to hear the pep band do their thing."

Ransom straightened. "I'll ask around, see if I can catch a ride."

Beau tapped his chest. "What time should I pick you up?"

Ransom and Beau hustled from the parking lot toward the light and noise coming from the football field. An announcer's voice rang over the crowd noise, calling the game. " *... ticking down the final seconds of the first half. Pomeroy's on the move. He's going long. Ramirez scrambles and ...!*"

The stadium exploded with cheers, and Beau grinned. "That's my little brother!"

A horn blared, and the band launched into their school's fight song. Beau pointed toward his family's stake in the crowded bleachers. "There's room!" he said, voice raised above the din.

Ransom shook his head and pointed toward the pep band. "I want to say hey to Timothy first. I'll catch up."

"I'll be praying." Beau thumped his back and moved off.

Ransom waded through the rush on the concession stand, making it to the sideline as the band marched onto center field. It took a while to pick out

Timothy in the sea of red, white, and brass. But once Ransom found him, he didn't look away. To his surprise, Timothy spotted him and sent an exaggerated eyeroll his way. Ransom signaled, trying to let him know he wanted to talk.

Timothy's eyes narrowed.

Hands up, Ransom arched his brows.

Another eyeroll and a smirk.

Ransom grinned. And while he waited his turn, a new thought occurred to him. Maybe Timothy wasn't Prissie's little brother's friend anymore. All the ice-breaking and hanging out during Zeke's camping trip had given him a different perspective. And they got along. Really well. The way friends should.

When the pep band quick-stepped off the field to make way for the cheer squad, Timothy waited in front of the stands. "Want something?"

"Kind of." Ransom followed Timothy around to the side of the bleachers and joined him in leaning against the supports. "It's been too quiet this week with you guys back in classes."

"Aww! You missed me?"

"Yeah."

Skepticism laced Timothy's response. "Because heaven needs more trombone players?"

Ransom shrugged. "That too, but the whole witty repartee thing is a plus. Seems to me, we could be friends. Provided you're willing to overlook the age difference."

"You're still trying to make a Christian out of me."

"That's not how it works." A whistle sounded out on the field, and a chant started up in the bleachers above them. "And considering both Zeke and Jasper are Christians, I didn't figure you'd hold my faith against me. Was I wrong?"

Timothy shook his head and started walking. "Game's starting. There's room if you want to sit with me."

"Sure!"

Ransom followed Timothy into the stands and joined him in raising a ruckus any time Zeke or Jasper did something noteworthy. They swapped game-related asides, but then Timothy said, "I don't remember. Were you on any of our teams?"

"I was never very good at team sports," Ransom said. "Sidelines made me … sad, I guess."

"All that white paint, mucking up the grass?"

He laughed. "More like … all that waiting around, hoping someone would need me."

"Sounds familiar."

"You, too?"

Timothy snickered. "I meant your love life. Or lack thereof."

"Ouch. We can add brutal honesty to the witty repartee."

"Can't take it?"

"We're good." Ransom gazed across the playing field to where Prissie sat with the Pomeroys. "And I went for track. Ran cross-country and long distance. Even did a marathon once."

"I'm still on the sidelines."

Ransom's attention snapped back to Timothy. "In what sense?"

"Stuck waiting and wondering."

"About what?"

"Stuff," Timothy replied shortly. "Being optional sucks."

"Guess so. But isn't that part of what makes being chosen special?"

Timothy stared at him for a long time. Finally he asked, "Is this about God now?"

"Well, that works. But I was actually thinking about my nonexistent love life again."

"One track mind." Timothy's laughter faded, and he said, "I don't think it'd work out with me and God. Long distance relationships also suck."

Ransom grinned. "So you're gonna leave Him on the sidelines to wait and wonder?"

"I can't believe you just *benched* God."

"It's an imperfect analogy. But this choice is yours, and it's life-or-death, which kinda explains why Zeke is so antsy." Ransom hoped he wasn't pushing too hard. "God's definitely hoping with the rest of us that you'll pick Him."

Timothy kept his eyes on the game. "To drag down the rest of the team? I don't think so."

"That's *really* not how it works." Ransom hoped Beau was praying hard because he didn't know what to say. "You know, I told her."

That got Timothy's attention. "Didn't think you had the guts. What happened?"

Ransom's hands floundered while he searched for an appropriate answer. "Not much. Best I can tell, she's trying very hard to pretend nothing happened."

Timothy's face turned to stone. "Do you think that means she doesn't care?"

"Nope. I *know* she cares." Ransom couldn't believe he was telling Timothy stuff he hadn't even admitted to Marcus. But there was such a hunger for more in this guy's eyes, like he needed to know. So Ransom kept going. "You should have seen her face. Stunned with a side of panic. And there I am, feeling guilty for putting her in an awkward position. I keep kicking myself for being selfish and impatient. Because now everything will change, and I might lose everything I was hoping for. And it's all my fault."

Timothy opened his mouth, then closed it. Then he swore under his breath. "You have *no* idea."

"Sorry?"

"Look, the game's almost over, so I don't have time for any more of this repartee you claim to be fond of. But I might drop by the bakery sometimes. If you'll make it worth my while."

"Like … feed you?"

"Perfect." Timothy fiddled with his spit valve. "I'll be there."

CHAPTER 13

THE BIRTHDAY WISH

Several members of the Pomeroy family's Hedge gathered on the lawn under Prissie's bedroom window. Most wore grim expressions. Taweel flat-out scowled. "A doe and a pheasant," he said gruffly.

"The doe may account for the hoof prints Ethan found by the machine shed." Othniel scratched at a bristling sideburn. "Any other signs?"

"Only a squirrel, but it was old." Lucan pointed toward the farmhouse gable. "Except it was in the gutter."

"Two more dead pines," offered Jude's Guardian.

Jayce's said, "A duck."

"A pigeon. But that was in town, on the bakery roof."

"Raccoon. Over behind the well house."

Othniel sighed as the death count mounted. "This demon certainly doesn't stay put for long."

Conrad lifted a hand. "One of the cherry trees is dropping leaves faster than its neighbors."

"The seasons are turning," Lucan pointed out. "Most trees are losing a few leaves."

"How are we supposed to know if a tree is suffering or settling in to sleep?"

"We can't," said Jayce's guardian angel. "But a Caretaker could."

"And where would he start looking?"

Just then, a leaf spiraled into their midst, landing at Taweel's feet. The big warrior's eyes narrowed, and he bent to pick it up. They whole group turned with him to stare at the nearest tree. Several of its branches were already bare.

Prissie woke earlier than usual. Dressing quickly, she wrapped a shawl around her shoulders, then stepped into her garden clogs. She wasn't due at the bakery for another couple hours, and she had the sudden urge to watch the morning glories open.

Early morning light sparkled in the heavy layer of dew. From the porch steps, Prissie scanned the farmyard for signs of her brothers. Tad and Jude would be up and about, along with Grandpa Pete. As she meandered toward the vegetable garden and its arbor of climbing flowers, she caught movement out of the corner of her eye.

She stopped and stared hard. There it was again! Someone was in the orchard!

"Fear not."

Prissie jumped away from Asher, who stood right next to her. "Honestly!" she exclaimed. "You can't sneak up on someone, then tell them not to be startled!"

The boy stood barefoot in the grass, his gaze fixed on the dark figure walking amidst the apple trees. "It is safe. You may proceed."

"Who's there?"

Asher smiled up at her. "Go see."

She picked her way across the lawn, drenching her feet in dew. Ducking under the branches of the first few rows of trees, she caught up to their intruder. And laughed in relief. "Good morning!"

Padgett turned and gazed at her with an expression that was difficult to read. "Hello, miss." The Caretaker's raiment gleamed with a light all its own, and his loose black hair grazed the tips of the grass. A few yahavim buzzed through the trees, and one rode in the basket he carried.

"No wonder Asher said it was safe," she said with a little laugh.

He hesitated, then asked, "Who?"

Prissie's eyes locked on the basket, and a half-forgotten memory stirred. "What are you doing?"

"Koji asked me to pick enough apples for a pie. Would you like to help me choose?"

"Yes, I want to help. Obviously. But Padgett," she clutched her shawl around her shoulders. "*When* will you give these apples to Koji?"

The Caretaker almost-smiled and answered, "Almost ten years ago."

Right after church on the last Sunday in September, Prissie waited on the porch steps for Beau to arrive with Ransom. The two had been spending more time together lately, and she was happy for her brother. Beau tended to bury himself in his studies, but Ransom wasn't shy about dragging him out of his little apartment. If you could tell a lot about a person by who their friends are, Ransom's new "gang" was an interesting mix—Marcus, Beau, and Timothy Grable. Angelic warrior, prayer warrior, and brat.

Beau's car rolled to a stop, and Ransom emerged with a battered picnic hamper. When he spotted her formidable backpack, his eyebrows shot up. "I thought we agreed that I'd bring lunch."

"These are other things." Prissie stood and smoothed the skirt of a flowered dress. "Necessities."

"How long's this orchard tour supposed to take?"

"We'll be back by sunset. Everything else will be ready by then."

Beau patted Ransom's back in passing, then touched Prissie's arm on his way up the steps. "Enjoy yourselves."

She dredged up a smile. "Be back soon."

"Let me take that, Miss Priss." Ransom shouldered her baggage with a grunt. "You don't pack light."

"I like to be prepared." She relieved him of his picnic basket and swept past him down the sidewalk. "Let's go, birthday boy."

Prissie wasn't sure how to act. Back when Ransom asked her to spend the day with him, it had seemed like a simple request from a friend. Not a man. But now, she was pairing off, going out, and heading away from a houseful of chaperones. She'd asked her parents about the potential impropriety, but neither of them was worried. Because they trusted Ransom.

When it came down to it, so did she. Ransom wasn't luring her into danger. Prissie worried it might actually be the other way around. Ethan walked before them, pink wings flowing like a cloak from shoulders. Their edges swept along the grass tips in a way that made her wonder if it tickled.

"Are you trying to outrun me? Because it's not working. My legs are longer than yours."

Prissie pulled up short. "Sorry. I'm just …."

"Awkward?"

"Very."

"If it helps, you could pretend we're old friends."

Her conscience twinged, and she nodded. All Ransom had wanted for his birthday was her company. By ignoring him, she was essentially abandoning a friend. And spoiling what should have been a gift.

Ransom kept talking. "And that I never noticed those three little curls."

"What curls?"

He slowly reached out with one finger and twirled a stray tendril at the nape of her neck. Clearing his throat, he said, "Maybe we should also pretend I didn't do that."

"You …! You're …!"

" … apologizing. Sorry, Prissie. I'll keep my hands to myself."

"This is ridiculous." She glared up at him. "We *are* old friends."

"Positively ancient."

"And it's your birthday!"

"Hence the upcoming party."

"Which I helped plan." Prissie's temper faded with a sigh. "If you were Koji, I know exactly what I'd do."

Ransom blinked. "I'm not him."

"No, but with him things like this were never awkward." And Prissie offered her hand.

"Is this a truce?"

Prissie shook her head. "It's what friends do."

Ransom lightly hooked his fingers with hers. "Do you and Marcus hold hands like this?"

"Just like," she retorted, even though the one time they'd held hands was a *long* time ago.

"Then what took you so long to include me?"

To Prissie's embarrassment, Ethan stopped walking and glanced back. Waiting for them. Guardians probably witnessed plenty of private conversations, so she couldn't exactly blame him for eavesdropping. Especially when his expression held so much compassion.

She tightened her grip and tugged him along. "Probably because you were always more of a hugger."

"Fair enough, Miss Priss." He hurried his steps to walk by her side and gave her hand a small squeeze. "So can I switch gears and ask an apple-related question?"

"Please do."

"Why are all yours missing? These trees are empty."

"The sections near the house are all picked over." She launched gratefully into familiar territory. Every Pomeroy could talk apples. "Did you want some?"

"It *is* an orchard."

Slowing to a standstill, Prissie asked, "What kind of apples do you prefer? Tart? Sweet?"

With a crooked smile, he said, "Turns out I like both."

Prissie got the distinct impression that he wasn't talking about apples.

Ethan gazed expectantly at them, and she discreetly indicated a westerly route. This time, her guardian angel fell in step behind them.

While they cut across rows, bypassing stacks of crates with the Pomeroy Orchard logo on them, Ransom kept his comments neutral. "So what did you pack?"

"Tarp. Blanket. A rolled screen so we can make our own shade. Pillows. A couple of card games. My folks come out pretty regularly on nice Sundays to read and nap under the trees."

"Sounds dangerous. What happens if an apple falls on your head?"

"You thank God for windfalls and eat it."

Ransom asked, "How often do you come out here?"

"A lot lately. Grandma Nell needs help with her picking since we still can as much applesauce as ever. But I also come out here to remember. And to pray."

Ransom turned so he was walking backward. "We could do that. I'd like that. Can we add that to the list?"

Her brows arched. "You have a list?"

"Don't birthdays usually come with a wish list?"

"Aren't wish lists usually written down?"

Ransom ignored her disapproving tone. "I like the flexibility of an unwritten list. It allows for spontaneity."

"Fine," Prissie sighed. "In that case, apple picking is now on the list, but applesauce is out of the question. I left my enameled pot at home."

"I meant *pray*, Miss Priss. Let's put that on our list."

"If you want."

Before long, they reached a place where the regularly spaced trees gave way to a gap. Prissie set down the hamper and walked up to a maple sapling that had been planted in the middle and patted it. "This is a crossroads. Four different sections come together here. Sweet, tart, mellow, and crisp—take your pick."

Ransom checked out the nearest tree, which had light green apples. "How can you tell if they're ready?"

From amidst the branches of a tree with dark red apples, she answered, "The color changes on those. Look for a touch of pink."

He rustled around, searching for a telltale blush. "Are we stopping here? Seems like a good spot for a picnic."

"Tad keeps it mowed because he brings his family here." Prissie caught up to him and presented three apples, one of each of the other varieties. "This is *his* spot. Don't you want your own?"

"I like that idea." Ransom stowed their apples in the basket and hefted it. "So do *you* have a spot?"

"Yes."

"Can I see?"

Prissie hesitated. "It's a long way from here."

"Too far?"

She shook her head. "Not if you don't mind the walk."

"We have all afternoon. So where is this place?"

"In the back forty." Pointing to the northeast, she added, "On the slope overlooking the fairgrounds."

Ransom backpedaled. "If it's private or anything, we don't have to …."

"If I wanted to keep it a secret from you, I would say so. It's something we can share." She reclaimed the picnic hamper from his grasp. "I promise, it's worth the walk."

More than an hour later, Ransom slipped free of his heavy pack. "Looks familiar," he remarked, nodding toward the barns and fences surrounding the county fairgrounds. "Is this your spot?"

"Not quite." Prissie beckoned for him to follow her toward the thicket that occupied this corner of the orchard. She enjoyed his stunned expression when they pushed through a seemingly impenetrable wall of wild apple trees and into the tiny meadow at its heart. Tangled branches offered shade, shelter, and the strangest sense of being far from the world. Under the trees, mounding moss crept up over a haphazard collection of stones, but sunshine poured in from overhead, filling the space with the scent of warm grasses and sweet apples.

"This is it," Prissie said in hushed tones. "My spot."

"Wow. You weren't kidding. I vote we stay here."

"Then it's unanimous." She unpacked the tarp, which he helped her spread in a dappled patch of clover. Shaking out a thick plaid blanket, she rummaged again and tossed a couple of small pillows at Ransom.

He kicked off his shoes and sprawled. "All the comforts of home!"

"Hardly surprising. This *is* my home." With a swish of flowery fabric, she sat next to him and smoothed her skirt. "But I'm willing to share. So make yourself at home."

"Will do," he said, closing his eyes.

To Prissie's surprise, Ethan approached the edge of the blanket and stretched his wings over them. Seeing her bafflement, the Guardian quietly explained, "Prayers bring us close."

Ransom was praying. But why would that affect Ethan? And then it hit her. Ransom was praying for her. She couldn't decide whether to be annoyed or grateful. Given everything that had been happening lately, the latter won out by a narrow margin.

At her sigh, he opened his eyes and smiled sleepily. "M'wake."

"Sunday's a day of rest, remember? Naps are allowed." Prissie hadn't noticed how tired he was looking. Probably because she'd been avoiding eye contact. "How many hours did you work yesterday?"

"Officially, or unofficially? Because I spent all afternoon helping Derick Matthews install a deck. And then I did stocking at the lumberyard until eleven."

"But your shift at the bakery started at four in the morning!"

"Yeah, yesterday was a long one. Feels good to go limp."

"You're doing odd jobs for Mr. Matthews now?"

"We're trading favors." Ransom folded his hands behind his neck. "I'm no carpenter, but that doesn't mean I can't sand rails and pound nails."

Prissie couldn't believe it. "Doesn't that mean you're holding down *three* jobs now?"

"Guess so."

"You shouldn't overdo!"

"Can't be helped. Down payment cleared out my savings. I'm a homeowner."

"Since when?"

"Yesterday."

Prissie grumbled, "No one told me!"

"You're the first to know. Well, except for Mr. Mailman, who found it for me, and Mr. Matthews, who did the inspection."

Curiosity bursting, she asked, "Where is it?"

"I picked something out in the country. It's a fixer-upper. Derick figures it'll take me until the snow flies to get the outside the way I want it, and then I can spend all winter working on the inside. Gonna learn as I go."

"Do you need help?"

"All kinds of it," he readily admitted. "I'll talk to Marcus about lending a hand. He's pretty good at this kind of stuff."

"Yes, he is." Prissie cautiously asked, "Is there anything I can do?"

"Not right off, but later I'll probably want some pointers."

"Oh." He'd bought a house. One he probably wanted to share with her. In a way, she was upset that he hadn't conferred with her sooner. But that would have been even more awkward. "So where is it?" she asked again.

"North of town."

"Up this way?"

"Kinda."

Prissie pushed for more details. "What road?"

With a sidelong glance, Ransom replied, "Orchard Lane."

"You bought a house on *our* road?"

"Small world!"

"But nothing's for sale," she retorted.

"Like I said, Mr. Mailman helped me work things out. He knew the owner was thinking of selling and introduced me."

Prissie's heart was racing now. "Which place?"

"The old school house."

"That property backs up to our orchard!"

"I know."

Prissie shook her head in disbelief. "Tad looked into the Pierce place back when he got married, but they weren't looking to move. That's why he ended up building on that parcel out on the highway."

Ransom was searching her face. "It has a big vegetable garden and a lilac hedge. Plus, I really liked the neighborhood."

"You took my advice?"

"Seemed like good counsel."

She looked away and awkwardly said, "Dad is going to be thrilled."

"Counting on it. I don't have a car yet, so I'm hoping he won't mind carpooling. Bicycle's not going to cut it once winter hits."

"How soon will you be moving in?"

"Immediate occupancy. I was planning to sleep there tonight."

If it wouldn't have taken so long, Prissie might have suggested they walk over there now. "So what's it like?"

"It's small, but it'll do for now. Derick suggested building off the north side of the house once there's kids."

"You really like to plan ahead, don't you?"

"These are hard decisions. And I'm trying to think of more than me." He sighed and asked, "Don't you want to get married, Miss Priss? In a general, hypothetical sense."

"I used to, but that changed."

Ransom sat up. "Why?"

"There was an age difference. He was way too old for me. And then, there was a compatibility issue."

"Weren't they a believer?"

"Oh, he's Faithful," she cheerfully replied. "And he loved me enough to overlook my foolishness. We became friends instead."

"And you still love this guy."

"Always and forever."

Ransom was clearly struggling. "You don't sound heartbroken over it."

Prissie laughed. "It would be ungrateful to complain about a love that will never fail. Besides, I still get to see him every day."

And he caught on with a groan. "You're talking about Milo!"

"My first love."

"Does Mr. Mailman know?"

"Yes, and he's kind enough not to tease."

Ransom held up his hands. "I wouldn't. But you're just friends?"

"Didn't I already say that?"

"Kinda. But I needed to make sure. I can't believe I've been living with your old flame."

Her laugh faded, and she ventured, "What about you? I know you didn't date in high school, but … after?"

Instead of answering directly, Ransom posed a question. "What do you think dating looks like?"

Prissie frowned thoughtfully. "Spending time with someone. Getting to know them better. Finding out if you have the right things in common."

"You and I did a whole lot of that in high school."

Which was true. Still, she rolled her eyes. "But there has to be *romance*!"

"Yeah, I had you pegged for a romantic. But you're really easy-going about hugs and hand-holding. And a farm girl with a patisserie in the family has all the flowers and chocolates she wants."

"Are you trying to say that I'm the only one you …." She couldn't finish the sentence.

"My first love also knows how I feel, and she's been nothing but kind." Ransom smiled wanly. "But I think my feelings make her uncomfortable. And I clearly fail at romance."

"Maybe this isn't such a good idea." Prissie fidgeted. "It took forever for me to get used to thinking of you as a friend."

"Then the hard part is already done. I think it's important to marry a friend." Ransom made a helpless gesture. "I never said anything because I thought you had your heart set on Marcus."

"He's not interested in me like that."

"Well I am."

"Since when?" she challenged.

"Senior year, I guess."

Prissie muttered, "It's hard to picture you pining for me."

"To keep from pining, I stuck to praying." In matter-of-fact tones, he said,

"Asking God to help me love you like He does. So I could be the kind of friend who'd make a good husband."

She gaped at him. "How can you say all that and not be embarrassed?"

Ransom shrugged. "I think husbands and wives should be able to tell each other anything."

She started to get up, but Ransom snagged the hem of her skirt.

"Don't go," he said.

"I'm not going far." Pulling free, Prissie concentrated on finding ripe fruit in the tangled branches of the thicket. She'd never been very successful at pushing Ransom away. His tenacity had always baffled her. But if his loyalty was based on love, it made more sense.

Prissie returned to the blanket with a handful of golden fruit no bigger than golf balls. "These are small, but they're sweeter than any other fruit in the orchard."

He nibbled and hummed appreciatively; he also watched her, waiting.

Taking a determined stab at diplomacy, Prissie changed the subject. "I like birthdays. Momma always found ways to make them special. I can see why she put so much effort into making them fit each of us."

Ransom balked. "You're *not* my mother."

"Obviously."

"And I'm not one of your brothers."

"I can tell. None of the Pomeroys have your nose."

"The Pavlos schnoz. Not my best feature."

"You *have* a best feature?"

"I can cook."

"Are you going to prove it anytime soon? I skipped breakfast."

Ransom's smile resurfaced and he started the painstaking process of unpacking his picnic. While he worked, Prissie studied him. He'd asked her to look at him differently. The first time she'd done that, the bane of her existence had become one of her best friends. Didn't that mean it was *possible* for her best friend to take on some romantic appeal?

He glanced up from his array of dainty foodstuffs and caught her staring. As usual, it didn't faze him a bit. Ransom simply held up a finger, then reached into the very bottom of the picnic hamper. With a waiter's flourish, he presented her with a bottle of cream soda.

Prissie accepted it with a soft giggle. "You remembered."

"Not likely to forget something that makes you smile!"

She hummed, then said, "Eyebrows."

His shot up. "What about them?"

"I think they're your best feature. Very agile. Expressive. They distract from your nose."

Ransom rubbed the offending feature.

Rolling her eyes, Prissie said, "I'm only teasing. Why are you so worried about your nose all of the sudden?"

"I've been worrying about all kinds of things I never worried about before." His hands gyrated between them. "You're driving me crazy all over again!"

"But I haven't done anything."

"*That's* been the hardest part!" Ransom grumbled, "You're enough to drive a man to prayer."

"I can't believe we're having this conversation."

"I'm so glad we're finally having this conversation," he countered. "It's important for us to talk it out. But there's a higher priority right now. I agonized for days over this menu. Eat!"

She accepted a plate and chose several items that could have been sold for top dollar in a Paris shop. Ransom was definitely showing off. Prissie did her part, repaying his efforts with lavish compliments, but once she'd made a proper fuss over every detail, the conversation swung back around.

"What if I said *no*?" she asked quietly.

Ransom took a swig of his own cream soda before saying, "It's too soon for you to make up your mind. Let's see what happens. Because once you get over the awkward parts, you'll remember the important stuff."

"Like what?"

"That you like me. That we share a lot of the same priorities. That we have fun together. And that I own a house on Orchard Lane."

"Is that supposed to be leverage?" she asked tartly.

Ransom smiled crookedly. "Love your neighbor!"

The sun was low on the horizon when Prissie ushered Ransom into the Pomeroys' crowded kitchen. Balloons and streamers festooned the room. Kids bounced around, full of giggles and questions, and at every turn, people called, "Happy birthday!"

Jayce and Zeke presided over a complex birthday cake. "Nine tiers, one for every missed birthday!" boasted Mr. Pomeroy.

"Wash up for dinner!" exclaimed Grandma Nell. She and Momma were putting the finishing touches on a celebratory feast.

Prissie quickly reached for an apron and joined them in squeezing everything onto the table. She was easing a bubbling pan of cheesy potatoes onto trivets when Zeke called, "Sis?"

"What?" she asked, only half paying attention. Where was she going to fit the cut glass bowls of refrigerator pickles?

"Sis," Zeke called louder, dragging out the single syllable in tones of disbelief.

"I'm right here."

"Sis!" he exclaimed more sharply, turning from the window and waving her over. "Am I seeing things?"

"What kind of things."

"A peddler toting his pack." Grinning now, Zeke said, "Wanna bet he's willing to sing for his supper?"

Prissie followed his gaze to the man strolling up their driveway. There was no mistaking the redhead with a guitar strapped to his back. "Baird!"

CHAPTER 14

The Bachelor Quarters

Tamaes stood at his post, alert for signs of a threat even though he couldn't know what form that danger might take. Blight's stealth was impressive. And cruel. Everything he'd touched was tainted, suffering, or dead. The Guardian shuddered to think what would happen if the demon found a way to reach Prissie.

Purple wings stirred the air as Taweel joined him on the barn roof, quickly followed by their captain's arrival. Tamaes acknowledged them with a short nod, but returned his attention to the cat picking her way along the edge of the duck pond.

"See anything?" asked Taweel.

Before Tamaes could frame a report, Jedrick said, "He's too focused to see anything."

Taweel grunted.

Picking up on the cherub's teasing tone, Tamaes favored him with a longer look. "Am I missing something, Captain?"

Jedrick chuckled. "We have all missed him."

Omri whizzed around Tamaes's head, all squeaks and somersaults. Then Taweel took his apprentice by the shoulders and turned him around so he faced the driveway. And the man who was bouncing up and down and waving with both arms. *Baird.*

"Baird!" shouted Zeke, who led the charge out the Pomeroys' front door.

As friends and family mobbed the redhead, a smile stole onto Tamaes's face. Their former teammate was back. Surely, God had Sent a good gift.

The kitchen emptied. Ransom moved to join the rush, but Marcus cut in front of him, aiming for Prissie. She still stood at the window, knuckles white from gripping the sill. Turning to Marcus, she asked, "Is it really him?"

"No doubt," said Marcus.

"Can he stay?"

"Good question. How about we ask Baird? Since he's here."

"To see me?" Prissie asked in a small voice.

"You're asking the wrong guy." Marcus took her elbow and steered her toward the door. "Come on. Both of you."

Following Marcus's lead, Ransom helped usher her out of the kitchen. He asked, "You didn't know he was coming?"

She shook her head.

Ransom said, "Looks like we'll have to wait in line."

The Pomeroys' unexpected guest was hidden from view by the welcoming committee. Hardly a surprise. Ransom had already been taller than Baird when they met. Those were good memories—hanging out with him and his band, listening to endless tracks at the music store, and having long conversations about the Bible over burgers or pizza. If you wanted to stick a Christian label on things, Baird had stepped up to disciple a new believer. But Baird had always treated him like a friend.

From the midst of the crowd, Baird exclaimed, "Zeke! Milo said you'd hit another growth spurt!"

"It's a family thing. Pomeroys are mostly tall!"

Baird made a joke about giants in the land, then asked, "Man, is that you, Jasper?"

"Hey, Baird," he replied, grinning broadly. "You sure do know how to put the surprise in party!"

"There's always something to celebrate!" Without missing a beat, Baird said, "And Timothy, it's good to see you again!"

Ransom caught the note of surprise in Timothy's reply. "You remember me?"

"I'd never forget a fellow musician. Maybe we can break out the instruments later!"

"Maybe."

Ransom and Marcus stopped short as Baird fought his way free. Ransom decided he hadn't changed much. Maybe a few creases beside his eyes. Laugh lines. And Baird's hair was longer than he remembered—cornrows in the front, loose in back. But he hadn't lost a bit of his enthusiasm.

"Prissie! Braced?"

"More like stunned." She managed a shaky smile. "My joy is full."

The redhead went up on tiptoe to fling his arms around Prissie's shoulders, and Ransom overheard him say, "For so many others who miss you back."

Prissie was laughing and crying, and Marcus stepped in, easing her away from the redhead.

Baird used the opening to jump to Ransom, thrusting out a hand. "Nice togs, Mr. Pavlos! Very chic boutique!"

Ransom grinned and used the handshake to pull Baird into a hug. "Missed you."

Holding tight, Baird sighed, "That's the stuff. I love this part."

"Which part's that?" asked Ransom.

"Reunions."

Baird stopped in the doorway and gawked at the balloons and streamers. "Okay, this is seriously decked! Whose party am I crashing?" But he was looking straight at Ransom. And the shine in his eyes said he already knew.

When Prissie explained, Baird zoomed in for another hug. Thumping Ransom's back, the redhead said, "So you finally fessed up?"

"Yeah." Ransom rolled his eyes in Prissie's direction. "She forced it out of me."

"And are you *happy* on this birthday?" Baird asked, suddenly serious.

Ransom pondered that a moment, then answered, "Mostly grateful, and leaning toward hopeful. But seeing you again is definitely a happy thing. Icing on the cake."

"Awesome!" Baird's attention was caught by Grandma Nell and Naomi, who were squeezing in another place setting at the table.

"Put your things anywhere and join us," said Prissie's mom. "There's always room for one more."

Baird said, "Mrs. Pomeroy and Mrs. Pomeroy, if you don't mind, I'd like to sing grace over the meal you prepared."

Permission was granted, and all the little-kid whispering and shuffling turned to wide-eyed awe. Ransom knew because he peeked. Baird stood in the middle of the crowd with arms outstretched, palms open, eyes shut, face filled with love and peace.

The sweetness of Baird's song was just like Ransom remembered. He'd spent so many afternoons in the youth center at the DeeVee's church offices down in Harper. And this was how Baird always was, prone to bursts of spontaneous song, never minding if he turned heads. The redhead always met comments and compliments with a grin, as if glad his antics had netted him an introduction. Living courageously. Never ashamed. Drawing in friend and stranger alike. Ransom admired Baird more than he could say.

During the meal, there was never a lull, which Ransom considered the best kind of fun. But he noticed that Prissie was unusually quiet. She laughed and smiled quite a bit, but she spent most of the dinner hour simply watching Baird. Ransom could have been bothered that the redhead had stolen so much of her attention, except Baird was sitting right next to him. So Prissie kept catching Ransom's eye, and she'd send these silent little messages. *Can you believe it? It's been so long. He's really, truly here! Aren't you glad? I wish we could keep him.*

Ransom finally asked the question Prissie was holding back. "How long can you stay?"

Baird sighed softly. "Not long. But it's not like I'll turn into a pumpkin at midnight or anything."

"Where will you stay?" Ransom asked.

"With you." Baird laughed at his expression. "Provided you're willing to put me up and put up with me."

"But I was planning to …."

The other conversations happening around the table dropped off, and Ransom found himself at the center of attention. He cleared his throat and said, "Guess this is as good a time as any to tell you guys. I was planning to stay at *my* place tonight. I bought a house, but it's empty. I don't know what to say, Baird. You'd be welcome, but I doubt you'd be comfortable."

"If I'm welcome, I'm there. Thanks for your hospitality!"

Ransom asked, "Marcus, you want to come over?"

"Sounds good."

"Can I?" Zeke quickly amended, "Can we batch it at Ransom's, too? Me, Jasper, and Timothy?"

Mr. and Mrs. Pomeroy traded glances. "There's school to consider, boys. Maybe you should …."

"Please?" interrupted Prissie. "Baird's only here for a short time, and Zeke and the boys can still catch their bus here."

"Here?" Jayce Pomeroy shot a puzzled look in Ransom's direction.

With a shaky laugh, he said, "Howdy, neighbor."

Zeke tossed another sleeping bag into Ransom's arms. "Sis washed these after the camping trip. They still smell like sunshine. Doncha love that part of laundry?"

"Never gave it much thought," Ransom said. "Are you sure you want to do this? I've got nothing to offer but a shed full of rusty garden tools and a leaky roof."

"No power?" Zeke checked. "I should grab lanterns."

"There's water and electric. And a clunky old fridge and stove that have been together longer than your parents." Ransom adjusted his grip on the growing pile. "But the cupboards are bare as the floorboards."

"Not much different than camping." Zeke stropped rummaging in the cedar closet to ask, "Pillows?"

Timothy leaned in from the hallway. "How many ways does he have to say he's got nothing? Bring enough for everyone."

A moment later, Ransom felt like he was on the receiving end of a one-sided pillow fight. Until Timothy started pitching pillows back at his friend. That left him in the middle.

Mrs. Pomeroy chased Zeke back downstairs, leaving Ransom and Timothy to pick up the scattered sheets. Ransom remarked, "I had no idea Zeke was passionate about bed linens."

"He also painted flowers all over his sister's bedroom. Yet no one questions his masculinity."

"I saw the roses. Impressive."

A finger collided with Ransom's chest. "You've been in Prissie's bedroom?"

"Once. She gave me the tour."

Timothy's smirk was all insinuation.

Ransom hit him upside the head with a pillow. "Don't you go there, because I didn't either."

"So your love life's still nonexistent."

"Nothing's changed, but things are changing."

"Can't argue with your strategy," Timothy said. "Buying a house out here gives you serious leverage."

Ransom's brows drew together. "I'm not trying to bribe her."

"You gonna deny you had her in mind when you plunked down your money?"

"I definitely chose with her in mind." He glanced into the hallway, then lowered his voice. "I want her to be happy."

Timothy scratched at his freckled nose. "She seemed happy to see Baird again. Doesn't that worry you?"

"Not even a little." Ransom firmly changed the subject. "Will your mom let you stay over tonight? I don't want to get you into trouble."

"She lets me crash with Zeke all the time." Timothy's smile twisted oddly. "Probably because I can't get into trouble up here."

There it was again. That note of regret. Ransom quietly asked, "Are you in trouble, Timothy?"

He hesitated just a little too long before answering, "Nope!"

"Cake time!"

Ransom grinned through a booming rendition of "Happy Birthday" and blew out twenty-six candles all in one breath.

"Did you make a wish?" asked Tad, who had a teasing light in his eyes.

"Does he get nine?" Beau asked.

Zeke said, "I wanna see that list!"

"I'll get paper," offered Jude.

While Jayce and Zeke carefully disassembled the tiers of their cake so everyone could sample all nine layers, Ida attempted to explain the redhead to the kids.

Ransom slipped over to Prissie. "Do your brothers always gang up like that?"

She giggled. "You're lucky Neil's not here. He's the best worst tease of the lot."

"Say, Prissie. I'd have thought you'd push to have Baird stay here."

"Baird said he's going to stay with you." Prissie gave a little shrug. "I can be happy for you."

"I still can't believe he turned up today of all days."

Prissie smiled softly. "He's a gift from God."

Ransom tapped her shoulder. "You love this guy."

"So much. Don't you?"

"Yeah. Baird was part mentor, part friend for a long time. Straight up until I left for Europe. Seems like we both dropped off the face of the earth at the same time."

"All the more reason to believe that he stayed around for your sake, then came back for your sake. The best birthday present you could hope for."

"Almost." Ransom gently tugged one of those little curls at the nape of Prissie's neck. "You're still my favorite part of today."

"Flattery won't get you anywhere," she warned.

"Good. Because I'm right where I want to be."

Ransom's party didn't so much end as change venues.

From the front porch, Prissie called, "Don't let them keep you up all night!"

Mr. Pomeroy said, "Ransom, I'll pick you up at four."

"The rest of you, be back here for breakfast," said Momma. "We'll make something extra nice."

"Like those little sausage patties?" asked Zeke.

"French toast?" wheedled Jasper.

From further along the driveway, Timothy shouted, "Blueberry *anything*!"

Ransom glanced back when Prissie called, "Baird!"

The redhead turned. "Right here!"

"Sweet dreams."

Baird laughed. "It's a promise!"

Ransom sighed happily as he trudged along, gravel crunching underfoot. This was his road. They were walking to his house. He lived in walking distance. Could it get any better than this? Well … maybe. But even though he was walking away from Prissie, Ransom was sure this was a step in the right direction.

Timothy slowed down to walk with him. "Your friend Marcus is okay."

"Already knew that, but thanks for noticing." Ransom asked, "So what did you guys do all day?"

"Grunt labor. Jasper and Marcus blew up balloons. I spent all morning passing Zeke stuff while he and his dad put that cake together." Timothy asked, "So how come you kept your birthday a secret for so long?"

"I didn't want to impose."

"Lame reason. I don't buy it."

Ransom chuckled. "You're the only one who didn't."

"I like the Pomeroys, but they're a little *too* good." Timothy kept his head down as they walked. "They don't have any concept of how it is for other people."

"Hey, I've seen them weather tough stuff. But you're mostly right. They do tend to think the best and see the bright side."

"So why'd you bury your big day for so long?" asked Timothy.

"I'd rather treat every day as special. Not save up for once-a-year recognition." Ransom added, "And it lends me an air of mystery."

"No, it doesn't." Timothy punched his arm. "Tell me."

Ransom said, "I don't have good memories of my birthday."

"How come?"

"When I was eleven, my mom threw me the biggest birthday party ever. Kind of like this one—balloons and streamers, friends from school, games and movies. It was the best day I ever had." Even thought it was dark, Ransom could feel Timothy's eyes on him. "When I woke up the next morning, the house was too quiet. My mom was gone. That's when I knew the party hadn't been for me. It was for her. That party was her way of saying goodbye."

"She left?"

"Yeah. I never saw her again." Ransom explained, "Me and my dad got tired of questions we didn't have any answers for, so he requested a transfer at work. They moved him to an office in Harper, but the apartments in West Edinton were cheaper. Been calling this home ever since."

"And ever after?"

"Yep." Ransom stopped at the end of his driveway, where the rest of the guys waited. "This is me, putting down roots."

"Huh," said Jasper. "It's … cozy."

Zeke stared fixedly at the ceiling, then poked one of the stained tiles just over his head. "Your house looked taller on the outside."

"It *is*." Ransom explained, "The ceilings in here are barely over seven feet. The original brick goes a lot higher."

Timothy folded his arms over his chest. "It's not so bad."

"For short people. Which we are not," said Jasper, who was developing a stoop.

Zeke pushed up one of the tiles and peered under it. "How come they hung these ceilings so low?"

"Derick Matthews did my inspection. He figures it's cheaper to heat the house in winter."

"What a way to skimp." Zeke wrinkled his nose. "Am I the only one who feels squashed?"

"View's good from here." Baird lay on his back in the middle of the room, arms flung wide. "Love the wood floors. Old school awesome."

Timothy snorted. "This *is* an old school."

The redhead grinned. "Ransom's gone *literal*!"

Ransom dropped his bundle of borrowed bedding on the floor and sat next to Baird. "I realize this isn't ideal, but it's fixable. Derick poked around, and there's lots of room between the drop ceiling and the roof I need to replace. He recommended opening everything up. Knock out these walls. Put in a stairway. Add a bed and bath upstairs."

"You're gonna gut the place?" Jasper asked, eyeing the wide window wells.

Zeke rubbed his hands together. "Need help? Because it's not every day I get permission to demolish stuff."

"Sure." Ransom lay back, tucking his hands behind his neck. "It'll be a bring-your-own-crowbar kind of event."

"I've been known to raise the roof, but this is something else." Baird sat up and snapped his fingers. The sound echoed slightly in the empty room. "Can I add your new sanctuary to my whirlwind tour?"

"You want to sing?" asked Ransom.

"Sing, shout, and sanctify." Baird bounded to his feet and paced off the room. "If you don't mind a little ruckus, I feel like celebrating."

So while Zeke and Jasper shook out blankets and created beds on the bare floor, Baird unpacked his guitar. The DeeVee's former worship leader plucked harmonies from his instrument while he sang of heavenly celebrations and unchanging faithfulness. Ransom hummed snatches. Nabbing a blanket, he sat against the wall and closed his eyes, adding prayers to the praise. He didn't realize he'd drifted off until Marcus woke him.

"Come on, ya lug. There's no way you'll outlast Baird." Soft strumming still came from the general vicinity of the kitchen. "Everyone else turned in ages ago."

"Gonna tuck me in?"

"And sing you lullabies." Marcus pressed a sheet of paper into his hand and asked, "What do you think?"

Rubbing weary eyes, Ransom fought for focus. This wasn't the first time Marcus had showed him some new pattern for a stained glass project. But none of them had been quite like this. Swallowing hard, he whispered, "Nice."

"It's yours if you want it."

"No, it's not. This is for Prissie."

"Is that a problem?" Marcus asked evenly.

Ransom blinked hard to hold back tears and muttered, "She'll think I put you up to it."

With a small smirk, Marcus promised, "I'll set her straight."

CHAPTER 15

THE HIDING PLACE

Blight's breath came in short gasps as he slunk through the midnight orchard. The Hedge was no closer to finding him than the day he was Cast into their midst. But that *cherub*! Hissing a curse, the Fallen pressed himself against the rough bark of a gnarled tree. Moments later, golden wings flashed past.

Seizing his chance, Blight threw himself across the open ground that lay between him and the machine shed. He pressed himself against the old building and held his breath. Something landed on its roof. Shoulders hunched, he squinted skyward. Was he found?

A deep voice came first. "What are you trailing?"

"Not sure. But it could be trouble." The soft *shing* of a drawn sword sent dread pooling in Blight's stomach. Then the horrible cherub said, "Let's take a closer look."

They landed in front of the building—the cherub and an ice-winged Guardian carrying two swords. As the crunch of gravel gave way to footfalls muffled by grass, Blight choked back a whimper and scuttled along the wall. Too quick. Too close. He wouldn't make it to the abandoned burrow near the end of the building.

"I smell fear."

"Yeah," replied the cherub, his voice heavy with disgust. "Be ready."

Burrowing into living tissue was much nicer than sinking into inert surfaces, but Blight had little choice. Lumber could fool a seeker with no Sending. With a frantic press, he shivered at the uncomfortable feeling of rusted nails and flaking paint.

Sounds warped, and woodgrain made it hard to see. But a moment later, Blight slammed down all his senses. He had no desire to see the gold-eyed cherub whose glare promised pain.

Prissie was pulling the last pan of muffins from the oven when Zeke thudded up the back porch steps and yanked open the door. Inhaling a deep, appreciative breath, he leaned back out to exclaim, "Told you she wouldn't forget your blueberry anything!"

Momma hustled everyone inside, and confusion reigned for several minutes while the boys herded through the laundry room to wash up. Jude sloped in a few moments later, full of questions about Ransom's new house.

Zeke said, "Old Ransom's putting himself out to pasture."

"Rusticating," agreed Jasper.

Timothy snickered. "More like laying siege. This is striking distance."

"But what's it *like*?" Momma interjected.

Choosing a more diplomatic route, Jasper said, "Well, ma'am, like Timothy said, it's real close."

"And historic," said Zeke.

"Which translates to *old*." Timothy dropped into a chair at the table and reached for the blueberry muffins. "It needs work."

Jude quietly pointed out, "Ransom knows how to work."

While Momma plied for more useful information, Baird sidled up to Prissie. "How's you?" he asked softly.

"I'm not even sure. Things always get a little confusing when amazing people drop by."

"I hear you've had your fair share of drop-ins lately."

Prissie turned to the refrigerator to cover her answer. "Some more welcome than others."

Baird said, "Want to talk it through?"

She passed him a pitcher of juice. "So much. Would you mind?"

"Wouldn't and will." Raising his voice to a more normal level, he remarked, "Though I feel a little bad for robbing fine gentlemen of your company. I have it on good authority that you're usually at the bakery at this hour."

Zeke piped up, "Yeah, Sis. How come you're not at work?"

"Daddy gave me the day off."

"How come?"

"For the same reason he let you sleep over at Ransom's. It's *my* turn to monopolize Baird." She turned to the redhead and asked, "Or … did you have plans?"

Baird shook his head. "Unless you want to go and do, I was planning to just be."

Zeke snickered. "I'm not sure Mr. Baird knows how to sit still."

"I don't think Mr. Baird knows how to sleep," said Timothy.

"Up all night," confirmed Jasper, who was making short work of a stack of french toast.

"And when he wasn't singing, he was scribbling." In tattling tones, Zeke added, "On the *walls*."

"Can't deny the truth." Baird led Prissie to the table and sat beside her.

She eyed the redhead. "You wrote on his walls?"

"Only the ones that won't be there once he wraps up his renovations."

"What kind of graffiti are we talking about?" asked Jude, whose hands were wrapped around a steaming mug.

"I left a few notes for Ransom," Baird said. "Words of encouragement. Prayers and blessings. Sage advice. Scripture verses. Maybe a few doodles."

Jude smiled. "I'd like to see that."

"I'd like to add to it!" Zeke said, raising his glass for a refill.

Timothy passed him the pitcher. "Gonna paint daisy chains?"

"Nah. He's got enough flowers around the place." Zeke took a swig of juice. "I was thinking more like advice on how to make the most of life in the country."

Jasper nodded wisely. "Take time to watch the grass grow. Beware of black-and-white striped kitties. Keep a weather eye on the sky."

"Isn't that one for sailors?" asked Timothy.

Prissie's curiosity was bursting at the seams. But Ransom's house would be there, and Baird's visit would be all too short. She said, "Keep a weather eye on the clock, boys. You have a bus to catch."

Jasper, Zeke, and Timothy crammed food in their mouths, and Jude reached for another muffin.

Momma spoke into the sudden silence. "Priscilla, make the most of your morning with Baird because Ida and Mel are bringing the kids over this afternoon. They'll want to play."

Baird raised his hand. "I'm totally available to play!"

Prissie laughed and said, "Of course, Momma. The more the merrier."

After waving off the school bus, Prissie showed Baird the tree where she'd first spotted Koji and told him about meeting a ten-years-younger Padgett. While they wandered along the edge of the yard, Baird entertained her with stories of his first time as a Graft.

"Do you miss it? Being here?" she asked.

"The toaster pastry withdrawal was brutal, but there were so many good things waiting for me. Streets of gold. Pearly gates. Crystal sea. And, man … I'd forgotten how much I love newfoundlings!"

"What are they?" Prissie asked.

"More of a *who*. They're angelic newbies." Baird added a skip to his steps. "The Caretakers find them and bring them to us. Adorable little guys, with their eyes all wide and their voices as pure and sweet as silver bells."

"You find them," Prissie murmured. "Oh, of course. New*found*lings."

"Oh, man. They make me feel ancient and wise, but then I end up acting all dippy and sappy because they are … I can't even begin!" The redhead twirled in place, then walked backward. "Not very long ago, they let me oversee a batch, and when they unfurled for the first time, I was sobbing so hard, the other zamarim sent for Kester. He scraped me off the floor and made up for my lapse in formalities by being amazing. And then we sang together, and it was like old times, and … words fail."

Prissie hadn't been much different when Asher first showed up, which had been similarly new and nostalgic. "So Kester's not your apprentice anymore?"

"Nope. When we left the DeeVee, he finally got an ear cuff and the newbie to go with it. Cute little button. And lucky as all get out to have a mentor like Kester. I've met Milo's and Padgett's apprentices, too."

Prissie stopped walking. "*Milo's*?"

"Oops!" Baird waved his hands. "You did *not* hear that from me!"

"But …!"

Baird zipped his lips. "Now's not the time. I'm supposed to be talking to you about *you*."

"We're talking."

He spotted the red bridge that spanned the Pomeroys' duck pond and jogged ahead. When she caught up, Baird said, "I would have liked to send Kester for this. You always opened up to him."

Prissie frowned. "It's not like I'm holding anything back."

"Sure about that?" Baird favored her with a long, searching look. "How are things with Ransom?"

She gaped at him. "You're kidding."

Baird drooped over the rail. "If it helps put things into perspective, you're not the first person to have a well-dressed, overly serious young man with a big nose show up on your doorstep."

"How did *you* know?" Covering her face with her hands, she said, "Wait. Nevermind. I suppose a little bird told you."

"Not so much." Baird gazed off toward the barn roof. "I was Ransom's mentor all through high school. Kester and I fielded most of those awkward, hypothetical questions that go along with being a teenage boy."

Prissie mimicked his pose, resting her arms on the bridge rail. While she appreciated his making himself available, she had *no* intention of talking to Baird about Ransom. She tried to put him off as diplomatically as possible. "I have a mother, Baird. She's always willing to hear me out."

Baird nodded. "But here I stand, as Sent as can be. So let's assume we're having us a teensy reprise. Remember that chat we had right before Koji had to go away?"

"Of course." Prissie's heart had been breaking, but Baird had been there to remind her that Koji was hurting, too. In shifting her focus from her own suffering to his, she'd been able to make the most of the time they'd had left.

"Well this is kinda like that, except not at all." Baird flip-flopped his hands as he tried to explain. "Because instead of facing the end of something, you're facing the beginning of something. And between you and me, I'm not sure which puts more knock in my knees. Change is all … different from before."

Prissie laughed softly. "That's the most honest definition of change I've ever heard."

"Does it help any?"

She doubted it. Ransom had told her he was afraid to push her away, and she was scared to lose a friend. This wasn't anything like before. Did God want her to put Ransom's feelings ahead of her own? That didn't sound right. Maybe it was a matter of looking at things from his perspective? Prissie shook her head. "This wouldn't be the first time I didn't understand the message of an angel."

"Kester is so much better at this stuff."

Prissie patted his arm. "Don't wish yourself away when I'm so glad you're here."

"Permission to gallivant is sweetness itself. Not gonna squander one second."

"And how do you propose we not-squander the rest of our morning?"

"Sing with me?"

"Here?"

Baird eyeballed the parking lot beside the apple barn and said, "Not if I'm going to cut loose. Can we go a little further afield?"

"Is it safe?"

"Should be." Baird waved cheerfully. "You have some serious back-up, Miss Pomeroy."

Prissie turned to find Ethan waiting at the foot of the bridge. Eight archers fanned out behind him, tall and stern. Well, except for Yannis—or was it Garrick—who winked and waved. "I'll sing if they do," she bargained.

Garrick—or was it Yannis—elbowed a Flightmate and cheerfully said, "Betcha didn't see that one coming. From back-up to back-up singers in the twinkling of an eye."

Prissie spent the rest of the morning learning a song she was pretty sure Baird made up on the spot. Ethan chimed in once he learned the melody, making them a trio, and their entourage of angelic archers hummed along and added rhythm with their heavy boots. Baird's elation was entirely contagious, and Prissie easily forgot every worry and care. He was the respite she hadn't known she needed.

After lunch in the apple barn with Momma and Grandma Nell, their Monday turned livelier … and much more crowded.

"Teams!" Josiah exclaimed. "I want Bennett!"

Nat said, "Shouldn't teams be big-and-little? Pick an uncle!"

"I'm bigger than Bennett," his younger brother argued.

"Only by nine days!"

Beau stepped in. "How about a team of three? I could use the extra help since I haven't played hide-and-seek in ages."

"Didja forget how, Uncle Beau?" asked Josiah.

"Let's just say I'm rusty."

"I want Auntie!" Juliette exclaimed, half wrapping herself in Prissie's skirt.

"That leaves Nat and Jude," said Prissie.

The final team bumped fists, and Josiah piped up again. "What about Mr. Baird? How come he's all alone?"

Baird jogged in place. "Because *I'm* going to hide, and *you're* going to seek."

Bennett cautiously raised his hand. "But that's not the rules of hide-and-seek."

"We're switching things around for fun," Prissie said. "Think of this as an outdoor game of hide-the-button, only the button hides itself!"

"I like it!" exclaimed Josiah.

Nat warned, "We'll have the advantage, Mr. Baird. This is our farm."

Bennett nodded. "We know all the best spots."

"Bring it on!" Baird did some exaggerated stretches, then asked, "How high can you count?"

Prissie giggled when Juliette held up four fingers.

"Okay, I need a slightly bigger head start. Plan B. Who can sing 'Jesus Loves Me'?"

So while the seekers covered their eyes and Baird hightailed it across the yard, Prissie and her brothers led the youngsters in a rousing rendition from *this I know* to *tells me so*. The whole lot doubled over with laughter when they spied Baird standing behind a tree that wasn't anywhere near wide enough to keep him out of sight.

Grinning broadly, Baird called for another song and took off again.

Nat's claim of a home field advantage was entirely true, but Prissie soon realized that Baird was getting insider information. Their Hedge must have been lending a hand because the Worshiper's hiding places were as clever as they were funny. He was up ladders and in trees. Locked inside the corn crib and on the chicken coop roof. They located him snoozing in Grandma Nell's herb garden with a butterfly on his nose. Nat found him in a borrowed flannel shirt and hat, pretending to be the scarecrow in Prissie's vegetable garden. From the daring to the endearing, Baird kept them running from one end of the yard to the next.

When they found him perched on the plank fence at the end of the driveway, everyone arrived on the scene in time for Milo to roll up.

"Teacher! Did you come to play?" asked Josiah.

"Please?" added Bennett. "You can, right?"

Milo quickly answered, "Count me in. I haven't played games with Baird in ages!"

Prissie glanced at her watch and said, "One more round, and then Mr. Leggett can join us for milk and cookies."

"Guess I'll have to make this a doozy-level hiding spot!" said Baird.

Josiah generously offered to be on Milo's team, and when their song came to an end, Baird was nowhere to be seen. Everyone scattered, but Prissie was in no hurry to follow. Juliette had been dawdling behind the rest all along. "Don't you like hide-and-seek?" Prissie asked.

"I don't," she said sadly. "I don't like *boo*."

"Does your brother like to scare you when you play?"

She shook her head, sending her pigtails swinging. "Uncle Zeke does!"

"Oooh, that makes sense." Prissie smiled and said, "I don't think Mr. Baird plays that way. He hasn't said *boo* once."

"Yes." Juliette tugged at her hand and whispered, "Can we find Mr. Baird first this time?"

"Let's do our best!" They walked a little faster, bypassing those areas where the other teams were already searching.

"How will we find him?" Juliette asked with a pout.

"Let's see." Prissie slowed her steps and considered their options. "I guess that if I wanted to find Mr. Baird, I'd use my ears. One time, I found him in the middle of the woods by following the sound of his guitar. The music led me right to him, and I'm not sure which of us was more surprised."

"Was it a good surprise?"

"Finding a friend where you didn't expect one—that's a very good surprise." Prissie held a finger to her lips. "Shall we try listening?"

The little girl closed her eyes and lifted her face. "Robin," she said.

"Yes, there's a robin in the big tree."

"Chicken."

Prissie hummed her agreement. "I hear them, too."

Juliette's face scrunched in concentration. "I don't hear music."

Although she was about to agree, Prissie hesitated as a faint whistle reached her ears. She turned her head, trying to figure out what direction it had come from. "Did you hear that?"

Opening her eyes, Juliette asked, "Do you hear music, Auntie?"

"Yes, I think someone is giving us a hint!"

Prissie strained her ears for another whisper of melody. Leading Juliette onto the grass so their steps were softer, she caught another trill that couldn't have come from a bird. Hauntingly sweet. Playfully captivating. But wholly unlike Baird's music. By the time Prissie understood that something was amiss, she was at the pond's edge, with the lower entrance to the apple barn straight ahead.

"Are you sure, Auntie?" Juliette asked. "I don't hear songs."

"You're right, sweetie. This isn't a place Mr. Baird would be."

"There you are!" Juliette's mother waved at them from the top of the slope. "Juliette, your Marmee wants to know if you want to help her serve milk and cookies."

"Can I wear aprons?"

Mel laughed. "Come, love. We'll both wear them."

Juliette trotted up the slope, but Prissie stayed put. "I'll catch up," she promised.

Once they were out of sight, a sing-song voice came from the shadows beyond the half-open door. "I knew a newfoundling with stardust in his lashes and stars in his eyes. Always reaching, ripe for teaching."

"Are you talking about Koji?"

"He loved me first. He was mine before you." The voice came closer to the gap in the door, which made his words clearer. "You sigh and cry. You loved him, too; he left you, too. We are the same."

Prissie's heart was hammering so fast, it was hard to breathe. She knew better than to go anywhere near that door, but he sounded close. Would he show himself? While it was possible that luring Blight into the open might help Ethan catch him, the truth was … Prissie was curious. Would she be able to see Koji's Fallen friend for herself?

The creak of rusty hinges made her jump.

"Hush, shush." Kind tones with a teasing lilt. Like this was a child's game, and she was silly to be afraid. "No fears, no tears, my Prissie Mae."

And he granted her wish, easing into the open and propping his shoulder against the door frame. Ankles crossed, arms folded, he invited her perusal with casual confidence.

Prissie hardly knew how to respond. She'd expected more. Or maybe less. Blight wasn't scary or scarred, gaunt or garish. Nothing about him seemed monstrous or malignant. Weren't demons supposed to be evil? But with his straight black hair and elfin ears, this Fallen reminded her a little of Koji. Paler, older, taller, and with eyes as blue as the forget-me-nots that grew under the honeysuckle bushes. Shouldn't she be afraid, even if he wasn't frightening?

She took a backward step.

Blight motioned with both hands, pleading for a little more time. "You are like my friend, and he is like you. Listening and lessening my loneliness."

"Ethan?" she asked softly.

"Call louder," Blight urged. "Bring him."

Prissie hesitated. Why did this feel like a trap?

"Cry out. Call him to your side." He straightened and strolled forward, slow and smiling.

"Why?"

Blight stopped within easy reach but made no move to touch her. "Don't you want him?"

"Obviously."

"Try and see," he coaxed.

And with a sudden burst of clarity, she saw the trick that made this a trap. "Ethan doesn't answer to me. If I need him, God will Send him."

"Brave girl. Bright girl." Leaning close enough to whisper in her ear, he whispered, "Braced?"

CHAPTER 16

THE PINK SHIRT

Ethan's wings stirred restlessly, but his boots remained on the barn roof. He'd been told to wait. This was obedience, and it was terrible. Not because he doubted God's wisdom or His timing, but because of what it revealed in himself. He felt like a dog straining at the end of its leash, still within the confines of obedience, but barely. And all because of Prissie.

Did she think he had abandoned her? Even though he wanted to rush to her side, from her perspective, he must seem late or lax or lacking. Would he lose her good opinion, perhaps even her trust? Ethan hung his head and faced an embarrassing realization. Blight was right.

A small hand slipped into his, and he glanced down. "Asher."

The young Caretaker asked, "Now do you see the danger?"

Ethan watched helplessly as Blight strolled toward Prissie. "She recognizes my voice and knows my name. Even though we are from different realms, our lives have touched, and we can talk. Prissie is not mine, but I want to keep her, to call her friend." His voice shook as he concluded, "Now I understand why Blight singled me out. We are the same."

Asher said, "Not the same. Not if you see the danger."

"I do."

"Then the snare cannot catch you."

Ethan gave the boy's hand a squeeze before letting it go. "I will not Fall."

Asher smiled. "Prissie also sees the snare. She refuses to call your name."

Would he have been able to remain in place if she'd cried out to him? Ethan wasn't sure. "Her wisdom may have saved me."

Going up on tiptoe, Asher said, "Listen."

But Ethan had already heard God's voice and taken the Sending to heart.

Prissie's knees were like water, but she held her ground. And prayed.

"Be friendly. Befriend me," coaxed Blight. "No one can Send me from your side. I will lessen your loneliness."

Sympathy bloomed in her heart, and pity replaced all her anger. This demon was bartering for something he'd lost. And his desperation showed just how precious the bonds of friendship were. She might miss Koji, but they shared a bond that would outlast Time. The Fallen had no such hope.

Her heart broke for him, but mercy wasn't hers to give. "I'm not lonely, Prosper. I've never been alone."

Blight's whole expression changed from confident mockery to tremulous joy. He reached for her with hands that shook. "You know my name."

Suddenly, pink light rippled between her and the demon, hiding him from view. Ethan's hands were on her shoulders, and his voice was in her ear. "Fear not, for I am with you. He cannot touch you, child of God."

Relief washed over Prissie, and she turned into the Guardian's waiting arms.

From outside the shelter of Ethan's wings, Blight spoke in approving tones. "Hearts race. Friends embrace. Let him. Like him. Love him."

Prissie wasn't sure if he was making fun of them or hoping to be included. Either way, his words bothered her. How could loving someone be as simple as letting them get close?

A few moments later, Ethan said, "He is gone."

Tears prickled behind Prissie's eyelids. Now that the danger had passed, she quietly fell to pieces.

When she sagged against him, Ethan scooped her up and started walking. "Did he hurt you?"

"I'm fine." After further thought, she remarked, "He seemed harmless."

"Do not be deceived."

Prissie wrinkled her nose. "I wasn't. He's creepy."

"I am similarly unsettled."

"Can I ask you something?"

Ethan searched her face. "I will answer if I am able."

"Is that what he *really* looks like?"

"When I first met Blight, he was newfallen. He is dim and diminishing, but not as ravaged as the demons I usually encounter."

Prissie fidgeted. "He has beautiful eyes."

"Does he?" Ethan asked, sounding surprised.

"I've always liked blue eyes."

"So have I." With a sheepish glance, he explained, "Zeke's eyes are blue."

She giggled, then sighed. "Ransom has brown eyes."

"Is that important?"

"Less and less." Prissie finally noticed that Ethan was carrying her away from the house. "Where are you taking me?"

"To a reasonable excuse for your late arrival." Ethan scanned the sky, then quickened his pace. "He is here."

Following his gaze, she caught a glimpse of gold through the treetops and groaned. "Oh, he is so going to chew me out."

Ethan set her on her feet. "In all likelihood, we will both be reprimanded."

Prissie hardly ever saw Marcus in armor. He made quite the spectacle as he stalked up their driveway with wings wide-flung and sword at the ready. Drawing up short, he demanded, "You okay?"

"Yes, of course," she replied, smoothing away the folds in her skirt. "I'm sorry to worry you."

Marcus's bristling tension dropped away. Sheathing his sword, he looked to Ethan. "Any problems?"

"Nothing we need to discuss now. Are you not Sent?"

Furled wings settled into zigzag patterns along Marcus's upper arms, shoulders, and back. Golden eyes darkened to commonplace brown. Jeans and a T-shirt replaced armor and raiment. Marcus shrugged into his brown leather jacket, then jerked a thumb toward the farmhouse. "Sorry to drop by unannounced, Prissie. Looks like I'm making you late for milk and cookie time."

The bell over the bakery's front door rang out, and Ransom broke into a smile. "You're early!"

Timothy leaned his trombone case in the corner and collapsed onto a chair. "My teacher's sick, my lesson's postponed, and my best friends have practice until the cows come home. I was bored."

"And hungry?"

"Maybe a little."

"What'll it be today?"

Timothy sat up straighter and asked, "Do you have any of those fancy seashell cake things?"

"Madeleines?"

"If you say so."

Ransom nodded. "Come on back into the kitchen, and I'll whip some up."

"Are you allowed to do stuff like that?"

Gesturing for Timothy to bring his gear, Ransom said, "If I wasn't, I wouldn't have offered."

"Hey, Mrs. Matthews," Timothy mumbled on his way through. Pearl smiled at him over her knitting.

In the kitchen, Ransom asked, "Doesn't Zeke ever bake for you?"

"We usually just clean out whatever's left in the case at the end of the afternoon."

Ransom pointed to one of the kitchen stools. "Sit. Or do you want to stir?"

"Nah. If you're gonna cater, get to it." Timothy glanced around. "Where is everyone?"

"Mr. Pomeroy and Prissie left early to spend time with Baird."

"Leaving you out?"

"It's no big deal. The guy's sleeping at my place again tonight, so I'll get my turn." Ransom pulled down a bowl and reached for ingredients. "Do you want to stay over again? I don't know if Zeke and Jasper mentioned it, but there's a hymn sing tonight."

"I told them I'd think about it."

"Do you have somewhere else to be?"

"You know I don't." Timothy sighed. "So what's a hymn sing?"

"A bunch of people get together to sing hymns."

"No kidding."

Ransom smiled broadly as he sifted flour. "What can I say? It's one of those self-explanatory things. Can you sing?"

"When absolutely necessary."

"I've been told I have more enthusiasm than skill."

Timothy snickered. "So we're talking religious karaoke night?"

"If it helps sway you, Mr. Pomeroy took home twenty balls of pizza dough."

"Guess I better let Mom know I'm staying over with Zeke tonight."

The Pomeroys' family room was bursting at the seams. Ransom wasn't surprised when Timothy stuck close since Jasper and Zeke weren't back yet from football practice. "More pizza?" Ransom asked as he crowded in next to Timothy on the floor in the corner of the family room.

"Is there any left?"

"Last two just came out of the oven. Get it while it's hot."

Timothy grinned and was gone.

Ransom stretched out his legs and watched Prissie, who seemed to be everywhere at once—collecting dropped napkins, mopping up spills, wiping kids' fingers, and somehow carrying on conversations with three people at once. He'd have felt entirely left out except she kept shooting him these quizzical little glances. Reaching for a napkin, Ransom scrubbed at his face. Just in case the seven-year-olds weren't the only ones with sauce on their chins.

When Timothy came back, his eyes were bugging. "Okay, that was more dangerous than anticipated. Help?"

"With?"

"Mr. Pomeroy decided to refill our drinks."

Ransom looked him up and down. "I see pizza and more pizza."

"Hood!" Timothy wheezed.

Laughing, Ransom rescued him from the four cans of cola that had him in a stranglehold.

Timothy mumbled his thanks around strings of mozzarella just as Baird angled over to say hey. Mouth full, the freckle-faced teen confined himself to a small salute.

Baird beamed. "I was hoping you'd make it! And you came prepared! That totally brings back memories. Kester hardly ever traveled without a few instrument cases." The redhead snapped his fingers. "Want me to work in a trombone solo?"

Timothy gulped. "Don't go out of your way."

"It's no trouble!" Baird exclaimed, already moving off in Milo's direction. "I'll give you time to think it over."

"That guy's a one man stampede," grumbled Timothy. "He didn't give me a chance to say *no*."

"I always thought he'd make it big in infomercials." While Timothy choked on his laughter, Ransom nabbed the top hymnal from the closest stack. "But he won't force the issue if you turn him down. Just tell him you don't know any of the songs."

"I can read music." Timothy leaned in to scan the pages as Ransom flipped through. "This stuff's simple."

"So it's stage fright?"

"I think you've got the wrong idea about me." Timothy crammed the last bit of pizza crust in his mouth and used a crumpled napkin on his fingers before holding his hand out for the book. "I'm a musician. This is what I do."

Ransom asked, "Then why don't you?"

With a wry grin, Timothy said, "Baird didn't give me a chance to say *yes*, either."

"Still sitting on the fence?"

"Looks that way."

Pointing to the empty plate, Ransom asked, "If pizza got you here, what's it going to take to get you to stay?"

By the expression on Timothy's face, he knew they weren't talking about camping out in the Pomeroys' family room. He stubbornly said, "Baird gave me time to think things over."

"You've had more than enough time. What else do you need?" Ransom kept his voice low. "Can't you trust anyone here with whatever's holding you back?"

Timothy's guarded gaze slowly opened. "Maybe. If it was you."

Ransom knew it probably would have been better to stay calm, but the glimmer of hope went straight to his head. Pulling Timothy into a headlock, he said, "Any time. Any where. Any *now*!"

But Baird chose that moment to strike a chord on his electric guitar, and Ida added a *ching-a-ring* on the piano to get everyone's attention.

Timothy elbowed his way free and muttered, "Later. Geez."

"Later," Ransom promised.

It was dark by the time Zeke and Jasper made it back from practice, and they fell on the leftover pizza like starved men. Timothy took his rightful place by their sides, but not for long. When the singing resumed, he returned to Ransom with a bowl of ice cream and a sly smile. "Did you notice?"

"Huh?"

"Prissie."

Ransom's brows furrowed. "What about her?"

"She's been staring at you all night."

"Yeah, I kinda noticed earlier. Seriously, do I have something on my face?"

Timothy snorted. "Is that an opening for a joke about your nose?"

"Do you think I'm in trouble?"

"Nope. But she might be." He pointed with his spoon as Prissie disappeared into the kitchen. "I think she wants to get you alone."

Ransom's confusion doubled. "What gave you *that* idea?"

"Her," Timothy said. "She told me to tell you to go to the kitchen for a minute. Please and thank you."

"In that case, I'll be right back."

"Beck and call."

"You make that sound like a bad thing," he said lightly.

Timothy's expression shifted subtly. "Nope. Don't make her wait forever."

Ransom found Prissie at the sink, filling water pitchers. She seemed preoccupied, staring at the water with unfocused eyes. "You okay, Miss Priss?"

"Umm … I'm not sure." She glanced between him and the door, then turned off the faucet. "I wanted to talk to someone who isn't … umm. Remember when you said you could talk about anything with me, even things that are a little embarrassing."

"Yeah."

"Well, I need to ask you about something that's been bothering me."

"Sure." He pointed to the kitchen table. "Is this good?"

Prissie shot another wary glance in the direction of the family room, where everyone had just launched into the first verse of "Great Is Thy Faithfulness."

Ransom hesitated when she headed for the back stairs, but she only went up half a dozen steps before taking a seat.

"It's too cold for the porch swing," she explained. "And I'd rather not be interrupted."

He lowered himself to the step below hers and leaned back on his elbows. "So what's up?"

"I heard this thing. Overheard it, really. And I wondered if there's any truth to it, even though they're … not someone I'd normally trust. At all." She took a breath and said, "Friends embrace. Hearts race. Let him. Like him. Love him."

Ransom fished for a little context, because he couldn't understand what had Prissie so wound up. "Sounds like random song lyrics. Is this about Margery again?"

Prissie smiled wanly. "No."

"Fair enough. But I'm not sure what you're asking."

"Friends embrace," she repeated. "We're friends, and we've hugged."

"Lots of times."

"And … I let you."

Ransom's eyebrows shot up. "Hey, it's not just me. You've initiated plenty of hugs."

"And I like you."

"Knew that." Ransom's heart jumped the gun, racing off even though he wasn't sure where Prissie was headed with this line of thought.

She said, "And as far as friends go, I'd even say I love you."

"Knew that, too. But haven't we been over all this before?"

"Yes," she sighed. "But the whole hearts racing thing. Shouldn't that happen?

Ransom tapped his chest. "I can vouch for palpitations."

Prissie's eyes widened. "Oh," she whispered.

"So what you're saying is … I don't make your heart go pitty-pat?" To Ransom's dismay, she shook her head.

"I'm comfortable with you," Prissie quickly explained.

"And you want a guy who makes you uncomfortable."

"No!" Prissie shuddered from head to toe before adding an emphatic, "*No*."

"So what are you asking, Miss Priss?"

She fiddled with the fabric of her skirt, eyes downcast. "Do you think if I let you get closer, it would change things?"

Ransom fought to keep a neutral tone. "Are you proposing a chemistry experiment?"

Prissie bristled and blushed. "That's a terrible way to put it!"

"We've already agreed that I fail at romance. But I think you have a valid complaint."

"I'm not *complaining*," she grumbled.

He eased up a step so he was at her side. "May I borrow your hand?"

"What are you going to do?"

"Hold it. It's a friendly thing we sometimes do. Remember?"

She sighed, then surrendered.

Ransom tucked Prissie's hand between his own, trying to warm her cold fingers while he gathered his thoughts. How could he explain without making things more awkward? With a swift prayer for wisdom and words, Ransom asked, "Do you remember way back, when you said that not-liking me was a habit?"

Prissie nodded.

"Well, for me, holding back around you is a habit." He explained, "It's no wonder your heart isn't keeping up with mine. I guess I'm way too convincing with the whole *just friends* act."

She asked, "What are you holding back?"

Ransom chuckled. "Miss Priss, that's a loaded question. Do I really have to explain?"

"I'm not asking for an explanation. I was hoping for more of a demonstration."

"This isn't like you, Prissie. What's the rush?"

Exasperation flashed across her face, and she tried to pull away, but he wrapped his arm around her shoulders and pulled her into a firm embrace. She was rigid, and he desperately hoped she was more annoyed than hurt. But experimenting on the back stairs would put everything he wanted in backward order.

Ransom said, "How about this? I promise to stop holding back so much, and sometime in the next month, I'll kiss you."

"A month?" Prissie peeked up at him. "Why so long?"

"Palpitations take preparation. And the waiting and wondering will probably work in my favor." Ransom settled her head against his shoulder. "Plus, this month is going to be extra busy, with all of us getting ready for the downtown Harvest Festival. Finding time to flirt might be a challenge."

"You're going to flirt with me?"

"Shamelessly."

"Is it too late to change my mind?"

Grabbing hold of a tiny burst of inspiration, Ransom said, "I'll give you a hint. I'll kiss you on a day when we're both wearing something pink. That way, it'll be a surprise, but one we agree on."

Prissie pulled away and headed downstairs. Pausing on a step that put her at eye level with Ransom, she said, "What if I wear blue every day in October?"

Ransom said, "You'll keep me in suspense."

"Do you even own a pink shirt?"

He waggled his brows. "Wait and see."

Late that night, Ransom trailed after Timothy, who was inspecting the walls at his place. He wanted to get back to their earlier conversation, but Timothy was carefully avoiding eye contact.

"There's a lot more writing already," Timothy remarked.

Ransom said, "Baird's scribbles started a trend. I'm pretty sure every Pomeroy has been through to add to my collection." He paused to read a scrawled note near the floorboards. "Check that. Pomeroys *and* Morrells. Nat and Josiah have left their mark."

Timothy found several rows written in red ink. "Yep. Zeke's aunt left you song lyrics. So you don't lock the doors?"

"Nope. This way, Derick, Tad, Marcus, and Pete can drop in at odd hours. They're all lending a hand with plans and changes."

"So how come there aren't any messages from Prissie?"

"Maybe she doesn't believe in defacement of property."

Timothy finally looked at him. "This is exactly the kind of gushy Christian thing her whole family goes for. What gives?"

Ransom peered around the cramped room with its low ceilings. "She hasn't been over yet."

"Why not?" The teen flung his arms wide. "All her brothers have been here except Neil, and he has an out-of-state excuse. Even her grandparents are leaving cutesy sayings on your walls."

"They were curious."

"And Prissie's not?" Timothy asked skeptically.

"Maybe she's not ready," Ransom ventured.

"Maybe she's not invited. Did you ask her over?"

"Not specifically."

"Don't you want her to see the house you bought for her?"

"Yeah, of course I do. But it's kind of awkward." Ransom leaned against the door frame of one of the old house's bare bedrooms. "How am I supposed to say, 'Come see the house I bought for you'?"

Zeke abruptly poked his head around the corner. "I like it. Short. To the point. What do you say, Mr. Reece. Should we write that over the front door?"

Jasper held up a fat marker. "In letters as bold as his declaration."

Baird wandered in, holding a fistful of markers in rainbow hues. "Hey, Timothy. What color do you want?"

"I don't need one. I've got nothing to say."

"That's not the impression I've gotten." The redhead's eyes sparkled. "You keep talking your friend into a corner. Might as well put a greeting there. Make him feel welcome."

Timothy grudgingly snagged a green marker.

Baird immediately switched gears. "Hey, Ransom? Is it okay if I go up into your rafters tonight? I want to leave some words on the boards and beams that'll survive the renovation."

"Fine by me. If you can find a way up."

"I'm on it," said Zeke. "Grandpa left a six-footer in the garage."

He and Jasper grabbed flashlights and raced out the door, but Timothy hovered awkwardly. Holding the green marker out to Baird, he said, "This probably won't work out. I don't know any Bible sayings."

"Not a problem. Your host might not have much, but he has what matters." Looking straight into Ransom's eyes, Baird said, "Give him a Bible."

Quickly crossing to the short stack of books in the corner, Ransom found a spare. Offering it to Timothy, he said, "You'll take it if it's from me, right?"

He stared solemnly at the book for several seconds, then took it. "If it's you."

Baird started humming and meandered toward the front door.

Ransom remembered the first time he'd held a Bible, a seemingly offhand gift that had changed everything about his life. "There's a Timothy in there. Two whole books."

"I know it's a Bible name. Zeke told me ages ago."

"Ever look him up?" asked Ransom.

"Nah."

"Want to?"

Timothy sighed. "Do we have to do this *now*?"

"I'm game."

"It's a school night."

Ransom conceded with a nod. "We don't have to go into it now, but I won't let it slide. Pick a day. When can we start?"

"Start what?"

"Bible study." He tapped the book's cover. "We'll read. I'll run through the basics. And you can ask questions."

"Maybe if you bake something insanely good that has a name I can't pronounce, we could meet up once a week." Timothy took his time checking the calendar on his phone. "Tuesday evenings?"

"Where? At the bakery? Marcus's place?"

"Here?" Timothy asked. "I don't want an audience."

"What about the two guys Baird's holding back at the front door?"

Timothy hung his head. "They're not an audience. They're the idiots who'll never let me live this down."

"Ever!" shouted Zeke.

Jasper boomed, "We're talking *eternity*, baby!"

Baird sang out, "Evermore and evermore!"

"Regrets," grumbled Timothy. "I can haz them."

Ransom chuckled. "If everyone can get permission, let's make it a weekly deal. A little home improvement, a lot of French baking, and a flexible course of Bible reading and discussion."

Zeke strode in with a ladder balanced on his shoulder. Face solemn, eyes wide, he asked, "Please, Timothy? Can we finally do this?"

Jasper punched Zeke's arm and shot him a warning look. Ransom understood. Peer pressure might send their friend skittering back to a safe distance. He glanced at Baird, whose gaze held so much compassion. How many times had the redhead helped teens wrestle through tough stuff and find their way to faith? Ransom only hoped he'd be half as good a mentor to Timothy as Baird had been for him.

Finally, Timothy groaned, "Why me?"

Zeke whooped, and Jasper accidentally punched right through a ceiling tile.

Ransom laughed so hard, he had tears in his eyes, which the teens took as permission to start the demolition. By the time the three of them dropped onto their makeshift beds on the floor in the first bedroom, no more ceiling tiles were left intact.

It was after one when Ransom finished bagging broken tiles. He smiled blearily at Baird, who was still writing things all over the central beam they'd exposed in their enthusiasm. "Do you ever sleep?"

"Not if I can help it," he replied with a wink. "Want me to sing you a lullaby?"

"Sure." He trudged over to the corner and collapsed.

Baird dropped lightly to the floor and bent to drag a blanket over Ransom.

He snorted. "I was kidding."

"I know."

The redhead sat, leaning against the wall as if standing guard. Ransom wasn't sure how much more his heart could take in one day. Prissie had thrown him for a loop, asking for a kiss. Then Timothy had sent his hopes soaring. And now sadness was creeping in. "Do you *really* have to leave tomorrow?"

"I do."

"Prissie thinks you came here to see me," Ransom said.

Baird asked, "What if she's right?"

"I'd wonder why."

The redhead propped his hands behind his head. "I have a doozy level question for you."

"I've asked you so many things over the years. I think you're allowed to switch things up."

"If you had those nine birthday wishes, what would they be?"

"Dunno," Ransom said candidly. "Seems a shame to wish for things I can work for. And it's best to pray for things you can only trust for."

"Should I be wondering why you're dodging the question?"

"Aren't doozy level questions supposed to be thought-provoking?"

"Just don't ponder so deeply, you start to snore."

Ransom glanced thoughtfully in the direction of the bedroom where his trio of house guests were sacked out. Both Zeke and Jasper were long gone, but Ransom was pretty sure Timothy was still awake and eavesdropping. But that didn't bother him so much. It wasn't as if Ransom had any secrets from him; he'd told Timothy stuff he hadn't told anyone else. Those confidences might have earned him some teasing asides, but they'd also stayed confidential. Timothy knew how to keep secrets.

"For starters, I'd wish and hope and pray that I'll be good enough," Ransom said.

"You are way open-ended. What are we talking here?" Baird asked. "A good *what*? Pet owner?"

Ransom rubbed at a crooked smile. "Man. Husband. Father."

"First one's a lock, but you're going to need help with the others."

"Working on it."

"Yeah?" Baird asked in knowing tones. "Got your heart set?"

"Figured that out, did you?"

"I might be privy to a little hearsay. Care to verify?"

"Verily, verily." Ransom sighed. "You know, I never understood Jacob like I do now."

"Oh, man. Don't tell me," Baird said, all sympathy. "Seven years of waiting?"

"It has been. But I'd wait seven more if Prissie needed the time."

Baird reached over to pat his shoulder. "That's some serious namedropping."

"Yeah. I'm serious."

"Good."

And that one word squeezed Ransom's heart to tightly, his eyes started to water. His father hadn't ever cared what he did so long as it didn't lead to trouble. So when Jayce Pomeroy had stepped in and taken a more fatherly role in his life, Ransom had grabbed everything he could get. But it wasn't like he could talk to Jayce about certain things. Especially Prissie-related things. So all his doozy level questions had gone to Baird.

"You know, I've always thought of Jayce Pomeroy as my second father."

"He's always treated you like a son."

"Which would make you my third father."

The redhead gawked at him. "I'm a *dad*?"

"Yeah. I'm bumping you to the top of my doozy level wish list. Honorary parental status for Mr. Myron Baird."

Chapter 17

The Golden Flowers

In the wee hours of the morning, Tamaes strolled along the orchard's edge, pacing off the boundary lines. It didn't take long. After more than two decades patrolling so much acreage, Ransom's property felt dainty by comparison. Eight hadarim were more than enough to stand watch, so Taweel had sent two Guardians aloft to stretch their wings.

From the darkest corner, under the trailing limbs of a large cedar on the northwest corner, Taweel strode into the open. Tamaes pulled up short and asked, "Finished your circuit?"

His mentor grunted.

"Does it feel strange, being the senior member of this Hedge?"

Taweel hesitated. "I would not be opposed to this post."

Eyes fixed on the grass at his feet, Tamaes ventured, "Do you think …?"

" … that our Sending will lead here?"

"Yes."

"Only God knows for certain." At his apprentice's impatient glance, Taweel's lips quirked. "Yes."

Gazing off in the direction of the Pomeroys' farmhouse, where Prissie slept under Ethan's watch-care, Tamaes asked, "Am I going to be like Lucan?"

"You would need a Weaver's help to achieve the hairstyle."

"I meant …." Tamaes rubbed sheepishly at the scar on his face. "Will I be the one to welcome in new Guardians? Will you be the one to lead them?"

Another grunt.

Stealing a look at the bronze-winged Guardian perched beside the house's cupola, he asked, "Is it too soon to make plans?"

Taweel followed his gaze toward Ardon. "We would be wise to prepare for *any* eventuality."

"See if Lucan can join us? And Jomei, if the Hedge can spare him." Then Tamaes spread his wings and sprang into the air, intent on joining Ransom's guardian angel. There was much to discuss.

For the entire first week of October, Prissie chose her clothes with scrupulous care. If Ransom was perturbed by the sudden absence of pink in her attire, he didn't let on. Nor did he wear anything pink himself. Not that she was checking *closely*. But Ransom mostly wore chef's whites at Loafing Around. Unless he spattered something pink on his apron, he was as pink-free as she.

"Does a flashlight count?"

Prissie frowned. "Excuse me?"

Ransom tugged the pink plastic flashlight out of his pocket so it dangled from his belt loop. "What do you think?"

"I don't think you can *wear* a flashlight."

"Nail polish?" he asked, casually checking her feet.

Prissie frantically tried to remember what color her toenails were at this moment. But with socks and shoes on, it was impossible to tell. "Only if it's showing," she said as her face heated.

"Fair enough." Ransom kept right on dolloping meringue on a long row of lemon tarts. But he didn't drop the subject. "You're blushing."

"That doesn't count!"

"It counts for something. But not for this."

Ransom chuckled in a way that made her suspicious. Had she just admitted to something?

"My socks," he said. "Just in case you're wondering."

She glanced warily at his feet, and he pulled one pant leg up far enough to expose socks with blue, purple, and pink stripes.

"I was feeling brave this morning."

"Those definitely required bravery," she said dryly. "Go you."

"You think it'll set a trend?"

She pretended not to notice his hopeful glance. "Marcus would never go for it."

Prissie quite enjoyed the look on Ransom's face when she breezed through the church foyer in her favorite pink dress. There was only one word for it. Tragic.

"You wore pink!"

"You didn't!" she replied sweetly.

"I gotta hand it to you, Miss Priss. That was gutsy."

"Not really. Zeke tipped me off."

Ransom whipped around and pointed to her brother. "Whose side are you on?"

Zeke held his hands up. "Wha'd I do?"

"She. Wore. Pink!" he said with all the melodrama of a bad actor.

"Sis does that. A lot."

"When did she call you?"

Prissie left Ransom to fumble through explanations. She'd known the trick would only work once. If it really *was* a trick. She had a strong suspicion that Aunt Ida would have called her a tease. Grandma Nell would have called her a flirt. Momma had her own way of looking at things. She liked to call this sort of thing the gift of encouragement.

Prissie reached for the apron she'd worn nearly every day since their little challenge started. Of all the aprons she kept at the bakery, it was the only one that didn't have any pink in the pattern. And it was missing.

"Zeke?"

"Yeah, Sis?"

"Where's my apron?"

His smile was too innocent. "Lots of aprons to choose from. You look great in those aprons."

"Zeke," she repeated. "Where's my apron?"

With a hangdog expression, he crossed to the sink, rolled up his sleeve, and pulled a dripping bundle of cloth out of a pot of soapy water. "I … uhh … washed it for you."

Thirty seconds later, Zeke was on the phone with his father. "Please, Dad? Just ask."

Prissie tapped her foot on the floor.

Zeke rolled his eyes toward Prissie and said, "Pink, huh? Okay. So before you get back, you need to trade socks with Ransom." After a short pause, he laughed uncomfortably. "Because otherwise, Prissie's gonna heap coals on my head, then slap me with the right hand of fellowship."

When the guys returned, Ransom looked uncomfortable, and Mr. Pomeroy spent the rest of the day wearing carnation pink socks and a bemused expression.

During the third week of October, Prissie was in her grandparents' kitchen, stirring a batch of pink applesauce. Grandpa Pete was idling over a cup of coffee as he chatted with his wife. Their conversation ranged from the upcoming *Messiah* rehearsal at the Presbyterian church to recent signs of construction—or deconstruction—underway at their new neighbor's house.

"The roof's gone. Nothing but tarps to hold the weather out."

Grandma Nell asked, "Will Tad meet the truck delivering lumber and shingles?"

"Not until tomorrow."

"Oh, that's right," the old woman murmured, taking a slow sip from her mug. "You know, I thought of another hymn to add to his wall. You remember, don't you? The one your mother used to play all the time."

As she and Grandpa Pete meandered down memory lane, Prissie's thoughts turned to Ransom's house. Nearly a month had gone by, and she still hadn't seen it for herself. Just because she'd been putting it off didn't mean she wasn't curious. But it would be uncomfortable asking Ransom for a tour. From the things she'd overheard Zeke and Jasper saying, it was awful. Prissie really didn't want Ransom to see her first reaction. What if she was disappointed? He'd know.

She asked, "Is anyone over there now?"

"What was that, sweetie?" her grandmother asked.

"Is anyone working at Ransom's now?"

"Tad's in the back forty today, and I didn't see Derick's truck." Grandpa Pete's eyes twinkled. "You might get away with it if you're quick."

Grandma Nell eased to her feet and joined Prissie in front of the stove. "Let me stir. Go while the getting's good."

Prissie kissed their cheeks, grabbed a shawl, and let the screen door slap shut behind her. Cutting through the orchard, she hurried between rows of trees that ran parallel with Orchard Lane. So intent was she on her goal, she started when Ethan dropped from the sky to join her.

That's right. The orchard wasn't necessarily safe. Prissie asked, "Is this okay?"

He nodded. "I will accompany you."

She brightened at the prospect of a partner in crime. Not that it was exactly criminal to sneak onto Ransom's property. He'd made it clear that the door was unlocked and the Pomeroys were always welcome. Stepping through the treeline into Ransom's back yard, Prissie considered the mess. A rented dumpster. Scattered shingles. Broken bits of plaster. Tufts of old insulation.

But the gardens were untouched. There hadn't been a killing frost yet that autumn, so while much of the greenery in Ransom's yard was dropping, enough cosmos still bloomed to give her an idea of how showy the flower beds must be in summer. "Pink," she whispered.

Ethan stayed by her side as she meandered through the yard, but he held his peace.

Finally Prissie said, "It's nice."

"You are pleased?"

"Maybe."

Ethan eyed the property lines with a critical eye. "With a few more guardians, this home's Hedge would be truly formidable."

"Zeke's been staying here every other night or so. Does that mean Tamaes has been guarding this house?"

"Yes."

Prissie wasn't sure how she felt about that. "Is he here now?"

"No," Ethan replied in gentle tones. "But Conrad is with us. On the roof."

She eyed the blue tarps. "I'm not sure that counts as a roof."

"Do you wish to go inside?"

"No one's here?" she checked.

"We are the only ones, seen or unseen," Ethan assured.

"Come with me?" Prissie dredged up a meager smile. "The last time I was in place with tarps for a roof, someone threw a sword at me."

Her temporary Guardian's wings swept outward. "Fear not."

Taking him at his word, Prissie tiptoed up the porch steps and tried the door. She knew she wasn't truly trespassing, but she felt sneaky and skittish. Creeping across the threshold, she stared around an echoing room with board floors. Scattered tools. Plaster dust. Power cords. Bare bulbs. Bent nails. She straightened and frowned. This wasn't a house; it was a work site.

How could Ransom possibly be living in these conditions? With growing indignation, Prissie marched to his kitchen. He had a sink and a toaster oven. "This is ridiculous!"

Ethan asked, "Is it?"

"Unbelievable!" She was both flustered and fuming. "Can he do laundry? And what about a furnace? Nights are getting so cold, and there's no roof!"

After a lengthy pause, Ethan said, "He does not complain."

She found the bathroom, which had an antique footed tub. "I guess it's not *all* bad."

"But you do not approve?"

"No!"

"He will be greatly disappointed."

Prissie blinked. "Oh, not the house! I don't know *what* to think about this place. I mean, the bakery was as big a mess when they redid everything, and look how beautiful that turned out. What I mean is … he's working too many hours, and he can't be eating correctly. I don't think Ransom should push himself so much."

"Even though it is for your sake?" Ethan searched her face. "Or *because* it is for your sake."

Angels certainly didn't mince words. Prissie stared at the makeshift bed in the corner. "How can he do all this without knowing if I'll accept any of it?"

Her companion remained silent, but not in an evasive way. Ethan nibbled at his lower lip as he considered her question. At times like this, Prissie really missed Koji. His insights had always changed her perspective. "You're my friend, Ethan. If you have an opinion, I'd like to hear it."

"This is love." With a shy glance and a small shrug, he said, "Not all who are loved accept the gift they are offered. Yet love remains."

"Like God's love?"

"In part." He turned to face her fully. "The usual comparison is Christ's love for the church."

Prissie knew which Bible passage Ethan was referring to. And it was one that talked about husbands loving their wives. "Is that what you see?"

"Do you see things differently?"

"No, but it's still strange. Like … I'm not sure I believe what I'm seeing."

Ethan walked along the wall. Finding a portion where Zeke had scrawled a verse, he ran his finger under the words. "I do not think Ransom labors in vain."

"Why's that?"

"Because you have given him hope."

"Well, I plan on giving him a piece of my mind. Living in this shambles is ridiculous." She marched over to a rolling rack that was covered with zippered plastic to keep out the dust. In full snoop mode, Prissie chanced a peek at the fabled Paris shirts and burst into giggles. Ransom owned no less than three pink shirts.

"Prissie?"

She carefully zipped shut the makeshift wardrobe. "He really has been holding out on me. Did my family leave any markers around?"

"Yes." Ethan strolled away and quickly returned with a pink one.

Her smile widened. "Your favorite or mine?"

"His."

Ethan had a point.

As she uncapped the marker, he asked, "What will you say?"

"Something … encouraging."

Prissie didn't mind that Ethan was reading over her shoulder. In fact, his being there made it easier to be bold. She finished her message with a tiny flourish, then capped the pink pen.

Ethan's chuckle must have elicited a response from his mentor, because the young Guardian looked up into the rafters and reported, "It says, *'Definitely the pinstripes.'*"

Prissie kept stealing peeks at Ransom while she waited for her batch of pastry cream to thicken. He had shadows under his eyes, but he stayed doggedly on task, measuring ingredients into the big stand mixer. Her concern for him increased every time he paused to check the recipe. Ransom didn't need that recipe any more than she would have.

He wasn't taking care of himself. She had half a mind to call in Marcus, whose protective streak was nothing to be trifled with. But their friend was probably in the middle of some kind of stained glass project, which meant it was up to her. "Time for an intervention," she murmured.

Pouring hot pastry cream into a bowl, she covered the pudding and stashed it in the fridge. Crossing to Ransom's side, she said, "I have storytime next. Will you be around for lunch?"

He blinked vaguely at the clock.

She put a hand on his forehead. "What's with you today? Are you getting sick?"

His gaze snapped to her face, and he said, "Sorry, Miss Priss. I have a lot on my … umm … what was the question?"

"Have you eaten?"

"Recently?" Laughing in the face of her indignation, he said, "Kidding, kidding. Yeah, I ate."

"Decent food?" she challenged, stepping away.

Ransom turned and leaned against the counter. "Not gourmet cuisine, but I'm getting by. Are you worried about me?"

"There's no excuse for skimping along. You should come over for dinner tonight. Let us feed you a proper meal. Maybe even bundle up some leftovers."

"Umm." Ransom's gaze drifted back to the clock, and he rubbed at the side of his face. "What's today?"

"Tuesday."

"Right. I trade my apron for a tool belt at two. And I can't make it on Tuesdays." He offered an apologetic smile. "That's when my Bible study group meets."

"I didn't know you were attending a study. Is it at the DeeVee?"

"Nope. It's kind of a private group. We meet at my place."

Prissie frowned, "Since when?"

Ransom said, "Three … maybe four weeks. It's kind of a blur."

"You never mentioned anything."

"Didn't seem like you'd be interested. It's a men's study." His smile deepened. "You want to be in the know whenever I plan something new?"

Her indignation fizzled to nothing. "Of course not. You don't answer to me."

"You sure? You seem miffed over being left out."

Prissie wrinkled her nose at him. "I'm not your keeper."

"I'd let you keep me."

Sticking to business, she asked, "How about Wednesday?"

"Can't. Derick's bringing a couple guys in to make my place weather-tight."

"Thursday, then? Oh, wait," Prissie interrupted herself. "We're doing hats for the harvest festival then."

"Friday?"

"Only if you're going to the *Messiah* rehearsal at Trinity Presbyterian," Prissie replied. "I'm babysitting Essie so Aunt Ida can sing."

"Yeah, no. I'm tagging along with Timothy to see the guys at an away game." He stepped forward and pulled her into a loose embrace. "Sorry, Prissie. Looks like I've been keeping you waiting. You even wore pink."

"Took you long enough to notice."

He tightened his hold. "Better late than never?"

Prissie hummed.

"Palpitations?" he checked.

"What if I said *no*."

Ransom's lips brushed her temple. "You're a terrible bluffer."

Was that cheating? She could feel her face heating. "Are you flirting?"

"Too tired to flirt."

"So you admit you're tired!"

"I admit nothing."

Prissie found herself smiling.

"Say, Miss Priss?" Ransom ventured. "If I can clear a whole day, would you spend it with me?"

"Are you asking me on a date?"

"Sure, we can call it that."

Prissie frowned. "What else *would* we call it?"

Ransom's hold tightened just a little bit more. "I'm going with … *worth the wait*."

When Prissie left work the following day, she wandered along the familiar path to Stained only to find Marcus's shop locked up tight. He'd left a note for her wedged in the door—*At Ransom's. See you at dinner.*

Prissie sighed. Ransom's fixer-upper had messed up her routine. She missed dropping in on Marcus, but what could she do? Ransom needed him. But did that mean she didn't? She took the note and drifted back down the sidewalk, eyes out of focus. Her little visits with Marcus probably weren't as important as getting a roof over Ransom's head. But did that mean their chats weren't important? Not a chance.

Rereading the note, she wondered which of her brothers had invited Marcus over for dinner. A small smile crept onto her lips when it occurred to her that he'd just probably invited himself over. Maybe she wasn't the only one missing their chats.

Dropping the note into her pocket, Prissie strolled back toward the bakery, but on impulse, she walked right on past her parking space. Today called for ice cream, and with any luck, Dill Brickle's would have cherry-nut in their freezer case.

She was halfway through the shop's door when Colin collided with her. "Prissie! You came!"

"Were you expecting me?" she asked with a laugh.

He wrapped his arms around her waist and squeezed tight. "You or someone." Lowering his voice, Colin explained, "I been praying for someone to come take me to the farm."

Margery turned from the counter with an iced coffee and an annoyed expression. "You ran wild at their place all last weekend. What more do you want?"

"That was *forever* ago!" whined Colin.

Prissie could remember when five days felt like forever. Smoothing the boy's fair curls, she said, "We're always happy for your visits."

"See, Mom! Can I visit them? Can I?"

"Let it go, already," snapped Margery. "Geez, you make me feel unwanted."

Colin looked ready to argue, but Prissie tapped a finger to her lips. Taking the hint, the boy's mouth snapped shut.

Margery rolled her eyes. "Oh, sure. *You* he listens to. I can't get him to shut up for anything."

Prissie eased the rest of the way inside so the door could swing shut. "How are you?"

"Sick to death of homework," Margery grumbled. "Online courses are such a bore, so I decided to take a coffee break. You?"

"Ice cream break," Prissie replied with a small shrug. "Then it's back home. Tonight, we're going to turn the kitchen into a milliner's shop. Getting ready for the Harvest Festival."

Margery perked up. "Hats?"

"This year, Momma decided to do a spin on the Mad Hatter's hat shop. We'll all wear big, wonderful hats, and there'll be lots more for customers to try on. Plus a spot for taking pictures." Prissie smoothly asked, "Would you like to help?"

"During the festival?"

"Then, too. But I meant tonight." Prissie couldn't believe she hadn't thought to invite Margery before now. "Colin can play with the boys while we girls have our fill of frills and feathers."

Margery's eyes widened a little. "Can I?"

Prissie tried not to laugh at how much she sounded like her son. Touching her old friend's arm, she said, "We'd love to have you. *Both* of you."

On Friday evening, Prissie paced the back of the sanctuary with Essie. The baby hardly needed the attention; she'd been asleep since the final notes of Milo's solo. But Prissie needed to keep moving to stay awake. They'd stayed up *much* too late the night before, filling the Pomeroy kitchen with laughter as they created flamboyant hats for the big downtown festival.

Prissie hadn't expected Margery to fit in so well with the circle of ladies, but they'd quickly found common ground. And no wonder. Ida and Mel both had seven-year-old sons, and Momma had raised her share of boys. Prissie could tell how much Margery had been craving this kind of camaraderie and encouragement.

"We won't leave her out anymore, will we?" she whispered to her sleeping cousin.

The choir director tapped his stand for attention, and when they moved on to another piece, Prissie did a headcount of Pomeroys. Grandpa Pete and Grandma Nell, Loren and Ida, Tad and Mel, Beau and Jude. Even Zeke would be taking part once football season ended. Grandpa Pete was proud as could be over ten-year-old Nathaniel's decision to join in this year. Nat was singing soprano with his mother. Tickling Essie's cheek, Prissie whispered, "Your big-big brother is doing us proud, Miss Esther."

Humming and swaying, Prissie made it through the long rehearsal. When she turned Essie over to Uncle Lo, she remarked, "The Hallelujah chorus may as well have been Braham's lullaby. She slept right through it."

"Maybe once we add the trumpet blasts and tympani rolls, she'll notice us," he replied with an easy smile. "Thank you, Prissie."

He moved toward the stroller in the corner, and for a few moments, Prissie tried to decide whether to join the group of church folks surrounding Milo. Instead, she slipped out the side door in search of a breath of fresh air. As she stepped through, she kicked a roll of paper on the carpet and bent to pick it up.

"Evening, Miss Pomeroy."

She glanced up and smiled at the church custodian. "Hello, Russ."

"Tell Marcus I found that blue he was looking for. The one that was out of stock."

"Oh, sure. I can text him for you."

"That'll do. Thank you kindly," he replied, continuing on down the hall with his cart of cleaning supplies.

Prissie reached for her phone, but the cast-off paper gave her pause. She'd assumed the scroll was some children's project made from construction paper, but the parchment was much heavier and had a finer texture. Unrolling the edge, she found a decorative border filled with intricate swirls and pretty flourishes. The pen-work reminded her of the playful illuminations Koji used to make along the edges of his notebook.

Heart beating faster, she unrolled the whole thing, revealing a work of art. The embellishments framed a poem about a white tower surrounded by golden flowers, lush meadows where bees buzzed, and a boy who was perfect in his innocence. The handwriting wasn't Koji's, but the poem was definitely about him. Which could only mean one thing. "Prosper."

Much more cautious now, Prissie tiptoed along the empty hallway. She rounded the corner, which put her at the foot of the stairway leading up to the balcony. A single golden flower lay on the bottom step.

Another was on the third step. Several more were artfully scattered on the fourth.

The flowers were just like the ones in the bouquet Colin had brought her several weeks ago. Slowly, she lifted her eyes. Strewn flowers littered the entire staircase. Delicate as buttercups. Lovely in every way. Yet dread washed over Prissie, freezing her to the spot. She was afraid to go up. She was afraid to turn around.

A patter of running feet came closer. Even though she knew someone was coming, she still jumped when a hand grabbed hers.

"Follow me," Asher said, pulling her down the unlit hall that led past Trinity's preschool rooms.

"What's happening?" she gasped.

"We are beset." The young angel's fingers tightened around hers. "I was

Sent."

Scuttling sounds and strange whispers echoed off the walls as Asher led her downstairs. The thud of boots chased them deeper into the church's south wing. Exit signs glowed red over closed doors, and faint light bled between blinds from the parking lot outside. Wind rushed past, as if a storm was brewing indoors, making Prissie sure they weren't alone. She ducked her head and prayed that Ethan and his Flightmates were okay.

They turned a corner into a short hall with no exit sign to point the way out. A dead end? With little more than Asher's raiment to light the way, Prissie didn't see the stone arch until they reached it. Stumbling through, she crashed to her knees on the other side and shivered in the sudden silence.

Chapter 18

The Many Hats

"Down!"

Ethan flattened as the trailing edges of cherub wings swept along his back, ruffling his hair.

A second call came. "Once more, friend!"

Arms tensed to push up froze as Garrick whipped past, twisted, and plunged down a stairwell. Then Ethan was on his feet and scrambling after his teammates.

Indoor flight required courage and creativity in equal portions, and the halls in the Presbyterian church were long enough for experienced warriors like Yannis and Garrick. The two burst through the narrow passages, forcing the enemy's retreat.

By the time Ethan reached the lowest level, his mentor was already there. No surprise. Conrad was lighter on his feet.

"She's gone," Yannis blurted.

"Safely," countered Conrad.

Garrick nodded. "That little Caretaker was Sent to her side."

Ethan felt the deep-seated tug that would lead him back to his charge.

Yannis growled, "But our enemy's gone to ground again."

"Here?" asked Ethan, giving the nondescript hallway a longer look.

"Who can say?" sighed Garrick. "This Blight is quick to vanish when a threat appears. And that would be us."

Conrad sheathed his sword with a snap. "We need to pin him down."

With a grim smile, Yannis said, "I'll drive the peg myself if you can get him to hold still long enough."

For several moments, Prissie lay in a graceless heap on a cold, hard floor. The chill was already seeping into her bones, but Asher knelt beside her and touched her shoulder. "Fear not. We are safe here."

Prissie's discomfort faded, and the frantic racing of her heart slowed. Easing off what felt like bare concrete, she sat cross-legged and pulled Asher onto her lap. "We're not at the church anymore," she whispered.

"No." The young Caretaker relaxed contentedly in her embrace and repeated, "We are safe here."

Prissie's eyes gradually adjusted. In the faint shimmer of Asher's raiment, she made out details about their hiding place. Metal walls. Wire shelving. Rubber mats. A familiar hum filled the cramped room, which smelled like cold cardboard and apples. She knew this place; they were at the bakery. "Why are we *here* of all places?"

Asher pulled her arms more snugly around his chest. "This is where I was Sent."

She hugged the young angel. "God told you to put me in the fridge?"

"Yes."

"Why?"

He shook his head. "I do not know."

A moment later, she groaned, "The door's still broken. Do you realize I'm locked in?"

"Yes."

"And nobody knows I'm here."

Asher tipped his head back to see her face. "Are you dismayed?"

"More like confused. Why would demons attack a church? Shouldn't it be automatically safe?"

"A building is only a building."

Prissie pointed out, "This bakery is only a building."

The young angel pointed at the low ceiling. "Your brother's prayers bring help near."

"Beau's home already?"

"Yes."

"Any chance we can get him a message?"

Asher hesitated. "I am not Sent to him. I am Sent to you. To keep you warm."

Prissie murmured her thanks, then asked, "What about your mentor? Does Padgett know we're here?"

"No."

"Won't he be worried?"

Asher answered with a small nod.

"And what about Ethan?"

"A Guardian always knows where to find his charge."

"Even if their charge is kidnapped by a Caretaker?"

He giggled softly. "Yes."

Prissie rested her chin on the boy's head, and he turned slightly, laying his head against her shoulder. With the beginnings of a smile, she said, "You're enjoying this."

After a lengthy pause, Asher said, "I wanted to see you."

"We're friends," she said, cuddling him close. "You can visit me any time."

"Only if I am Sent," he replied. "I have waited many days."

"Waiting isn't easy, is it?" Prissie murmured sympathetically.

He blinked up at her. "Are you waiting for something?"

"Yes."

Asher asked, "What?"

"For pumpkin pie season. For Christmas lights. For reunions that don't have goodbyes attached to them."

"Is that all?"

Prissie was also waiting for pink pinstripes to make an appearance, but she wasn't about to admit it out loud. "I'm looking forward to lots of things, but it's your turn. What are *you* waiting for?"

"To give a name. To touch a star." With a shy squirm, he added, "To taste a pie."

"I used to bake with Koji. Back then, most of my pies were flops."

"He speaks of them with great fondness."

"Would you like me to bake you a pie?"

Asher whispered, "Very much."

All of the sudden, Prissie's phone trilled. While she fumbled for it, she muttered, "I am so dense. I could have called Beau ages ago! Oh, it's Marcus."

"You may answer," Asher said calmly.

"Hello?"

"Yo. You okay?"

There was a lot of noise in the background, other voice clamoring for attention. She easily recognized Zeke's laughter and Jasper's cheerful tones. "You went to the away game?"

"Tagged along, yeah. You okay?" Marcus repeated, his tone edgy.

"Safe. Asher's with me."

"Good. Giving you over to Ransom."

There was a short pause, and then Ransom's voice came on. *"Hey, Miss Priss. We're in the parking lot at Trinity, but it looks like we missed rehearsal. Russ said he thought you left, but your car's sitting here. Do you need a lift?"*

"Not exactly. I'm at the bakery."

"Want some company?"

Prissie laughed weakly. "You could say that."

Ransom's voice shifted. *"Prissie?"*

"I'm here. I'm fine. But I need a little help."

"On my way!"

She heard a car door slam, and the call dropped. Prissie let her head droop. "This is going to be hard to explain. Or live down. Or both."

Asher quietly said, "I will leave you now."

She released her young rescuer. Immediately, a shiver ran down her spine and her skin broke out in goose bumps. Catching Asher's hand, she gave it a squeeze. "I won't forget about that pie."

He kissed her cheek, stepped back, then vanished, taking all the light with him.

But not for very long. Prissie squinted against the sudden glare when the door swung open.

"Prissie!" Ransom exclaimed. "What are you doing in here?"

"Nothing m-much," she managed between chattering teeth.

"How long have you been locked in?" he asked, rushing forward to help her to her feet.

"Not sure."

Then the door slammed shut, plunging them both into darkness, and Ransom cleared his throat. "That was probably not the smartest thing to do."

"I'm in no position to c-criticize."

He laughed, but then his hands closed around one of hers. "You're freezing! C'mere."

Prissie shuffled closer while Ransom rubbed her arms and back. And then she heard his jacket zipper, and he pulled her snug against him, wrapping her up as best he could with the open flaps. She leaned into his warmth, winding her arms around his back and rubbing her cold nose against his shirt. He was breathing hard from the three-block run from Trinity Presbyterian's parking lot.

She asked, "Did you t-tell the guys where you were going?"

"Not exactly." Ransom's voice was tight. "But I'm pretty sure Marcus was following me."

"He doesn't have a key."

"Zeke does. Or the lights are on in Beau's place."

She ducked her head, waiting for him to point out that she could have called for help. But he simply curled around her, as if trying to lend her all his warmth. His cheek brushed hers, and she could feel the scratch of whiskers. "Sorry," she whispered.

Ransom didn't answer, which was vaguely unsettling since he was never at a loss for words. She tried to look at his face, but it was no use in the dark. Her nose bumped his jaw. His hand touched her hair, and then his knuckles trailed along her cheek. "Prissie," he said, still a little breathless.

"Still here."

His nose nudged her cheek. "There's something you should know."

"Oh?"

"Yeah." He dipped closer and mumbled, "Heaven help me."

Maybe God listened because Prissie didn't move; she didn't want to. The first brush of his lips across hers was barely there, too light to even count. But the touch sent her heart tripping.

Ransom pressed his lips to the corner of her mouth. "I think I'm going to kiss you."

Going to? Leave it to Ransom to say something ridiculous. "Aren't you getting ahead of yourself?"

"Not a chance." The next kiss landed on her cheek, light as a feather. "Otherwise you'd have slapped me by now."

The romantic tension evaporated, putting an end to Prissie's palpitations. She pinched him. "Did you even *check* to see if I was wearing pink today?"

"Forgot." His cheek rested against hers. "Are you?"

"Yes," she sighed.

Ransom chuckled. "Then I'm definitely going to kiss you."

His confident tone put a distinct flutter in Prissie's stomach. "If you're sure."

This time, his lips lingered longer, but the kiss ended too quickly because he was smiling.

"What?" Prissie grumbled, her cheeks flaming. "Are you laughing at me?"

"No, Miss Priss. I'm happy," he said. "And more than a little relieved."

"Because I let you kiss me?"

A rap sounded on the door, and the lights flicked on. Prissie disentangled herself, and both of them winced against the sudden brightness as Marcus leaned into the fridge. "Yo."

"Saved!" Ransom exclaimed, placing one hand over his heart, the other across his forehead.

Prissie's exasperated look didn't make it all the way to its intended target, snagged as it was by pink pinstripes. Dragging her eyes back to the smirking cherub, she warmly added, "Our hero."

Marcus shook his head at them, then called over his shoulder, "They're in here, Boaz!"

Prissie was more than ready to leave the confines of the refrigerator, but Ransom held her back. With a quick glance to make sure Marcus wasn't paying attention, he set her straight. "I'm *happy* because you kissed me back."

On the last weekend in October, all of West Edinton turned out for their annual Harvest Festival. Based on the crowds clogging Main Street, most of Morrow and half of Harper were also in attendance, making it a true Tri-City event.

"Okay there, Priss?" asked Tad.

She glanced up at her big-big brother, whose oversized top hat was decorated with an assortment of cogs and gears. "I'm fine," she assured, piling more individually-wrapped cookies into the basket he carried.

"Have you taken a turn up and down Main Street yet?"

"Not yet. We've been so busy!"

"You should go." With a thoughtful look at her ensemble, he suggested, "Have Ransom take you around. He'll want to."

Detecting a teasing note, she asked, "And why's that?"

Tad just smiled and shrugged, then ambled down the line, offering free samples to those waiting to enter the bakery.

Prissie ducked back inside, where Momma and Pearl presided. The Mad Hatter's hat shop was a dress-up dream come true, with everything from bowlers and boaters to tasseled tams and jeweled turbans. Margery and Ida managed the photoshoots, dishing out fashion advice and juggling camera-equipped technology with ease.

Uncle Lou lounged at his usual table, decked out in a tweed cloak and deerstalker. Prissie had no idea how he managed to talk with a pipe clenched between his teeth, but his *indubitably*s and *elementary*s were well-received. Behind the counter, Jayce Pomeroy was resplendent in an ensemble Mel defined as "steampunk airship admiral." But in actuality, the bakery's owner had been reduced to register boy. The frivolous little cakes he and Ransom had collaborated on for the event were a hit, especially since Jayce wrapped them up to go in miniature hat boxes.

Delivery complete, Prissie took care navigating through the kitchen door. A serious challenge, given the size of her own hat, and nearly ran into Timothy.

"You look like a musical theater escapee," he said, staring owlishly at her through a pair of aviator's goggles. "Very *My Fair Lady*. Or maybe *The Music Man*."

"Is that a compliment?" she asked, eyebrows arching. Having Mel around had definitely elevated the authenticity of their costumes. Part and parcel with having a theater major in the family.

"From me?" He grinned and shook his head in a way that made it hard to guess what he was thinking, then quickly retreated to his post beside Zeke at the back door.

Prissie rolled her eyes. Timothy might be meeting with Ransom and the rest for weekly Bible studies, but he was still Timothy.

From out back, the screech of a steam-powered pipe organ resumed. The old instrument had been resurrected from the basement of a church down in Morrow. Grandpa Pete had gotten wind of it through a friend of a friend, and for the past three years, it had taken up a corner of the hayloft while Tad tinkered with the inner works. He and Grandpa Pete had found a way to make it portable, but the refurbished organ was destined for a permanent home in the apple barn.

Zeke's playing was full of sour notes, but artistically so. Anyone with an ear for music could tell he knew better and was flubbing on purpose. His act was made all the more impressive by Timothy's trombone playing, which Mr. Pomeroy generously compared to a heartsick moose. The racket was doing a good job of piquing curiosity about the bakery's creepy steampunk sideshow.

Prissie slipped back out front and rejoined Jude. Her youngest brother cut a dashing figure in his black and silver magician's ensemble, complete with swallowtail coat and velvet-lined top hat filled with bunnies. With shy smiles and patient reminders to be gentle, Jude allowed children to touch their soft fur.

A telltale jingling announced Ransom's return. He walked with a deliberate bounce, all mischief in his jester's get-up. He'd been roving all night, drumming up business with a sheaf of fliers. Holding up empty hands, he announced, "The deed's done, your Admiral-ness, sir!"

"Fair enough. Maybe you could …."

" … take Priscilla around!" Mrs. Pomeroy smiled sweetly at her husband. "Your daughter hasn't seen Main Street yet."

"Sure, sure," Mr. Pomeroy murmured, glancing around. "Are any of our lot in need of an escort?"

"They're all with Beau and Lo." Shooing at Ransom with both hands, Naomi said, "Take your time. We're fine here."

Bouncing over, Ransom swept into a bow. "Are you ready for a stroll?"

"Yes, please." Prissie let him lead her out the front door and right into the middle of the road. Traffic had been diverted, and downtown was lined with food carts and carnival games.

Ransom's get-up kept drawing stares.

"I can't believe Mel talked you into the tights," Prissie teased.

"At least my hat doesn't double as an umbrella." Ransom tapped Prissie's brim. The elaborate concoction of tulle, ruffles, and feathers was easily as broad as her shoulders. "Is this thing designed to keep guys away?"

"Why would you want to get any closer?"

His eyebrow quirked. "Gonna leave that to your imagination, Miss Priss."

She laughed and turned her attention to the crowds. Most people wore costumes, which varied widely from the handmade to super store specials. Those without a taste for masquerade wore T-shirts promoting local businesses or hometown sports.

They strolled past a face painting station, where artists added glitter and faux gems to their handiwork. Vendors sold glow-in-the-dark balloons and bracelets. A roving polka band meandered past, and at every door, they were greeted by barkers with bowls of candy.

In front of the corner store, Ransom fished through a bucket and came up with a cream soda flavored sucker. "My treat!"

A little farther along, Prissie found a display of masks. "You should get one of these. Add to your mystique."

"You think?" Ransom investigated the masks, which came in several styles and sizes.

Prissie found a wine-colored satin mask with gold trim that would frame his eyes. "This one would match."

He pulled off his hat in order to get its elastic band around his head. Turning to her with eyebrows lifted, he asked, "What do you think?"

"You have hat hair."

"The *mask*."

She smiled. "Roguish with a smidgeon of rakish."

"It's a keeper, then?" Ransom patted his hips awkwardly. "Whoops. My wallet's in my other set of tights."

"My treat." She fished out a few dollars. "What next?"

They sampled street food, greeted friends, and explored the displays set up in other stores along Main Street. Prissie was enjoying the leisurely stroll, right up until the swirl of a deep purple cape caught her eye.

Not a cape. *Wings*.

Two cherubim flanked the entrance to one of the alleys, and if she and Ransom continued along their present course, she'd pass right under the angels' noses. The warriors gazed out over the milling crowd, probably alert for signs of the enemy. Garrick and Yannis didn't seem to have noticed Prissie, even though she was close enough to touch.

Stretching out her arm, she let her fingers brush across Yannis's knuckles.

The Protector started so violently, he nearly dropped his bow. "Prissie!" he exclaimed.

Garrick quickly reached out, so their fingertips connected in passing. He dimpled and said, "Peace, friend."

Prissie smiled at them over her shoulder, so she saw Garrick point at the clock tower. Tipping her head so she could see past her hat, her steps slowed. The clock tower. The gazebo. The trees. One by one, she was able to pick out six more sets of vibrant wings. Ethan's eight archer friends were in attendance.

Ransom checked his pace and tried to follow Prissie's gaze. "What are you smiling at?"

"Light. Colors. Stars," she answered vaguely. He quirked a brow, and Prissie shrugged. "I'm happy, that's all."

In front of the next shop, Ransom ran into an acquaintance from the hardware store. While they chatted, Prissie's attention drifted to the lawn in front of Town Hall. Strings of lights stretched between the trees, banishing some shadows while deepening others. Beyond the far edge of the crowd, a lone figure loitered against the dark building. While she watched, he pushed off and walked their way.

Prissie glanced away, but something drew her eyes back to him. Was he someone she knew? Or maybe another friend of Ransom's? Then why was she suddenly on edge?

She checked on Ransom, but he was listening intently to his friend, who was in the middle of a story involving power tools. The other guy kept right on coming, showing no signs of rush or hesitation, and now that he was closer, Prissie could make out more details. Dark coat. Pale skin. And a mask similar to Ransom's, only this one was stark black, which set off eyes in a startling shade of blue.

"Be right back!" she whispered to Ransom.

He nodded, and she backtracked toward Garrick and Yannis. They were still posted by the alley, and they weren't alone. She reached them in a rush and grabbed their captain's arm. "Tycho! I saw him! He saw me!"

The three Protectors brought their wings up, shielding Prissie and perhaps hiding her from passersby. "Explain," ordered Tycho. "Please."

"Prosper. Blight." Her voice began to shake. "He's on the lawn in front of Town Hall."

Yannis gripped his bow and growled, "Send us, Captain."

"Go."

"Peace, friend," whispered Garrick, and he was gone as well.

Turquoise swirled around Prissie, but Tycho's wing wasn't close enough to touch. Not that she needed swaddling. Wondering at the discreet distance, she glanced up and found the archer contemplating her hat. Maybe Ransom was right; the thing *was* designed to keep anyone from getting close. A half-hearted laugh bubbled up. "Do I look foolish to you?"

Tycho held her gaze for a moment, then graciously sidestepped the loaded question. "You were wise to flee from danger." He turned and signaled, and a set of pink wings detached from the bakery roof across the street. In a gusty rush, Prissie's Guardian arrived.

"Prissie!" Concern creased Ethan's face, and he wasted no time tugging her hands into his own. "Fear not. I am with you."

"*We* are with you." Tycho nodded to his Flightmate. "Blight is too close for comfort. Stay closer."

Ethan drew his sword and nodded. "Prissie, you should return to Ransom."

Ransom! Prissie gathered up her full skirts and hustled back the way she'd come. In leaving his side, had she left him in danger?

The drooping peaks of his jester's cap soon came into view, and her steps slowed. He was still talking, though he glanced her way as if he'd been watching for her. Prissie offered a small smile, and he excused himself. "Something the matter, Miss Priss?"

She shook her head. "I saw someone whose costume gave me the creeps."

"I know you're no fan of the frightening," he said, reaching for her hand. "How about we pay Marcus a visit?"

"Can we?"

He steered her toward the well-lit windows of Stained. "Yeah, of course. Best for last."

"Success!" Zeke declared, rubbing his hands together. "And a fair chance at victory!"

Mr. Pomeroy pointed to the remaining stack of hat boxes. "Instead of resting on imaginary laurels, get the rest of these into the van. Everything else can keep until tomorrow."

"You wait! We'll be in the *Herald* on Monday!" boasted Zeke.

Prissie smiled tiredly. It would be fun if they won one of the local paper's prizes. But their dad was right. It would keep. She was grateful that the long, crazy evening was over and the bakery doors were locked up tight. Clean-up and tear-down crews were busy up and down Main Street, and stragglers trouped to their cars. By opening time on Monday morning, they'd all be back to business as usual.

Warm and worn out, Prissie eased through the kitchen door and found Ransom draped on a folding chair, his long legs stretched out in front of them. Smiling sleepily, he patted the seat next to his. "We done? Or just done in?"

"Both." Prissie joined him and began the painstaking process of removing the pins that kept her hat in place. She lowered it onto its hat stand with a sigh of relief.

"Glad to be out from under that thing?" he asked.

"It's not very practical."

"Depends on the goal. In my opinion, that thing's a menace."

"What do you have against pretty hats?"

"That brim's at nose level," Ransom complained. "I had to stoop to make eye contact."

Prissie shrugged. "I'll grant you, the hat has visibility issues."

"And this." With a twinkle of jester's bells, he leaned close and kissed her cheek. "Love you."

She was about to fend him off when another voice broke in. "Since when?"

Prissie's eyes widened. "Daddy!"

Ransom scrambled to his feet. "Sir! I've been meaning to talk to you about … this."

Surprise slowly faded into a bemused smile. Pointing to Ransom, Mr. Pomeroy addressed his daughter. "This clown?"

"Ridiculous, isn't it?" she said with a huff. "I was waiting for a prince."

"Hey, don't knock my pedigree, Miss Priss," Ransom protested. "I have direct ties to the Prince of Peace. He's like a brother to me."

Mr. Pomeroy rubbed his chin, and as he slowly backed out of the kitchen, he gruffly said, "We'll have that talk, Ransom. Soon."

CHAPTER 19

THE PAINT SAMPLE

"Do we have time for this?" Marcus asked, pushing his way into frostbitten bushes.

"Warriors must train," Jedrick replied.

"I get that. What I *don't* get is why I'm scrubbing for arrows."

"You can learn much from these archers."

"I've tried archery. Tamaes is better than fair with the bow."

Jedrick inclined his head but didn't back down. "Tycho and his Flight are superior. What do you see?"

Marcus straightened and looked back at the eight archers who bent their bows with deceptive ease. With a shrug, he said, "Garrick and Yannis are pretty funny. Easy to like."

"What do you think of their archery?"

The purple-winged cherubim radiated strength and a singularity of focus as they sized up their target. Marcus said, "They're scary good."

"Look at their stillness."

Garrick's muscles were taut, poised at the point of release; Yannis matched his steadiness. They loosed their arrows in unison, blowing away a winter apple from a half an acre.

"They have patience," Jedrick said pointedly.

"Meaning I don't?"

"You have always been eager to turn the tides of conflict. You seek change."

"Is that a polite way of saying I rush in where angels fear to tread?"

Jedrick's lips quirked. "As it happens, these cherubim are formidable hunters. Tycho and his Second have offered to teach you the skills required for tracking the enemy through various territories. Interested?"

Marcus's slow smile tilted into a smirk. "Guess I could make time for that."

Ransom asked, "Do you think this is romantic?"

Beau considered the teddy bear, then him. "That all depends on whose expectations you're dealing with. Jude might go for it, but if you're asking me, I'd really rather have a book."

Tossing the stuffed animal back onto the shelf, Ransom moved the shopping cart on down the aisle. "I seriously doubt that the way to Prissie's heart is through her brothers."

"Agreed." Beau followed him down the next aisle. "Seems to me, romance is mostly an impression left behind by a thoughtful gift or a kind word. If a girl notices an effort to please her, she responds favorably."

Ransom frowned thoughtfully. "How come you're such an expert?"

"Books mostly."

"No practical experience?"

"Prissie likes to say we're the family's maiden aunt and bachelor uncle." Beau met Ransom's incredulous look with a calm smile. "Compared to various other family members, we're behind schedule."

"Isn't Neil single, too?"

"Only on a technicality. He's planning to meet his girlfriend's s family over Thanksgiving break. All signs point to a proposal."

Ransom sighed. "Good for him."

Beau smiled faintly. "So if the old adage is true, and it's the thought that counts, what were you thinking when picked up that teddy bear?"

"That it's the sort of thing most guys buy for most girls."

Pausing to add cans to their cart, Beau counted under his breath. Once he'd checked the item off their list, he remarked, "I've never known you to fall in step with the world any more than Prissie does. You know her. You know what she likes. Start there."

"You're talking sense, but I'm still failing at romance."

Beau said, "Why don't you ask Sis what she finds romantic?"

"Isn't that cheating?"

"It's called communication. Often heralded as the firm foundation upon which healthy relationships are built. Also easier than omniscience. Or are you a mind-reader?"

Ransom grinned sheepishly.

In the next aisle, they caught up to Zeke, who was working from the other half of their list. "You want white or beige for the switch plates?"

"White."

"Decisive!"

"About the basics, sure." Ransom pulled a folded catalog out of his back pocket and thumped it against Zeke's chest. "But this stuff? Too many choices."

The teen flipped through the catalog, which contained countless examples of scrolled woodwork and ornamental trim. "Gonna put gingerbread in the peaks of those new dormers?"

"If it was a cake, I would." Ransom shrugged. Tapping one of the Victorian-inspired designs, he asked, "Do you think Prissie would like this one? Or the one with spindles? And what if I chose the wrong one?"

"The world as we know it would end." Zeke scanned the page and said, "I'd go for this one, but I'm not Sis. You want me to show this to her?"

"Based on your brother's wise words, I don't think secondhand is the way to go."

"Beau's wise? Since when?"

After a short scuffle that drew a few stares from other customers, Ransom aimed for the registers. "Let's get out before they toss us out."

Zeke grinned unrepentantly, then poked Ransom's shoulder. "You know, Sis is in the middle of canning right now. She recruited helpers, so you wouldn't have her to yourself. But you could probably barter opinions for a turn at the food mill. Wanna come over?"

"I have a couple hours before Derick's supposed to drop by."

"Well, there you go. Consider yourself invited!"

The scent of apples wafted from the farmhouse kitchen as soon as Zeke opened the door. "Smells good!" he exclaimed, effectively announcing his return. "Whatcha making?"

"Applesauce!" chorused the passel of apron-clad kids.

Ransom should have figured there'd be obstacles. He'd have to wade through the entire Pomeroy brood to get to Prissie's side. Nat and Josiah. Bennett and Juliette. Margery and Colin had also wrangled an invitation, adding to the merry "more" Naomi Pomeroy loved so well.

On the upside, Prissie was right next to the food mill. Maybe Zeke's plan was solid.

Beau meekly joined the ranks of peelers at the table, but Zeke rolled up his sleeves and jumped into the fray. "Need help with that, Ida? Lemme have a turn, Mel."

While the teen barged in between his aunt and sister-in-law, Ransom snagged a chair. Moments later, he was embroiled in a silent competition with Beau and Grandpa Pete to see who could remove apple peels in an unbroken spiral. This stuff still amazed him. Four generations pitching in to fill long rows of tiny jelly jars. This batch of pink applesauce was so smooth, it had a glossy sheen. He blinked as realization struck. "You're making baby food?"

Ida's laugh bubbled up. "Only the best for Essie! And there'll be *another* mouth to feed before next harvest."

Mel smoothed a hand over the bump showing under her apron. "Homemade is best."

With a pointed look in Ransom's direction, Margery piped up. "Hey, who knows? There could be *three* babies by this time next year."

Ransom's gut did an interesting little lurch and plunge at her insinuation. Was she talking about him? His sidelong glance was met by an arch look. Margery was laughing at him, but her jab seemed to be a friendly one.

The subtext went right over Prissie's head. She said, "Oh, Mel! Wouldn't it be fun if you had twins?"

Margery rolled her eyes, and Ransom sighed his relief. Sure, it was mathematically possible for him to be a father by next harvesttime, but it would take a Christmas wedding to even have a chance at pulling it off. For the space of time it took him to peel six apples, Ransom allowed himself to daydream about a whirlwind courtship. But common sense put a wry smile on his lips. Prissie didn't like to rush, so he'd take it one day at a time. And *today's* question wasn't the popping kind.

"Say, Miss Pr– "

"Uncle Ransom," Jude interrupted.

When he looked up, Prissie's brother was already mid-handoff. Automatically reaching back, Ransom found himself with his arms full of Essie.

"Thanks," Jude murmured. "Gotta check the animals."

"Can I come, Farmer Jude?" shouted Colin.

"Me, too!" echoed Bennett and Josiah.

"Not so fast. Turn in your aprons, boys," Mrs. Pomeroy ordered. "Boots and coats. Then you can take these peelings to the chickens."

The three boys rushed to not be left behind, and in the aftermath, Nat sidled up to Ransom. He reached down to tickle his sister's cheek before asking, "Do you know about babies?"

"Sure I do. Your mom taught me when I was the same age as your Uncle Jude." Ransom waggled his eyebrows. "You were itty-bitty like Miss Essie."

"You held me?"

"Lots of times. I let you drool on me and everything."

Nat was soon leaning against Ransom's shoulder. "I don't remember."

"I'm not surprised. You were still just a little guy when I left for school."

"Did you go to college like Uncle Neil?"

"In my own way. Cooking school instead of medical what-not. I'm better at Turkish delight than tourniquets."

A hand pressed onto the shoulder Nat hadn't borrowed, and this time, it was Prissie. She smiled softly at him and Essie. "Did Jude leave you holding the baby?"

When Ransom met her gaze, it occurred to him that Jude had his older sister pegged. Subtext was pointless. If you wanted her attention, small animals and cooing babies were definitely the way to go. And pink pinstripes.

"Say, Miss Priss. Can you reach the paper in my shirt pocket? My hands are full."

She dipped in and extracted a folded sheet of graph paper. "What's this?"

"Take a look. I was hoping to get an opinion or two." Checking to see if Prissie's mother and grandmother were paying attention, he raised his voice slightly. "Maybe even three."

Mrs. Pomeroy drifted over as her daughter unfolded Derick's unfinished plans and notes.

Grandma Nell ambled over, her blue eyes sparkling with curiosity. "What's this now?"

"We gutted the kitchen at my place, and we can pretty much put stuff back any way we want. I'm having trouble deciding what's best."

Prissie took a cautious tone. "You're a patisserie, and you don't know how you want your kitchen laid out?"

"I know how I like stuff at work, but I want the house to feel homey." Ransom took a deep breath and boldly continued, "Derick says it's good policy to keep wives, moms, and mothers-in-law happy, but I'm fresh out. Would you ladies be willing t–"

"Stove first." Grandma Nell tapped the paper. "It's the hub of any home."

"What about the kitchen sink?" asked Mrs. Pomeroy. "Cupboard space. Counter space."

Grandma Nell clucked her tongue. "Where's the laundry?"

Prissie peered over her mother's shoulder. "Is there going to be a pantry?"

And just like that, all the women were crowded around the paper. Even Margery barged in with her two cents' worth. Ransom eased out of his chair and escaped with Essie to a safe distance.

Zeke grinned and said, "Smooth."

A rap at the back door announced Milo's arrival. The mailman paused at the threshold to breathe deeply. "I thought I smelled something good."

"From the end of the driveway?" challenged Zeke.

"Like a sweet-smelling offering," Milo cheerfully assured. "What's cooking, my 'Eke?"

"Stay a while, and I'll make you some biscuits, My 'Lo."

"I could be coaxed." Milo skirted the table, where the women were thoroughly entrenched in a discussion of the pros and cons of double ovens. Offering both hands in a silent plea for a turn with Essie, he whispered, "What has them so excited?"

"They're mapping out the perfect kitchen."

"Perfect for whom?"

Ransom pointed to himself.

"And what makes it perfect?"

Without batting an eye, Ransom pointed at Prissie.

Milo followed his gaze and quietly asked, "Does she know that yet?"

"Probably somewhere deep down."

The mailman swayed and smiled at Essie, who gurgled and cooed, her eyes were fixed on a point just past Milo's shoulder. His smile was serene. "Perhaps you should pray that hidden things come to light?"

"Every day, Mr. Mailman." Ransom hooked his thumbs through his belt loops and waited for Prissie to make up her mind about the broom closet, the butcher's block, and him. "Every day."

A few days later, Ransom did a double-take when Prissie turned up at Porter's Farm and Home with Zeke. "Hey, what's up?"

"Grandpa Pete is fixing the refrigerator door. He sent me for parts," said Zeke. "Sis is just being nosey."

Ransom quirked a brow at Prissie, whose cheeks took on a faint pink cast. "It's almost impossible to picture you in a hardware store. I wanted to see for myself."

He twirled, showing off his uniform—a chambray shirt stitched with the store logo, a tool belt, and a nametag with bold letters announcing, *Hi, my name is RANSOM.*

Zeke laughed. "Betcha don't even know how to use all the thingamabobs you stock."

"This may not be my area of expertise, but I'm getting along." Ransom tucked Prissie's arm through his and said, "Do you mind coming with me for a sec? I need some advice."

"Go for it, Sis. I'll take care of this stuff." Zeke waved his list and disappeared down the first convenient aisle.

"What kind of advice?" Prissie asked.

"Paint colors." Ransom escorted her to the colorful display of rainbow-hued paint samples. "Or not-colors. Did you know they make twenty-six shades of white?"

Prissie reached out a tapped a few of cards—burnt orange, deep purple, emerald green. "Is it already time to paint rooms?"

"Upstairs and down." Ransom shrugged. "Maybe it's because the house is small, or maybe it's because Marcus works around the clock. Everything's falling into place ahead of schedule."

Her eyebrows arched. "Upstairs? Since when do you have an upstairs?"

Ransom grappled against a burst of dismay. He'd hoped Prissie would take more interest in the house. "Since last week, when Derick added the stairway. Before that, I had a decent view of the rafters. But I have ceilings again, and they're high enough that Jasper doesn't walk around with a hunch."

Prissie peeked at him out of the corner of her eye. "So you're going to paint over all the graffiti?"

"Already did. Base coat went up after Tuesday's Bible study." He slipped his phone from his back pocket and pulled up a photo. "But not before acquiring photographic evidence."

Her expression wavered between exasperation and embarrassment. "So you *did* see it."

"Hard to miss. Happy to oblige." Ransom pocketed the phone and waved a hand at the vast array of choices. "Do you have a preference, or should I be looking for pinstripe wallpaper?"

She wrinkled her nose, but she didn't turn him down.

"Did you ever see finer customer service, Clyde?"

"Escorted her down the aisle, just like a real gentleman." Clyde's grizzled beard didn't hide his smile. "Rex, we should make Ransom here Employee of the Month. He's truly going above and beyond!"

Ransom groaned inwardly. One of the things that made Rex and Clyde so much fun to work with was their constant joshing. But he didn't know how Prissie would react to being on the receiving end of their teasing ways. To Prissie, he said, "My bosses, Clyde Porter and Rex Porter. They own this place."

"And who might this be?" asked Clyde, a twinkle in his eyes.

Rex elbowed him. "Don't play dumb. She's Pete's granddaughter. Jayce's girl."

"Prissie," she said with a smile. "I see you at the bakery every Monday. You always buy three boxes."

"Muffins for morale," said Rex.

"We like to keep our employees happy." Clyde's gaze swung to Ransom. "So how did you and Miss Pomeroy become acquainted?"

"We went to school together," Ransom said easily.

"Started out as classmates. Now that's an old, old story." Clyde elbowed his brother. "You and your wife were high school sweethearts, ain't that so?"

"Ayup," said Rex, his moustache twitching.

"Ransom and I weren't sweethearts," Prissie quickly corrected.

Rex nodded wisely. "You remember, Clyde. She's seeing that boy with the wild hair."

Prissie bristled. "Marcus and I are *friends*."

Ransom decided it was high time he stepped in. Draping an arm around Prissie's shoulders, he said, "Now, sirs, don't tease her. That's my job!"

The oldtimers laughed and moved along.

"They're great guys," Ransom said apologetically. "But they do love gossip."

"Welcome to West Edinton," Prissie said, shrugging out from under his arm. "Have you forgotten how things work in small towns?"

"Nope. I like getting personal with people. And the folks here have been incredibly generous with advice. They're making sure the house is solid." With a nudge, he added, "But I still want your input."

She reached for a rosy paint chip and smiled sweetly. "I suppose pink is out of the question."

"It would be hard to live down."

"Something warm?" she suggested, her finger trailing along the row.

"I like warm."

Stopping over a soft, buttery yellow, she asked, "This?"

He looked intently between her face and the sample card. "You like it?"

Prissie plucked her choice from the rack and tucked it into his pocket. "I like yellow in a kitchen. But I think we should sneak in some pink. Especially since the house is surrounded with it."

Ransom dared to say, "Sure. We should have some pink."

When she didn't argue the *we*, a few lingering fears ebbed away. Prissie was warming to the idea. Someday, his house *would* be their home.

An insistent knocking dragged Ransom from the first floor bedroom where he'd been fast asleep. He opened his front door to find Timothy on his porch. "Hi," said the freckle-faced teen.

"Hey, Timothy." Ransom looked past him to the white minivan parked in the driveway. "The guys aren't here. We're supposed to meet up in the morning."

"I know." Timothy hunched deeper into his jacket and glared. "So can I stay here tonight?"

Concern crept into Ransom's heart. "Is something wrong?"

"Can I stay or not?" he snapped, bordering on belligerence. "Because I have to text my Mom one way or the other."

"Yeah, of course. Come in."

Timothy dragged his feet past the doorstep, then busied himself with his phone. "There. She knows I'm here."

"Does she think you're with Zeke?"

"I'm in his general vicinity."

"You're a quarter-mile away from the truth." Pointing to the phone, he said, "Tell her you're *here*, and give her my number if she freaks out."

Although his glare was rebellious, Timothy followed through.

"You should probably introduce me sometime. Or are you ashamed of me."

He showed Ransom his phone. His mother texted, *Knew it. Naomi tells me things. If she trusts Ransom with Prissie, I can trust him with you.* His phone buzzed again, and a second text came through. *Mind your manners.*

"Satisfied?"

"We're good."

Timothy started to shrug out of his jacket but made a face. "How can you live like this? It's freezing!"

"The new furnace arrives next week." Ransom gestured toward the first floor bedroom. "No sense running all the space heaters when it's just me. Come on, it's warm in the bedroom."

Dropping his coat by the door, Timothy shuffled after Ransom, rubbing his arms the whole way and grumbling under his breath. Just inside the bedroom door, he hauled up short, his eyes on the neat stack of paint cans. "You bought pink paint?"

"Can't deny it."

"Which room is gonna be pink?"

Ransom knew what was coming. "Upstairs."

"Do I wanna know why you decided on a pink bedroom?"

"Prissie chose it."

"Oh." Without another word, Timothy went to the closet and pulled out sleeping bags.

"Just *oh*?" asked Ransom, surprised at the lack of smirking and insinuation.

"You need to hear me say it?" Timothy straightened and stared at him. "It's a lock. The girl you've been waiting for is going to be your wife."

Grabbing a couple of pillows, Ransom tossed them at Timothy. "Yeah, I think so, too."

Timothy made his bed against the wall closest to the space heater and sat. Pulling a spare blanket around his shoulders, he took out his phone and stared at it with glassy eyes.

Ransom asked, "You okay?"

"Nope."

"Are you sick?"

"To my stomach." Timothy grimaced. "I'm gonna tell you something. And before I do, let's get some stuff straight. It's a secret."

Ransom sat on the edge of his cot. "I can keep secrets."

"And it's bad."

"Bad stuff happens."

Timothy looked positively queasy. "And my friends will *hate* me if they ever find out."

"That's … hard to imagine." At the teen's flat look, Ransom tried again. "You and I are friends, and you're trusting me with your secret."

"Feel free to prove me wrong. Don't hate me."

"Okay." Ransom abandoned his seat and crossed the room. Sitting on the floor next to Timothy, he promised, "I won't hate you."

With a gulp, Timothy started talking. "There was this girl at band camp. Kinda quiet, kinda pretty. Really talented. She was officially there with the flute, but she could play six kinds of woodwinds. Plus the ukulele." Dragging in a shaky breath, he explained, "Her whole family is musical, so she lives and breathes the stuff. She made it look so easy, and that made it hard to look away."

"What happened?"

"Nothing at first." Timothy stared at the floor. "Later I found out she was watching me, too. Turns out she likes freckles."

Ransom made a soft sound, encouraging Timothy to keep going.

"She did some switching and made it so we were using the same practice room. My slot was right after hers, so I said hi. We talked a little, talked some more. Then we shared the time slot, messed around with our instruments."

There was a long silence. Ransom cautiously said, "Duets are cool."

Timothy's face crumpled.

"Something bad happened?"

He shook his head. "Something *amazing*. She told me she loved me."

Dread was building up in Ransom's gut. "Yeah?"

"Yeah. So we started to find other ways to meet up. Learned more about each other. She had big plans. A college all lined up, a scholarship, connections." Timothy talked faster, getting it all out in a rush. "I was ready to follow her, apply for scholarships, move to another city, play in the same orchestra. It was perfect. *She's* perfect."

Ransom silently watched Timothy's face.

"After camp, we stayed in touch. Phone calls. Texts. Dumb jokes and funny pictures. But then it all stopped." Timothy pulled his knees to his chest. "Her parents pulled the plug."

"Why?"

Timothy's breath came in short puffs, like he was trying not to cry. "Her dad called my mom, and then he came to our house. I thought he was going to kill me." His voice cracked, and a tear slipped into view. "She dropped out of school. Had to quit symphony. Lost her scholarship. All because she decided to keep the baby."

Ransom's eyes widened. "You're a father?"

"Figured that out, didja?" Timothy's laugh was short and bitter. "I never told anyone, not even my best friends. Mom made me swear."

"You have a baby." It was more a statement than a question, but Ransom was still incredulous.

Timothy snorted. "No, Cookie. My first—and only—trip to band camp happened when I was fifteen." He pulled out his phone and swiped a few times and held it for Ransom to see. The screen was filled with the face of a laughing boy. Timothy said, "I have a toddler."

"What's his name?"

"She named him after me, but they call him by his middle name—Charles. Charlie for short."

"Do you get to see him?" Ransom asked.

He shook his head. "They live in another state, and Emmie's parents won't let me see her until I graduate. But she sends me lots of pictures and a freckle count every night."

Flicking through more pictures, he stopped on one of Emmie holding up her hand for the camera. "I had to mail her a ring."

"You're getting married?"

"Aren't you paying attention?" A stubborn glint showed in Timothy's eyes. "I'm the worst thing that ever happened to her, but she's still perfect."

Ransom shook his head. "You're *engaged*."

"Yep. Way ahead of you."

"And you don't really hate kids."

“Are you kidding?” Timothy cradled the phone to his chest, head lowered as he gazed at the picture of his son’s face. “They scare me to death.”

CHAPTER 20

THE WISH LIST

Prissie had slipped into enough true dreams to recognize the sensation of being whisked into a heavenly haven. But this setting was unfamiliar. The tower rose upward, tier upon spiraling tier. No roof intruded upon her view of the swirling sky. Brilliance found its way into every nook and cranny. Darkness and shadows had no place here. Only light … and music.

The hem of Prissie's white dress brushed her ankles as she followed her ears. Two alcoves over, she came up behind a man and boy sitting together on a piano bench. Both wore raiment. Angels, then.

Tapping the sheet music spread before them, the man said, "Mind the timing. Try again."

"It is difficult," sighed the boy. "Can I sing it first?"

"You may."

Prissie bit her lip, holding back the call that would have interrupted the lesson.

The boy sang the notes, substituting *la-la-la* in place of words. With a mellow *do-do-do*, his mentor added harmony.

"Now with your fingers."

This time, the boy played through the simple piece correctly.

"Very good. Again." And the tall angel stretched an arm around, playing notes both above and below his student's melody.

Prissie giggled. Leave it to Kester to skip straight from duet to trio. The music cut off, and both Worshipers turned to consider their audience. Kester smoothly rose, arms outstretched. She rushed into them, mumbling, "Hello again."

"It is a pleasure to find you here."

From his seat at the instrument, the boy asked, "Why would a dreaming woman be in our tower?"

Happiness crinkled the corners of Kester's eyes. "That is a long story. Perhaps Prissie and I should tell it together."

Prissie woke with a start and a vague sense of loss. Details from dreams she shared faded too quickly, but her heart felt light. Pulling her pillow close, she started to drift.

The soft tap came again, followed by a husky voice. "Sis?"

"Judicious?"

He opened the door a crack, and quietly asked, "You awake?"

"Am now. What day is it?"

Her younger brother ducked his head. "Your day off."

"And you're waking me … why?"

"You have a guest."

She threw an accusatory look at her alarm clock. "It's not even seven."

"Sorry, Sis."

"What kind of human is up before seven on my day off?"

"Farmers and bakers, mostly."

With a soft groan, she pulled her blankets over her head. But the damage was done. She was awake. "Should I be curious or worried?"

"Nothing's the matter," Jude quickly assured. "I got the idea that Zeke's behind this neighborly visit."

That confirmed her suspicions. Sitting up, she asked, "Did Ransom say why he's here?"

"Not exactly. But I doubt it's to help me with chores." Jude leaned further into her room. "He asked me to wake you, so maybe he needs a friend."

"I'll be right down."

"I'll let him know."

Prissie stepped into her slippers and hurried down the hall. No matter how much she wracked her brain, she couldn't come up with any good reason why Ransom would drop by at such an early hour. While she washed up, she glanced at her reflection in the mirror and wrinkled her nose. Not a pretty picture. But she wasn't going to waste time primping. Pulling on a heavy robe,

Prissie headed for the back stairs. She was still knotting the ties when she shuffled into the kitchen. "Ransom?"

He'd been staring into a coffee mug, but he glanced up and froze. Except for his eyes, which widened considerably. Abandoning his chair at the table, he stopped in front of her with the funniest expression. "You have bedhead."

"Happens every night." Prissie pushed impatiently at the disarray. "Jude said you needed me?"

But Ransom clearly wasn't ready to change the subject. Gently smoothing his hand over the top of her head, he murmured, "I've never seen you with messy hair."

"Ever?"

He shook his head.

Prissie sighed. "Well now you know the terrible truth."

Ransom's expression shifted. "Knowing is one thing. Knowing what to do about it … not so easy."

"It's not your job to fix my hair."

He blinked, and his attention shifted back to her face. Pulling her into a tight hug, he said, "How do you do that?"

"Do what?" she mumbled against his shoulder.

"Say the exact thing I needed to hear."

Prissie didn't have an answer for that, so she hugged him back and asked, "Is something wrong?"

"Long night." Ransom kissed the top of her head. Setting her at arm's length, he took another step back before adding, "Love you."

Her eyes narrowed. "Something happened."

He nodded.

"Something you want to talk about?"

He shook his head.

Prissie moved toward the coffee pot and diplomatically changed the subject. "Isn't today supposed to be your big painting day?"

"It is. But my crew claims to be one brush short." Ransom dropped back into his chair. "They refused to let me help, and then they kicked me out of my own house."

"Sounds like mutiny."

"More like a conspiracy." Ransom waited until she sat in the chair across from his. "I've been informed that you have the day off. I know this is short notice, but … I do, too. Do you have anything to occupy an otherwise unoccupied patisserie? Or did you make other plans?"

"I have plans, but you could be part of them. Tag along. Talk over options. Tote bags." Prissie smiled over the rim of her cup. "It's more fun to shop with somebody."

"I can handle shopping. Where to?"

"Oh, I had a few different places in mind. I think you'll really like one of them. There's a new restaurant supply store that's open to the public. Worth the drive." She explained, "That's where I always do my Christmas shopping for Dad and Zeke.

"You go Christmas shopping in November?"

"Every year." She checked the clock. "Momma's taking my place at the bakery, so it's just Jude and me this morning. Why don't you make enough breakfast for three while I get ready?"

"Fair enough. Any requests?"

Prissie pushed back her chair. "Something simple is fine. It's your day off."

"Your definition of simple needs work."

Ransom's grin reached Cheshire proportions. "That recipe only has five ingredients. You can't get much simpler."

Prissie kept her eyes on traffic. "You were showing off."

"Does that mean you were impressed?"

"Didn't Jude and I shower you with enough compliments earlier?"

Ransom chuckled. "Hey, you're the one who keeps bringing it up."

"Only because I like your attention to detail." Plus she wanted him to make it again sometime. Prissie hit her turn signal. "We're here. You're going to love this place."

She parked in the lot behind an unassuming brick building. The weather was cooperating so far, but a few snowflakes showed white against the gray sky. It wouldn't be long before winter took hold.

The front doors opened with a soft whoosh of warm air, and Ransom whispered, "Whoa."

"Three floors of everything that makes a culinary sort's heart beat a little faster. And we have all day."

"I think we should have brought the van."

She laughed and grabbed a hand basket.

He snorted and grabbed a full-sized cart.

They walked up and down the aisles, exclaiming over everything from cooling racks and offset spatulas to nesting bowls and measuring spoons. Prissie cooed over cookie cutters and pie birds, ramekins and custard cups. Ransom scrutinized timers and thermometers, decorating tips and spring-form pans.

Halfway through the second floor, Ransom started jotting down a wish list.

He said, “I think I’m in love.”

“You’re not alone.” Prissie tested the heft of an enormous spatula. “I can lose Dad and Zeke in here for hours on end.”

When she pulled him into the tiny shop on the third floor that sold colored sugars and cookie sprinkles, edible pearls, gold leaf, and glitter, he whimpered.

“I don’t think I’ve been this happy in … wow.” Ransom’s eyes took on a puppy-dog quality at the sight of hundreds of colors and styles of cupcake papers.

She finally dragged him away in favor of a break in the coffee shop. Over tea and tartelettes, they compared notes.

Ransom groaned. “You should probably hold onto my wallet or I’m going to bankrupt myself. I have a house payment to make next week, and I want to stay on the bank’s good side.”

“It’s easy to get carried away in the moment.”

To Prissie’s surprise, Ransom sobered up. The pensive expression he’d been wearing earlier was back, as if she’d brought up a bad memory.

“It’s not that I don’t understand,” she said, trying to keep her tone light. “But if you slow down and think about how many cakes and cookies we actually sell each month, what’s already in the pantry that needs to be used first, and what our regular customers like, it’s easier to say no.”

“I usually stick to my budget, but … tart pans may be my downfall.” Holding up a teensy lemon tart so he could see its underside, he asked, “Do you think they sell these?”

“They do, but don’t bother. We have that set.”

“At the bakery?”

“Nope. Home collection.”

“As soon as I have an oven, I’m going to beg a loan.”

Prissie hummed agreeably, but her attention was mostly on her shopping list. Two options for Dad. Half a dozen possibilities for Zeke. Narrowing it down to one gift each was going to be tricky.

“Say, Miss Priss. What do you want for Christmas?”

Sitting back in her chair, she entertained and eliminated several of the items she’d seen today, but none of them were really worth mentioning. With a small shrug, she said, “I have everything I need.”

Ransom slouched casually in his chair. “Nuh-uh. I didn’t ask what you *need*. I asked what you *want*.”

“I want … enough faith for one more day. And for the day after that. And then another.”

“Are you waiting for something?”

“Isn’t everyone?”

"That's not an answer," he scolded. "Stop dodging simple questions."

Prissie's gaze turned inward. "Did you ever feel like you're missing something? Or at least missing out on something."

"Sure, I know what that's like."

"Lately, that's how it seems." Prissie toyed with her napkin, pleating it into a fan. "I want to remember how much I have to be grateful for … and to appreciate it. To enjoy things like I used to."

Ransom rubbed his hands together. "Let me help! You tell me what's missing, and I'll shore up the gaps."

"It's little stuff," she protested. "Silly stuff."

"My specialty. Seriously, Prissie. Give me something to do, or I'll go crazy."

Startled, she said, "I haven't been ice skating in years. Or built a snowman."

"Easy." Ransom gestured for her to keep talking.

Lowering her gaze to her cup, she searched her memory for other possibilities. Ones she'd done before as a child. Others she'd only heard about and dreamed of doing. "I want to see the northern lights. And eat a winter picnic. Maybe have a winter bonfire. And go caroling. Things like that."

"Hang on."

Prissie couldn't believe it. He was actually making notes.

"This is great!" he exclaimed. "Prissie, the next several weeks are gonna be jam-packed. All we need now is a little planning and some snow."

"Snow," she whispered, staring in awe.

"Snow," Ransom echoed, managing to sound smug.

Prissie had to step quickly to catch up. "This won't stay, you know. It'll melt before Monday."

"O, ye of little faith," he countered. "But even if it does, there's definitely more where this came from. And now I'm looking forward to it."

They'd each spent and splurged, and Ransom insisted on carrying most of the bags. Thick snowflakes drifted lazily around them, sticking to their hair and piling up on anything that wasn't moving. While Ransom loaded the trunk, Prissie brushed off the windshield, and then they were underway.

"You'll have to shovel your own sidewalk and driveway this year."

Ransom grinned. "Yeah. Amazing, isn't it?"

She shook her head. "You're determined to enjoy it."

"Every bit of it. Especially the little things and the silly things."

On their way through West Edinton, Prissie asked, "Do you want to check on your mutineers?"

"No." Ransom stared out the passenger side window. "Miss Priss, would you be upset if I asked you to wait a while before I show you the house? I was thinking that a tour would make a good Christmas present."

"I like that idea," she assured. "Should I drop you off?"

"I'd rather help you carry your bags to the house. I'll walk home after."

"After dinner?" Prissie invited, continuing on home and pulling into the machine shed.

"Not this time." The seriousness was back in his gaze. "You planned a good day. Let me plan the next one?"

"Oh?"

"Yeah. I'd like to invite you to a concert in town. It's big stuff. An annual tradition." He waggled his eyebrows. "Maybe you've heard of it since it's something of a classic—Handel's *Messiah*."

"I'm already going."

"Sure, but I want you to go with me. In a more formal capacity."

Prissie nodded. "I'd enjoy spending the evening with you."

They sorted whose bags were whose, and Ransom escorted her up the steps and onto the back porch. The door was locked, so she had him put her bags on a bench while she fished for her key. A hand on Prissie's arm stopped her from going inside. "C'mere," he said, pulling her into his arms.

She huffed but let him hold her. "Relax, Prissie. It's called a hug. An expression of affection."

"I know how they're supposed to work."

"Am I doing it wrong?" He rubbed her back and repeated, "Relax."

"Bossy," she murmured, leaning into his hold.

Ransom chuckled. With a playful tug on her long braid, he coaxed her to look up. "I'll keep saying it until you believe me, Prissie. I love you."

"That's been made abundantly clear."

"Good." His lips brushed her cheek, and he said, "You're all rosy."

"Your favorite color."

Ransom gave her hair another tug. "We're going to be okay, Miss Priss. I promise."

"I might believe you."

"And I'm going to marry you, Prissie Pomeroy."

She arched her brows. "Is that supposed to be a proposal?"

"Not a chance. The look in your eyes says you'll turn me down flat."

"Maybe I'd accept just to prove you wrong."

He laughed. "You're good at keeping me off balance."

But his next kiss left *her* reeling.

She would have happily continued, but Ransom whispered, "One last kiss.

I need to leave."

"Why?" she complained.

"Because I don't want to." And with a fleeting caress, he turned his eyes skyward and prayed, "Thank you, God. This day has been an unexpected gift in so many ways. I know Zeke would love to take credit, but the snow's all You. And I'm all Yours. And hers, if Prissie will have me. Please give her a glimpse of how much she's loved. I'm *more* than happy to help in that department. But if something's missing, You're the best possible Provider. Help us trust you for each new day. Neither of us wants to miss out on the good You have in store."

"Amen," Prissie whispered.

Ransom turned her toward the door. "See you at work in the morning."

"Yes," she murmured, letting herself in. He was already halfway down the sidewalk when she called, "Ransom?"

"Yeah?"

"Love you," she blurted before taking refuge in the kitchen.

She counted to ten before risking a peek at Ransom's retreating figure. Just in time to see him fling his arms wide and whoop to the sky. His joy was sweeter than any kiss. Ransom wasn't romantic, but his love was so honest. As straightforward as his prayers. As staggering as his kisses.

"Priscilla?" Momma came into the kitchen. "Was that Ransom?"

"Y-yes. He … umm."

Her mother joined her at the door. Peering out the window, she asked, "Was it a nice date?"

Prissie gave in to the wild impulse to *tell* someone. "Momma, I think I'm going to marry Ransom."

"Want to talk about it?"

"Please?"

Her mother smiled. "I'll put the cocoa on if you'll explain why that nice young man tied a knot in your hair."

Prissie reached back and found it was true. Her braid was in knots. And her heart was well and truly his.

Midnight found Prissie in her windowseat, watching snowflakes drift through the downcast beam of their yard light. The shadowy silhouette of a cat slunk across the illuminated patch, probably after the mice in their corn crib.

Tap, tap.

She turned her head to the door and quietly called, "I'm awake."

"May I come in?"

"Ethan?"

The young Guardian eased through the door. "Verrill and Raz are here. They would like to offer greetings."

"Of course. I'd love to say hello."

The Messengers dropped in from above with a whispery flutter of wings. "Fear not!" Raz said, upholding tradition.

"Greetings *and* a song, if you'll permit it," said Verrill, who'd brought his harp.

"May we join the song?" came a voice from overhead. Prissie gasped as Yannis landed on her braided rug, then stepped aside to make room for his mentor.

"Peace, friend." Garrick offered his hand, and she gladly touched her fingertips to his.

"And me!" Asher clambered up onto the windowseat with Prissie.

She shook her head wonderingly. "Am I dreaming?"

"No, Prissie Pomeroy," said Jedrick, who entered through the door. Scanning the room, his lips quirked. "I see news travels fast."

Milo slipped through the ceiling, resplendent in raiment. "Especially good news," he said, moving to stand beside his captain.

Prissie looked from face to face. "What's going on?"

A streak of light zinged through the open door. "Omri?" she gasped, trying to get a good look at the excitable little angel. She'd almost forgotten how bright he was. And how happy he made her feel.

Asher giggled and pointed, and Prissie turned in time to see Taweel attempt to straighten. Even hunched, his wild black hair brushing the angled ceiling.

His name came out like a sob as Prissie jumped from her seat and stumbled into his arms. The big Guardian lifted her up, sheltering her in the folds of one purple wing.

"Taweel," she choked out. "I've missed you *so much*!"

"I am never far." He touched her hair, then turned so she could see the latest arrival. "We are ever near."

Jedrick and Milo flanked Tamaes, whose bittersweet and amber wings trembled. Prissie held out her arms like a child, and her guardian angel needed no further invitation. He cradled her close, not letting her go even when his teammates helped him to a seat on the floor.

Ethan knelt before the two and extended his palm. "Prissie, your name is still under my hand, but God is gracious."

Finally, Tamaes found his voice. "I am Sent to sing."

"Is this evensong?"

He shook his head and quietly explained, "Your heart is safe. I rejoice because you rejoice."

Prissie leaned her head against Tamaes's shoulder and studied his tanned face. The old scar. The gentle gaze. The fond smile. "You're happy for me?"

"I am."

She placed her hand against the armor that guarded his heart. "I love you."

"I know it."

"And I think I'm in love."

Tamaes's smile widened, but all he said was, "Ah."

Every angel in the room was so intent on their reunion that no one noticed how hate glittered in the blue eyes of the cat crouched on the limb of the tree outside Prissie's window.

CHAPTER 21

THE SNOWY DAY

Jedrick addressed the matter on all their minds. "She still has the scroll."

Ethan nodded. "Prissie keeps it on the dresser in her bedroom."

"She hasn't mentioned it to me," Marcus grumbled. "Maybe she forgot about it?"

"No." Pink wings shifted uneasily. "I have seen her gaze resting on it more than once."

"Does she treasure it?" asked Jedrick.

"If anything, I would say Prissie fears it," said Ethan. "She has not touched Blight's scroll since the night it was given."

Marcus asked, "Does it pose a danger?"

Ethan quietly said, "That depends on what it contains."

With a frustrated huff, Marcus snapped, "Anyone know what's written in the thing?"

Silence stretched until Jedrick asked, "Has anyone been Sent to deal with it?"

"Guess we wait and see," grumbled Marcus.

Jedrick inclined his head. "And hope."

Ethan quietly added, "And trust."

Winter made its move, burying Milton county. A foot of snow fell overnight, and the long-range forecast had locals reminiscing about the crazy weather from ten years ago. On the Sunday before Thanksgiving, Ransom woke early. His internal clock was set for pre-dawn, even on his day off.

"For being a morning person. For hand-me-down quilts. For central heating."

Pulling on heavy socks, he padded out of the downstairs bedroom where he crashed each night and skirted a pile of crown molding, boxes of light fixtures, and a line of cabinet doors. Even with as much as they'd accomplished in eight weeks, there was so much left to do.

Ransom's voice echoed slightly off bare walls that still smelled like fresh paint. "For orange juice. For Jayce's potato rolls. For plastic. Never underestimate the power of plastic."

The new furnace kept things comfortable, even though the deep window wells marching along both sides of the old schoolhouse still lacked glass. Heavy plastic let in weak, gray light and kept the wind at bay, but the heavy covering blurred the world beyond. Ransom pulled an apple from the bottom drawer in his fridge and took a bite.

"For progress, in more ways than one. For potluck Sundays. For local produce."

Pomeroy apples grew in his back yard. You couldn't get much more local than that. Wondering if he'd need to shovel himself out, Ransom opened the front door to a blast of frigid air. Snow wasn't so much falling as flying, and a knee-deep wall of the white stuff barred his way.

With a shiver, Ransom backtracked to the bedroom while voicing one more triad of gratefulness. "For owning a snow shovel. For the strength to use it. For thermal underwear."

An hour later, Ransom had fallen into a rhythm. The soft *shuff* as his shovel bit into the drifts. The gritty scrape as he pushed is across icy concrete. The muffled impact of snow on snow as he pitched the shovelful off to one side.

He was almost to the end of his sidewalk when he caught the low rumble of an engine. Turning toward the road, he stepped back when a tractor pushed up his driveway. A wave of snow curled away from the blade of its plow, and in one fell swoop, the rest of Ransom's work was done.

Grandpa Pete touched his hat before backing up for another pass, widening a patch for parking. When he finished, Ransom stepped closer, and Pete Pomeroy cut the engine so they wouldn't need to shout.

"Thanks so much!"

The old man waved off his gratitude. "Been plowing this driveway since before you were born. Since before Jayce was born, for that matter."

"Being neighborly?"

"I like to think we Pomeroys take care of our own."

Unsure how to take that remark, Ransom stammered, "Th-thanks, sir."

With a harrumph, Grandpa Pete said, "I've a message from Jayce. No church today on account of the weather. And Prissie says for you to come on over and spend the day."

Ransom inadvertently finished a third round of gratitude by repeating, "Thanks. I will."

The storm came in unpredictable waves—gusts and gaps. Ransom's cheeks stung from the driven snow, but then the wind would drop off, and he could hear the *crunch* and *squeak* of his boots as he trudged along the single lane left behind by Grandpa Pete's plow.

In a lull, Ransom paused, listening for signs of life. No cars. No birds. Only the whisper of snow as it brushed past his ears and stuck in his scarf. Nature had brought the world to a standstill, and Ransom found peace in the stillness. His thoughts turned to God, then turned to prayers.

He'd been in a rush to answer Prissie's call, his thoughts in a whirlwind of wants and wishes. But as he prayed now, his soul settled. And when the wind whipped up again, their roles were reversed. A confusion of new flakes and blown snow tore at him from every side, but he walked right on through. Calm. Confident.

When Prissie opened the kitchen door, she laughed her good morning, then pressed her hands to his face. "You must be freezing," she said, smoothing her thumbs over his cheeks. She smelled like lemon peel and dish soap. And her cardigan was an inviting shade of pink.

Three seconds. That's all Prissie needed to destroy Ransom's composure. He managed an inarticulate, "Uhh … hmm."

She laughed again and pulled his arm. "Come in and warm up. Breakfast's almost ready."

While ridding himself of boots and coat, Ransom's focus widened enough to notice that he and Prissie weren't alone. Far from it. Her parents sat together at the table, Jayce hiding a rueful smile behind his coffee cup while Naomi cheerfully elbowed him.

Zeke was grinning from ear to ear as he handed Ransom an oven mitt. "Don't let my stuff burn while I'm helping Jude finish his rounds." To Prissie, he added, "Hey, Sis. Do you remember which box the mistletoe is in?"

"Of course I do. I'm the one who did the packing." Prissie calmly retreated to the kitchen counter, which was stacked with everything from glace cherries to white chocolate. “Hurry back and you can haul it down for me.”

Ransom caught the strains of Christmas music coming from the direction of the family room and finally asked, “Are we running a little ahead of schedule this year, or did I sleep through Thanksgiving?”

Prissie said, “Since we’re stranded for the day, we decided to get a head start on the holidays. Still interested in a tour of the attic?”

Elated that she’d remembered the months-old promise, Ransom said, “Sounds good.”

Crouched before a squat half-door at the opposite end of the house from Prissie’s room, Ransom muttered, “How awesome is this?”

“Want me to go first?” Jude asked. “The stairs are steep enough to count as a ladder, so be careful.”

Ransom glanced Prissie’s way. “Ladies first?”

“Not a chance,” she replied.

“Oh. Is this a heights issue?”

Hands on hips, she said, “More of a skirt issue. After you, gentlemen.”

Crawling through the opening, Ransom slowly straightened. Cold air trickled down a short staircase barely wider than his shoulders. The only way to make room for Jude was to start climbing. After weeks of renovation on his own place, Ransom noted several similarities in the old farmhouse’s construction. Stout beams. Brick and boards. Wrapped wires. Antiquated fixtures. Creaking floor.

The attic roof angled so low, Ransom stayed slouched. In the gray light filtering through cobweb-clogged window panes, he made out a maze of boxes, trunks, and mysterious lumps draped in sheets. “Oh. I thought it would be bigger.”

Jude pushed the button of an outdated switch, and a bare bulb lit overhead. “Our attic is elevated a half-story and takes up about a quarter of the top floor. Past this wall, it’s bedrooms.”

Prissie caught up and eased past. Pulling a faded quilt off a stack of boxes, she said, “Judicious, do you mind …?”

“Happy to.”

“Be extra careful with mine, please.”

“I know, Sis. Precious cargo. Handle with care.”

After Jude disappeared downstairs, Ransom asked, “*Your* boxes?”

“My ornament collection.” She opened one lid and lifted out a fragile sphere of sky blue glass swirled and dappled with white.

“Looks like you have enough for a whole tree.”

"Oh, no. These hang in a much safer place. Boys and glass don't mix."

"Tell that to Marcus."

Prissie laughed softly. "He's the exception. In this house, Zeke is the rule."

Jude reappeared, quietly collecting another box, and Ransom asked, "What should I do?"

"I've got this," said Jude. "Sis is going to give you the tour."

Prissie eased past a squat desk and pulled the sheet off a dollhouse. She sighed and smiled. "This brings back memories." She knelt and began rearranging furniture that looked to be handmade.

Ignoring the dust, Ransom sat beside her. "You invited me over to play house?"

Her flat look faded to something fonder. "No. But once upon a time, this was one of my treasures. It's special." Then Prissie's expression turned sad. "And not just to me. This dollhouse was Aunt Ida's before it was mine. Just like my room."

Unsure what to make of her mood shift, Ransom kept his tone light. "This is pretty foreign to me. I never had family traditions or legacies. If I'd known attics were important, I would have asked Derick to work one in."

Prissie pushed tiny chairs around a toy table. "I worried so much about giving up my treasures." She set flat buttons and bottle caps at each place setting. "A year ago, it broke my heart to think that I'll need to move into the spare room of the house across the yard. Which is exactly what Aunt Ida had to do when I was little."

"Not sure I'm following." Ransom asked, "Is there a house swap in the works?"

"Maybe not right away, but yes. We all know that this will be Tad's house." Pushing tiny chairs into position in front of a miniature fireplace, she said, "I hated the idea of giving up my room, even if it was to Juliette."

"But that was a year ago." Choosing his words with care, Ransom asked, "Does that mean you see things differently now?"

"I do see differently." Her gaze flitted to the opposite corner of the attic. "Things I never thought I'd see."

Jude came and went without intruding. After the dollhouse, Prissie showed Ransom more pieces of Pomeroy history. A bird cage. Framed photographs. Embroidered handkerchiefs. A child's tea set. Scrap books dating back fifty, seventy, and ninety years. And from a trunk near the diminishing pile of Christmas boxes, she withdrew a velvet-covered box. "Let's head back down," she said.

Warmth, light, and the smell of popcorn hit Ransom when he emerged from the attic door. Jude offered a hand up, and Ransom's eyebrows lifted.

"Don't tell me Ida's here."

"Oh, no. It's just us." Jude held a finger to his lips and softly said, "That's Auntie's protégé on the piano. Didn't you know Zeke could play?"

"I've heard his off-key organ music." Ransom helped Prissie through the low door. "I seem to remember his friends mentioning a hidden talent."

"Zeke's good. Better than good," said Prissie. "But he usually only plays the keyboard in his room. Momma must have sweet-talked him into dusting off his Christmas repertoire."

Ransom listened with growing amazement. "I'm surprised. Zeke's not shy about showing off his other skills."

"It's hard to explain." Prissie hugged the velvet box to her chest. "He puts a lot of time into it, but he doesn't want attention. I think … piano is how Zeke prays."

"How do you know?" asked Ransom.

She shrugged. "I asked."

"Speaking of asking," said Jude. "What's next, Sis?"

"I'll be hanging ornaments. Will you set up the nativity in the family room?"

Jude nodded. "Yep. First I'll bring you the short ladder."

Ransom raised a hand. "And me?"

"You're my able assistant."

"Is that like trusty minion? Or more of an unpaid lackey thing?"

Prissie breezed past, and he trailed after. Her bedroom looked the same as the last time he'd been invited in. Except for the neat stack of boxes at the foot of her bed. Aquila greeted them from the windowseat with a squeaky meow, and Ransom ambled over to scratch the big, orange cat's ears. For several moments, his purring was the only sound.

Jude dropped off a short stepladder, and Prissie lifted the lid on the first storage box. Spools of ribbon, scissors, and fishing line were followed by a box of white hooks. Prissie murmured, "I might need to add another line this year."

Ransom looked up at the dozen stained glass diamonds currently occupying one corner of Prissie's window. They only accounted for a quarter of the hooks lining the ceiling. "Anything I can do?" he asked.

"Yes, please," she replied distractedly. "You can take the sun-catchers down to make room for these."

He set up the ladder. The second step put him in easy reach, but he hesitated to pull them down willy-nilly. But then he realized that each hook was labeled. Scrutinizing the faint pencil marks, Ransom recognized Marcus's handwriting. Only instead noting colors, Marcus had written names. Ransom tilted his head to the side as he deciphered a very familiar list—Harken, Milo, Baird, Kester,

Abner, Padgett, Koji.

"Huh." Unhooking an emerald green diamond, Ransom asked, "Who's Jedrick?"

Prissie made a funny little squeak.

"You okay?" he asked. At her mute nod, he reached for the next one. "Taweel. Is that even a name? Guess it must be if Mr. Ranger and Mr. Mailman are up here, too."

"They're friends," Prissie said, her voice hitching oddly. "I told you before. Marcus made those to remind me that I have friends."

"Should I be offended that I'm not in the mix?"

She shook her head. "Marcus left himself out, too. It's hard to explain."

"You don't have to." Ransom's brows knit as Prissie alternately blushed and paled.

She kept her gaze firmly fixed on the ornaments she was unwrapping from tissue paper. "I guess they're a little like Zeke's piano playing. Something so personal, it's difficult to share. That's why I keep them in here, where no one else can see."

"Should I be apologizing?"

"No. I wouldn't be sharing all my treasures with you if you weren't among them."

Ransom's heart slammed into overdrive at her quiet admission.

It took him a bit to realize why they were mired in an awkward silence. The piano had stopped, and a moment later, feet thudded up the stairs. Zeke leaned through the door. "Sis! Popcorn balls are ready, and Momma brought out a puzzle. She says to come down once you're done messing with her wedding stuff."

"She didn't say that," retorted Prissie.

"Wedding stuff?" Ransom followed Zeke's gaze to the velvet box on the bed.

Prissie said, "We'll be right down. Now git."

"Gone!" Zeke laughed.

Ransom stepped off the ladder and held up his hands. Sun-catchers dangled from all his fingers. "Where do you want them?"

"Dresser."

"So what's in the box?"

Prissie opened it, lifting out a small crown of gold and pearls. "Do you remember?"

"Sure. From Koji's painting."

She tilted it this way and that. "I used to sneak up into the attic and put this on."

"Another of your special treasures?" he asked as he carefully lined up glass diamonds on the center of her dresser.

"Definitely. For a girl of six, this was proof that I was a princess." With a far-off look in her eyes, she said, "I suppose it's true in a roundabout way."

"Daughter of the King!"

"And Zeke was teasing because Momma wore this tiara on her wedding day. Back when I showed Koji, he quoted verses about Jesus and His angels coming to claim His bride."

"He knows his stuff."

"And then …." Prissie's eyes narrowed in thought, then slowly widened. "He set this on my head and looked me in the eye. And said he'd be at my wedding."

Ransom smirked. "You wouldn't be thinking of marrying me just so you can see him again."

Prissie blushed.

She had such a penitent look in her eyes, Ransom had to laugh. "You are so busted, but I won't hold it against you. In fact, I'd hand letter his invitation if it would get him here faster. Might take him a while to read my scrawl, but hey. You can't beat a personal touch!"

Prissie was staring at him, her forehead scrunched in concentration.

Ransom quickly placed the last glass diamond on her desk, bumping a scroll in the process. "Speaking of Koji, is he still sending you stuff in the mail?"

"Yes, of course."

Holding up the scroll, he asked, "Is this from him?"

"No." She took it from him and stared at it. "A hand-written invitation," she whispered.

"If that's what it takes," he said, unsure why they were whispering.

And suddenly, Prissie flung her arms around him. He wasn't complaining, but she seemed to be trembling. "Hey now, Miss Priss. Are you … crying?"

Prissie tilted her head back to look at the ceiling. Blinking tears from her eyes, she laughed shakily and said, "Thank you, God. I know what to do!"

With a mystified shrug, Ransom added a hearty, "Amen!"

A couple days later, Ransom loaded a fresh tray of cookies in the bakery case, then strolled to the corner of the dining area where Milo and Beau had taken over one of the larger tables. Books and notebooks on Milo's side. Keyboard and tablet on Beau's. "You guys need a refill?

Milo glanced up. "You don't need to serve us, Ransom. It's after hours."

"It's no trouble. Another cappuccino, Beau?"

"Yes, please." He pushed back his notes and stretched. "But I'll get it myself. More tea, Milo?"

"I appreciate your hospitality."

Beau laughed and carried both cups behind the counter, leaving Ransom wondering if he'd missed the punchline of a private joke. He asked, "So what are you guys working on?"

"Next week's lesson," said Milo.

"And plotting our spring themes based on Pastor Bert's preaching schedule." Beau snagged a plate and loaded it with almond scones. Bringing it back, he set the goodies atop a pile of commentaries and backtracked for the drinks.

Ransom noted the titles on some of the more hefty volumes. "Isn't this a little chewy for the age range you guys teach?"

"Nope." Beau set tea and honey in front of Milo and slid into his own chair. "I have to know what I believe before I can teach someone else."

Milo chuckled. "Especially children. Their questions don't always fall in line with lesson plans."

"Any chance you're referring to my dear brother?" Beau pushed out the chair beside his, encouraging Ransom to join them. "Milo's stories about Zeke are unreal."

Folding his hands around his mug of tea, Milo smiled. "I wouldn't exaggerate."

"No need," said Beau. "Zeke is walking hyperbole."

"I learned a lot about teaching from him. He kept me on my toes."

Ransom elbowed Beau and asked, "Weren't you in Milo's class, too?"

"Yes. But there are no wild stories about my escapades."

"Everyone has a story." Milo propped his chin on his hand. "As if I'd forget. You were the quiet boy in the back corner who already knew most of the answers, yet took each lesson to heart. Back then, you were afraid to speak up; now you're a teacher."

"The teacher who can offer fair warning." Beau mimicked Milo's casual posture. "Next year, you'll have your hands full with Bennett, Josiah, and Colin."

"Sounds wonderful," Milo replied mildly.

Beau gazed at the ceiling for a moment. "I do hope Margery stays put. For Colin's sake."

"Amen and amen," murmured Milo.

Ransom's lips quirked, hearing the mailman say something Marcus often did.

A knock at the bakery's front door interrupted them, and Ransom's chair scraped back. Strolling to the door, he lifted a hand and spoke through the glass. "Hey, Margery. We're closed."

"Open up," she ordered. "I want to talk to Prissie."

"Sure, sure." Ransom let her in.

Margery pushed back her hood and loosened her scarf. "Isn't this cozy?" she drawled, looking from Beau to Milo and back again. "You two look right at home."

Beau smiled. "I do live upstairs."

"Oh, I know," she drawled. "You're two of Main Street's most eligible bachelors."

Milo smiled and shook his head, and Beau blinked.

"Well?" Margery shifted her weight. "Is she here?"

"Miss Priss is one pie duty. Pecan and pumpkin are in high demand this week. For obvious reasons."

"Are you bums loitering while Prissie does all the work?"

Ransom knew for a fact that Prissie was sitting at the back counter, leafing through catalogs while keeping an eye on the timer. But he held his peace. "Hang on. I'll let her know you're here."

Margery joined Milo and Beau and pointed to the scones. "Can I?"

Bumping through the kitchen door, Ransom checked the oven timer. Eight minutes and counting. He'd be glad to call it a night. Or at least switch gears. He and Marcus would be working until all hours back at the house. "You have company, Prissie. Margery's here."

"Oh!" she held up a chocolatier's catalog. Tapping the photo of a box of truffles, she said, "We should try these. Blueberry has been really popular this year."

Ransom took it and studied the page, drifting after Prissie. He was only half listening to her and Margery's conversation, until the latter's tone sharpened.

" … on and on about Uncle Pastor and you sharing a birthday. I tried to tell him yours was after Christmas. But he won't give me any peace until I prove him wrong."

"Oh, that," Prissie said, taking a cautious tone. "He's talking about our spiritual birthday. It's coming up the first week of December."

"Are you kidding?" Margery asked, her gaze sliding to Beau. "You guys actually made up a religious holiday for yourself?"

Beau laughed. "Don't act so surprised, Margery. You know our family doesn't need much of an excuse to celebrate."

"And it's hardly a religious event," Prissie said. "If the ice on the pond is thick enough, we were leaning toward a skating party. And Colin's invited."

"We should build a snowman while we're at it," Ransom said.

Prissie's surprised look tilted toward something softer. She nodded and said, "That would be fun."

"I guess that's all right, then," Margery said. "Hey, if I can't be there, could he sleep over or something. I could do my Christmas shopping while he's out from underfoot."

"You know he's always welcome," Prissie assured.

Margery's lips twisted into something close to a smile. "You actually mean that."

"You know I do."

She shook her head. "You're a weird bunch. But he likes you."

Ransom waggled his eyebrows. "Like mother, like son."

Prissie giggled. "Of course Margery likes us. We have scones!"

"Iced coffee, right?" asked Beau, hopping up to get her something to drink.

Margery grumbled some, but she stuck around for a second scone.

Thanksgiving with the Pomeroys was nothing new for Ransom. Being friends with Prissie, he and Marcus had been invited over every year. A few others shared the standing invitations, like Timothy, Milo, and Padgett. This year, the park ranger had brought along a kid with long black braids. Ransom hadn't caught the whole story, but the boy was apparently a relative who was in town for the holidays. And predictably, he latched onto Prissie.

Snow didn't put a stop to the family's annual football game in the side yard. Grandpa Pete's plow took care of most of the accumulation, leaving snowbank-style bleachers on either end of the field. Zeke groomed the rest with a snow blower.

As soon as everyone could budge after the midday meal, they bundled up and chose sides. Zeke was quarterback for the Young Bucks, which was pretty much every unmarried male over the age of fifteen. Jayce led the Dads and Lads, which included the remaining men and boys, plus Mel, who excelled at team play and mercilessly teased her young brothers-in-law.

The ball snapped, and she shouted, "All right, boys! Once more into the fray!"

Zeke groaned. "Theater majors. What're ya gonna do?"

"Avoid at all costs," said Beau. "Mel plays for keeps."

"I thought she was pregnant," said a wary Timothy.

Jude said, "That's never stopped her before."

Ransom found that the game had changed since he was away. Back then, the toddlers went down for naps. Now, whenever he caught a pass, he had seven-year-olds wrapped around his legs. Chugging toward the goal line was like wading through molasses.

But the Young Bucks held their own. Zeke had confidence, and Jude had some serious reach. Milo was fast, and Marcus proved he could jump over your average seven-year-old.

On the sidelines, Juliette sat on her grandmother's lap. "Go, go, Mommy!" she cheered, earning a double-wave from her mittened mother.

"Good catch, Nat!" Prissie called.

"You did good, too, Uncle Grandpa!" Ida added in teasing tones.

Mr. Pomeroy grinned at his little sister, then called for a huddle.

Ransom's attention veered back to Prissie, who'd bundled up with Asher. Padgett's guest had politely declined all invitations to join the game. Maybe it was the dark hair or the solemn gaze. Or maybe it was Prissie's peaceful expression. Either way, Ransom couldn't shake the impression that the kid was a lot like Koji. "How'd they get so close so fast?" he murmured.

Timothy overheard. "Kinda obvious, isn't it? They're friends."

"They just met."

"Doesn't matter." Timothy pulled off a glove to scratch his nose. "Haven't you ever met someone and stuff clicked? You skip over all the awkward beginnings and *be* friends."

Ransom quietly asked, "Is that how it was with Emmie?"

"Nope. Zeke."

"And me?" Ransom asked, half teasing.

Timothy snorted. "No resemblance. You shoved your way in and refused to back off."

"As long as I'm *in*."

"More like *in for it*."

Ransom wasn't sure what Timothy meant until the Pomeroys straggled inside and Mr. Pomeroy's hand dropped heavily onto his shoulder.

Guiding him firmly into the kitchen, Jayce said, "I need a few minutes of your time."

"Sure." As soon as he was through the door, it was obvious that he wasn't being called upon to assemble sandwiches. All the Pomeroy men waited at the table, seated in age order from Grandpa Pete down to Jude. Except Timothy had been included.

"Sit here," Jayce said, indicating the chair at the end of the table.

"Thanks." Ransom scanned the group. Tad seemed amused, but Beau's gaze was more sympathetic. Jude's expression could be defined as thoughtful, but Zeke and Timothy had that whole wicked gleam thing going for them. Clearing his throat, Ransom asked, "What's up?"

Taking the seat across from Ransom's, Mr. Pomeroy said, "I told you we'd be having a talk soon."

Ransom sat a little straighter. Was this some kind of trial by committee? He was well aware that Prissie was Jayce's only daughter and that everyone assembled cared about her future happiness. But so did he. So why the inquisition? He pointed at Timothy. "If this is about that, why's Timothy here?"

Zeke said, "We nominated him to stand in for Neil. He'd definitely give you a hard time if he was here."

Grandpa Pete harrumphed. "I only have one thing to say. If you do anything to compromise my daughter's reputation, I'll run you off our property with George."

"Who's George?" asked Ransom.

Jude whispered, "Tractor."

Tad spoke up. "If you break Priss's heart, I'll hoist you into the barn rafters by your belt loops."

"And I'll pitch you in the pig sty!" Zeke said cheerfully.

"Do we have a well?" asked Timothy.

"Yep," said Jude.

"Can we throw him in?"

"Best use the pond, Mr. Grable," said Grandpa Pete. "It'd be a shame to sully the drinking water."

"Kinda not feeling welcomed into the fold here." Ransom leaned forward, hands outspread. "Guys, you know me!"

"We *thought* we knew you," Zeke countered, playing up the drama.

Beau chuckled. "It's simple, really. If Prissie will have you, we'll take you. If not, we'll take you down."

Everyone started talking at once, and Jayce raised his hands for silence. Fixing Ransom with a stern look, he said, "Ransom Pavlos, it's come to my attention that you might wish to date my daughter."

"No, sir. I want to marry your daughter."

Grandpa Pete harrumphed. "Honorable intentions."

"Hard worker. Good provider," said Tad.

Beau added, "Longtime friend."

Jayce said, "But he kept all this a secret for longer than I like."

Zeke laughed. "You didn't notice, Dad. That's not the same as being sly."

"Sly?" Prissie marched through the kitchen door and exclaimed, "Ida was right! She said you and Grandpa Pete did the same thing to Uncle Lo when he started making sheep's eyes at her."

"It's a father's duty to …"

"Oh, honestly!" she snapped, grabbing Ransom's arm and dragging him to safety.

Before they were out of earshot, Beau raised his voice. "That settles that! Sis took him."

Chapter 22

The Better Offer

"Sent?" A slim angel with long silver hair peered down his nose at Asher. "He says he's Sent?"

"Quite adamantly."

"But you can't confirm it?"

"No, sir," sighed Padgett. "Which is why I wanted your advice."

Icy gray eyes blinked several times. "Padgett, I'm not in the business of Sending angels."

"And yet you have guided many apprentices."

"You then. Asher was it?"

"Yes, sir."

"Not you, too! Call me Abner."

"Yes, Abner," Asher replied.

"Are you Sent?"

"I am."

Abner turned to Padgett. "He says he's Sent."

"Yes, sir. That's why we're here."

"Oh? Was he Sent to me?"

Asher vigorously shook his head.

Padgett shifted from foot to foot. "Was I ever this precocious?"

"Never." Patting his former apprentice's shoulder, Abner said, "You were an obedient little tuft of reliability."

"Tuft?" asked Asher.

Abner explained, "Early on, Padgett's hair was unusually short for members of our order."

Asher gazed up at his mentor. "May I call you Tuft?"

At Padgett's blank look, Abner stepped in. "Best not, Asher. Your mentor deserves an appellation of surpassing dignity, symmetry, and irony. If I might presume to make a suggestion, why not call him *sir*?"

Everyone pitched in with necessary chores around the farm, then lingered into the evening hours. Laughter erupted at regular intervals from the kitchen, where a card game was underway. A quieter group had taken over a corner of the family room, working on a new jigsaw puzzle. Grandpa Pete and Padgett had the chess board set up over by the wood-burning stove. Tad dozed on one couch, and Ransom had fallen asleep in the recliner. So for the moment, Prissie had Asher all to herself.

They nestled together on the loveseat, flipping through one of the family photo albums. "There, see?" Prissie murmured. "This was at Christmastime."

Asher studied the group photo closely. "He is happy."

"Yes. You can't see it, but Koji's holding my hand." Prissie felt Asher's hand slip into hers and smiled. "He was so pleased to be in a picture, we took more after this. See? Here he is again."

"Pajamas." In the picture, Koji and a much younger Zeke and Jude sat in front of a blanket fort. Asher sighed, "I wish to try pajamas."

"Your sweater looks very nice," she said. "Did Padgett help you choose?"

"He did." Asher plucked at the cable knit. "This pattern is worthy of Weavers."

Prissie flipped to a picture of her, Ransom, Marcus, and Koji studying at the kitchen table. She wasn't smiling. Back then, it had been so hard to smile.

Pointing to a figure in the background, Asher said, "His eyes are open."

"Beau's?" Thinking back, Prissie nodded. "He knew a little by then. Although I don't think he realized yet that we had an angel on our refrigerator."

Asher's head popped up, and a moment later, Beau strolled into the family room.

"There you are, Asher," he said. "Milo wanted me to let you know that he's doing storytime upstairs."

Prissie nudged the boy. "It's okay if you want to join the other kids. Try something new."

"No, thank you." Asher moved even closer to Prissie, making room for

Beau. "I am where I belong."

Accepting the seat, he offered his hand. "I know there are a lot of us to remember. I'm Prissie's brother Beau."

Asher clasped his hand and held on. "I like you."

"Likewise, young sir," Beau replied easily.

"You have been Prissie's comforter and friend. Well done."

Beau's brows knit, but then his gaze locked with Prissie's. "Oh," he breathed. "Oh, I see."

"Yes." Asher let go and leaned into Prissie's side. "Your eyes are open."

"Again, Sis?"

Prissie wrapped her arm around Asher and whispered, "Amazing, isn't it?"

"If that's the case, young sir, may I ask why you've joined us?"

"I am Sent."

"For how long?" asked Beau.

"I come and go. I am a visitor." Patting the photo album on Prissie's lap, he said, "I cannot stay as Koji did."

Beau asked, "Do you know why you were Sent?"

Asher shook his head. "God knows, and His purposes will become clear."

Prissie would have left it at that, but her brother pressed for more.

"Then may I ask why you shared your secret with me?"

The young Caretaker placed his hand on Beau's arm. "Because you will need me."

"When?"

Asher's eyebrows lifted. "God knows, and His purposes …

" … will become clear," Beau finished with a chuckle. "So be it. I am in His hands."

On the night before her spiritual birthday, Prissie sat up late. The house was packed in anticipation of tomorrow's festivities, so it had taken a while for everyone to settle down. Nat, Josiah, Bennett, and Colin had claimed the bunk beds. Beau had taken Zeke's spot in with Jude because Jasper, Timothy, and Zeke were over at Ransom's.

In the quiet, Prissie waited and wondered. Several days had passed without much angelic interaction. She hadn't spoken with Ethan since the night he'd brought Tamaes to her. The past two weeks had hardly been empty, but the silence was beginning to echo in her soul.

Gazing at the shadowy ornaments hanging over her head, Prissie reminded herself of all the reasons she had to be glad. Tomorrow was a special milestone. She'd been wanting to skate. Padgett had accepted their invitation to his "nephew," so she'd see Asher again. And Ransom would join the party after the Saturday rush at the bakery. All good things.

But now that Prissie had a plan, she was restless to put it into motion; however, she was also second-guessing herself. Maybe her idea wasn't good enough for God to use. Was this His way of closing a proverbial door? Prissie wished she could ask someone.

While Milo and Marcus weren't avoiding her, she was never alone with them. If only Ethan would check in. But as much as Prissie wanted to call out for him, she kept her mouth firmly shut. When the time was right, an angel would be Sent. They came and went at God's whim, not hers.

So she prayed.

Her thoughts touched on each member of her family, then meandered to Colin and Margery. Prissie offered a general prayer for the strength and courage of the guardian angels in their Hedge. Then for Ethan and the other members of Tycho's Flight. Name by name, she counted them off on her fingers … and came up one short. Trying again, she was still missing one of the eight cherubim.

Something flashed outside, and Prissie checked the sky. Golden light dipped back into view, and she pressed her hand to the window in a breathless greeting.

Marcus landed lightly on the steep slope of the roof and gestured for permission to enter. At her nod, he sprang into the air; a few moments later, he dropped through her ceiling. "Yo."

"Is something wrong?" she asked. "What's happening?"

"Take it easy, kiddo. It's a quiet night." He waved at her perch in the windowseat. "I was stretching my wings and spotted you. What's up?"

"Besides me?"

Marcus dropped to the floor, stretching out his legs as he slouched against her bed, managing to look comfortable despite wearing armor. The drape of his luminous wings took up most of the floor space. "Take your time. I won't be missed until baker's hours."

Prissie hesitated. "Were you Sent?"

"Not like you mean. But I don't need to be Sent to a friend. Or friend*s*." He glanced toward the door and asked, "That you, Boaz?"

With a tentative rap, it opened to reveal a wide-eyed Beau. "I saw a light under Sis's door. And it felt … heavenly."

"Good eyes." Marcus crooked a finger. "Good timing."

"Am I intruding?"

"Get in here," said Prissie. "I could use the company."

"Thanks," he murmured, quietly closing the door behind him. Beau's eyes remained fixed on Marcus. "Seeing you like this brings back memories. And worries. Is there anything I can do?"

Prissie stirred. "Is it okay if I show Beau the scroll?"

Marcus's gaze snapped to her face, but his voice remained soft. "You've never mentioned any scroll."

"But you know about it, don't you?"

"Yep. Known for a while now." Marcus reached over and tapped the side of her dresser. "Figured you'd mention it when you were ready."

Beau picked his way along the edge of the room and located the rolled parchment. Marcus helpfully lifted his wings and increased the wattage. For several moments, the scroll was forgotten as Beau admired the cherub's display. "Still wish I had a camera."

Marcus snorted. "Focus, Boaz. You're holding something that's potentially dangerous."

He blinked at the scroll, then sniffed lightly. Nose crinkling in distaste, Beau asked, "Who wrote this?"

"A demon," Marcus said flatly.

"Sis," Beau said slowly. "Why would you be in contact with a demon?

"It's a long story, but it's not like I wanted his attention," said Prissie. "He chose me."

"When?"

Before Prissie could answer, Marcus said, "Since summer. And it's *not* her fault. But I'd like to know why she's been holding onto that scroll since October."

Beau put the question more directly. "Sis, why would you hang onto his words?"

Prissie's shrug was more of a squirm. How could she explain such an obvious compromise? Yes, the writing was Blight's, but the story was her friend's. Yes, Prosper had become Blight, but she understood his affection for Koji, sin-twisted as it had become. But to crumple the scroll or cast is aside would be like saying she didn't care about Koji. So she'd kept it. She finally admitted, "I kept it because he wrote about Koji."

Tilting the scroll toward the light, Beau took the time to scan the message. He shot an incredulous look at Prissie, then reread before saying, "On the surface, this reads like a love letter. But it's hard to tell if this demon is enamored of Koji or my sister. I'm uncomfortable with the implications." Looking to Marcus, he asked, "Is Prissie leading him on?"

Marcus shook his head. "I think it's pretty clear where Prissie's heart lies, but that won't stop Blight from developing a case of false hope."

"Prissie," Beau sighed, setting the scroll aside. "I wish you'd trusted me with this sooner."

She looked away, stung by his disappointment. "I'm sorry."

Beau took two steps and pulled her into a clumsy hug. "I'm not blaming you, Sis. He exploited your biggest weakness. Koji is precious to you."

Hauling her hurt into line, she nodded. "Keeping Blight's scroll was probably a mistake, but I learned from it. Will you listen to my idea? I think I have a plan."

"For dealing with this demon?" Beau joined her on the windowseat, then gestured to Marcus. "Shouldn't we leave that to the experts?"

"So far, the experts haven't had much luck," Marcus said. "Go ahead, Prissie. I want to hear your idea."

She pointed to the scroll. "Blight's gift tells us what he treasures—words, beautiful writing, and the memory of friendship."

"No doubt," Marcus said. "Even Fallen, he still acts like an Observer."

Prissie dared to hope she was on the right track. "I think Koji would be able to lure him out. Blight wouldn't be able to resist."

"One problem," said Marcus. "Koji's not Sent to us. And he won't be."

"I wouldn't *want* to lead him into danger," she quickly assured. "But what if I asked him to give me a scroll?"

Sitting forward, elbows on knees, Marcus scrutinized Prissie's face. "You want Koji to write a letter to his old friend."

"Yes." Prissie's heart fluttered under the cherub's intense gaze. Marcus might spend his days creating delicate works of art out of colored glass, but he was an angel of war. And it showed. "And if I tell Blight about it ..."

" ... he'd do anything to get his hands on it."

Prissie nodded, but Beau raised his hand. "I foresee a small problem."

"Yeah?" asked Marcus.

"The part where this demon will do *anything* to get his hands on it." Beau's expression was grim. "Doesn't that put Prissie in a great deal of danger?"

"There's a bunch of us willing to keep her safe."

Some of the tension left Beau's shoulders. "Yourself included?"

"You know it," Marcus said. "So let's get word to Koji."

"I've been wanting to!" Prissie exclaimed. "But how am I supposed to get a message to him?"

Beau chuckled. "I've got this one." Pulling his phone from his pocket, her tech-enamored brother flicked through his contacts list and tapped the screen. "I just happen to be best friends with a divine Messenger."

He set the phone against Prissie's ear, and she could hear a low tone. It was already ringing. And then Milo's voice spoke in her ear. *"Beau?"*

"N-no. It's me," Prissie stammered. "But Beau's here with me. And

Marcus."

"Miss Priscilla," Milo said, his tone calm yet concerned. *"What do you need?"*

"Can you get a message to Koji for me?"

After a moment's hush, Milo answered, *"Yes. Prepare your letter, and I'll personally place it into his hands."*

Even with Beau's prayers and the comforting curl of Marcus's wings around her shoulders, Prissie had struggled with her letter to Koji. Her neatest writing paled in comparison to an archivist's elegance. There was no way she could fill the empty spaces with flourishes or artwork. And this was her first letter to him. After ten years of his faithfulness, why had she never written? Wasn't it selfish to only reach out now that she needed a favor?

Heart in a bind, stomach in knots, Prissie framed her request in plain words. Even so, by the time she'd finished, her cheeks were wet and tiredness made her head ache. At breakfast, she was lightheaded and left all the speechifying to Beau.

"Sis and I are close in age."

"Like me and Bennett?" Josiah interrupted.

Beau chuckled. "Not quite. But right now your Aunt Prissie and I are both twenty-four."

Colin's forkful of eggs paused halfway to his mouth. "You're twins?"

"Almost. Sis turns twenty-five in January, but I'll stay twenty-four. We're only the same age for seventy days. When I was little, I didn't really understand. I wanted to stay twins for always."

Prissie poured herself some coffee while the questions kept coming. Beau was incredibly patient with children. With anyone, really. God had given her bookish brother a pastor's heart, and she was proud of the man he'd become.

Jude joined her at the kitchen counter and nudged her arm. "Okay there, Sis? That's your second cup of coffee."

"I'm fine, Judicious. There's just so much happening, I had a hard time falling asleep."

He studied her face for a moment, then nodded. "Maybe you should join Juliette for naptime later."

With a burst of affection for her baby brother, Prissie brushed her fingers against the back of his hand. "I might just do that."

Beau was saying, "But my mother is a wise lady."

"Marmee?" asked Juliette.

"Yes, your Marmee is my Momma. And she had a good idea."

Prissie's attention sharpened, if only because she'd so recently shared her own good idea.

Beau met her gaze across the room and smiled warmly. "Even though I couldn't go back and change my birthday to match my sister's, we could share a different kind of birthday."

"Your spiritual birthday," Nat said wisely.

"That's right. We both prayed to let Jesus know how much we love Him on the same day. He saved us, so today, Sis and I are celebrating our spiritual twinship. Our party is how we're telling God thank you."

"A thank you party?" Bennett asked.

Momma said, "We Pomeroys celebrate all kinds of things. Why not a party to thank God?"

"It's a good idea!" said Josiah. "Especially on account of me loving skating!"

"Me, too," said Prissie. "Let's have a good day."

"Starting after a good breakfast," Grandma Nell interjected. "Who needs more?"

While the kids ate, the conversation rotated around the table to the other adults. Momma shared about when she first heard about Jesus, and Grandma Nell told funny stories about church camp. Even Grandpa Pete took a turn, telling about growing up on this very same farm with a whole passel of fussing sisters.

Good memories. Embarrassing moments. Tricky choices. And shining through every story, a thread of faithfulness. God's toward them. Theirs to God. Prissie loved her parents, her grandparents, and the legacy they lovingly passed along.

About the time Beau and Prissie had all the kids fitted for skates, Marcus arrived on foot. "Yo."

"Will you be on the ice with us?" Prissie asked.

"Yep. If I can borrow gear."

So while Beau and Jude escorted the youngsters down to where Tad was already grooming the pond, Prissie led Marcus back toward the barn. She asked, "Is everything all right?"

Marcus shoved his hands deep in his jacket pockets and stared into the sky. "Better than usual. You've about tripled the Hedge with this party of yours."

"Good," she breathed.

A car pulled into their driveway, and Marcus smirked. "And they tip the scales into the over-abundant category."

Padgett parked in front of the barn, and Asher bounced out of the vehicle, only to pause midway through his rush to get to Prissie. The young Caretaker lifted his foot, then placed it on the ground, took a couple of steps, then peered over his shoulder.

Marcus asked, "Strange to be leaving footprints in this realm?"

"Very," Asher replied seriously.

Padgett said, "Good morning, miss. Thank you for your kind invitation."

"I was about to be fitted for skates," said Marcus. "Care to join me?"

Asher grabbed Marcus's hand, but Padgett said, "I'll greet your brothers and find a place to watch."

"Tad and Zeke set up benches last night, so there are places to sit," said Prissie. "We'll join you shortly."

In the barn's tack room, a ticking space heater made jackets optional. It had been many years since the narrow room had been needed for harnesses and saddles, but the smell of oil and leather remained, thanks in large part to the collection of ice skates that hung in rows overhead.

Marcus remarked, "There are more than last time I was in here."

"Grandma Nell and Momma watch for them at thrift stores and garage sales, and Grandpa Pete fixes them up good as new," Prissie explained. "He likes to keep everything ready for his grands and great-grands."

Asher spotted the rows of snowshoes lining the far wall. "Koji sings of snow and ice, joy and danger."

Prissie gently tugged the boy's glossy black braid. "After today, you'll have memories of your own. Ice skating. Snowman building. And knowing the boys, a snowball fight."

"Will you fight?" Asher asked.

"No." She pulled off his boot and measured his foot. "But I'll show you how to make snow angels."

"Thank you," he breathed. "Koji warned me that skating is difficult."

"At least you know that going in. But I'll stick close and keep you on your feet." Marcus boosted his young teammate up onto the workbench and tweaked his braid. "Can't get over the makeover. You look like a mini-Padgett."

"He is meant to be my uncle."

"Definitely seeing a resemblance," Marcus said. "But green suits you better."

Asher tipped his head to the side. "And you are most yourself with gold."

"Yep. Hey, Prissie, let me finish up here."

"No need. This won't take long."

"I've been doing this for the runts since forever," he insisted, taking a pair of child-sized skates from her hands. "Besides, Ransom's here."

"This early? How do you know?"

He shrugged. "I have connections. Go to him."

She made it outside in time to see Zeke's taillights leave the driveway. Ransom was halfway up the sidewalk, a stack of pastry boxes in his arms. "Hello!" she called, waving. "You're early."

"Your brother insisted," he answered. "Be right there."

While he vanished inside the house, Prissie crossed to the plank fence beside the barn. The spot afforded an excellent view of the frozen duck pond and its red bridge. Beau was leading Juliette by the hand, and Jude skated backward, Colin in tow. The other boys had more experience and zipped back and forth under the bridge. Tad and Padgett chatted on one of the benches along the pond's edge, but they weren't the only watchful eyes.

Ethan sat on the bridge's rail, flanked by two purple-winged cherubim.

Prissie relaxed against the fence and breathed a prayer of thanks. After such a long lull, it was reassuring to see him again. For an instant, her conscience pricked. Was she placing too much importance on the presence of angels in her life? But no. Prissie was quite sure she'd been missing him the same way she missed any of her friends. He was a gift from God that would last forever.

But it was almost time for goodbye.

From the start, Ethan had told her his protection was a temporary thing. Prissie understood that when this mess with Blight was settled, he'd be Sent from her side, and everything would return to normal. Glimpses of pink wings would be rare. Like the members of Jedrick's Flight, he and his Flightmates would become a treasure waiting for her in heaven.

"I don't like goodbyes," she whispered.

Heaving a sigh, she pushed the thought aside. Today was special, and she wanted to make sure everyone had fun. Prissie turned her attention back to the skaters only to find that Ethan was no longer lounging on the rail with Yannis and Garrick. He stood on the rail, tension radiating from his outspread wings.

Ethan's gaze locked on hers, but he didn't budge from his position. It was as if he wanted to fly to her side, but his feet were stuck. Prissie's confusion changed to a sick sense of dread when she heard a low growl. Whipping around, she faced a strange dog. Head low, hackles raised, the blue-eyed dog inched forward.

"Prosper?" she whispered.

The dog's snarl vanished, and its tail swayed.

"You're not supposed to be here," Prissie muttered dazedly. "There are Guardians everywhere."

Slinking toward the fence, the animal fixed its eyes on the pond. Laughter hissed against Prissie's ears, and Blight's disembodied voice chanted, *"Itty.*

Bitty. Bitter. Bite."

"No!" Before the stray could climb between the planks, Prissie pushed it aside with her boot. "Stay away from them! Go away!"

He skipped backward, turned tail and trotted away. But she didn't get the impression that she'd scared him off. For all she knew, he was circling around the barn to come at the kids from the other direction. So Prissie chased after him.

Ethan caught up to her at the far corner of the barn. "Wait!"

"He's here!" she gasped. "He's inside some poor dog."

He gripped her shoulders. "Prissie, I know. But while I am Sent to you, I am not Sent after him."

"But if I go, you can follow, right?"

"That is true," Ethan said, voice low and tense. "But our plan did not include allowing Blight to lure you from our midst."

Prissie touched his arm. "But he's in the open. Isn't this the chance your Flight's been waiting for?"

Ethan let his arms fall to his sides. "Garrick and Yannis are with me. They will follow if you choose to pursue this enemy."

"I need to try!" she begged.

He stepped back with a nod, but before she could follow, Ethan caught her coat sleeve. "Be wary. He is clever."

Prissie accepted that with a nod, then hurried to follow the animal tracks veering off into the orchard. All the while, she reminded herself that she wasn't alone. She didn't need to be afraid. She was safe. She could do this.

The laughter and chatter coming from the direction of the skating pond soon faded. Prissie slowed as a sense of isolation settled around her. She found herself stepping with slow care. Hand pressed over her thudding heart, she took deep breaths. "How much farther?" she whispered.

Ethan only pointed with his drawn sword.

A snarl ripped through the air, and she jumped back, knees shaking. When the growl changed to doggish yips of pain, the only thing that kept her on her feet was Ethan's hold on her arm. The sudden silence was almost a relief. Sagging against her companion, Prissie quavered, "Wh-what happened?"

"This trail ends in death."

Prissie crept through the next row of trees, brushing aside grasping branches until she spotted a dark lump. Blood streaked the churned snow. The stray dog was no longer a threat. But he was also no longer a hiding place. "Where did Blight go?"

"Not far," Ethan murmured.

Any of the trees. A passing bird. A hibernating animal. Maybe Blight could even invade the snow at their feet. Prissie swallowed against the queasiness in her stomach. She was safe with Ethan. Wasn't she?

"Dear ones. Drear ones." Blight's voice skipped around, jumping from tree to tree. "Come away. Come and stay."

Ethan's mouth pressed into a grim line as their quarry stepped into the open.

Prissie edged closer to the Guardian and glanced at the sky. Where were Yannis and Garrick?

Blight's wary expression dawned into beautiful delight. "Are you here for her, friend?"

"This child of God is under my watch-care," Ethan answered stonily. "You cannot touch her."

As the demon strolled closer and reached out, Prissie could feel Ethan's tension. But he didn't do anything. Prissie couldn't understand. Why wasn't he *doing* something?

Blight didn't actually touch her, but his hand slipped through the air beside her face in a near-caress. "Hold her. Scold her," he crooned. "Blame her. Tame her. Tell her why there is peace between you and me."

Ethan's eyes blazed, but he didn't say a word.

Stepping back, the demon bowed at the waist and spread his arms wide. "He is not Sent to me."

Prissie's eyes widened. Ethan had said as much earlier. He'd tried to warn her, but she hadn't listened.

Blight continued, "Were *you* Sent, pretty Prissie?"

"Yeah. She was." Marcus dropped from the sky, landing beside Ethan and Prissie in a rush of golden wings. Armor and holy anger. Blade and blazing eyes. Turning his back on the enemy, Marcus asked, "You need me to repeat myself, kiddo?"

Prissie gaped at him, shaken by her friend's rarely-seen intensity. "M-me?"

"Ransom's here. Go to him." With a trace of something kinder, Marcus added, "Thus spake the cherub."

He drew his blade and leveled it at Blight, and Prissie fled toward home. Tears blurred her vision, turning the world into dark and white. But she didn't really need to see in order to stumble in a straight line. Eventually, she needed to cut across the rows of trees, and that's when she ran into trouble.

One thin branch slapped across her face, making her cheek sting. In flinching away from the sudden pain, she lost her hat to another branch. And in backing up to rescue it, she snagged her hair. Within a minute, she was hopelessly tangled. Surrendering to a sob, she waited limply for Ethan to come to her rescue. Then she could apologize.

The expected sound of footsteps came with an unexpected voice. “Prissie?”

Turning as far as the snarl of twigs allowed, Prissie saw Ransom. She doubted anyone could have duplicated the gymnastics his eyebrows went through. But then he was at her side and babbling something about missing persons, tracking skills, rabid dogs, and answered prayers. Keeping up wasn’t possible, so she waited numbly for the verbal onslaught to end.

“Hey.” Ransom pocketed his gloves and gently touched the top of her head. “Hey, it’s all right. I’m here. Hang on a sec, and I’ll untangle you.”

She dabbed at her nose, then fished a packet of tissues out of her pocket. But the minute she cleaned herself up, fresh tears began to fall.

Ransom asked, “You okay, Miss Priss?”

All she managed was a tiny shake of her head.

“M’kay,” he sighed. “I’ll try to be quick. Can I dismantle this whatever-you-call-it?”

She shrugged, and he began to steal the pins from her hair. Ransom kept right on talking, but not to her. True to form, he had switched to prayer.

He thanked God for sending him to her side and admitted feeling like a total fumble-fingers. “I’m used to putting the knots in, Lord. Not coaxing them out. Is this what they call poetic justice? Maybe we’ll be able to laugh about this later, but right now there seem to be a lot of tears. And you know how Prissie’s tears do a number on me. Any help You can offer is much appreciated.”

Dropping the hairpins into his pocket, Ransom unraveled the thick coil of her braid, teasing strands free. Little by little, he pulled Prissie loose, then tugged her away from the low-hanging branches. She stepped straight into his embrace and hid her face against his shoulder.

“Want to talk?”

Prissie shook her head.

“Fair enough.” Undoing the last of her braids, he took to playing with her hair. He threaded his fingers through its length as if searching for stray twigs and tangles.

Clinging to the comfort he offered, she relaxed enough to notice more details. Like Ethan’s quiet presence a short distance away. The Guardian’s relaxed stance communicated safety. And she caught a distinctly familiar smell, like honey and coriander, sweetness and light. Without a doubt, the scent was coming from Ransom.

Unable to hide her surprise, Prissie looked up and asked, “Why do you smell like heaven?”

Ransom’s eyebrows vaulted toward his stocking cap, but he answered seriously. “I was baking all morning. It’s this thing I do—baking. Maybe you’re hungry?”

"Oh. No thanks," she mumbled, feeling increasingly foolish. "But it's nice. The smell."

"Good to know."

Prissie's breath caught. Up until now, only Tamaes had ever looked at her with so much love. Did she deserve this much goodness?

"Ready to go back?"

"Do I look like I've been crying?"

"Afraid so." He kissed her nose and said, "We can walk slowly."

They'd barely taken three steps when Marcus jogged up, coming from the direction of the barn. "You found her."

"Yeah, she totally pulled an Absalom. Took forever to get the tree to let her go."

Prissie stared determinedly at the ground, too ashamed and embarrassed to meet Marcus's eyes. But he forced his way into her personal space.

Dropping to one knee in front of her, he looked up into her flushed face. "You okay?"

"Mostly."

After a small pause, he asked, "We okay?"

"Is there any reason we wouldn't be?" she countered, so afraid of his answer. The mistake was hers. Would he blame her for being foolish?

"Nope." Reaching up to give her hand a squeeze, Marcus included Ransom in the renewal of an old promise. "Long haul."

CHAPTER 23

THE FINISHING TOUCH

Milo stepped into Koji's alcove and inadvertently kicked a scroll. The entire floor was littered with rough drafts and spattered paper. Crouching to pick up a crumpled section of parchment, he found blue-lined notepaper underneath. Undoubtedly a relic from Koji's school days.

"I haven't seen a mess on this level since the last time I was called up by Gabriel," Milo announced.

Koji finished a line, set aside his pen, and carefully capped his ink before turning. "The prince of heaven who serves the malakim?"

"That's the guy," Milo said, reaching for another page. "He has an archivist's love for records, but none of your orderliness."

Swinging his legs around, Koji hopped off his bench and dropped to his knees on the thick rug. He gathered up more of the castoffs, hugging them to his chest.

Milo asked, "Did you have trouble finding the words?"

"I have always known the words. Putting them in the right order took many tries."

"Are you satisfied?"

Koji hesitated. Putting his clutter on a low table, he anchored them with a large key, then returned to his desk. Dark eyes skimmed the page, and then he carried it to Milo. "I will be satisfied if you are satisfied."

"If you're certain …?" Milo checked.

"Indeed."

Surrendering what pages he'd managed to collect, Milo sat on the rug and turned his attention to the lengthy missive. He finished with a sigh of mingled sorrow and satisfaction. "It's good."

Koji nodded and held out a length of yellow ribbon. "Then it is finished."

Ransom fell asleep in the passenger seat on the way home from Porter's Farm and Home. But a hand on his shoulder and a shake roused him enough to yawn and stretch. "Sorry, Beau. I'm not much for company after double shifts."

"You've earned a rest, though it may still be a while in coming." Beau leaned forward, hugging the steering wheel as he peered out the windshield. "Looks like we caught a pair of Christmas elves at work."

All thoughts of weariness were quickly replaced by wonder. "Is that Tad?"

"On the ladder," Beau acknowledged. "And wherever our big-big brother goes, Jude is sure to follow."

The tall teen waved as Ransom emerged from the vehicle.

"We were hoping to be done before now, but it took a little longer than we thought. But I promise, we're almost done," Jude said, rambling a little in obvious embarrassment. "Umm. Surprise?"

"You put lights on my house?" Every window—upstairs and down—was neatly outlined in white lights.

Jude nodded. "Tad put in the hooks when we were taking the plastic down."

"How long have you been planning this?" Ransom asked.

"Since the Thanksgiving inquisition."

Tad climbed down from the ladder and offered a hand. "Sorry to intrude on your evening."

"No need to apologize for a gift this amazing!" Ransom countered. "But why would you guys go to all the trouble. You can't even see my place from the road."

Jude and Tad traded a look.

"What?" Ransom asked, glancing at Beau for help. "Am I missing something?"

Tad explained, "This whole scheme was Grandpa Pete's idea. Once he caught wind about your windows, he made us his minions."

"Grandpa Pete's a romantic," Jude added.

"Thoughtful," agreed Tad.

Ransom stared blankly at the house. "Since when are white lights romantic?"

"Go inside," said Tad, who turned back to the ladder.

Jude added, "Don't mind us. We'll be done and gone soon."

Beau steered Ransom toward the house and said, "Trust us, you'll like this. And Prissie will love it."

Inside was cool and hushed, and Ransom automatically reached for the lights so he could turn up the thermostat.

Catching his wrist, Beau said, "Not so fast. You'll kill the romance."

And then Ransom realized what Prissie's brothers had done. Kicking free of his boots, he padded deeper into the house, admiring the effect. Marcus and his friend Russ had only finished installing the last of the windows two nights ago. Soft light through stained glass scattered colored diamonds on the old plank floors.

Ransom said, "It's beautiful."

"Very. When are you going to show Sis?"

"Tour of the house is supposed to be my Christmas present."

Beau said, "I *highly* recommend giving that tour after dark."

Making up his mind, Ransom said, "Christmas Eve."

The next day found Ransom sitting on a secret he wanted desperately to share with Prissie. But he somehow managed to bite his tongue and bide his time. During Pearl's and Prissie's lunch break, he manned the front register. Two boxes of delicate Christmas-themed tarts went out the door at the same time a new customer strolled in.

A passing look turned into covert scrutiny as Ransom tried to figure out why the man looked so familiar. "Can I help you, sir?"

He stopped ogling pies and grinned. "Did you just call me sir?"

For a surreal moment, Ransom wondered if this was one of Zeke's pranks. There was no mistaking the gleam in those blue eyes. Which could only mean one thing. "Neil?"

"Guilty as charged."

"I didn't recognize you under all that beard!"

The Pomeroy family's second son laughed. "Grandma Nell likes my new 'chin whiskers,' but Momma's already hinting that I should shave. Tad is calling me 'old man,' and Zeke has pledged to grow his own over Christmas break."

"When did you get in?"

"Late last night. I'm home for the holidays."

"Welcome back."

"Likewise." Neil leaned forward and lowered his voice. "I hear I missed the inquisition."

"And endured one of your own?"

"Yeah, that was something. I had to face the ladies of the family—two sisters, three aunts, and a truly ferocious grandmother. So I'm letting you off easy." Pulling two forks from the inside pocket of his jacket, he said, "How about we settle for splitting a pie?"

"Take your pick."

With a sly smile, Neil pointed out one of Prissie's candy apple pies. "Whip up some cream to go with it?" he wheedled.

"You got it!"

Minutes later, Ransom returned with a heaping bowlful. Neil poured coffee, and they took over a table. After an initial foray into the pie, Ransom asked, "So how's stuff?"

"Big changes. Last semester of school. Job already lined up. Marriage proposal accepted. And I signed the lease on an apartment close to work." Neil tapped the tines of his fork against his lower lip. "I didn't realize when I went away for school, it would be for good."

Ransom said, "I didn't realize I'd be back. Guess you never know what'll happen."

"True." Neil prodded the pie. "I have a feeling every family vacation in my future will bring me back here."

"Regrets?"

The sparkle in Neil's eyes was pure happiness. "None. So what are you up to?"

"Showed up here unannounced. Found out an old hope had a chance. Started working three jobs. Bought a fixer upper."

"I heard about the wall-scrawl project from Zeke."

Ransom said, "We saved some space on the rafters if you want to leave your mark."

"That'd be good." Neil shoveled more pie, then chewed thoughtfully. Finally, he said, "I want Prissie to be happy."

"Me, too."

"You gonna propose while I'm home?"

"How long are you staying?"

Neil held up three fingers.

Ransom slowly nodded. "Yeah, three weeks would about do it. Were you scared?"

With an expressive groan, Neil said, "I lost so much sleep. Worried myself sick with plans. Tried to make sure everything was perfect, then felt like I was gonna empty my stomach. I had such cold feet, I was shaking. But she laughed at me, and then I was laughing at myself. And suddenly, everything went back to normal again. Only better."

"Sounds worth it."

"No doubt."

The afternoon of the *Messiah* concert found Ransom clumsily assembling a brand new ironing board while Timothy pulled pins out of a new white dress shirt.

"You are so lucky," Timothy grumbled. "Everyone's pushing you toward the girl you want to marry."

"While I appreciate their support, it's Prissie who has the final say."

"Which is why you are really lagging behind. Is this really your first date?"

Ransom tackled the box holding his new iron next. "Umm. Depends, I guess. We've been out together a handful of times."

"Going for sandwiches at Dill Brickle's doesn't count."

"Shopping?"

"Was it work-related shopping?"

"Hey, I bake for fun, too."

Timothy held up a hand. "Fail. How can a guy who fails so hard still get the girl?"

Ransom scanned the iron's instruction manual. "It's not so much about *getting* as *agreeing*. Marriage is about two people sharing one vow."

Snatching the iron, Timothy went to the garment bag hanging nearby and pulled out a small bottle. With a pitying look, he explained. "Distilled water. It goes in here. And *this* is spray starch."

"And here I thought Zeke was serious about laundry."

"This is business." Timothy plugged in the iron and fiddled with the settings. "I wear formal stuff all the time. Tours. Concerts. Recitals."

"I suppose you own your own tux."

"So?"

Ransom shook his head at Timothy's defensive tone. "I'm impressed. And grateful. I didn't realize that my chauffeur could double as a valet."

"Like I said, you're lucky." Timothy draped Ransom's shirt over the ironing board and uncapped the spray starch. "Do you think it's because of God?"

Mentally retracing the course of conversation, Ransom asked, "Me and Prissie?"

Timothy nodded. "Yeah. Like she's some kind of gift you're getting because you've been good. And if you'd blown it, she'd be gone now. And you'd be alone. And everything would suck."

"You're asking a guy who considers everything a gift from God. But yeah, there was a time when I thought she'd be gone." Ransom leaned against the wall, watching the iron spit out puffs of steam. "We've both spent years wondering if we'd ever be with the person we love."

"So don't be stupid tonight."

"Nope. Stupidity isn't on the agenda." Ransom asked, "Say, when did you propose to Emmie?"

Timothy looked away. "On her birthday."

"I was thinking about doing that, too, but it might happen sooner. My birthday."

"Cookie, I was at your party in September. Next fall isn't soon."

"I meant my spiritual birthday. The anniversary of the day I prayed with Jayce to become a Christian."

"And when did that go down?" asked Timothy.

"Christmas Eve."

Candle wax and pine boughs. Rustling programs and subdued voices. Crowded pews and poised musicians. Ransom knew he should be soaking up the holiday ambiance, but he was caught up in appreciating little things about Prissie. Like the scent of warm vanilla that tickled his nose and the faint rustle of her full skirt. The tiny tendrils he'd grown so fond of were escaping her upswept curls, and her happiness left him giddy.

While they waited for the concert to begin, he noticed how her gaze kept returning to the church's stained glass windows. Floodlights outside the building made the biblical scenes on each window shine as if cut from jewels.

Keeping a casual tone, he asked, "Was your window like that?"

"Not really." Prissie used her hand to form a diamond shape. "The panes were about this size, and the colors were softer and more transparent. Mostly pastel colors. Blue and green. Yellow and peach."

"No pink?"

"I used to wish there were pink panes, but no. No pink."

Ransom hadn't been so excited for Christmas to come since he was really small and his parents were still together. Inside, he was a kid again, counting down to a day full of gifts and treats. But he'd done enough waiting to know its worth. So he forced himself to relax and look around.

By some miracle, he had Prissie to himself. They were only two rows away from the rest of her family, but Naomi Pomeroy sweetly insisted on giving them some space. Jayce occasionally glanced their way, and Ransom heard the occasional *click* and *snap* of phone cameras.

Prissie's attention kept straying to the same window, and Ransom finally asked, "Got a thing for Daniel?"

In a way." Leaning into his side so he could follow her gaze, she pointed. "Do you see that piece of orange glass in the lion's mane? It kind of looks like a leaf."

"Sure."

"That piece is my special favorite."

"And what makes that piece of glass better than all the rest?"

"Nothing." Prissie smiled softly. "It's not better, but it's needed. The lion's mane wouldn't look right without that piece, and without the panes of glass around it, that piece wouldn't make sense. Because they're together, they're able to tell a miraculous story."

"Daniel's story," Ransom said. "An amazing testimony of faithfulness and trust."

"And angels."

"Well, yes. I suppose you could say he and Gabriel go way back."

She laughed, then straightened and gave a little bounce as the choir filed into position. "Doesn't Nat look handsome in his new suit? And look! They did decide to let Neil sing!"

Prissie's eyes shone with love and pride throughout the applause that heralded the conductor's entrance. And when the overture began, Ransom reached for her hand and whispered, "This is one of your treasures, too."

"Yes. Obviously."

Lacing his fingers through hers, he gave a gentle squeeze. "Thanks for sharing it with me."

After the concert, Mrs. Pomeroy beckoned for Prissie and Ransom to take part in the annual group photo. No one missed the significance of his inclusion as a member of the family. And yet no one mentioned it. Not even Zeke. Ransom's respect for Prissie's mother went up a couple more notches.

Prissie touched his arm and said, "I want to talk to Milo."

"I see Timothy in the back," he replied. "Catch up to you later?"

"Thanks!" And she slipped away.

Even before Ransom reached the back pew where Timothy lounged, he was sure something was wrong. Freckles stood out against paled cheeks, and Timothy watched Ransom's approach with mournful eyes.

"You okay?" Ransom asked.

Timothy waved him off. "You're in the middle of a date. You don't want to disappoint Prissie."

"She's with friends and family. I wouldn't be surprised if she mingles until they lock the doors." Ransom joined Timothy on the pew. "Are you familiar with Handel's *Messiah*?"

"There's no trombone part."

"So … no?" Ransom pressed a little farther. "Have you ever been to church?"

That earned an eye roll. "I've been in plenty of churches for all kinds of performances. They're like mini concert halls."

"Good point. But you gotta realize by now that they're more than that."

Timothy smirked. "Yeah, I hear they're real popular for weddings."

"Duly noted," Ransom said dryly.

Smile fading, Timothy said, "Does it ever bug you how happy they are?"

"Guess it used to, but not for a long time now. Somewhere along the way, I decided to make them my goal."

"By marrying up?"

"Nothing like that. But the way they do family is the way I want to do family, if I ever have one of my own."

"Makes sense," Timothy said bitterly. "You're just like the rest of them. All polite and kind and truthful."

Ransom wasn't sure if Timothy was headed somewhere or simply complaining. Slouching more comfortably into the pew, he asked, "And these things bother you … why?"

"Because I'm sarcastic, selfish, and secretive. And I don't want them to know what I did."

"Do you really think Zeke and Jasper would turn on you?" Ransom challenged. "Is that the kind of people they are?"

"They'll be shocked."

"I was shocked."

"They'll look down on me."

"They're taller than you."

Timothy's glare begged for understanding. "They'll think less of me."

"Why?" Ransom kept his tone even. "For owning up to a mistake? For staying true to Emmie? For keeping track of every freckle on your son's nose?"

By now, Timothy was almost bent double, elbows on knees, hands locked behind his neck. "You think?" he asked hoarsely.

"I know. And so do you, but I'll say it again anyhow," Ransom said. "They love you. Probably as much as you love Emmie. But not nearly as much as God loves all of us."

"Even me."

It wasn't a question. If anything, it was resignation. Maybe Timothy's skepticism was finally tipping toward belief. With his gaze on the pane of orange glass in the main of Daniel's lion, Ransom said, "Promise me you'll have a talk with them."

"If I get the chance."

"Fair enough."

The crowd dwindled and dispersed before Ransom and Timothy left the building. On the front steps of the church, they peered up and down Main Street. Colored lights winked in shop windows. Garlands dipped between streetlights, and white lights lined the gazebo in front of town hall.

"So where's your date?" asked Timothy.

Ransom paused to listen. "Do you hear singing?"

"Parking lot."

They circled around back and immediately slowed their steps. A small knot of people stood in front of a white mini-van—Milo, Beau, Marcus, Padgett, Asher, Neil, Jasper, Zeke, Jude, and Prissie. And they were belting out a carefree reprise of *Messiah*.

This wasn't a performance. It was pure enjoyment. Smiles and exuberance. Playful shifts. Ransom was quite sure Jasper and Neil were trying to outdo each other on the bass line. Zeke was singing soprano in a passable falsetto.

"That guy could go pro," muttered Timothy, pointing at Padgett.

Ransom had rarely heard the park ranger talk, let alone sing. "Who knew?"

Zeke noticed them first and beckoned for Timothy to join the huddle. Ransom worked his way around to where Prissie was tucked between Marcus and Milo. Just as he'd done months ago at the football game, Milo caught his eye and lifted a finger as if to say, "Right this way, sir. I've been holding your place."

With a grateful nod, he came closer and realized that Prissie's arm was tucked through Milo's.

Milo turned sideways and extended his free hand. Bringing Ransom into the group, he smoothly made a transfer, setting Prissie's hand into Ransom's and stepping back. Not one word was spoken, yet Ransom felt certain that Milo had just entrusted him with something precious.

CHAPTER 24

THE MIDNIGHT CLEAR

Beau had visited Milo's apartment a grand total of three times, and that included this one. They generally met at the bakery, but the mailman's note had been clear.

Can you meet after work? My apartment. Let yourself in. Make yourself at home. (Ha.)

As Beau climbed the stairs leading to the living quarters over Stained, he smiled at the parenthetical laughter. Milo had been using the same mailing address for nearly two decades, but he didn't really live in his tiny apartment. The space was a practical necessity, the trappings of humanity. But homey? Not by a long shot.

Letting himself in, Beau noted the same battered old table in the center of the room. Notebooks, pens, church bulletins, and lesson folders littered its surface, just like always. But sometime in the last two years, Milo had brought in a second chair. The addition was made obvious by the little boy who knelt on it, tracing a finger over the writing in a notebook as he mouthed the words.

Beau wracked his brain, trying to place the child. He wasn't one of Jasper Reece's nephews, and Mickie's son was only four. Was there some slim chance that Harken Mercer's kin were visiting the area?

But that was barely plausible. Especially since the boy was dressed in a shining tunic with sky blue stitching at the collar. Beau's every suspicion was confirmed the moment the boy looked up. With a silent explosion of sapphire light, the mystery child vanished inside the trembling cocoon of his wings.

With measured steps, Beau crossed to the table, pulled out the other chair, and sat. Propping his chin on his hand, he waited for Milo.

A ripple. A ruffle. The luminous bundle unfurled enough for a pair of wide eyes to peep out.

Beau and the child were still gazing at each other when Milo returned.

The mailman drew up short. "Beau?" he ventured, his usual cheerfulness a trifle strained.

"Yes, Milo?"

"How are things?"

"Things seem to have taken an interesting turn." Indicating the child, he asked, "Is he yours?"

"As a matter of fact, he is. God saw fit to Send me an apprentice. He's called Silas." Milo scooped up the blue bundle and worked a finger between the seams. "Did you remember your first words, wingnut?"

Safe in his mentor's arms, Silas's wings slithered apart, but the youngster didn't answer the question. Hiding his face against Milo's uniform, he shook his head.

Beau took matters into his own hands. He stood and stepped close, saying, "That's okay, Silas. I remember what to say." Offering his hand palm up, he said, "Fear not."

Silas touched fingertips with him and shyly replied, "B-b-beau."

Prissie took a deep breath and smiled. This was how winter should smell, like snow and pine and icy apples. Trekking into the orchard by snowshoe brought back so many good memories. Ransom had chosen the Sunday afternoon before Christmas for their winter picnic, and she was grateful for the softness in the air.

"Hey, Sis," Zeke called from his place in line. "I think Ransom's doing it wrong."

She craned her neck to the front of the line, where Ransom led the way. "What do you mean? He knows how to snowshoe."

"Not that. This! He can't count this as a date if he brings along the girl's parents and all five brothers!"

Beau, who plodded along between them, said, "He's only doing it wrong if his goal was to get Prissie alone. Think about it, Zeke. What's the real gift here?"

He lapsed into silence, but from the tail end of the line, Jude spoke up.

"Momma cried when Ransom invited her and Dad. This might be for them."

"It's for all of us," Prissie said. "We won't have many chances after this."

"You trying to make me feel guilty, Priss?" asked Neil, who walked in front of her.

"Don't be ridiculous," she said tartly. "We're celebrating with you. Just like always."

"Yeah." Neil hitched up the pack on his back. "Ducks in a row. Just like always."

Ever since Neil's arrival, he'd been fighting like crazy to pack in as many memories as possible. Prissie knew he'd spent time in the attic, the hayloft, and the chicken coop. He'd swung from ropes in the barn, piggybacked all the kids who called him uncle, and challenged Zeke to the silliest competitions. There were also plans in the works for winter camping, a sledding trip to Sunderland State Park, and a Christmas Eve bonfire.

And he wasn't the only one moving on.

Zeke would spend a year at Bible college, to be followed by a stint in the same culinary institute Ransom had attended. And Beau had casually let slip that his choice in seminaries for his doctoral program would take him away.

When Ransom had proposed the winter picnic, Prissie knew his gift wasn't just for her. But his thoughtfulness was better than any romantic gesture. Ransom was playing host to the seven of them. No one else. So when leaving the farmyard, Momma had called her children to order the same way she'd done when they were little. Like ducks in a row, they followed their parents in age order—Tad, Neil, Prissie, Beau, Zeke, and Jude. With Ransom along as coordinator, caterer, and photographer. And the giver of a good and perfect gift.

Prissie left work and walked over to Stained. The chimes over the door sounded, and she almost laughed at how normal it felt. "You're actually here!"

Marcus carefully set aside a wisteria-themed lampshade. "Nice to see you, too."

"Aren't you usually at Ransom's at this hour?"

He shrugged. "Not much left for me to do."

"Is it done?"

"Close enough to count." Marcus stood and crossed to a cluttered workbench in the corner. "I think Zeke and company are helping with finishing touches for your tour."

"Is it nice?"

"Depends on your definition of nice."

Prissie asked, "Is there furniture yet?"

Marcus shoved something into his pocket and said, "You'll find out soon enough."

She pouted, and he took her elbow. "Come on. Time for a blast from the past."

"What are you talking ab–" Her throat closed on the rest of the question. Against the wall in the back room were two doors. One green and ordinary, one blue and anything but. Carved leaves, fruit, and flowers created an elaborate border around the image of two trees with intertwined branches. The blue door's knob was shaped from a luminous opalescent crystal.

"Oh," she breathed. "It's back."

"Remember how it works?" Marcus asked, mimicking the turning of a knob. "I know it's been a while."

She cuffed his shoulder, then laughed when he pushed a tissue box into her hands.

"Go ahead, Prissie. Milo's waiting on us."

So she touched the knob, which sent a musical thrill through her body, right down to the soles of her feet. With a twist and *click*, the door swung away, and Prissie blinked in the wash of heavenly light. She stepped through onto soft grass. The forest glade hadn't changed at all. Shedding her coat, boots, and heavy socks, she ran barefoot to where Milo chatted with half a dozen fluttering yahavim.

"Milo!"

"Hey, Miss Priscilla. Marcus. You, too, Ethan."

Prissie turned to find the pink-winged Guardian standing at Marcus's side. She waved, then turned back to Milo. "This is a wonderful surprise!"

"The first of three."

Marcus stepped forward. "Ethan and I have an early Christmas present for you. It's not much."

He passed along a small bundle of tissue paper, and Ethan added, "I believe you will understand."

She slowly unfolded the delicate wrappings and made a soft sound caught somewhere between happiness and dismay. Finding the fine strand of filament, Prissie lifted a stained glass diamond. Soft pink with pearlescent beads along the edge, it was a perfect match for both her set back home and for the angel it represented. "Pink for my borrowed Guardian," she said. "Thank you both!"

"Seemed like a good idea," Marcus said gruffly.

Ethan wasn't so reticent. Stepping forward, he wrapped her in arms and wings and held tightly. "I will miss our talks," he whispered.

Prissie asked, "Are you Sent away?"

"No. But I believe it will be soon."

"I think so, too," said Milo, who touched Prissie's shoulder. Ethan released her, and the Messenger continued. "For this is your third gift."

He placed a heavy scroll in her hands. The ribbon-bound parchment shone like raiment, shimmering faintly. Turning it, she found a small inscription and immediately recognized the neat script and accompanying flourishes.

Koji had written, *May Prissie Mae prosper.*

Before sunrise on the twenty-fourth of December, Prissie woke when two hands closed around hers. Small. Childish. Warm. She opened her eyes and blinked at the soft glow of angel raiment. Asher's face came into focus, and she whispered, "Is it time?"

"The time has come," he replied formally. "Dress warmly. You must walk to the appointed place."

Prissie rushed through her usual morning routine, then pocketed Koji's scroll. "I'm ready," she whispered. "I hope."

A stone arch appeared, and Asher led her through. Temperatures plunged, and the scent of hay assaulted Prissie's nose. "The loft," she whispered.

"Welcome, Prissie Pomeroy," said a familiar voice. She turned to find Jedrick, Marcus, Tycho, and Ethan waiting. Jedrick continued, "Your plan has found favor in the eyes of God Most High. We are your support."

"Only I can't hold your hand this time," said Marcus.

Tycho inclined his head. "You must appear vulnerable."

"But he can't touch me," Prissie said quickly. Looking to Ethan, she added, "And you'll be near."

"I will be near," he promised.

Prissie hesitated. "How long do you think this is going to take? Daddy gave me the day off, but I'm supposed to help Momma and Grandma Nell with brunch."

Asher said, "You will return before you are needed."

"Then I'm ready." Prissie looked from face to face. "Where do you want me to go?"

"Into the orchard," said Marcus. He steered her toward Asher's arch, and Jedrick and Tycho preceded them through.

In a twinkling, Prissie was beside the pond with its red bridge. "Any particular direction?" she asked.

"You may choose," said Tycho. "We will adjust our plans accordingly."

"That way, then," Prissie said, pointing northeast.

Jedrick's expression softened. "So be it."

Prissie kept to one aisle, taking the most direct route toward her favorite corner of the back forty. Deep snow made for slow going, but she trudged along, ears straining for any hint of mockery. But there was only the sound of her boots and her breath.

Acre by acre, she walked past stark branches and withered fruit. Based on everything around her, it would be easy to assume that winter was the end. But farmers had faith in springtime. Prissie trusted the seasons and the trees to do what they were made to do, but she was less confident in herself.

Little doubts stirred up. What if she was wasting everyone's time? What if she couldn't coax Blight out of hiding? What if she only made things worse? Prissie might have counted several angels as friends, but that didn't make it any easier to face a demon like Blight. He might not be frightening to look at, but she knew he was dangerous. What if she messed up somehow? What if he turned the tables?

"Peace, friend."

Prissie doubled her pace to reach Garrick. He offered his palm, and she grabbed hold with both hands. "I'm so glad to see you," she gasped out.

"Why are you frightened?" He swiftly scanned the surrounding trees. "Did you encounter our enemy?"

"No, no. I think maybe I frightened myself." Prissie looked back the way she'd come. "What if something bad happens?"

"God's plans are always good." Garrick dropped to one knee. Even though he was still taller than her, Prissie didn't have to look up quite so high.

"I thought this was my idea."

The warrior's dimples made an appearance. He gently rearranged their hands so that his large brown ones enfolded her smaller gloved ones. "Even so, your plan fits within His purposes."

Prissie laughed softly. "I needed to hear that."

"Then that is why I was Sent."

"God Sent you to encourage me?"

Garrick's smile widened. "Are you encouraged?"

Patting her chest, Prissie said, "I feel a little braver for what's ahead."

"Then your courage will increase as you go." The cherub pointed farther along the row. "Look there. Yannis is waiting."

Prissie looked ahead, to where another pair of purple wings showed bright against the snowy landscape. God was helping her along in an unexpected way.

"Goodbye for now, Prissie."

His tone caught at her heart, and she realized what Garrick's words must mean. He and his Flightmates had been Sent to serve as her guide and guard, but God was also allowing them to say goodbye. Holding tightly to his hands,

Prissie asked, "Are you encouraged?"

"Abundantly." Garrick's wings swept up and out, fanning wide before settling in a loose circle around her. "Eternity is vast, but I will find you there."

"Peace, friend," she whispered and walked on.

They awaited her at regular intervals along the path. Each time she touched their hands and offered thanks, they shored up her resolve and lent her their courage. She'd never liked goodbyes, but these were different. They pointed to one bright, shining truth. Her protectors could withdraw because the battle was ending. Success was assured. This was victory.

Alone once more, she arrived at the thicket. Her own special place. Pulling off her gloves, she took out Koji's letter and chose a seat on the nearest snow-covered jumble of stones. Cradling the precious scroll to her chest, she gave her enemy time to make the next move.

"Prissie is waiting. Prissie is wanting." Blight's sing-song chant ended with an upward inflection. "Prissie is willing?"

"No, but I brought something. A gift."

Blight's voice came from a different direction. "For me?"

"I'm not entirely sure. I haven't opened it yet." She offered a little shrug. "I was waiting for you because of the inscription."

"Show me." Blight stepped out from behind a tree, clutching a bouquet of golden flowers.

Prissie held up the scroll. "Come closer. He used small letters."

His eyes darted skyward. "Trickery? Trappery?"

"Honestly," she muttered. "I thought you missed Koji as much as I do."

"More!" he snapped. "He was mine first!"

"Obviously." She toyed with one end of the scroll's ribbon. "Come closer, and we can see what he wrote."

"Too soft, too sweet, too giving." Blight circled closer, his bare feet not making a single dent in the snow. "Your lies are fragile things. They melt like snowflakes on skin. I will burst them like bubbles and break them like butterfly wings."

"I haven't lied."

Lifting one pale hand, he pointed to the scroll on her knees. "That is a lie."

"Koji wouldn't lie either."

Blight's lips thinned, but he crept even closer, his eyes fixed on the shimmering parchment. Prissie turned it so he could read the inscription, and childish delight dawned on his face. "My words! My name! Prissie Mae and Prosper."

"I'll admit, I hoped he would come himself. But isn't this the next best thing?"

“Words,” Blight breathed reverently.

Prissie’s gaze dropped. While she hadn’t lied, her intentions were far from friendly. She needed to lure him out and distract him long enough for Tycho’s Flight to close in. If Blight was as clever as everyone said, he had to recognize such a simple plan. But Koji had given her the perfect bait. She doubted the demon could resist.

When she looked up, it was straight into blue eyes. She gasped and leaned back.

“Come closer, you said.” The teasing lilt was back in Blight’s voice. “I am here, Prissie Mae. I accept your gift and will give one in exchange.”

She eyed the golden bouquet. “I don’t want anything from you.”

“Not a thing. A secret.” He straightened and checked the skies again. “There are tales I can tell. There is a place I can show.”

Prissie shook her head.

“Not far.” Blight stepped back and dropped a flower, then another. Edging toward the thicket, he left a trail of blossoms in the snow. “A good place. A sweet place. Like home.”

When he vanished between the tree trunks, she stood and called, “I know there’s a meadow there. I come here as often as I can.” She didn’t like having the tables turned, but she followed the scattered flowers. “Are you running away?”

Blight called, “This way, Miss Mae.”

He was waiting between the trunks of two of the oldest fruit trees in the thicket. Beckoning urgently, he said, “Here is the door. Only here. Right here.”

Prissie wasn’t sure what she was getting herself into, but he couldn’t harm her. And as far as she knew, stepping between two trees wouldn’t put her out of reach. “There’s no door,” she said. “The tower’s long gone.”

The demon laughed, stepped backward, and vanished.

She inhaled deeply, breathed a prayer, and followed.

Warm air. Soft breezes. Buzzing bees. For the first time, Prissie understood where Blight had been getting his golden flowers. She stood on the edge of a meadow carpeted with them. These must be the last vestiges of beauty left behind after Shimron’s tower moved on.

“Like home,” Blight repeated.

Recalling the demon’s own scroll, Prissie asked, “Was that part true? That Koji grew up in a place with golden meadows and bee hives.”

“And a stream.” With a faraway look in his eyes, the demon traced a wavering line across some imagined landscape. “Water over white stones.”

“I had no idea this was here.”

“Seek and find. Catch and keep.” Turning to her with an eager expression,

Blight said, "Give and take."

Prissie gripped the scroll tightly. "Not so fast. You can look, but don't touch. Let's find a place to sit down, and I'll read it to you."

He considered her for several moments, then sighed. "There. A stone for a throne."

She waded carefully into the flowers, which came to the tops of her boots. Loosening her coat and uncoiling her scarf, she took a seat and smoothed out her heavy skirt. Blight reminded her of the children who came to the library for storytime, for he sat at her feet. As the ribbon slipped and the parchment unrolled, he gazed at her with a strange combination of hatred and hunger.

The letter was much longer than anything she'd received. These weren't Bible verses or song lyrics; they were Koji's own thoughts and feelings. His memories vibrated with affection and flowed like poetry. In many places, he spoke with gentle familiarity, as if chatting with an old friend, and Prissie found herself lapsing into his speech patterns.

All the while, Blight remained riveted.

When she paused to uncurl the parchment, the demon fidgeted and hissed. "More," he ground out. "There must be more."

Prissie didn't care for the way his eyes blazed, and she began to fear what would happen when all Koji's words were used up.

Koji's gift held one last surprise. Unrolling the final section of parchment, Prissie found a small square of delicate paper. Flipping it over, she gasped at the colors revealed. "A painting."

Blight's hand inched toward the hem of her skirt, then twitched beside her knee. He didn't go so far as to touch, but he clearly wanted to snatch this new treasure from her grasp. "Don't," she snapped.

"Show it! Give it!"

Could such a scene be real? Golden hoops spun from the branches of candelabra-like trees, and the air was strewn with bits of rainbows, as though prisms scattered the light. And in the bottom corner, a name. Prissie nodded. "Yes, this was meant for you."

She held it out, but another hand intercepted the transfer. "Do *not* reach out to him."

Prissie blinked up at Ethan, whose expression was one of stern exasperation. "How long have you been here?" she asked.

"I am ever near." Extending the painting, he said, "This gift is for Prosper, the angel you were, the friend Koji loved."

Blight crouched, ready to spring away. "A trick! A trap!" he shrieked.

"A mercy. A memory." Ethan tilted the paper so the demon could better see his gift. "Do you want it?"

"I want it." Blight trembled like a mouse who knows the hawks are circling.

Ethan promised, "You shall carry it with you into the Deep."

Eight arrows the size of javelins dropped from the sky, thudding into the earth, sizzling with holy light. The demon shrank from the bright cage, which the cherubim swiftly reinforced with a second volley.

Blight reached for Prissie. "Friend of angels, be mine. Speak for me, and I will be saved!"

Prissie shook her head.

Twisting toward Ethan, the demon's voice broke. "Friend?"

As eight warriors arrived with a powerful backbeat of wings and bows taut, Ethan stepped forward and silently offered the painting. Blight only resisted for a few seconds before snatching the gift and turning his back on both of them.

Ethan nodded to his Flightmates, scooped up Prissie, and carried her away.

Prissie might have spent the rest of the day trying to sort out her feelings, but Koji's letter came with a postscript. *Do not weep as one without hope. I love you.*

During a lull between board games late that afternoon, she stole up to her room. With a sense of finality, she bound Koji's scroll with ribbon and added it to her collection. Then she carried Blight's to the family room and added it to the fire.

Ransom ambled over. "Need help?"

"With this? No. But you could lend a hand with sandwich assembly."

"More exciting than puzzles. Less arduous than dragging brush for the bonfire." Clapping his hands and rubbing them together, he said, "Count me in. Unless …."

"Unless?"

"Would you like a tour of my house?"

She glanced out the window. "It's almost dark already. Shouldn't we wait for daylight?"

"I've been informed that evening is my best hope for a good first impression."

"Why?" she asked suspiciously.

He made a juggling motion, as if sorting through all the possible answers. Finally, he said, "Let's go with *ambiance*."

"Fine," she sighed. "I'll grab my jacket."

"Hold that thought," he said, pulling out his phone. "Let me see if we're good to go."

"Who are you texting?"

"Your brother."

"Which one?"

"Zeke offered to help me get stuff ready. He, Jasper, and Timothy have been at my place for about an hour."

"Oh! I thought he was helping Neil and Jude set up for tonight's bonfire."

"He made sure we had enough sticks for roasting marshmallows before he took off. And we'll all be back in plenty of time for the festivities." Ransom's laugh was a little forced. "Small house, short tour."

Ransom's phone buzzed and he checked the screen. His eyebrows did a funny jiggle, and he said, "Zeke needs half an hour."

"Trouble?"

"How much trouble could Zeke get into in an hour?"

Prissie laughed. "Are there power tools, paint cans, or small kitchen appliances in this house of yours?"

Ransom groaned and texted back. A few seconds later, he cleared his throat and showed Prissie his phone. "Should I be worried?" he asked.

Zeke's return message was one word. *Pray*.

Neil and Jude were putting the torch to a heap of brush and old wood when Prissie followed Ransom down the back steps. Her big brother whistled and waved, and she waved back. "You must have some serious pull with Zeke for him to give up fire-starting."

"He has a vested interest," said Ransom. Instead of turning down the driveway as Prissie expected, he aimed for the machine shed. "After all the hours he put into fixing up my place, he has a right to be proud."

"If you're not careful, he'll take over the tour."

"He won't." Ransom sounded distracted when he added, "He knows the plan."

Prissie didn't see any signs of angels in the vicinity. Not that she expected to after saying farewell to most of Tycho's Flight. A part of her was satisfied with how things had ended, but … she would have liked to talk to Verrill and Raz once more. And neither Ethan nor Asher had said goodbye. Would they simply fade into the background so that life could return to normal?

"Prissie?" Ransom stood by a gap in the snow piles left from Grandpa Pete's plowing. "It's this way."

"This goes to your house?"

"Obviously," he answered in teasing tones.

The entrance was shoulder high and wide enough for two, so he tucked her arm through his and proceeded. Once they were past the initial pile-up, the snow dropped to knee level beside their old plank fence, which was lined with white lights. Their glow stretched on ahead, lighting their way.

"How long has this been here?" she asked.

"Neil finished the plowing yesterday. Beau and Jude strung the lights."

The path fit snugly between the wide swath of trees and shrubs that lined the north side of Orchard Lane and their orchard's edge. In spring, this would be a bower, and in summer, a green tunnel. Peering up at the gentle arch of branches overhead, Prissie said, "These have been recently pruned."

"That would be Tad's doing. And the whole plan was Zeke's idea." Ransom searched her face. "He thought you'd like having a lane through the trees."

"He's right."

"Good. Because this is your brothers' Christmas present to you. Or us. Either way, I'm grateful."

"Me, too. This is so pretty." The sun was fully set now, but they strolled slowly along the shining path that connected their homes. Suddenly, Prissie stopped and listened. "Do you hear … singing?"

Ransom held his breath for several moments, then shook his head. "Nope."

"Can you hear it?" came a voice from behind them. Prissie turned slightly and stared into Ethan's shining face. He said, "We sing for joy. We sing for Timothy."

"Timothy," she gasped. Pulling on Ransom's arm, she hurried him along.

"What's wrong?"

"Nothing!"

She broke away and rushed the rest of the way. Ethan flew ahead and waited for her at the end of the long line of lights. And not alone. A taller Guardian with wings mingling bittersweet and amber leaned against one of the venerable cedars on the edge of Ransom's property. "Are you trading back?"

Tamaes nodded, and Ethan said, "Now is not the time to talk."

Prissie's heart latched onto the implied promise of a later chat.

Ransom caught up with a breathless laugh. "That's a good sign. The house is still standing."

Black against the sky, the silhouette of the old schoolhouse's steep roof showed against a backdrop of stars. But the only visible light was coming from a camp lantern sitting in the snow a few feet in front of the porch. Zeke, Timothy, and Jasper waited together on the top step.

Prissie marched over and bent close. Even in the dim light, she found confirmation in their eyes. Flinging her arms around Timothy's shoulders, she hugged him tight. "Welcome to the family."

Jasper chuckled. "She has him pegged."

"How'd you know?" exclaimed Zeke.

"The angels are rejoicing," Prissie said. "Their joy is full."

Ransom said, "She did say she could hear singing."

She squeezed Timothy once more, then straightened. Planting her hands on her hips, she added, "And it's obvious that you've all been crying."

Ransom asked, "Does she mean what I think she means?"

Timothy innocently answered, "She just welcomed *me* to the family. Guess you're out of luck, Cookie."

Prissie pulled Timothy's hat down over his eyes and tweaked his nose. "You're still a brat, but you're ours for keeps."

"Say it straight," said Ransom. "Tell me the good news."

Zeke flung an arm around Timothy's shoulders and proudly announced, "This is our brother Timothy. He's prayed up and in."

"By which he means saved," Jasper added. "And on his spiritual father's spiritual birthday, no less."

"Appropriate, isn't it?" Zeke asked.

"Providential," said Prissie, turning to Ransom with a smile.

He was staring at Timothy, jaw working. Heaving a shaky breath, Ransom asked, "Do you mean me?"

Timothy ducked his head and muttered, "Duh."

Jasper scooted over and thumped the porch, and Ransom sat heavily. For a while, they stayed like that, shoulder to shoulder. But once he'd collected himself enough to talk, Ransom pulled Timothy into a headlock and lifted teary eyes. "Lord, this is my friend Timothy. He's smart and funny and loyal …"

"Don't forget freckled," interrupted Zeke.

Timothy snorted, and Ransom kept right on praying. "He's got verbal sparring down to an art form, and I've been enjoying his company for months. I'm not sure how many prayers we've all brought to You about him."

Zeke said, "Probably more than he's got freckles."

Ransom laughed, and Prissie saw tears on his face. "Lord, I want to thank You for answering those prayers. Because this is my brother Timothy."

"Son," corrected Jasper. "You're not weaseling out of fatherhood, Pavlos."

"Fair enough," Ransom said hoarsely. "If I played a part in God's plan, it's like Miss Priss said. My joy is full."

"So … why are all the lights off?" asked Prissie.

"You'll see, Sis." Zeke held up the end of an extension cord. To Ransom he said, "We shoulda brought a blindfold."

Ransom returned to Prissie's side. "That's a little extreme."

Prissie supposed she was in for some kind of light show. "How about I promise to keep my eyes shut until you say so?"

"Guess so," Zeke said.

"Sure, sure," agreed Ransom, guiding her forward. "Three steps up."

Across the porch. Over the threshold. Into a room that smelled of varnish, pine, and something sweet. "Did you bake?"

"A cake."

Ransom led her far enough from the door that Prissie guessed they were in the middle of his front room.

"I had trouble sleeping last night, and baking relaxes me," he explained. "You'll have to see it. I want a little crazy with the frosting. Showing off my mad piping skills."

"See it? I want to taste it."

"Fair enough. We'll call it Timothy's birthday cake."

Prissie lifted her face toward the sound of his voice but kept her eyes closed. "It's also your spiritual birthday."

Ransom's hands settled on her shoulders. "That too," he whispered.

Zeke's voice came through the door Ransom must have left partly open. "You guys ready in there?" he hollered.

"Almost!" In softer tones, Ransom asked, "Can I tell you one thing before they light it up?"

Prissie hummed. "Of course."

"I'll love you forever," he said, all seriousness.

"Promise?"

"I'm prepared to formalize it before God and witnesses."

She felt a little silly standing there with her eyes shut. Of all the times to bring up marriage, why do it when she couldn't even see his face? "Was that a proposal?" she asked lightly.

"Unless it's too soon."

"No."

Ransom sucked in his breath. "Wait. Was that *no* as in 'no, I don't accept,' or 'no, it's not too soon'?"

Prissie laughed. "If you want a clearer answer, maybe you should ask a plainer question."

"Marry me?"

With equal simplicity, she answered, "Yes."

A short hug. A breathless laugh. A totally inappropriate increase in volume. "Go ahead, Zeke! We're ready!"

Ransom turned Prissie so they were facing the same direction and wrapped his arms around her shoulders. Meanwhile, Zeke cheerfully yelled, "Five! Four! Three! Two! One!"

The countdown ended, and light bloomed against Prissie's eyelids.

Eventually, Ransom asked, "So …?"

She sighed. "Hard to say. I promised to keep my eyes closed."

With a small groan, Ransom said, "Open them, Prissie."

Prissie stopped breathing at the beauty set before her. Gentle light poured through windows set with diamond panes. The colors of her lost treasure were all there—blue, peach, green, yellow. But more colors had been added to the design, like lavender and aqua. Even pink. Prissie pulled free and shuffled to the nearest window. She traced the edges of a rosy diamond with a growing sense of awe.

"So?" Ransom repeated.

"Perfect," she whispered, looking down the line. Five more evenly-spaced windows scattered rainbow light through the dining area and into the kitchen. "I never imagined anything so perfect."

He bent close to see her face. "You aren't marrying me for my windows, are you?"

"Were they Plan B in case I refused?"

"Would that have worked?"

She laughed. "Possibly."

Ransom reached for her hand. "Marcus gave them to me, but they were always for you. They're the same on the other side of the house. Upstairs, too."

"Can I see the rest?" she asked.

"In a minute. This first." Then Ransom pulled something from his coat pocket and slipped it around her ring finger.

Prissie watched in disbelief as Ransom tied the length of pink ribbon into a floppy bow. "I didn't want to choose rings without you, so this'll have to do."

"You did this once before," she said wonderingly. "Back before we were friends."

"Before you *admitted* we were friends."

All of a sudden, droves of yahavim burst into Prissie's periphery. Scattering. Twirling. Dancing. Whirling. Their midair antics brought enough of heaven's light into the room to give her a few glimpses of her future home. A place where angels would always be welcome.

They also drew her attention to another arrival.

Fighting for a serious expression, she turned to Ransom and asked, "Can I tell you something before Zeke barges in?"

"Anything."

"I love you, too." Prissie kissed her future husband's cheek and whispered, "And there's an angel sitting on your refrigerator."

Koji's eyes took on a faraway look, as if he was seeing past the dusty attic into heaven's glories. "When your Bridegroom comes to claim His bride, He will be attended by His angels."

Prissie laughed a little. "So I guess that means you'll be at my wedding."

The young angel's eyebrows rose slightly. "Indeed."

excerpted from "Gold and Pearls," a Threshold Series Outtake.

More outtakes can be found at ChristaKinde.com.

EPILOGUE

THE PROMISE KEPT

"Well?" Abner folded his arms across his chest and narrowed his eyes. "What's wrong?"

Koji swayed in place, eyes locked on his feet. They suddenly felt so far away. "Are you certain th– " he began, then slapped a hand over his throat, eyes widening further.

"Certain this is necessary? Quite." Abner placed a steadying hand under Koji's arm. "Human boys grow into young men over the course of a decade. You can't show up at Prissie's wedding looking twelve. Or sounding twelve. Congratulations, you're a tenor."

"Thirteen," he said, wincing at the unfamiliar tambour. "I was meant to be thirteen."

"Details, details." Taking Koji's hands in his own, Abner took a step back. "Come along. Get a feel for the future model."

While Abner led him in a wide circle, Koji took a cautious inventory. Longer limbs and bigger feet made him feel stretched and clumsy. He tripped over his own toes and pitched forward. The hair that swung into his face was much longer than it had been.

"I assumed you'd let your hair grow," Abner said.

Koji pondered that. Did hair grow because he let it? Growing seemed to happen whether he noticed or not. He tucked the straying locks back behind his ear and stopped for two reasons. His fingers were too long. And his ears were too short.

"I'll put everything back where it belongs after your visit."

"Thank you." Koji flexed his fingers, unsettled by their unfamiliarity. Could these hands hold a pen or brush? If he was this clumsy with new feet, was he back to blotting parchment and dribbling paint? Reining in the urge to go check his penmanship, Koji whispered, "Abner?"

"Yes?"

With a small shrug, Koji asked, "Will she know me? I barely recognize myself."

Abner's eyebrows arched. "You are and will always be you."

Although he hadn't quite answered his question, Koji took comfort from Abner's confidence. "Yes. I am myself." With a faint smile, he added, "Who else would I be?"

At long last, God was honoring a decade-old promise. Koji had left West Edinton knowing that he *would* return one day. But not *when*. Everything depended upon the man Prissie would choose for a husband. Koji often pondered his restlessness for her bridegroom's appearing. Did believers await their soon-coming King with equal anticipation?

"You're tottering," sighed Abner.

"The floor seems quite distant."

"Yet your feet still touch the ground. Relax. Find your balance."

Firming his resolve, Koji bounced on the balls of his feet, then took a few longer strides. "Yes. With more practice, I will adapt."

"More?" Abner shook his head. "You have barely enough time to run to your room and collect your baggage."

"Now?" Koji reached for the wall, suddenly needing its support.

"Your ride will be here momentarily."

"Ride? Will you not make a door for me?"

"Not this time." Abner shooed him toward the stairs. "Jedrick insisted, so hurry along. You don't want to keep your captain waiting."

Prissie perched on the plank fence behind twin mailboxes, waiting for Milo. Bees buzzed among the purple coneflowers, and locusts put up a racket in the trees. She appreciated the faint breeze, but she rustled as much as the leaves overhead. Of all days for the mail to be late!

But before she could fly to pieces, the sound of an engine and the rattle of gravel announced his approach. Her stomach plunged. He was alone.

Milo waved as he drove past and circled around to park along Orchard Lane's cul-de-sac. With a slam of his car door, he strolled over and joined her on the fence. "Good afternoon, Miss Priscilla."

"Why aren't you in uniform?"

"I'm off duty."

"But what about the mail?"

"Oh, I imagine my substitute will be along in an hour or so. She doesn't know the route as well as I do, so she's a little behind." He casually asked, "Why, were you expecting something?"

"Don't tease." She struggled to quell her disappointment. "I thought you were bringing Koji."

"Fear not." Milo let his shoulder bump hers. "On paper, I have the day off in order to pick up an old friend at the airport. But miracles aren't always a matter of plane tickets and passports."

Prissie's breath caught as the sky exploded with color.

Milo cheerfully said, "There's his Flight now."

Koji's color guard was a mix of familiar and new—Jedrick, Taweel, a cherub with lemon yellow wings, and an ax-wielding Guardian with red wings. With a small nod, Jedrick set down a slender young man in ordinary clothes and stepped back.

Prissie could feel her cheeks heating. Her forever boy had grown up. Straight black hair caught in a low ponytail. Windblown bangs framing a solemn face. Dark eyes that missed little. Quashing her sudden bout of shyness, Prissie eased off the fence and offered him a small bouquet of golden flowers tied with a pink ribbon. "Welcome back."

Recognition and delight lit up his features. "Where did you find these?"

"There's a hidden meadow in the back forty. If you're up for a walk later, I'll show you."

"Yes, please."

Easing closer, Prissie whispered, "Is it really you?"

Koji's fingertips brushed the back of her hand. "Indeed."

"I'm going to hug you now."

His eyes sparkled. "I am prepared."

And with a teary laugh, Prissie pulled him into a fierce hug. After a few moments, she could feel Koji's arms around her back. His bowed head touched her shoulder, and she felt warm droplets. "Why are you crying?" she asked.

"Because I cannot stop."

Prissie held him close and hummed her prayer song, silently thanking God for her very best friend and for all the things that would never change between them. But her efforts didn't sooth Koji. His hold tightened, and he sobbed. She looked to Milo for help, but the Messenger's eyes were politely averted as he brushed away the tears on his own cheeks.

Eventually, Koji was able to hum a few notes, picking up the melody where she left off. Milo joined in, and Jedrick and his companions added their harmonies. Then with artless joy, Koji gave words to the song in an earnest offering of praise. Gifts and giving. Faith and faithfulness. Reunions and rehearsals. Virtue and vows. Love and the Beloved.

After the final amen, Prissie stepped back, keeping hold of Koji's hand. "Now for next things. Do you *know* how hard it is to plan a party when your guest of honor doesn't schedule his flight in the usual way?"

Koji blinked. "Am I late?"

"Of course not. The wedding isn't for three more days. But I *knew* you'd come today." Prissie pulled him toward the house and Milo fell in step beside them. "Everyone's here. We baked you a cake, but there's also apple pie. Just in case."

"Why today?" asked Koji.

Prissie squeezed his hand. "Because it's your birthday."

"I hear the organ," Margery leaned to the side so she could see the barn from Prissie's bedroom window. "Say, is your foreign musician friend still single?"

"Leave him be," Prissie sighed. "I told you, Kester is a confirmed bachelor."

"But he's so good with Colin!"

Prissie bit her lip. It wasn't as if Kester couldn't take care of himself. So she simply switched the topic. "If the music has started, it's almost time."

"Almost done," promised Ida, who was arranging Prissie's curls around the tiara of gold and pearls.

A soft tap sounded on her bedroom door. "Sis? I brought your flowers."

"You can come in, Judicious. I'm ready."

"*Almost* ready," said Aunt Ida with a bright laugh.

Jude eased into the room and gazed at Prissie with a thoughtful expression. Nodding to himself, he said, "You're happy."

"Are you?"

He handed her a generous bouquet of pink cosmos. "Some happy. Some lonesome. Mostly proud."

Zeke barged in. "You ready already? Come on, Sis! Ransom's gonna think you left him at the corn crib!"

Ida swatted his shoulder. "Yes, she's ready."

"Great! Let's go!" Despite all his talk of rushing, Zeke led her slowly along the upstairs hallway. "Betcha he keels over at the sight of you."

"Don't be ridiculous."

He chuckled. "Okay, maybe he's not the swooning type. But you're beautiful, Sis."

"Thanks," she whispered.

Beau waited at the top of the front stairs. "Watch your step," he murmured.

"Impossible. I can't see my feet."

"Which explains why I'm here. Hold onto me."

Billows of white swished softly as she carefully descended.

"You know, a couple of special guests showed up a little while ago."

"Oh?"

"Milo introduced me to Mr. Mercer's 'nephew,' also named Harken. Quite the coincidence, isn't it?" Beau patted her hand. "And Ranger Ochs is here. He and Grandpa Carl hit it off. When I left, they were talking about natural wonders and national parks."

"I can't wait to see them."

Neil whistled loudly when Prissie stepped into the kitchen. "Nice!"

She curtsied. "You're looking quite well yourself."

"You think?" Neil made a face as he fiddled with his tie. "Because … pink pinstripes."

"I happen to love pink pinstripes," she said haughtily.

"No doubt. I'll survive the day somehow." Neil led her out the back door and down the porch steps. "Be good to Ransom. Like I've been saying since the beginning, he's a good guy."

Prissie squeezed his arm. "Yes, he is. And I will."

At the end of the sidewalk, Tad awaited his turn. "All right there, Priss?" he asked.

"Yes." She gathered up her skirts for the walk to the big barn. With Kester's help, their rustic cathedral was finally a reality, for organ music spilled from the loft. She could feel it in the air, and it made her heart beat faster.

"I'm glad you'll be close," Tad said.

She nodded. "Our apples didn't fall far from the tree."

"Deep roots, good fruit."

They strolled slowly, giving Jude and Zeke time to escort Margery inside. Beau and Neil caught up and hurried to their places in the family section. Which left their father. She laughed weakly at the look on his face. "Daddy, don't you dare cry. If you do, I might."

"I can be brave, my girl." Mr. Pomeroy straightened his shoulders and grinned boyishly. "It's only that you look so much like your mother. Any tears will be happy tears."

"*No* tears," she repeated.

"Sure, sure," he promised.

Aunt Ida helped pull forward Prissie's veil and fussed with the drape of her skirt. With a whispered word of encouragement, she hurried away. The music shifted, and Ida started Juliette down the aisle. As Prissie's lone bridesmaid, her aunt followed a few steps behind.

Mr. Pomeroy led Prissie into position, and she could see all the way to the front where Ransom waited with his two groomsmen and Pastor Ruggles. Marcus elbowed Baird, who remembered he wasn't supposed to put his hands in his pockets. Craning his neck so he could see, the redhead beamed at her.

"You missed earlier," her dad leaned down to say. "When Ransom first came in, he explained to everyone that Marcus was Best Man and Koji was Best Friend. He had the whole room laughing."

No wonder everyone was smiling. Ransom had put them at ease.

As much as she adored Aunt Ida, the only person Prissie wanted in the place of honor was Koji. She tipped her head to better see her best friend, whose boutonniere of white cosmos set him apart.

Koji mimicked her head tilt, then looked pointedly at the groom, as if to remind her where her focus belonged. So as the organ fanfare swelled and the congregation rose, Prissie met Ransom's gaze and took a step of faith. And of hope. And of love.

I will greatly rejoice in the Lord, My soul shall be joyful in my God; For He has clothed me with the garments of salvation, He has covered me with the robe of righteousness, As a bridegroom decks himself with ornaments, And as a bride adorns herself with her jewels. –Isaiah 61:10

If you enjoyed this addition to Prissie's story,
please take the time to leave a review.

Discussion Questions

1. When Prissie asks Ransom if she seems lonely, he points out that it doesn't matter how full our days are. "When something's missing, we feel it." How does loneliness creep in and steal the good stuff? Do *you* have everything you need?

2. Prissie struggles with Margery's casual attitude toward commitment. What are your ideals for marriage?

3. The cherubim uncover a room filled with proof that the Pomeroy family isn't perfect. How would you feel if your sins, secrets, and shortcomings were written out for anyone to read? Why did Jedrick call it a "graceless record"? How did God deal with it through young Asher's Sending?

4. Why did Prissie feel like she was falling behind compared to Margery? Of these two young women, whose example would you rather follow? Are either of them perfect?

5. Having faced her share of demons, Prissie *knows* what it means to have an enemy. What happens during the county fair when she realizes that she's been treating Margery like an enemy?

6. Jude's comfortable talking about apples and chickens, but when it comes to talking about his faith, he struggles. Can God use us even if we're nervous and unsure?

7. Why does Ransom say he shied away from team sports while in school? Do you ever feel like you're stuck on the sidelines? On the flipside, have you ever "benched" God?

8. Ransom admires Prissie for her compassion. At the same time, Blight is eager to exploit her merciful heart. How can a strength become a weakness? Can your weaknesses become strengths?

9. Do you agree with Prissie's definition of dating? What about Beau's explanation of romance?

10. Think it through. Why didn't Ethan stop Prissie from chasing the stray dog into the orchard?

11. If you could have added to the "wall-scrawl" project, what would you write?

12. Are the Pomeroys too good to be true? Ransom's made them his goal. "The way they do family is the way I want to do family, if I ever have one of my own." What parts of their lifestyle do you want for your own lot?

About the Author

Behind the scenes, I'm a cheerful homebody whose many talents include dish-washing, laundry-sorting, and the weaving polysyllabic words into everyday conversation. First to know, last to tell, happy to try, and always true. A plotter and a plodder, a dabbler and a devotee. Weaknesses include bright colors, crazy socks, and alliteration. More to the point, I spend my days planning studies, plotting stories, and putting my nose to the proverbial grindstone … because as much as I loves writing, it's work. Finding the perfect word, turning a phrase so it sparkles, giving a plot just a bit of a twist—they're worth every iota of effort. I'm delighted to have discovered what I want to do when I grow up!

Christa also publishes family-friendly fantasy under her maiden name. If you like magical master sculptors, shape-shifting brothers, stowaways with secrets, and mythical creatures, let your curiosity lead you to CJMilbrandt.com.

Threshold Series art, outtakes, and postcards await you on Christa's website. Be sture to drop in for milestone parties, character Q&A sessions, and news about upcoming and ongoing stories.

ChristaKinde.com
Facebook /ChristaKinde
Pinterest /christakinde
Twitter @ChristaKinde
Twitter @BAIRDjustBAIRD
#ThresholdSeries
#PomeroyLegacy

Adventure Begins at the Door

Prissie never expected to stumble into an adventure on her way to the mailbox. Invisible doors, angels in disguise, kidnapped comrades, demonic minions, divine messengers, sword fights, winged rescuers, shared dreams, and apple pie. The Threshold Series by Christa Kinde is appropriate for readers aged eleven and up. Complete in four volumes from Zonderkidz.

Three Free Short Stories

Angels All Around – A divine Messenger becomes one little girl's prince, and a fledgling Guardian becomes their knight.

Angels in Harmony – Angels have always served in pairs, but Baird is sure there must be some mistake when Kester shows up on his doorstep.

Angels on Guard – Tamaes only understood part of what it meant to watch over one precious life. The rest he learned on the day he almost lost her.

Also Available

Rough and Tumble – Zeke Pomeroy's parents always joked that it would take a miracle for their rough and tumble son to reach adulthood. Unbeknownst to them, that miracle's name is Ethan. Follow one little boy's adventures as he turns his guardian angel's life upside down.

Tried and True – Taweel is Sent to watch over a young girl, but when her life ends, his heart shatters. Bitterness, anger, and despair leave him vulnerable. But though Taweel's need is great, the One who provides is far greater. The grieving Guardian's life undergoes a slow and steady transformation after he meets a yahavim named Omri, a pair of heavenly Weavers, a Worshiper whose songs are laced with sorrow, and two little boys with auburn hair and wide brown eyes.

Angel on High – As the newest member of his order, Koji is eager to learn what it means to be an Observer. But looking and listening lead to trouble when he spots danger and overhears secrets. Heaven's archivists weren't made for battle, but Koji will need a warrior's courage to be ready for the unusual plans God has for him.

Family Friendly Fantasy

Christa writes family-friendly fantasy under her maiden name, C. J. Milbrandt.

Byways Books. Three brothers with a magical inheritance take sibling rivalry to new lengths as they race each other across their homeland. [A multi-book series for kids who are ready for chapter books.]

Book #1: *On Your Marks*: The Adventure Begins
Book #2: *Aboard the Train*: A Ewan Johns Adventure
Book #3: *Over the Bridge*: A Zane Johns Adventure
Book #4: *Up the Mountain*: A Ganix Johns Adventure
Book #5: *Inside the Tree*: A Ewan Johns Adventure
Book #6: *Into the Hills*: A Zane Johns Adventure
Book #7: *Across the Line*: A Ganix Johns Adventure
Book #8: *Down the Stairs*: A Ewan Johns Adventure
Book #9: *Through the Notches*: A Zane Johns Adventure
Book #10: *Back on Track*: A Ganix Johns Adventure

Galleries of Stone. Of all the world's treasures, none are more valuable than stone from the Twelve. Children on all four continents are tested for affinity, for the mountains hold magic. But in the foothills of the Gray Mountain, no one remembers stone lore. The majestic Statuary is forgotten, as are the wonders that fill its galleries. Only rumors remain, and those are used to frighten children. For it's said that a monster lives in the heights.

Freydolf serves as the Gray Mountain's Keeper. Exiled. Feared. Unwelcome. But necessity drives him into a Flox village to hire a boy to fetch water and tend fires. Tupper Meadowsweet isn't the cleverest child, but he's brave enough to follow his new master up top. In the Statuary, Tupper finds hints of faraway lands, diverse races, long histories, unique customs, and danger.

Book One: *Meadowsweet*
Book Two: *Harrow*
Book Three: *Rakefang*

CPSIA information can be obtained at www.ICGtesting.com
Printed in the USA
LVOW10s1846060716

495334LV00026B/1297/P